Law was certain he'd fallen into some alternate universe at some point in the past five minutes. Or maybe he'd hit his head and was hallucinating. Could be one of those fugue states, even—were there hallucinations in fugue states?

Nia pressed her lips to his and he groaned, opening his mouth.

*Slow down—think—*

Except he was pretty certain that wasn't possible. Thinking. Slowing down.

And what in the hell was there to think about, anyway? She wasn't drunk—she was clear-eyed, sober, and that long, coffee-and-cream body was pressed against his, warm and sweet and naked and he wanted her like he wanted his next breath.

It was more than a want—it was a blinding, desperate ache and what was there to think about?

Gliding his hands up over her sides, along the curve of her rib cage, up until he could cup her breasts in his hands, he plumped the warm, soft weight of her, stroked his thumbs over her nipples.

She whimpered into his mouth, then tore away, her head falling back on a ragged sigh.

"You sure about this, Nia?" he rasped, staring at her through slitted eyes.

By Shiloh Walker

*If You Hear Her*
*If You See Her*

# IF YOU KNOW HER

## SHILOH WALKER

BALLANTINE BOOKS • NEW YORK

A Ballantine Books Mass Market Original

Copyright © 2012 by Shiloh Walker

Published in the United States by Ballantine Books, an imprint of The Random House Publishing Group, a division of Random House, Inc., New York.

BALLANTINE and colophon are trademarks of Random House, Inc.

ISBN 978-0-345-51755-5
eBook ISBN 978-0-345-51759-3

Printed in the United States of America

www.ballantinebooks.com

9 8 7 6 5 4 3 2 1

Ballantine mass market edition: March 2012

To my family, always to my family—I thank God for you. Every day, and it's still not enough. I love you all.

To friends who helped out along the way. Friends like Nicole, Natalie and Lime—rush jobs and crazy questions, they never faze you.

To my agent Irene, who helps keep me sane, and my editor Kate, who has been so excited about this book, even from day one.

# IF YOU
# KNOW HER

# CHAPTER
# ONE

Jolene had been dead for six months.

Six long months.

Nia Hollister lay on her bed, staring up at the ceiling as she tried to will herself to sleep, but sleep wasn't coming. It wasn't getting any easier. *Nothing* was easier. Sleeping. Living. Moving on with her life.

But how was she supposed to get on with her life, when her cousin, her best friend, her only family was gone? Murdered . . . dead and buried, brutalized by some monster for reasons that Nia couldn't even fathom.

Even after six long months, she still felt like she had a hole in her chest the size of the entire state of Virginia.

The fact that the man who'd killed Joely was dead made no difference, not to her. It changed nothing. It helped nothing, eased none of her pain. Not even watching as they'd lowered his worthless corpse into the ground had helped.

That should have helped, right?

He was dead—the man who had killed her cousin was dead. That should give her closure, right?

*Closure*—

Shit.

Did people really think having *closure* helped?

It sure as hell wasn't helping her. Knowing who did it . . . how did that help?

Exhausted, sick at heart, and still as miserable now as she had been the day she'd found out the truth, Nia sat up in her bed and rummaged around on her bedside table until she found a mangled pack of cigarettes.

She'd stopped smoking three years ago. She'd started again five and a half months ago. She kept telling herself she'd stop, and she knew she needed to, but she just couldn't work up the energy to care.

Right now, she couldn't quite give a fuck if she was polluting her lungs—what did it matter? Right now, she was having a hard time finding anything that mattered.

Sighing, she lit a cigarette and climbed out of bed, moved to stare out the window. It was dark and quiet. She was far enough outside the city that the lights from town were muted and she could see the stars.

There had been a time when she had loved nights like this.

Now she hated them, hated the quiet, hated the peace. It seemed like that was when she heard it the loudest. Heard *her*. It was just her imagination, but it seemed so real.

Joely's screaming . . . God, how she must have screamed. Had she begged? Had she pleaded?

"Shit."

Heedless of the smoking cigarette in her hands, she pressed the heels of her hands against her eyes, as though that might keep her from hearing the screams, might keep her from thinking about her cousin.

Her best friend.

The woman who'd been murdered by some sick-ass bastard who was now rotting away under six feet of dirt. She should take comfort in that, Nia reckoned.

But she couldn't. Didn't. It just felt too . . . unfinished.

Blowing out a breath, she lowered her hands and eyed the cigarette. "Going to catch my damn hair on fire," she muttered. Putting it between her lips, she inhaled. As the smoke filled her lungs, she tipped her head back and stared up at the darkened ceiling.

Yeah, it felt damned unfinished.

But Joe Carson had been found with Joely's watch on him, and her clothing and other evidence had been found at the cabin where he'd been squatting.

What were they supposed to do?

In some sick, convoluted way, it even made sense, once somebody had explained things to her.

Hope Carson had left her abusive ex-husband and spent two years on the move, because she feared he might come after her. Finally, she'd decided she was going to settle in with her friend Law Reilly. The ex must have been watching her pretty damn close. Timing-wise . . . no. Nia didn't quite buy the timing bit, because her cousin had been grabbed *before* Hope had arrived in Ash, Kentucky, but the cops had shrugged it off.

*There wasn't any secret that she was friends with Reilly. Reilly had confirmed she had been making plans to come stay with him.* They'd speculated that Carson had just made a lucky guess, or suggested maybe he'd had some inside knowledge—their suggestions hadn't meant shit to her.

So, Hope arrives in Ash and her ex-husband waits until she sort of settles in, and then he kills Nia's cousin. Leaves her body right where Hope can all but trip over it. Trying to scare Hope into running . . . just trying to scare her? Warn her? *This will be you if you don't toe the line?*

"It's all so fucked up," she whispered. "Damn it, Joely, what am I supposed to do? Why can't I let go?"

But there wasn't any answer.

Leaning her brow against the chilled glass, Nia smoked her cigarette and suffered the miserable silence alone.


Her name had been Mara Burns.

She'd been his first—a man didn't forget his first. His first fuck. His first love. His first wife.

His first kill.

He'd had different firsts . . . Mara had been his first kill, and she'd been . . . sweet.

It hadn't been planned.

At all. It had been back in college and she had been a hot, sweet little bitch, but the first few times he'd tried to ask her out, she hadn't given him the time of day.

That changed his senior year—and she'd been the one to ask *him* out. As a ploy to make a boyfriend jealous, mostly, and he had known. They'd gone out, fucked in his car. Then she whispered for him to hit her. To choke her.

He hadn't. But he'd imagined it.

When he took her home, she'd mocked him, but he'd been so caught up in those images, he had barely noticed. That night, he'd dreamed about it. Choking her. Hitting her.

Thoughts of it consumed him.

Weeks passed, turned into months, they rarely spoke, but he saw her, and each time, it made those fantasies burn hotter. Brighter.

One night she'd been walking home from her job. He'd seen her . . . because he'd been watching. Watching. Dreaming. He had offered her a ride. Because it was starting to rain, or maybe because she wanted to taunt him some more, she'd accepted. But then he hadn't taken her home and she had put her bitch-face on. He'd backhanded her.

Instead of getting pissed, or scared . . . she'd been turned on.

They went back to the quiet, secluded little area outside of Lexington where they'd fucked that first night, and they went at each other like animals. They started out in the back of the car, moved to the trunk, and eventually ended up on the ground.

He'd hit her, and she would come. He'd squeeze her neck until she almost blacked out, and she'd come harder. For hours.

But then, toward the end of the night, as he was driving into her, chasing another climax, his fingers digging into her silken neck, he'd squeezed, and squeezed, and squeezed . . . he'd let go, watched as she sucked in a ragged breath of air right as he climaxed so hard it had almost hurt, and he'd thought about how he hadn't wanted to let go.

Then, when she was smiling at him, he'd closed his hands around her neck.

For reasons he couldn't understand then, he'd started choking her again. And that time, he hadn't stopped. Not when her heels beat on the ground, not when she had torn at his hands with her nails, real fear beginning to flicker in her eyes. Not even when her bowels and bladder had released.

His mind had remained cool, detached throughout all of it, even as his heart had raced at the thrill.

His first kill.

Yes . . . Mara had been one of the most beautiful firsts of his life. A man didn't forget his first. He'd worried for years somebody would discover her, discover what happened to Mara, and somehow link her back to him.

But in the end, she wasn't the one who was coming to haunt him.

Hers wasn't the face he dreamed of at night now.

And she wasn't the reason he had been forced to put a stop to his games for a while.

Because he couldn't indulge in those games, he was all but burning, all but dying to feel that thrill again, the pleasure he found only when he took a life. She wasn't the reason he felt like a ticking time bomb, one that burned hotter, brighter, every damn day.

No, that honor belonged to one Jolene Hollister and one Lena Riddle. Jolene had almost gotten away from him, had screamed bloody murder . . . and Lena had heard her screaming, had called the cops, had stirred up too much attention.

Six months. It had been six months.

He knew how to wait.

Sometimes he felt like a lump of coal under extreme pressure, like he'd emerge a diamond—after a bit of polishing and cutting down.

Other times, he just felt like he was going to explode and right now was one of those times. Six fucking months.

It was worse being in here in this crush of people.

A wedding was a big deal in a small town like Ash, though, and Lena and Ezra hadn't spared any expense. The Inn was full to bursting. The reception had been going strong for more than an hour and he had no doubt it would keep going for another hour at least.

He couldn't even make a quiet escape, though. It would be too easily noticed.

So he waited, chatted, and danced.

He danced with the bride, he danced with the bridesmaids, he danced with the flower girl, he danced with the married women whose husbands wouldn't dance, and he danced with the tittering, blushing girls who were still learning how to flirt.

He danced with so many women . . . so many.

Tall, short, lean, lush.

Short hair that barely brushed their jawline, long hair that fell to their hips. Hair upswept to leave their shoulders bare. Jewelry sparkled and glowed against toned and tanned flesh.

Over by the bar, he spotted Roslyn Jennings talking with the bride, her curves poured into a dark green dress that clung so lovingly. Gold glinted at her neck, ears, and wrists.

On the dance floor, he saw Hope Carson, dancing with her beau Remy Jennings, wearing a dress just like Roslyn's, the same deep, deep green. But where Roslyn looked like a witch, Hope looked like some fey woodland nymph. Sweet and innocent and lovely. She wore little jewelry, but there were flowers in her short, shiny hair.

Then there was the bride, her deep red locks glowing against the white of her dress, pearls at her neck, gold on her fingers.

All the women . . .

Hunger pulsed inside him, driving him mad, making him greedy and desperate.

Desperate—but not too desperate.

Not so desperate he'd get foolish again. Not here. Not now.

At present, he had a girl—just barely out of college—wrapped around him, and it pissed him off. Perhaps it turned him on a little as she pressed her breasts against his arm, smiling up at him and trying to act like she was so much older than she really was. But she was just a child. Besides, he also had a lady nearby who would notice before much longer and although she would understand, he didn't want her upset.

Especially not by an obnoxious little bitch like this.

As she swayed a little too close, he dipped his head and murmured, "Estella . . ."

"Star. I'm going by Star now. Estella is so *old*," she

said, giving her lower lip what she probably thought was a seductive stroke of tongue.

"Estella Price," he repeated. "I don't know why you keep rubbing against me like that. I've known you since you were in diapers. I'm pretty sure I probably even changed one or two."

He hadn't. But it had the desired effect. She turned almost as red as the lipstick she'd slicked on her mouth and jerked away from him. Suppressing a chuckle, he lost himself in the crowd and headed toward the cash bar. He needed a drink, and he wanted to see if he couldn't work his way out of here yet.

If he didn't escape soon—

This wasn't where he wanted to be . . . wasn't where he *needed* to be. Except the whole damn town was here.

There were places a guy wanted to be in life—in bed with a long, lean woman wrapped around him? That topped the list, as far as Law Reilly was concerned.

Although he wouldn't mind a cabin in the mountains, just him and his laptop. He'd be fine with swapping out the laptop for a long, lean woman.

Or even a shack on a beach, just him and his laptop. Again, the swap-out—his laptop for a long, lean woman? That would work. And some beer on hand.

The place he didn't want to be, though?

A wedding in small-town Kentucky.

Namely, Ash, Kentucky, where he'd been living for the past ten years. Long enough that he could call the place home, long enough that most of the people knew him by face, by name . . . and by bank account, even if most of them didn't entirely know where the money came from.

They just knew he wasn't hurting for cash and at a wedding with a lot of single women, and that was always dangerous. Even if he'd been in his sixties, balding, and carrying a spare tire, it would be dangerous.

But Law was thirty-four, still had a full head of hair, and while he might not see himself as the cover model for any magazine, he didn't have a spare tire, either.

Yeah, this was a dangerous place to be, and he was in a lousy mood, anyway. His mood got darker and uglier each time one of the single women would come up and flirt, attempt to make some sly remark about his single status.

He could handle this—get through the reception. He just had to have a game plan, and be cautious.

Things had been going fairly well, too, for about the first hour.

At a wedding, a guy didn't want to make eye contact, didn't want to stand around looking like he might be anything resembling lonely. None of that stuff, because sometimes, the single women got ideas in their heads.

If he wanted to make it out of there sane, and without making himself look like an ass at his best friend's wedding, he had to exercise caution.

Sometimes, caution could serve a man well.

And sometimes, so could throwing caution to the wind.

Law Reilly was tempted to throw caution to the wind and just get the hell out of the Inn, especially after Mackenzie Cartwright came simpering up to him, pressing her breasts against his arm, angling herself so he could see clear down to her belly button if he wanted.

He looked—hell, why not? She put herself there on display.

But she was also in the mood to dance . . . and maybe leave early . . . weddings always made her . . . She'd actually trailed off with a suggestive giggle as she slid her hand down, resting it on his hip.

Shit.

"Part of the wedding party, kid," he said, tacking the *kid* on just to annoy her. She was twenty-three, definitely too young for him, although hardly a *kid*. "I think I'm supposed to hang around awhile."

Then he put some serious floor space between them and wondered how long he needed to hang around. He didn't want to be there. Didn't want to watch as Lena Riddle snuggled up against Ezra King for what had to be their fiftieth damn kiss. But she wasn't Lena Riddle now. She was Lena King.

And he wasn't jealous—exactly. Well, he was.

He was damn jealous, but not because he wanted to be the one she was pressing her pretty mouth against. There had been a time when that was exactly what he wanted.

But he wasn't the one for Lena.

Lena was happy with the guy, happier than Law had ever seen her. He couldn't begrudge her that happiness, even if once upon a time he'd imagined himself in Ezra's place.

There was an ache in his heart, though. Yearning wisps of envy that had him wishing he was anywhere but here. Okay, anywhere but here or anywhere with Mackenzie.

Home, alone, sounded good.

Weddings weren't exactly his favorite way to pass the time, but this was one of his best friends . . . and even though once upon a time he'd desperately loved her, seeing her happy was important to him.

With just about anybody else, he could have ignored the invite.

Except he was the one who had given away the bride. Hard to ignore the invite when that was the case. Sighing, he tipped his beer back and counted down the minutes until he could make a polite escape.

For Lena, he could be polite.

"You look about as happy to be here as you'd be at your own funeral," a soft, quiet voice said.

Glancing down, he made himself smile.

Hope Carson stood barely five foot six, even in the three-inch heels she'd worn with her maid of honor dress. She was slender . . . and she was the only other person in the entire world with the power to get him into a monkey suit.

Her dress was as green as her eyes and gleamed against her pale skin. She'd always had that delicate beauty, but tonight, he had to admit, she looked amazing.

And every guy who looked at her longer than two seconds probably felt the lingering stare of her boyfriend, the county DA, Remy Jennings.

Well, every guy but Law. Law was nothing more than a brother to Hope, like she was nothing more than a sister to him, a fact that Remy was more than well aware of. So when Hope leaned against him and hugged him, Law wasn't overly concerned when Remy's eyes lingered on them. Hell, he enjoyed needling the guy anyway.

That was what had him leaning down and pressing his mouth to Hope's. Pissing the DA off was a favorite pastime of his. Had been for a while. Passing a hand over Hope's hair, careful not to dislodge the delicate spray of flowers near her right ear, he said, "You look amazing, sweetheart."

"Thanks." She smoothed a hand down one narrow hip and sent a look over her shoulder, smiling in Lena's direction. "It looks like her day went well, right?"

"Hell, she's married. That was the goal, right?"

Hope rolled her eyes. "You're such a guy. Yes, she's married . . . and that's the goal. Sort of. But getting there, how they do it, the memories . . . it matters."

"Whatever." Law took another drink of his beer, shooting Remy another look. He was talking to one of his cousins, Carter Jennings—Roz's husband.

Hank Jennings was also there with some woman Law couldn't immediately place. Hank was the mayor, and in

Law's opinion, a class A asshole. Although he'd gotten a little better over the past few months.

The Jennings clan—the whole damn county was lousy with them. Three cousins served on the town council. The vice principal of the high school was also a Jennings. Several of the county cops were Jennings by blood, a few were Jennings through marriage, and at least one person on the minuscule city police department.

A quarter of the people in Ash were related to the Jennings clan in some way, shape, or form. Hope would be one of them before another year was out, Law had no doubt about it.

"Speaking of goals . . . you thinking you might make a run for that goal with Remy any time soon?"

Hope blushed and hunched her shoulders. "I . . . I don't know."

"You haven't talked about it?"

Her blush deepened.

Law laughed. "That's a yes." And knowing her as well as he did, he suspected she was terrified and excited. Dipping his head, he kissed her again, this time, pressing his lips to her brow. "Go for it, kid. You know you're not going to find another guy who'll love you the way he does. And you're never going to love anybody as much as you love him."

She sighed. "No. You're right. I just . . ."

Something dark and ugly moved through her eyes, memories that would take a lot longer than a few months to fade.

"He's gone, kid. Dead and gone."

"I know. It's just . . ." She didn't have to say.

Law knew her as well as she knew herself sometimes. Hope and Law had gone to high school together, back in Clinton, Oklahoma, a small town that was pretty much dominated by one family, kind of like the Jenningses seemed to dominate Ash, Kentucky. At least in size.

But the Carson family wasn't a kind dictator.

Hope had married the golden boy, Joseph Carson, not too long after they'd graduated. His control over her had been subtle at first. *Dress how I want you to dress. Act how I want you to act. Wear your hair the way I want.*

And when she didn't, that's when the real abuse started.

Years passed and it got to the point where Hope felt the only escape was through killing herself. She'd tried . . . and failed. Her ex-husband had been a cop and he'd abused his badge and his family's name, managed to get her locked away in a mental institution.

When she got out, the abuse had gotten so much worse.

It wasn't until Law finally managed to get back in touch with her after a few years of sketchy communication that he realized just how bad things had been. He no longer gave a damn about any so-called power the Carson family might have had, and at that point, he'd been more than capable of causing his own brand of trouble.

He'd gone looking for Hope, and he would never forgive himself for not doing it sooner. Once he realized how bad things were, Law had been ready to kill Joe.

Although Hope had never confirmed it, he suspected that was what had given her the courage to leave. Not fear for herself, but fear for what it would do to Law's life.

Why in the *hell* hadn't he gone back sooner? Why hadn't he known? She'd gone through hell, and if he'd listened to his gut, he could have done . . . something. Anything.

Like kill the bastard. He could have killed the bastard, and saved Hope all that heartache. Damn the consequences.

A storm of memories burned in the back of his mind, memories he struggled to hold at bay. Fuck that bastard to hell and back—

"Law."

A soft, cool hand touched his cheek and he looked down, met Hope's sad eyes.

"It's not on us, right?"

He just stared at her.

"You keep telling me, I can't blame myself for what he did. I can't blame myself for Nielson being dead, and I can't blame myself for how he killed that girl."

Nielson—the cop who'd died saving Hope when Carson came after her.

And Joely.

*That girl* . . . the memory of the woman who'd lost her life was imprinted on his mind forever—a wound he'd carry for always. *That girl.* Swallowing, he looked away. His voice was gruff as he said, "Her name was Jolene. Joely Hollister."

"Joely." Hope looked away. "I know. I know her name. But you keep telling me I'm not to blame. How can I believe that, though, when I look at you and see just how much you blame yourself?"

Swearing, he shoved a hand through his dark, over-long golden-brown hair, only to have it fall right back into his face. Closing his eyes, he shook his head. "It's not the same, Hope. Damn it, I *knew* something was wrong, and I didn't listen to my gut. I didn't *do* anything . . ."

"Neither did I," she said flatly. "All the times he left bruises on me, I didn't just *know.* I had proof, physical proof. I could have left, I could have come to you—even a phone call would have been enough. But I stayed. I can try to move past my guilt, but it's going to be damn hard to do it, if I see my best friend wallowing in his."

He narrowed his eyes at her. "That's pretty damn manipulative."

"Yeah. It is." She cocked a brow at him. "But if it works . . ."

Then she shrugged and pushed up onto her toes, pressed a kiss to his cheek. "Stop brooding. Go talk to people. Ethan's here . . . that deputy from the sheriff's office. You two hang out some. Go talk to him. Have fun. You look like you're facing an IRS audit or something."

Law grimaced. Shit. He'd rather face that. He had an accountant he paid to handle that shit.

But he couldn't pay somebody to handle this for him.

# CHAPTER
# TWO

SHE WAS SLEEPING WHEN HE CLIMBED OUT OF BED.

By the time he came out of the shower, she was stirring and he knelt by the bed, pressed his lips to hers. She turned her head aside so his lips brushed her cheek. "Morning breath," she muttered.

He laughed.

"You going to call me when you get to the hotel?"

"Yes." Although he already knew the answer, being ever dutiful, he knew he had to ask. "You sure you don't want to come with me?"

In the dim light filtering from the hallway, he could see her grimace. "No. Not my thing. You know that. But you go . . . have fun."

He kissed her again. "I'll try. I'll miss you."

"Hmmm. You do that. Bring me back something pretty . . ."

"You know I will."

In his mind, he was already making plans.

He was heading to Chicago. It was a big city, one he was familiar with, and although he'd miss the pleasure of a leisurely hunt, he couldn't keep putting this off. The urge was a hungry, boiling need inside him . . .

By the time he was ready to head out the door, she was

already lost once more to sleep. He paused to look in on her one more time, smiling absently at her. Then he left, impatience building, burning inside him.

He needed to be gone, away from here and gone.

He hadn't realized it would be this hard to stop . . .

Her name was Katia. Or at least that was the name she'd given him. He didn't know if that was her true name, and just then, he didn't care. All he cared about was getting her out of this club. Getting her to a quiet, private place.

She didn't know her time was running down. He figured that the one thing she was aware of was the need for sex—he could see it in her eyes. It probably had something to do with the pills she'd been popping. He didn't much care for that, but in the end, it wouldn't matter. She'd still fight—he could see it in her eyes. He knew which ones would fight.

A fast hunt wasn't the same as a leisurely one, but there was pleasure in it just the same. A lot of pleasure.

They were walking down the block—or rather he was walking, she was stumbling while he held her up. One of her hands kept sliding down to rub his cock through his jeans and despite the need, he was a little disgusted with her. Beggars couldn't be choosers, though, and he knew Katia was ideal for his needs. Ideal . . .

Abruptly, she giggled and grabbed his hand, jerking him into an alley. "Let's do it in here."

"Wouldn't you rather get a hotel?" he asked.

"No." She grabbed the hem of her short dress, pulling it up to show that she wore no panties. Faint light fell across her hips and thighs, revealing her waxed cunt. "I want to do it here." She licked her finger and touched herself. "If you're good, then I'll let you get me a hotel. Later."

He lifted a brow and followed her deeper into the shadows. This . . . well, this could be a new challenge altogether. He had some of his tools secured inside the leather jacket he wore. It wasn't much, but it would suffice.

It wasn't like they were in a *quiet* area of town. He'd heard sirens three different times in the past ten minutes, all from different directions. Voices rising and falling, the occasional yell, the pump and blast of music coming from somewhere close—very close. Another club, he assumed.

Behind him, he heard footsteps, a shout. Automatically, he lowered his head, hunched his shoulders. Hiding his height, his face as much as he could as he moved across the busted-up pavement, feeling the crunch of broken glass under his feet.

She smiled at him and rubbed herself harder. "You want to fuck me in here?" she whispered, batting her lashes at him, giving him what she must assume was a seductive smile.

He smiled back and slipped a hand into his pocket. He needed a rubber. And a gag.

"Yes." He leaned in, kissed her, taking pleasure in it, giving her pleasure in return, smiling inwardly as she stilled, then sighed and shuddered against him. She whimpered in pleasure, and that pleased him.

All the while, her hands ran all over him and he let her do just that. When he pulled a rubber from his pocket, she grabbed it from him and put it on him, although he was careful to catch the wrapper, tucking it inside a zippered pocket, keeping it nice and safe.

Couldn't leave any fingerprints lying around after all. After he dealt with the wrapper, he found a thin pair of gloves, balled them up in his fist, so she wouldn't notice, wouldn't see.

She curled her hand around him, started to stroke, but he stopped her by reaching down, cupping her. She wasn't wet enough, not yet. Oh, he couldn't have that. A bit of finessing, a bit of patience . . . and a few more kisses and she was mewling into his mouth, shaking and rocking against him, desperate, all but begging. He made certain she came before he did anything else.

That was one of his favorite parts.

Now it was almost time for the next favorite. He pulled his gloves on, quickly, quietly, kissing her to keep her from paying attention. Although she was so strung out, and still riding high on the orgasm, she might not have noticed anyway.

When he leaned back, her lashes were low, shielding her eyes.

He reached up, stroked a hand down her cheek. Then, as her lashes started to flutter, he fisted a hand in her long golden curls and slammed her head back against the brick, once, twice, three times.

Hard—hard enough to stun her and as she sagged against him, silent, he slipped the gag into place. Once that was done, he glanced around once more.

Dark, damn dark.

She moaned, her head slumped against his chest. He steadied her, lifted her. Waited until she roused before he did anything else. It just wouldn't be much fun unless she was awake. Who wanted to fuck a motionless stick?

Her lashes lifted and he saw the moment fear began to slide into her eyes. That was when he pushed inside.

She didn't start to fight right away though.

She was still confused, thanks to the drugs in her system, and the blows to her head probably weren't helping. To aid that confusion along, he stroked her clit and murmured, "I love a bad girl who likes to play games."

She blinked and looked delightfully confused over the gag and as he started to pull out, she tightened around him—a startled, harsh moan ripping from her behind the gag.

She reached up, tried to pull it away. He caught her hands in one of his, slammed them over her head. Watched as that flicker of fear bloomed into something larger. She tried to pull away.

"No, Katia . . . it's part of the game. *My* game." He laughed as she started to struggle in earnest.

Watching her, he rested a hand on her neck, lightly at first, as he peered into her clearing eyes. No longer clouded by lust, no longer clouded by pain, and even the lingering effects of the drugs she'd been tossing back were clearing. Adrenaline could do that.

It wasn't fun, though, to let it end too fast. He let her have one hand free, resting his own on her neck.

He squeezed and watched as she reached up, raking her nails across his hands. Or trying to. She felt his gloves and freaked out. He chuckled as she started to fight. And that really did it for him. As his cock swelled and his balls drew tight, he wedged his forearm against her neck and whispered, "Didn't your mama teach you not to talk to strange men, Katia?"

Her name was Kathleen Hughes, not Katia.

But Kathleen was such a boring name . . . such a good girl name and she was so tired of people thinking she was a good girl.

She was twenty-four, damn it. Living on her own, having a good time, living her own life, living her own life and having fun. Tired of people expecting her to do what *they* wanted, tired of people expecting things of her, or even just being disappointed in her when she fucked up.

That was what she would have said if anybody had asked a few hours earlier.

So what if she was a little bit miserable lately? So what if she was missing her mom? Missing Jared, too . . . Jared—the bastard. And that was why she'd been popping those pills, because she'd been thinking about him, missing him, thinking about calling him.

But he wouldn't want her back . . . miserable thoughts that only made her more miserable, which made her pop more pills, and now she was out here, struggling to breathe, struggling to see, to think, to function.

She would have given anything to be back home, listening to her mother tell her, *You shouldn't dress that way . . . you should try to find a nice boy, Kathleen . . . not* those *kinds of boys. Kathleen, please . . .*

Would have given anything to be back with Jared, where she felt safe . . .

She tried to scratch, tried to bite, but her attacker just laughed. And he slammed into her, brutally—what had felt so good, even if a little wicked a few minutes ago, now hurt and tore and burned and she moaned, tried to pull away. Tried to think past the pain in her head, between her legs. Tried to think past the fear—

She needed to get away from him. Needed to scream for help.

But she could barely breathe. The gag. She tried to spit it out but that didn't work. Tried to pull her hands away from his, but his grip was brutal, merciless. Whimpering, she stared at him, tried to beg him silently to let her go.

And then he dipped his head, gave her one of those sweet, tender kisses, pressed lovingly against her neck even as his body tore into hers. When he lifted up and smiled down at her, Kathleen struck out at him with her head, slamming her forehead against his. But he evaded, as though he'd known exactly what she was going to do. Slumping against the wall, tears trickling down her cheeks, she shuddered and tried to twist away when he started to touch her again—this time gently. Even as pain was ripping through her.

*NO NO NO NO . . .*

He was fucking *laughing* at her . . . turning her body against her.

Bastard—

Fucking bastard . . .

Through a red haze, she glared at him and with a strength she didn't know she had, she wrenched against his hold. Her wrists, slippery, slick with her sweat, twisted and she got one free. Blindly, she swung out, driving her fist into his neck, then again into his nose.

He snarled and swore, but didn't let go. He fisted a hand in her hair, slammed her head back against the wall again, harder this time. A second time. A third.

By the fourth time, she was no longer even aware of what he was doing.

By the fifth time, she was unconscious. There was a sixth . . . a seventh . . . an eighth time. She never knew.

Kathleen died of a brain hemorrhage before he was even done using her.

"Cunt," he muttered, kicking her side as he let her fall to the ground. His throat still ached from the jab and his nose was tender, puffy. Not broken, thankfully. That would have been harder to explain away. But the little slut had gotten a few good blows in.

Swearing, he knelt and wished he had the time to let her wake up. He'd do it all over again, but this time, he'd make her hurt more. There was no time, though. Closing a hand around her mouth and nose, he squeezed. A few seconds passed before he realized she wasn't breathing.

Swearing, he jerked his hand away, stared at her face. Her eyes were closed. Her face slack. Shit.

He lifted one lid. Stared at her pupil, stunned when there was no reaction.

Lifeless.

Still not processing it, he rested his fingers on her neck, searching for a pulse that wasn't there.

Nothing.

Disgust rolled through him as he realized he'd been fucking her corpse.

Swearing, he grabbed her shoulder and rolled her over, and that was when he saw the back of her head. Saw the damage. It was all pulpy and misshapen, the bones of her skull pulverized.

Fuck . . .

He surged to his feet and cast a quick glance around the alley. Although every instinct screamed for him to get the hell away, he needed to be careful. Very careful. Shit. He'd screwed up. Screwed up bad. Had let his anger get the better of him, had been in too big a hurry, hadn't taken his time, hadn't been *careful*. That was the bottom line—he hadn't been careful. Then, when she'd managed to get a hand free and hit him, fight back, she'd caught him off guard.

He'd fucked up.

When the cops found her, he knew they'd examine her.

Would they realize penetration had happened after her death? Or while she died? Shit, he wasn't a fucking necrophiliac. She'd been alive when he started on her. Fucking cunt. Damn it.

Too screwed up. This was all too screwed up. All this time, he'd been so careful.

Ever since the mistakes he'd made with Mara, he'd been careful not to do it again. But lately it seemed like his entire house of cards was about to come crashing down around him. Shit, shit, shit.

"Get it together," he told himself. He made himself take a deep breath, calm down . . . think.

And that was when he realized.

Maybe if they thought he'd taken her *after* she'd died . . . well. That wasn't a bad thing for *them*. What did he care if they thought he was into fucking stiffs? They'd be looking for different crimes, then. Different sort of criminal. That wasn't a problem. Not at all. If they were looking for a different sort of criminal, how likely were they to find him? Even if they were looking?

He'd only have problems if he lost control of the situation and he wasn't going to do that. He wasn't going to do that at all.

Nobody would know he had been here, nobody would connect the man who'd left the club with this girl to who he was. Nobody.

He just had to keep calm. Keep cool. Do that, and nobody would be any wiser.

His hands were steadier as he freed the gag from her mouth. It had her blood on it. He'd have to get rid of it. But later. A lot later. Crouching by her side, he drew a ceramic knife from the inner pocket of his jacket and caught one lock of hair. He did love that knife . . . made it so much easier considering how many places used metal detectors these days. And he wanted his souvenir.

It wasn't a neat job—too much of her hair had blood and brain matter matted in it so he couldn't cut all of it the way he usually did. Just a nice, gleaming hank that was free of gore. He didn't like making a hatchet job of it, but this girl was so fucked up from his normal, anyway, what did it matter?

He'd be more careful in the future. More careful, he'd plan better. And control things better—couldn't risk getting that angry again.

This wouldn't happen again.

He'd have to find a new MO, a new way to hunt his

girls—replan, reformulate. Reorganize. No more mistakes. No more losing control.

Tucking away the hair and the knife, he removed his gloves and tucked them inside his jacket as well. He donned a new pair before he attended to the final task—this was easy. He had known she was the one the moment he saw the diamonds glittering on her wrist. Real diamonds, despite the pink pleather dress. He didn't know where she'd gotten the bracelet, but it was his now. Another souvenir . . . a special gift for the special girl in his life.

Once he had it tucked away, he made his way to the mouth of the alley.

He had to get back to his hotel. Needed to destroy these clothes, shower . . . And he still needed to get some sleep before all those damned meetings tomorrow.

# CHAPTER
# THREE

Two months later

WITH HER HEAD PROPPED ON HER FIST, NIA HOLLIS-
ter surveyed the crime scene photos and police report
of yet another raped, murdered woman. She'd gone
through half a pack of cigarettes, two cans of Monster,
and she knew she couldn't stay awake too much longer.

Knew she couldn't keep this up too much longer.

*You can't keep this up,* her common sense argued.
*How much longer are you going to let this take over
your life?*

"For as long as it takes," she muttered, taking another
drag on the cigarette.

At least when she was looking for some indefinable
*something,* she felt like she was *doing* something. Felt
like she was making steps toward wrapping up the unfinished mess that was her cousin's murder. It didn't
matter that they had closed the case, that they had a
name for the killer, that the killer was dead.

It didn't matter . . . because it didn't feel *right.* Nothing felt right, nothing felt finished, or complete—it all
felt *wrong.*

Her eyes were bleary with exhaustion and her head
ached. Her belly was an empty, shriveled knot, but she
wasn't leaving her desk until she'd finished going through

these files. She'd spent the past two weeks in Europe on assignment, hadn't been able to do a damn thing with all the information that kept coming her way, and she was going to make a dent in it.

*How?* Somewhere, she still possessed the ability to be rational. It was fading, and fading fast, but she could still do it. And that rational part of her brain was demanding how in the hell she could make a dent in the dozens and dozens of files she had sitting all over her office. Cases about women raped, and murdered. She'd tried to keep the scope relatively narrow—young, attractive, from the Midwest.

There were still too many. She felt raw inside. Her on-again, off-again boyfriend had walked in on her a few hours earlier after taking one look at the files.

"When are you going to let this go? They found the guy."

*No, they didn't,* she wanted to argue. But it wouldn't matter if she argued or not. He wouldn't believe her. And it didn't matter if he did or not.

He'd stared at her, something in his eyes that was pity, anger, and sadness. Then he'd turned and walked out. Somehow, she'd known he wouldn't be back.

It didn't matter. Nothing did. Except the search. She had to keep looking. Keep searching. For what, she didn't know. But Nia couldn't let it go. She couldn't leave it alone.

It didn't matter that they had found the guy. She had to keep looking . . . it was like the monkey on her back, riding her, pushing her, driving her. She had to keep looking, had to, had to . . .

Eyes heavy and gritty, she flipped through the file of a twenty-one-year-old nursing student who'd been assaulted and killed in St. Louis. They hadn't found the killer. Nia's heart ached for the girl. But beyond the grief, the heartache, she felt nothing when she read the reports, looked at the pictures.

Nothing that told her *this* was what she was looking for—*this* was what she needed to find. Not that she was *expecting* to feel something. She just . . .

Shit. She didn't even know what she was expecting. Looking for. Hoping to find. She reached for the nearly empty can of Monster, took a sip, and then reached for the next in her "hopeful" pile. But exhaustion made her clumsy and she ended up knocking over the "hopeful" and the "not-so-hopeful." Swearing, she made a mad grab at fluttering pages, eyeing the mess around her desk.

"Hell." Pushing her hair back, she hoped the people who'd sent her all these files had some recognizable sort of organization. With a groan, she scooted away from her desk, tempted to just ignore the mess and head to bed.

She might have just done that, too. She was so tired, so damn tired.

But a picture caught her eye.

She couldn't say why.

Staring at it, though, she *felt* something.

A burn. That *thing* she'd been waiting for—*this* was what she'd been searching for, *who* she'd been searching for. There wasn't anything really intriguing about the woman's face. She looked nothing like Joely.

She had hair so pale a blond, it didn't seem natural at all. Big blue eyes, big round breasts . . . a lot like a Barbie doll, right down to the bright pink-and-white sundress that barely skimmed her ass. Everything about her sparkled, her smile, her eyes, the diamond bracelet on her left wrist.

Her name was Kathleen Hughes.

The next picture of her wasn't quite so attractive.

She was lying on a slab, her skin that pale, bluish-gray

color of death, and the pink pleather dress she wore was splattered with blood, gore, and dirt.

Nia sifted through the files, finding everything pertaining to Hughes and then she started to read. She had nothing in common with Joely, other than being physically attractive, and young. Joely had excelled in all things—this girl was big into partying, hard and fast, making up for what looked like a relatively normal, borderline-boring childhood. She'd barely been coasting along in college and had been working some on the side at a club as a stripper.

Nothing in common with Joely.

But looking at Kathleen's face, Nia's gut twisted, burned, and adrenaline roared inside her. It couldn't be anything, though. Because Kathleen had just died two months ago.

Joe Carson had been dead now for nine months.

Still . . .

Unable to resist, she continued to read. Brutally raped. Drugs in her system. Roommate confirmed she'd been using for a while. No boyfriend—her last serious boyfriend had a solid alibi—he was an ER doctor at a hospital in Detroit, a Dr. Jared Roberts, and he'd been working in said Detroit hospital the night Kathleen died . . . in Chicago.

She'd been seen leaving the club with a guy—only description was "an older dude."

Nia frowned, checked the info in the folder on the ex-boyfriend. Somehow pink pleather Barbie didn't look like the sort of girl a doctor would date. He was thirty-five . . . and originally from Kathleen's hometown of Madison, Indiana.

Eleven-year difference. Would that count as an older dude? Then she sighed. Didn't matter. He was alibied. And why did it even matter?

But she couldn't stop reading.

She read through the medical examiner's report, her head pounding, her heart racing.

One line caught her eye. She found herself stumbling over it. Again. And again. Even as her mind tried to process it, Nia found herself seeing her cousin. Lying on a slab . . . just like Kathleen. Her hair . . . shorter than Nia remembered. A lot shorter.

Nia hadn't thought much of it. Not then.

But now . . . Her breath hitched in her chest, right next to that burning ache. Swallowing, she rubbed her eyes and made herself read it one more time. Kathleen Hughes's hair had been cut sometime that night. Not completely—just a section toward the front, a six-inch-long section.

Her hand shook as she reached for her cell phone.

It took three tries to actually get her hands to cooperate long enough to call Bryson. Before her cousin died, Bryson had been Joely's fiancé, and a casual friend of Nia's. The two of them had tried to keep in touch for a while, but both Nia and Bryson had finally realized their memories were too painful.

Needless to say, he wasn't pleased to have her on the phone. "Nia . . . it's late."

She glanced at the clock, winced when she saw it was past eleven.

"Sorry. This won't take long. I just . . . ah, well. I had a question. Had Joely gotten her hair cut recently?"

"Her hair? What?"

"Yeah. A haircut. Had she gotten it cut before she . . . ah . . . died?"

He sighed. "No. She hadn't. She wanted it long for the wedding—something . . ." His voice half broke. "Shit. No. I don't know what the hell this is about, but she hadn't gotten her fucking hair cut."

"Okay. Thank you."

He hung up without saying another word.

Nia put her phone down and continued to stare at the report. This didn't mean anything. She waited for that rational voice to murmur an agreement, waited for that voice to tell her to dump this file, just like she had dumped so many others.

But for once, that voice was silent.

Completely and utterly silent.

The house was silent . . . completely and utterly silent, save for the slow, measured sound of Law Reilly's breathing as he lifted the bar up, lowered it, lifted.

Sweat rolled down his brow, along his arms. He ignored it, focusing on the weighted bar. Just like he ignored the trembling in his arms—especially in his right. That arm, still trying to heal from that bad break, didn't seem as strong as it should be, and by the time he was done with the third set of reps, his muscles were quivering, all but begging for a rest.

He ignored them, moved to the next set of exercises, and the next. It wasn't until he'd worked his body into a numb state of exhaustion that he let himself leave the gym he'd set up in his basement. On his way down the hall, he passed by a closed door.

Months ago, it had been his office.

Now, it was nothing but unused space.

Awhile back, he'd finally admitted the obvious and moved his books and everything else out of the room, turning his living room into his office. Wasn't like he had a lot of company out here anyway.

There was just no way he could work in that room again, that room where a man had died, slowly, painfully. Although the professional team had gotten the blood out of the floor, although he'd redecorated, even put down a new floor, he couldn't look at the room without seeing it the way it had been that night. Without seeing the blood.

Shit, there were days when he didn't even want to live in this house—it wasn't just the office, but the *house*. But Law wasn't about to give in to that—wouldn't let the bastard win that battle.

He'd keep his damn house, but the office . . . no. He wasn't fighting that one. He couldn't stand to go in there—even though it no longer looked anything like it had looked all those months ago. Law still couldn't look at that room without seeing blood.

Without remembering how a guy he'd known in elementary school had killed a cop in there, then tried to kill Law, and Hope. Shit, there were days when he thought if he had any sense at all, he would tear this damn house down, build a new one.

Screw tearing it down—burn it and salt the earth, make sure no demons from the past could rise to haunt them. Then he'd move to Fiji, buy a shack on the beach, and write from there.

But he was too fucking stubborn to do that. Too stubborn, too determined.

And he knew the demons would still be there anyway.

The demons lived in his memories, not in the house, not in the earth. He couldn't eradicate them from his memory, so he'd just have to deal with them, live with them.

Those memories weren't going to win, damn it. They weren't.

Joe was dead, Hope was safe, and she was happier than she'd ever been in her life. It was over. Completely over.

He'd just started up the steps when the phone rang.

His muscles turned to lead as he turned to stare. It was late. There had been a time when late calls wouldn't faze him, but after the past year, it was hard to ignore the dread creeping through him. Hard to ignore the worry, the fear.

Not too many people would be calling him. Not too many people had his number. Hope and Remy. Lena and Ezra. His agent. A few friends. That was about it—and none of them would call him this late unless it was an emergency.

Scowling, he moved to the phone, stared at the caller ID.

Virginia. Did he know anybody in Virginia?

The machine picked up and he stood there, dumbly, as a voice rolled out. Low and smooth, soft and sexy as black velvet draped over a woman's nude body.

"Hello. I'm . . . looking for Law Reilly. My name is Nia Hollister. I . . . ah, we met a few months ago . . ."

Yeah. He hadn't forgotten. They'd met the day she accused him of killing her cousin. The day she'd punched him, drawn a gun on him—not exactly the sort of woman a guy was going to forget.

Without realizing what he was doing, he reached for the phone.

"Hello."

"Ahh . . . Mr. Reilly?"

He just waited.

"Ah . . . hello. This . . . okay, this is awkward. My name is Nia Hollister. We met a few months ago—"

"I remember." Short, silken, dark hair. Big gold eyes. A mouth that he would have given his right arm to taste. Long legs. Attitude. Grief. And a gun . . . mustn't forget that gun, or the fact that she'd come onto his property ready to kill him, and Hope, if she'd decided they had something to do with her cousin's death.

Stupid, he knew, being that hung up on a woman with that kind of reckless disregard. But he couldn't help himself, couldn't stop thinking about her, even months later.

Even now he found himself wondering what that mouth of hers would feel like pressed against his. How she would taste. How she would feel if he pressed her up against a wall, then pressed himself against her . . .

"Yeah. For some reason, that doesn't surprise me," Nia muttered, her voice low and soft. Then she cleared her throat. "Look, I'm sorry to be calling so late. I just wanted to . . . well . . ."

Her voice trailed off.

Law cocked a brow and leaned back against the wall. "You wanted to what?" he asked when her silence stretched from a few seconds into nearly a minute.

"I . . . shit. Has anything else, um, weird happened in Ash since, well, you know, that shithead died?"

"Weird." Law ran his tongue along his teeth and tried to get his brain to think about something *beyond* the physical images. But he wasn't having much luck. "Define weird."

She muttered under her breath and then abruptly said, "You know what? Forget it."

And just like that, she hung up.

# CHAPTER FOUR

*DEFINE WEIRD*, HE TELLS HER.

Nia was still trying to decide if Law Reilly had been trying to piss her off or if he'd been serious.

Weird was *weird*. What was there to define? But screw it. She'd just check things out herself. And that was what she was doing, why she'd spent the past eleven-something hours on her bike, driving from home to Ash, the small town almost an hour outside of Lexington.

She wanted answers—she'd get them. Wasn't like she had anything better to do, not really. She couldn't focus, couldn't concentrate, and it was finally starting to show in her work, as evidenced by the fact that the last job she'd tried to get, they'd given it to somebody with half her experience, half her talent. But more heart, that much Nia could admit. She had no heart left, not for this at least.

She'd spent so many years building her career in photo-journalism, but lately, all she was doing was flushing it down the drain. She didn't give a damn, either.

She had to find closure, find some way to make herself accept this, or her life, as she knew it at least, was just going to stay in limbo. So she was back here. Whether or not she'd stay for long, Nia didn't know. But the trouble had started here, so this was where she would start.

For now.


This was . . . unexpected.

He watched from the café as she rode into town. He'd seen her before. But the last time she'd been in town had been months ago . . . not long before things had come to a head.

Everything was over now. Why was she here? Why now?

For reasons that he couldn't really understand, the sight of her had him . . . twitchy.

"One hell of a bike, huh?"

He glanced over as a couple of deputies came out. Giving them a smile, he shrugged and said, "I guess. I don't know much about motorcycles."

"I bet it would be a hell of a ride," Ethan Sheffield said, a wide, wicked grin on his face. "The bike. The babe."

Kent Jennings, a member of the city's finest, smacked Ethan in the back of the head. "Your wife would kill you—over the bike *and* the babe. And you wouldn't consider either of them—you're too damn whipped."

"Yeah. But I can think . . . right?"

Joking with the rest of them, he still watched her, watched as she pulled up in front of the sheriff's office . . . watched.

Wondered.


"Okay, Joely . . . I'm trying," she muttered, climbing off her bike and staring up at the courthouse.

Nia could all but feel the eyes crawling all over her as she started toward the sheriff's office. She knew she wouldn't find Dwight Nielson in there. She'd attended his funeral, although she'd kept to the back and left without speaking to a soul.

What she'd known of the guy, she had liked. It bothered her that the guy who had killed her cousin had cut such a wide swath of death. A sheriff, a deputy, her cousin . . . and he'd almost killed Hope Carson, as well. If it wasn't for the sheriff, Hope would have died, too, probably.

Hope had survived, though. She'd survived and because of the sheriff, the son of a bitch Carson was dead in the ground.

Still, it just didn't sit right. Nia just couldn't buy it.

*That* was why she was here.

It didn't matter that she didn't belong here. It didn't matter that they had told her that her cousin's killer was dead. It didn't matter that everybody else insisted that things fit—that it was over.

It didn't *fit* for her. Nia liked it when things fit into a certain order and for some reason, these things didn't fit into the order they were supposed to fit, and *damn* it, she wasn't going to get whatever closure she needed until those pieces fit.

It was just . . . too easy, she guessed. Something that was too easy didn't settle right with her.

Besides that, her instincts were humming. Nia trusted her instincts. Even though right now, she knew it might be grief pushing her to cling to something . . . anything.

But she didn't think that was the case.

As she started toward the sheriff's office, something shivered down her spine and her instincts went from a hum to a scream. Casually, she reached into her hip pocket and tugged her iPhone, pulled it out. Pretending to study it, she lowered her head. Using the phone as camouflage, she looked around without moving her head, tried to isolate just where that feeling was coming from.

Somebody was watching her. Staring at her—*hard*. She could all but feel the heavy intensity of that stare. But try as she might, she couldn't figure out where it was coming from.

"Sheriff."

Ezra still had to fight the urge to flinch when she said it in that tone of voice. He kept expecting Ms. Tuttle to throw him out on his ass for being an impostor. And honestly, he felt like one.

Plastering what was most likely a very false-looking smile on his face, he met her bright, impossibly vivid green eyes and said, "Good morning, Ms. Tuttle. How are you doing?"

"Not running late, as you obviously were."

A dull red blush crept up his cheeks—he hadn't been late.

His hours were typically from eight in the morning until five and he had been in this damn seat by 7:53. Normally, he was here at 7:30, the same time as Ms. Tuttle, because she terrified him. But that morning . . . well, Lena had slipped into the shower with him. He had lost track of time.

Without looking away, he said, "I was attending to an important personal matter."

For a split second, he thought he saw what might have been a smile tugging at her stern mouth. But then it was gone—gone before he could be sure. "Hmph. I'm sure you were. Well, I hope it was very important. Now . . . I assume you're ready to handle *business* matters, Sheriff. There's a young lady here to speak with you. Claims she knew Sheriff . . . Sheriff Nielson."

Ms. Tuttle's eyes gleamed brightly for a second, too brightly, and she looked away. To give her a moment, Ezra frowned and pretended to study the ruthlessly organized calendar she always provided for him.

"I don't see anybody on my schedule."

"Hmph. Like you would know what to do with that schedule if I didn't *give* it to you," she muttered. Then she sighed and reached up, patted her hair. "She's not on the schedule, Sheriff King. Her name is Nia Hollister—"

Ezra looked up. "Hollister."

"Yes."

Their eyes locked, bright and snapping green with dark, deep forest green. Ezra looked away first.

That name would echo through this county for decades. None of them knew the woman who had died here. Died in their town. But none of them would ever forget her either.

"Nia," he murmured. "That would be Jolene's—the victim's—cousin."

"Yes. Do you have time to speak to her?"

Although it was a question, it was asked in such a way that Ezra knew if he said no, he might as well hold out his knuckles to get them rapped. Not that he'd planned on saying *no*, anyway.

Still, he couldn't let her think she had him completely cowed. Right?

He folded his face into stern lines and met her gaze somberly. "I'll make time. But we need to try to stick to the schedule."

"I make the damn schedule," she sniffed. Then she turned on her square heels and let herself out.

Letting his head fall against the back of his chair, he muttered, "Dwight, I appreciate you leaving me the dragon, but geez. How do I rein her in?"

There wasn't an answer, of course, and three minutes later, he forced himself upright as he heard the familiar *tap-tap-tap* of Ms. Tuttle's heels on the tile floors. He didn't hear anybody else behind her, although he imagined Joely Hollister's cousin was there.

And she was . . . A second later, the door opened and

Ms. Tuttle stepped aside, allowing a woman to enter before she closed the door and tap-tapped down the hall.

Once Ms. Tuttle was gone, he focused on his visitor.

She was tall—that was Ezra's first impression.

She was gorgeous—that was his second impression.

She was heartbroken—that was his third, and final, impression.

Even after all this time, she was still broken inside. And there wasn't much of anything he could do to help her with that, either. He couldn't give her the closure she needed, because he was still having trouble finding it himself.

"Sheriff King, right?"

He rose from behind his desk. "Yes, that's right. And you're Nia Hollister."

She gave him a tight, strained smile. "Yes. Thanks for seeing me like this."

"Not a problem." He gestured to the seat across from his desk and waited until she'd sat before he lowered himself back to his chair. As she crossed one jean-clad leg over the other, he folded his hands. "What can I do for you?"

She swallowed and looked down, studying the black messenger bag she carried. "I . . . this isn't easy," she said quietly. She looked back at him, once more giving him that tight, strained smile. "I usually have something of a reputation for being very calm, logical . . . rational. I don't . . . well, I don't know exactly, but lately, I'm so paranoid, I'm even annoying myself and that's not like me."

Ezra cocked a brow at her. "Why don't you just tell me why you're here?"

She reached inside the black bag, pulling out a file folder. "I . . . I don't know if you know much about my cousin."

"There's not a person in this town who doesn't know about your cousin, Ms. Hollister. We're all terribly sorry," he said softly.

"Thank you." She nodded, gripping the folder so tightly her toffee-colored skin went bloodless. "I . . . I'd been out of town for a few weeks before she was killed. And not in very good contact before that. It had been probably close to three months since I'd seen her. Her fiancé, well, he just—he couldn't cope with anything after he was told she'd died, and she was in bad shape. We had a closed casket ceremony."

She stroked the folder, her gold eyes staring off into the distance, seeing something. Memories, Ezra assumed. Unpleasant ones, he suspected, judging by the way her mouth tightened, the way her lower lip trembled as she fought against tears.

"Three months," she whispered again. "When I saw her the day I came to identify her, I didn't think about her hair."

Something inside Ezra went cold. "Her hair?"

Nia's eyes cut to his. "It was short—too short. I'd thought maybe she'd gotten it cut . . . they were getting married soon, and I thought . . . well, I wasn't really reading e-mail much, deleting a lot. Not keeping an eye on Facebook or anything either. I just didn't think. But her hair was too short. And she didn't cut it."

"How do you know?"

Nia cocked her head. "I asked her fiancé. Joely wanted long hair for her wedding . . . and if that's what she said she wanted, she wouldn't have cut it on a whim. Not my cousin." With a strained smile, she said, "Joely didn't do whims. She just didn't. I might react on a whim and go short with my hair, but once she made up her mind, she didn't change it."

Tucking that information away, Ezra studied her face.

"Okay. I'm trying to understand why you're telling me this, but okay."

"I think her killer did it." Then she reached inside the folder and pulled out a picture. It was a close-up of a woman's necklace—a gold heart, simple, elegant. Nothing particularly unique about it. "And her necklace is missing."

Ezra frowned, studying the little bit of gold. "No necklace was reported on her or near the victim. We found a pair of earrings, an engagement ring, and her watch. But no necklace."

"I know. I'm the one who claimed her personal effects. But she would have worn that necklace. It wasn't in her car, her home, and nobody has reported it in the days since she died. I think the killer took it."

Now the ice in Ezra's gut was a cold fire—cold, but ready. Just like him. He felt strangely excited . . . tense but somehow loose. Even as he tried to tell himself to let it go, to move on. "That's a possibility, but unless we find where he kept his . . ."

"Trophies?" Nia offered, lifting a brow.

He didn't respond, wasn't entirely sure *how* to.

"I'm telling you this to give you another tool *to* find him," she said softly.

"Find him," Ezra repeated.

*Find him*—fuck, he wished he could just write her words off. Find him—Joe Carson didn't *need* to be found. He was buried in Clinton, Oklahoma, and half the town there was cursing the people of Ash, Kentucky, while the other half was secretly crowing in delight or thanking God and muttering about just rewards.

*Find him*—according to the way the case went down, Jolene Hollister's killer didn't *need* to be found because he was already dead. He'd been found with those personal effects, personal effects that had belonged to

Jolene Hollister. It had been enough to incriminate him. Questioning after the fact revealed he had been seen in town, often, and he was also staying in a motel in another small town twenty miles away—the room had been in his name for several weeks. Before that, there was no record of him in Ash or even near the town, but if a cop couldn't cover his tracks, who could?

Oh, yeah, Ezra wanted to think that Nia was paranoid, even waited a few seconds to give his brain a chance to conjure up the appropriate, noncondescending response.

It wouldn't come.

As he stared into golden eyes, all he could feel was a faint, excited hum in his blood . . . one that was all too familiar.

"Exactly why do you think I need tools to find him?" he asked finally, leaning back in his chair, keeping his poker face on.

"Well, at least you're not patting me on the head and reminding me that you guys buried somebody, somebody you think did it," she muttered, more to herself than him.

Ezra chuckled. "I get the feeling that if some guy tried to pat you on the head, he might draw back a bloody stump, Ms. Hollister. And you haven't answered me."

"I'm still trying to figure out how to say it. I was prepared to come in here and have you throw me out on my ass, seeing as how you were probably involved in closing that case."

"No." He shrugged. "I just stepped into this slot at the beginning of the year. The deputy sheriff, Steven Mabry, took over the job temporarily, but he was only willing to do it until they found somebody else. It's not a job he wanted for the long haul just yet."

Nia lifted a brow. "I take it you're the somebody else?"

"Yeah." He grimaced, absently reaching down to rub his leg. "I'm the somebody else."

"So maybe that's why you're not throwing me out on my ass. You haven't been involved in this from the get-go." She inclined her head as she spoke.

Ezra grinned at her. "Oh, no. Make no mistake. I couldn't have been any more *involved* in this if I'd asked. And I didn't ask—didn't want it, either. Now that you're done stalling, why don't you tell me just why you think I need to find a killer when the record says he's already been found . . . found dead, by the way?"

A straight shooter, Nia surmised.

A drop-dead gorgeous one, too. Under normal circumstances, she'd like to see him in front of her camera. Those deep green eyes, that wide, somewhat wicked smile.

But Nia's life was so far from normal . . . Still trying to find the words, she looked around his office. Absently, she glanced down, saw the glint of gold on his hand. "You're married."

"Yep. Few months ago. And you're still stalling."

"Not . . . stalling. Formulating." Nervously, she rose from the chair and started to pace. Her messenger bag bumped against her hip as she did and she rested a hand on it, on the files inside. "This . . . shit. I was out here before, back when Sheriff Nielson was trying to find my cousin's killer. Did you hear about that?"

A faint grin curved Ezra's mouth up. "Enough to hear that you've got a mean right hook."

"I take it you and Reilly are friends." She blushed hotly and looked away.

"Of a sort. Yeah, I guess. He's one of my wife's best friends. And because I love her, I try not to hate him."

Curious, she glanced back at him. "Ah, why would you hate him for being friends with her?"

"Because he had a thing for her when I first moved here." Then he scowled. "Shit, you got a way of making people tell you things, you know that."

He glanced down, studying a picture frame on his desk.

Nia followed his gaze. "Is that your wife?"

He nodded.

Nia waited, but he didn't hold it out to her. She lifted a brow. "May I see?"

"You don't want to see." There was something in his voice . . . something strained, she realized.

It made a shiver of cold race down her spine for reasons she couldn't understand.

"Why not?" Nia asked, ignoring the voice that whispered, *Leave it alone.*

Ezra studied her face with narrowed eyes. "Did you come out here to talk about your cousin or study my wedding picture? I'm just curious."

"The case. But now I'm curious why you think I shouldn't see the picture." She ambled up to the desk, reaching out, slowly, deliberately.

Ezra didn't stop her as she traced a finger down the smooth crystal, then lifted it. It was the fancy sort of frame somebody would buy as a wedding gift—heavy and solid and expensive.

"It will hurt you," Ezra said quietly. He reached out, wrapped his fingers around her wrist. "I promise you that."

Then he shifted his gaze to hers, and once more, she saw the compassion there. Swallowing, she tugged away from his grasp, still holding the picture. At first, her brain couldn't quite process what she was seeing. Not at first.

It was a trick—had to be. The framed picture was a collage. The largest image was like a punch straight to her gut and she almost doubled over from the pain.

The second image showed the woman with her back to the photographer, a pale, smooth back. That alone had Nia biting her lip, hard enough to draw blood. *It's not her, girl. It's not her, it's not Joely . . . it's not, it's not . . .* Her back, long and slim, left bare by her wedding dress. Nia could see her shoulders, and they were unmarked, pale as porcelain.

No butterfly tattoo.

The strength drained out of Nia's legs and if the sheriff hadn't come around the desk, she might have ended up on her ass, right there on the floor.

He caught her arm, eased her back. "I'm sorry," he said gruffly, catching the frame as it slipped from her numb fingers.

"Who . . . who is that?"

"It's my wife," he said gently.

Nia lifted her head, staring at him, feeling so battered, so drained. "Your . . . your wife. She's your wife."

"Yeah. I can't imagine how much it hurts. When I—when I first saw the picture of your cousin, I couldn't quite get over it myself. That's why I didn't really want you seeing her picture."

"She—I, well." Nia nodded, pressed her lips together. "I can see the differences, but it's spooky."

"You're telling me." Ezra grimaced. Then he paused, studying her face. "Are you okay? Do you need a drink?"

"Fuck, no." She winced and muttered, "Sorry. I can't put anything in my stomach, though. I'd puke all over the floor."

"Okay." He leaned back against the desk, setting the picture down, angled away so Nia couldn't see it.

Not that it mattered. She wasn't likely to forget there was a woman out there who was almost her cousin's twin. A woman who lived in this town where her cousin had died.

This was too much— She wanted out of here. *Now*.

But she wouldn't do that. Not until she'd done what she came for. She'd come for a reason and Nia didn't walk just because things got hard. She didn't do it.

Taking a deep breath, she reached into her bag and pulled out the folder. "I know whoever took over after Sheriff Nielson died says they closed the case. But it doesn't sit right with me. I can't buy it. Something . . . shit. I don't know, it's like there are pieces missing from the puzzle and until I've got those pieces, I can't find whatever so-called closure I'm supposed to find to get on with my life. So . . . well, I've been digging around."

Ezra narrowed his eyes. "Digging around how?"

"Online, mostly. Phone calls, sometimes. People give me information—providing I don't do anything with it." She gave him a tight smile. "I know people. I'm a photojournalist. For a while, I thought I wanted to be an investigative reporter, but then I figured out I preferred to capture the story from behind the camera. And I'm better at it. Still, I've got decent instincts and I know people. Called in some favors."

She licked her lips and looked down at the folder. The one holding the information on Kathleen Hughes. With a shaking hand, she held it out to the sheriff, watched as he took it. But as he flipped it open, she looked away, unable to watch his face. "I've been following up on missing persons reports and women who've been assaulted and murdered. Nothing really clicked with anybody until I saw her. She doesn't really fit the profile right. She doesn't look anything like my cousin. She was younger, into parties, living hard. If I had been looking to connect them, I never would have."

From the corner of her eye, she saw him flipping through it.

"So why did you?" he asked, his voice absent, distracted.

She wasn't fooled. When she shot a look at him, she could tell he was taking in everything. Everything about the victim—about the information in his hands.

She saw the exact moment he found what had jumped out at her—what had made *her* connect things. And then she waited for him to tell her she really needed to let go . . . to move on her with her life.

Instead, he cocked his head and plucked the report out, reading it over a second time.

"Her hair was cut," he murmured. He flicked a glance at her.

She swallowed and nodded.

"Not all of it—the guy probably didn't want to get anything on him. Looks like . . ."

"He messed her up good," Nia said, shrugging. "I'm not delicate, Sheriff King. I've seen a number of dead bodies, more than I care to remember. But I'm not delicate. She would have had blood and brain tissue all over her. If he'd been found hauling *that* around . . ."

"Wouldn't be wise," Ezra murmured.

"There's more," she said quietly.

He flipped it over and when he came to the part where a roommate mentioned a bracelet missing, his eyes narrowed.

"She was wearing some pretty expensive bling—the bracelet was made custom for her, although it wouldn't have been obvious at first—it was engraved on the inside with the words, *For my angel*," Nia said.

She hadn't known about that until she talked to the woman's roommate a few days later. It had been inscribed with *For my angel*—it had been a gift from an old boyfriend, the doctor in Detroit. She'd dropped the boyfriend, kept the bling. Nia had gotten a few more details from the roommate as well—the bracelet *wasn't* one of a kind, but there were two details that might as well make it that way.

It had been inscribed and set with a stone . . . on the inside. A sapphire, a small one.

Kathleen's birthstone. Apparently the doctor had wanted her to have something unique—she'd wanted the bracelet, but he'd wanted it to be special for her. But Nia kept that bit of information quiet.

"You can see that she had on some pretty expensive jewelry. Some earrings worth two or three hundred, at least. A necklace that would have sold for three or four. A mess of rings. The only thing missing was the diamond bracelet."

"She wasn't mugged, then." Ezra nodded absently, still studying the report.

"No."

Slowly, Ezra blew out a breath and laid the report facedown on the folder. Then he looked at her. "I can't say I blame you, still following up on this—if she'd been my cousin, I don't know that I could let it go, either. And I can also see why this is screaming at you. But it might not mean anything. There was good, *solid* evidence on Joe Carson."

Nia tilted her head, holding his gaze. "I've also been following things that have taken place around here. Law Reilly's girlfriend was set up, made to look like she'd attacked him. Although that mouse couldn't hurt a fly."

"Girlfriend . . . mouse . . ." Ezra shook his head. "You're talking about Hope, I assume. She's not his girlfriend, and Nia? That girl might be quiet, but she's not a mouse."

Nia shot him a scowl. "Keep up, okay? Somebody leaves my cousin's body on Reilly's property. It's pretty clear to me that somebody is . . . or at least *was* screwing with law enforcement, doing whatever they could to throw people off the trail. Who is to say this isn't just more of that?"

Ezra stared at her. His green eyes were hard and flat.

And although he didn't say it, she saw something in his eyes.

He had a good game face, but she could read people . . . and she knew what she saw in his eyes.

He was worried, all right—worried about just that.

# CHAPTER
# FIVE

Edgy and restless, Law left Lena and Roz in the café while he headed down to the post office. There was no real reason for him to go down there. Hope had already been out there this morning, but he couldn't stay in the café, either. He needed to get out of the crush in there—seemed like half the damn town had shown up.

Roz was chattering on about a couple of weddings she had coming up, Lena was talking new menus. If he had to hear any more inane chatter about roses, champagne brunches, and the like, he was going to go stark, raving mad.

Or maybe he was already getting there.

Normally, he could tune them out, talk with Carter, or just zone, focus on one of the books, something, anything besides the chatter—hell, there had been a time when just being with Lena had been enough for him.

That had changed. Shit, everything had changed, and not just because she was married, and not just because he realized he wasn't in love with her.

He was edgy and he didn't really know why.

He was edgy and he couldn't focus on writing, couldn't focus on anything.

He was edgy . . . restless, like something was nipping at his heels.

As he passed by the sheriff's department, he absently glanced toward it. Sometimes he still half-expected to see Nielson striding out of there—he didn't know if he'd ever get used to not seeing that guy.

As he went to look away, though, he found himself freezing.

Doing a double take.

Shit.

It was *her*.

Nia.

Nia Hollister.

Fuck . . .

The air dwindled down out of his lungs. At the same time, he felt his heart start to race in his chest. Shit. Son of a bitch. What in the hell . . .

That was when he noticed Ezra, walking along beside her.

Ezra caught sight of him and then he glanced past him, toward the café. Something dark flashed through the other man's eyes—something Law couldn't quite define. Worry. Nerves.

What the fuck . . . he didn't care about Ezra. She was here. What was she doing here?

As they came to a stop in front of Law, he stared at her, into those pale golden eyes.

"Hey, Law." Ezra gave him a tight smile. "You heading back to the café?"

He shrugged. "In a bit. They're still talking—some big wedding coming up." He needed to quit watching her. She was busy looking anywhere *but* at him and he was going to look like more of an ass than he probably already did, but he couldn't quit staring. "Hi, Nia."

She slanted a look at him. "Mr. Reilly."

"Law." He tucked his hands into his pockets, glanced between her and Ezra. "What brings you back to Ash?"

She shrugged, still not looking at him. Then finally, her shoulders rising and falling on a sigh, she met his eyes. "Personal business, Mr. Reilly."

"Law," he said again.

Ezra glanced past him again, toward the café, then met Law's gaze. "Ah . . . Nia, can you give me a second?"

She shrugged.

Law scowled as Ezra grabbed his shoulder and all but dragged him about fifteen feet away. "Get back to the café and keep Lena in there."

Law glared at him. "Excuse me?"

"Damn it, would you just *do* it? I'll explain later."

Curling his lip at him, Law jerked his arm away. "What's the matter, you getting bored with marriage already?"

"What . . . are you nuts?" Ezra stared at him like he'd lost his mind.

Law wasn't so sure he hadn't. But he had a very hard time thinking clearly around Nia—something he'd demonstrated the one time he'd been around her before now. Rubbing his temple, he shook his head and glanced back at the café, then at Nia. "What's the deal, Ezra?"

"Would you stop being so fucking obvious and just get to the café?" Ezra asked. "Please? I'll explain—shit."

Nia was sauntering toward them.

That look in her eyes—a glint of trouble, sparking there like an ember. She glanced from Law to Ezra, then down the street. A grim smile curled her lips and she walked right past them—straight toward the café.

"Shit," Ezra muttered, rubbing the back of his neck. Then he shot Law a glare. "Could you have been a little *more* obvious?"

"What?"

Ezra just shook his head and muttered under his breath as he started along behind Nia.

"Damn it, what in the hell is going on?"

Ezra shot him a narrow glance and then stopped. "Nia's cousin."

"What about her?"

Ezra glanced up as Nia started across the street. "She looks enough like Lena that they could have been twins. I'd hoped . . . well. Hell. Doesn't matter now."

The second she stepped foot inside the café, Nia knew why the sheriff hadn't wanted her in there. The woman sat along the back wall, a pair of black glasses shielding her face.

From across the room, the similarity was eerie—the same deep, gleaming hair, although this woman's might have a little more red. The same clear, milk-pale skin. The shape of the face, the mouth.

So much like Joely.

Nia stared at her, hard, fast. Part of her wanted to hope, to pray . . . wanted to think maybe it *was* Joely, even though she knew better.

But it was easier, for that moment, to just pretend.

*Look at me . . .*

If the woman would look at her, then maybe Nia could quit pretending. Maybe. She'd have to face reality, have to take that stab to the heart, accept it, and move on. But she continued to chat with her friend, some blond lady, totally oblivious of Nia standing there, with her heart lodged in her throat, and her heart aching, breaking . . .

Just then the bell over the door jangled. And the dog lying by the redhead's feet sat up. Until that moment, Nia hadn't even seen the dog. Now it was staring at the door, tail waving back and forth.

Apparently, something about it caught his owner's attention, too, because now the woman's face was turned toward them.

That was when Nia realized Lena King couldn't see her.

"Your wife's blind," she said as Ezra came to stand beside her.

"Yeah, I think somebody mentioned that to me somewhere. Look, Nia, you don't need to do this to yourself."

She swallowed. "You know, if I'd seen her on the street, it would have been harder."

"Not very likely. You don't live around here," Reilly muttered.

She glanced at him, then at Ezra. No. She didn't live around here. But she wasn't leaving, either. Not until she found out something—more of that indefinable, insubstantial closure. Which meant the likelihood of her running into Lena King on the streets was higher than they thought.

But they didn't need to know that. Yet.

Slipping back outside, she started to walk. Blindly. She didn't know exactly where she was going; she just needed to get away from there. Ideally, she'd like to be very, very far away, but there was no way she could leave. Even if she was willing, and she wasn't, she couldn't very well ride just then.

The tears blinded her so that she wouldn't even be able to see the road.


"Why do I get the feeling she's not leaving town?" Ezra muttered to himself as he watched Nia stalk out of the café.

Then he glanced toward Lena. She was gazing his way expectantly—Roz had pointed him out after Puck had noticed him, catching Lena's attention. "I'm going to say hi—and do me a favor, yank your head out of your ass and don't mention Nia. Lena doesn't need to know she . . ."

"Know what?" Law asked, his mouth twisting in a wry smile. "Need to know you were talking to a beautiful woman or that your beautiful wife looks just like her dead cousin . . . ? Which don't you want her knowing?"

Ezra glared at him. "Again, take your head out of your ass and figure it out. What in the hell is your problem, anyway?"

As Ezra headed over to his wife, Law rubbed the back of his neck and wished he could figure it out. Shit. That woman—she came around and his brain went the way of the caveman. He stopped being *able* to think.

Hell, why was he acting like he'd caught Ezra and Nia going at it? He knew better. Ezra would cut off his arm before he'd hurt Lena like that. Swearing, he glanced out the door. Saw Nia pacing aimlessly around the square.

Then, without a backward glance, he slipped outside.

He just needed to talk to her. A minute. Without anybody else, see if maybe he could manage to get his brain cells functioning on any level resembling normal.

She should have known she couldn't be alone.

Not in Small Town USA. Or Ash, Kentucky, as it were. Ash, Kentucky, was the epitome of Small Town USA, too. And there, damn it, was the epitome of some things that could go very, very right in Small Town USA, she guessed, watching as Law Reilly ambled her way, that loose, easy gait, all lean, long limbs, the sunlight glinting off his hair

Damn. He was pretty, she thought, the observation winging up out of the blue to catch her off guard. She had an eye for attractive or appealing types—it was just part of her job. He was definitely attractive and appealing. Usually, neither one was enough to hit her low in the gut, though. Something about him did—hit her low and hard, making her go all warm and tingly.

Except she didn't have a right to be feeling this way, and she knew it. Pushing it aside, she tried to focus on anything *but* those warm tinglies. It was harder than she'd thought it would be, considering her ex-boyfriend hadn't made her feel much of anything.

His hair had grown out since the last time she'd seen him. Almost down to his collar, and shot through with threads of gold, darker strands of brown. Nice hair, she thought. Nice face . . . nice eyes. Nice everything, really.

Just looking at him did bad, bad things to her. And damn, that was a shock.

It had been a long, long time since she'd felt anything other than grief, or rage. That low-level sexual attraction was a pleasant surprise . . . for a few seconds anyway.

Then guilt kicked in. She couldn't do this—couldn't feel this.

She was here for a reason, and even if she was inclined to lose her head for a few minutes, she sure as hell couldn't do it with him. Definitely not with him.

She'd made a complete fool of herself with him already, and she wasn't here to look at him, wasn't here to repeat those mistakes.

Definitely wasn't here to ogle him . . . but that's what she was doing.

Her mouth was dry, she realized. Turning away from him, she tried to find something else to stare at. Something else, anything else. There wasn't anything else. Just a lousy picnic table.

Desperate, she settled on it, clutching the edge of it in her hands. It was worn smooth from years of use— damn good thing, too, because the way she was gripping it, she would be lucky if she didn't have a forest of splinters in her hands.

"Can't be easy."

The table groaned a little as Law settled down beside her. Shooting him a look from her eyes, she said, "What can't?"

"Seeing her . . . ah, Lena. Ezra mentioned that, she . . . well, looked like your cousin. I'm sorry. I . . ."

She sighed and rested her elbows on her knees. "Stop, okay? I figured out why he didn't want me going in that café."

"So why did you do it?"

She shrugged. "Couldn't stop myself." Closing her eyes, she buried her face in her hands.

"What was she like . . . your cousin?"

Nia lowered her hands. "Joely?"

"Yeah."

"Why? Why are you asking?" She turned to look at him, trying to figure out where he was going with this, what he wanted.

Law shrugged. "Why not? You look pretty shaken. Just sitting here isn't going to help. Talking might."

"And why in the fuck should it matter to you if I'm shaken or not?"

He watched her, a look of compassion on his face, and Nia felt the knot in her throat swell until it threatened to choke her.

Shit.

"Ah, hell," she muttered. "I'm sorry."

He shrugged. "You don't need to be sorry. Not like you haven't had a lousy deal lately." With his weight braced on his hands, he leaned back. "So what was she like?"

Nia stared at him for a long moment and then abruptly, she sighed. "Joely . . . she . . . she was my opposite. Everything I'm not. Cool and calm, where I'm hotheaded and always ready for a fight—I can be as logical as I want, but I'll still be spoiling for a fight at the end of it all. I looked for the bad shit. She saw the good."

"You were close."

"Like sisters. She was all the family I had," she whispered. Tears threatened, but she blinked them back. "Shit, I still can't believe she's gone."

"I could tell you that it will get better eventually—the pain will start to fade. And it does fade, but not because it gets easier. You just learn to live with it," he said gruffly. "I know that's probably not what you want to hear."

Nia sniffed. "Actually, that helps a hell of a lot more than somebody telling me that this will get *easier*. She was raped and murdered—*nothing* about this should be easy."

With shaking hands, she dug into her pocket, desperate for a cigarette only to realize she'd smoked the last one. *Shit.* Feeling the weight of his gaze, she slid off the picnic table, desperate to put a few feet between them. She needed to say something, anything—needed to stop feeling so fragile, and she needed him to stop looking at her like . . . hell, what was the look on his face anyway? She couldn't quite figure it out.

Scowling, she shoved her hands in her pockets and turned away, staring toward the sheriff's department and her bike.

Anywhere but him.

"I need to apologize to you again for what I did last year," she said, the words coming out of her so fast, they tumbled over each other. "I was wrong and I'm sorry."

"Okay."

She turned and stared at him. "Okay? I pull a gun on you and your girlfriend and you say . . . *okay*?"

Law cocked a brow. "Hope's not my girlfriend. And what do you want me to say? Tell you to take your apology and shove it?" He shrugged. "I know where it came from—I know Deb Sparks. She had it in her head I was guilty and Deb . . . well . . ." He stopped, ran his tongue along his teeth and shook his head. "Well, once she gets an idea in her head, there's nothing that can be done to get that idea out, not until she decides she wants it out. And it's not like you were exactly in the best state of mind that day."

"Gee, thanks," she muttered.

Staring at her averted face, Law tried to figure out just what in the hell she wanted him to say—what she wanted him to do. *Would* she be happier if he just told her to shove her apology?

Hell. This wasn't familiar territory.

Looking away, he rubbed the back of his neck. "Look, I just . . ." Her gold eyes cut his way and he blew out a breath, struggling to find something, *anything* to say. "Would you feel better if I told you to just fuck off?"

To his surprise a faint smile appeared on her face, tugging up the corners of her mouth for the briefest of seconds before dying. "I don't know if I'd feel better, but it seems a lot more plausible than you telling me *'okay.'* I know *I* sure as hell wouldn't be saying *okay* to somebody who pulled the crap I had."

"Maybe you'd surprise yourself," he said softly. If she'd seen the way she looked . . . And damn it, he needed to quit thinking about that. Like now. Although really, it wasn't that much better to think about how she looked now, either. Even with that irritated look on her face, there was something so damn appealing about her.

"I don't think so." She shook her head. "I rarely surprise myself." Then she sighed and flicked her fingers through her hair. "I have to go. I'd say it was a pleasure seeing you but . . . well."

"You'd be lying," he finished. "How about interesting? I can't say it's ever been *not* interesting."

"Well, seeing as how you've met me all of twice." The smile on her face now was a real one, at least.

He tucked the memory of it inside his mind as he watched her walk away. He also lingered long enough to enjoy the view . . . hell, he was a guy, and it was too nice of a view to *not* watch it.


Her name was Nia Hollister.

Nia Hollister—Jolene Hollister's cousin. Jolene's cousin—explained perfectly why she'd been in town *last* year, but didn't explain why she was here *now*.

He might not have worried if all he'd heard about her was that she'd been seen in the Circle K picking up some cigarettes—Marlboros, not the cheap stuff for her. But no, she hadn't gotten her cigarettes and headed out of town.

After she'd bought her cigarettes, she'd checked into the Ash Hotel. *That* had him worried. Very worried, and it didn't make him feel better once he started digging around and finding out more about her. Oh, he had learned some interesting things about her, too.

When he plugged her name into a search engine, he wasn't bombarded with *Did You Go To School With*. No, she actually had information online. A photojournalist. A bit more research revealed where she lived, as well as a variety of links to her work.

So many things could be learned on the Internet these days. Still, the one thing he needed to know, that eluded him.

What he didn't know was why she was here. Why she was back in Ash.

He'd made another trip back to town, under the guise of being lazy on a day off. Had a late lunch at the café, hit the bookstore, a few other places, chatting people up.

Yes, she'd been noticed by quite a few people. But nobody knew why she was here. Back in *his* town.

Nobody was talking. Not the boys from the sheriff's department, not the local gossips, nobody.

There was speculation. But nobody *knew,* which meant whatever her business was, she was keeping it close to her chest. He'd learned a long time ago how to separate the facts from the fancy and all there was now—it was just fancy.

Nobody *knew.*

Coming to a stop in front of the hotel, he let his van idle as he peered down the side.

He could see her bike, but not her. She was already checked in, tucked into her room. She'd have the door locked, probably. Both the chain and the deadbolt in place, her being a city girl.

Not that it could keep him out, but he couldn't exactly go and do something that blatant, now could he?

Still, he needed to know why she was here.

The small hotel wasn't much but Nia didn't need much. It was clean and it was quiet. That was all that mattered.

It faced away from the street, and the woods that rose at the back provided some extra shade against the bright summer sun. When she pulled the curtains, it darkened the room so that she could barely see her way to the bed. She didn't need to see—stripping her clothes away, she left them in a trail on her way to the bed and paused only long enough to pull the blankets back.

She needed sleep, desperately. Sleep, then she'd figure out where to go from here.

What to do next . . .

Sleep . . .


Nightmares chased her. Taunted her. Haunted her.

In the dream, she was no longer herself, but Joely. Running—breathless and terrified—through the trees, no idea where she was going, just certain she had to get away.

And he followed along behind.

Nameless.

Faceless.

A malicious, dark presence that watched, waited . . .

She could feel his eyes, all but crawling along her. All but touching her.

Waiting . . . waiting . . .

She wanted to scream, but didn't dare. Keeping it trapped in her throat, she bit her lip almost bloody to keep it locked inside. If she screamed, it made it that much easier for him to find her.

Not that he wouldn't find her anyway.

It was just a matter of time—didn't matter where she went, where she ran, she couldn't escape . . . this was his town . . .


She came awake to complete dark.

As a sob tried to tear its way free, Nia fought loose from the blankets that had wrapped around her like chains. Standing by the bed, nude and shaking, she wrapped her arms around herself.

*Calm down . . . you have to calm down . . .*

The dream replayed itself through her head over and over. She saw herself—but it wasn't her. It was Joely. Running, trying to get away.

No shocker, there.

Joely hadn't been always ready to pick a fight the way

Nia would, but she wouldn't back down from one, either—she would have fought. And fought hard.

It was disconcerting, though, the way she found herself remembering . . .

*This was his town . . .*

Blowing out a breath, she bent over and snagged her shirt from the floor, pulled it over her head. She didn't give a damn what the official reports said and she didn't give a damn what so-called evidence had been found when Joe Carson's body was found.

She wasn't buying it. The killer was local.

In her gut, she knew it.

Which meant the killer wasn't Joe Carson . . . and was still out there. Somewhere. She shivered, rubbing her neck. The hairs on the back of her neck stood up, made her feel like somebody was watching, staring at her. Waiting.

"You're paranoid," she muttered even as she shoved upright and went to go check the locks on the hotel door, and the curtains. The curtains were closed up tight, and the door was locked securely, the deadbolt in place. No way somebody could be watching her unless they'd bugged the damn room, and she shouldn't even be *thinking* about that, as antsy as she was.

Throwing a look at the clock, she wondered if it was still possible to get food around here. It was a little after 8:30 on a Monday. Was there any place *open*?

Her belly rumbled.

Only one way to find out.

She came sauntering into Mac's Grill and if she realized everybody in there was staring at her, she didn't pay them any attention. He suspected she noticed. Suspected she'd even noticed him, sitting in a booth and chowing down on wings. She wasn't one to miss things.

That bothered him, even as it excited him.

She'd be a fighter, like her cousin. It was a thought that thrilled him, frustrated him. He wanted her, could already feel that burn—but knew he couldn't risk this. Not after Jolene. Not only would it throw doubts on everything he'd done when he'd killed Carson, but there was no way he could take somebody like Nia and not expect it to be noticed—*very* noticed.

The sort of notice that he would do anything to avoid. So he would keep his distance, and he would content himself with his memories of her cousin . . . and thoughts of what it might have been like. There wasn't much physical similarity between the cousins. Next to none.

But he could see . . . something.

Attitude, perhaps. Arrogance. And strength.

She wasn't here to leave flowers in her cousin's memory.

He watched as she slid onto a bar stool, watched as a few men shot her considering looks. Three of them were married. Two started toward her side anyway. He was considering moving to that empty spot himself. He could be friendly, make small talk. It would be amusing, he thought, talking to her, trying to figure out just why she was here, even though he suspected he already knew.

But one man beat them all.

Law Reilly.

Law had been shooting pool with a couple of the numerous Jennings boys when Nia Hollister came into the Grill.

Silence fell.

Even though music still blasted from the jukebox, there was an odd hush. He wasn't fooled into thinking she didn't notice. Still, she didn't seem to pay any attention as she slid onto a bar stool and smiled at Leon, the bartender who had been working behind the counter for as long as Law had lived in Ash. Law didn't think Leon had aged a day since Law had met him. He was also sure Leon hadn't smiled once in those ten years.

"Damn, ya see the ass on her?" Ethan Sheffield muttered. One of the deputies from the sheriff's department, he was young, happily married, and one of the biggest flirts in the whole damn town.

And while his wife understood Ethan's harmless flirting, Law didn't want the guy anywhere near Nia. Smacking the deputy in the belly with his cue stick, he said, "Play the next round without me."

Without waiting for a response, he headed over to the empty stool next to Nia. It wouldn't stay empty for long, he knew. Even as he settled on it, he saw a few familiar faces hovering close by, almost as if they were waiting to see if he struck out.

Screw 'em.

"Didn't know you were hanging out around town," he said as Nia's gaze slid his way.

"You didn't ask."

"True." He nodded at Leon and the bartender brought him a beer. "I'll tell you, if you're out looking for wild nightlife in Ash, you already found the hot spot."

Amused, she glanced around the small bar and grill. With the music blasting from the jukebox, the empty stage, and the booths roughly half-full, it was actually fairly busy for the small place. But he knew what it looked like—dead.

He liked it.

"I'll try to contain my excitement," she said, leaning in closer.

He told himself it was so she wouldn't have to raise her voice over the music. And maybe it was. It also brought her close enough that he could smell the scent of her skin, her hair . . . nice . . .

"You want to get excited, hang around a few weeks. We start our county fair. That gets really exciting."

"Hmmm. What's the highlight . . . cow-tipping?"

He chuckled. "Nah. We save that for the yokels who don't live close to Lexington. We're classy here. Something to do with horses. Not entirely sure what, though. Can't say I've ever been." He tipped his beer back, desperate to wet his throat. It didn't do much good, though.

"That's not very neighborly of you." She smiled, her lashes low to shield her eyes. "Your own town and you don't go out there to show your support."

"I show my support by coming into town on Mondays and drinking beer, buying hot wings. It's good for the local merchants." He grinned and gestured to the menu chalked up over the bar. "Hard to believe, but Leon's got some of the best wings around here."

She wrinkled her nose. "That's not hard to believe. The only places I've seen serving wings are chain joints. Those aren't good wings."

"This being your first night in town, how about I buy you dinner?" He wondered if she had any idea how damned nervous he was, just saying those words. Law didn't do nervous. Granted, he also hadn't asked a woman out on a date in . . . shit. A couple of years? Even then, he didn't think he'd been *this* nervous. And this wasn't even a date. He was just being neighborly, right?

"Dinner." The faint smirk on her mouth curled into an all-out smile and she glanced down at herself. "I'm not sure if I'm up to dinner at such a classy place. But what the hell. I think I should buy, though. It's the least I can do."

Law opened his mouth to argue. Then he snapped it shut. Hell, she was sitting there next to him. That was what he wanted, right?

Sitting there . . . and waiting for him to take offense. "How about this, you get this one . . . and let me take you out sometime? Assuming you'll be in town."

"I'm not going anywhere," Nia said.

For some reason, he wasn't surprised to hear that.

# CHAPTER
# SIX

SHE SHOULDN'T BE SITTING THERE.

Nia knew that.

Not because she wasn't worried about Law Reilly. She actually worried about Law Reilly a lot, and in a lot of ways.

She should worry about Law Reilly. She also knew that. Law Reilly was bad for her state of mind—and her hormones. Law Reilly was just plain bad for her. And maybe, later, when she was back in her room and her hormones had cooled off, and her brain had settled and she had a chance to get herself back on course, maybe then she would convince herself that she needed to worry about Law Reilly.

Worry about things like staying away from him.

But just then, all she wanted was one night where she didn't think. Didn't think about *anything*.

What was so wrong with that?

She hadn't enjoyed a night with a guy in months. Eight months. Not since her cousin died. Hell, longer than that. Before Joely had died, Nia had been so fucking focused on her job, she hadn't been thinking about anything *but* the job. The few nights she'd had with her last boyfriend, it had been more about scratching an itch than anything else.

Empty—her life had been empty and she hadn't even realized it. Empty, except for her cousin, and now it was too late to tell Joely how much she'd meant to her. Now, with Joely gone, all she wanted was her cousin back. A chance to spend time with her again. To live, to think about things other than a job.

A chance to watch Joely walk down the aisle. Throw a bachelorette party for her. Take her to the store and watch her do all that goofy bridal shit. Things Nia had dreaded. Now she wanted them more than anything and she couldn't have them.

But she could have a nice night with a good-looking guy. She could do something about the raw, empty ache of loneliness in her heart. Nothing was stopping her. Except herself, and she wasn't going to let that happen either.

Glancing at Law, she found herself thinking about the girl . . . Hope. Hope Carson—timid, quiet, that petite, delicate type—the kind a guy would want to rescue. Nia hadn't ever needed rescuing.

But she supposed guys might find it appealing—the damsel in distress thing. Law had said she wasn't his girlfriend. She wanted to ask more about that, but just then, she didn't care. Well, not true. She did care, but she didn't want the truth to ruin things. Didn't want the truth to mess up her night.

She needed her night, needed to enjoy it. So she shoved those questions aside and decided it didn't matter. Nothing mattered but now. Having a few beers, having some hot wings, and enjoying talking about nothing in particular with a hot guy who seemed to enjoy looking at her.

As the evening wore on, people came in and out of the Grill.

At some point, they moved from the bar to a booth.

Finally she found herself alone in there, just Law, the bartender, and her, and she realized the time had slipped away without her even noticing. That hadn't happened in . . . months.

"Where did you go?"

She glanced up, looked into Law's intense hazel eyes, found herself caught up in them. Then she looked away. "What do you mean?"

"You went away," he said.

Frowning, she started to count the bottles in front of them. Eight beers. They'd put away eight beers, and she suspected she'd probably drunk half of them.

As she spun around to put her feet on the floor, the room tipped around her. "I didn't go anywhere," she said, taking great care not to slur her words. "I've been right here."

"Yeah. You're right here, all right," Law said.

She thought she might have heard laughter in his voice. Shooting him a dark look, she snapped, "I'm not drunk."

He lifted his hands. "I didn't say you were."

"Want me to take her home, Reilly?"

She shot the bartender a dirty look. "Like I'd let you."

Big, bushy brows rose over his eyes.

Law lifted a hand. "I'll take care of her, Leon."

Nia snorted. "Yeah. Right." She reached into her pocket, digging out her keys. In the back of her mind, an alarm started to sound—images flashed, but they were too vague, too blurred, making no sense. Clumsy, fat fingers closed around the keys and she jerked them out. "I'm going to my hotel," she announced, flashing her keys at Law.

"Uh-huh."

Two seconds later, her hands were empty.

She wiggled her fingers, looking for the keys.

They weren't there. Frowning, she checked her pocket again, then the floor. Where had they gone?

They jangled and she looked up, scowled when she realized Law had them.

"Come on, gorgeous. I'll get you back to the hotel. You can thank me in the morning when that bike of yours is still in one piece . . . and you are, too." Law slid an arm around her waist.

She started to jerk away from him. "I don't let anybody touch my bike." But even as she started to pull away, she relaxed against him, wondering why she would want to pull away. He smelled . . . wonderful. Like . . . well, a guy. Warm, sexy, like soap, grass, and beer. Something else, too . . . hmmm, books, she thought. He kind of smelled like books. She liked it. A lot.

Turning her face into his neck, she breathed him in. "Hmmm. You can't touch my bike," she said. "But maybe you can touch me."

Law grimaced as she slid a hand under his shirt. Her fingers were cool, sleek, and wicked against him, tracing along his skin with no hesitation and all sorts of determination.

If he lived through the night, he deserved a nomination for sainthood.

Maybe he should have told Leon to call it quits before she'd ordered that fourth round. But right up until she'd gone to slip out of the booth, she'd been steady as rain. Barely even a glint in her eyes to betray that she was anything beyond sober.

But then she slid off the seat and although she wasn't slurring her words, wasn't tripping over her feet, it was pretty clear she wasn't sober. There was also the fact that she had her hand under his shirt, sliding over his belly like she was petting a cat.

Damn—he wouldn't mind being a cat, for her.

Aw, fuck . . . now she was toying with his belt buckle. It was his turn to stumble a little as he led her over to the door. Yeah, not entirely sober, there, and damned if he wasn't going to suffer for it.

"I like the way you smell," she muttered. She tipped back her head to stare at him. "Like it a lot. You gonna come to the hotel with me?"

"Yeah. I'll come back with you." *To tuck you into bed . . . right before I go home and take a cold shower, jack off.*

A wide, wicked grin spread over her face and she wrapped her arms around his neck. "Oh, really . . . ? Aren't you going to talk me out of it? Tell me how I've had too much to drink and I don't know what I'm talking about?"

*Oh, you've definitely had too much to drink,* he thought. He just barely managed not to whimper like a baby as she arched her hips against him.

"A pretty lady wants me to take her to her hotel," Law said after he took a moment and swallowed, hoping he could talk without his voice cracking. "Who am I to argue?"

From the corner of his eye, he saw Leon watching the whole thing with a look of amusement on his face.

Then Nia slanted her mouth over his and Law forgot where he was. Who he was.

Oh, shit.

Her lips parted against his, her tongue slid across his lower lip and without waiting a beat, she pushed inside his mouth. There was no hesitation in her kiss, nothing shy or slow . . . nothing but a determined, sexy woman and he was all but helpless to resist.

Helpless—

*Fuck it, Law, she's plastered—*

He told himself that. Twice.

Then he reminded himself why she was here—why she'd come to town.

And just when he thought he was going to totally lose control, she pulled away and settled back to look at him with a smile. "Come on, then."

Without saying anything else, she pulled away and sauntered out of the Grill.

Law clenched his hands into fists, digging the ridged surface of her keys into the palm of his left hand—hoping the pain might clear his mind a little.

"You *are* just planning on getting her to the hotel, right?"

Shooting Leon a dark look, he snarled, "Yes. I'm not a total asshole."

"Nah. I know that. But you're a guy. And hell, I don't know if *I* could walk away after that. Glad I ain't you."

Law groaned and scrubbed a hand over his face. Shit, right then, he didn't want to be him, either. Get her out to his car. He could handle that.

Get her to the hotel.

There wasn't even much of a question *which* hotel, because they had only *one* hotel.

Unless she meant the Inn . . . and somehow he doubted it. If she'd been at the Inn, she wouldn't have bothered coming into town, because she could have gotten something to eat there, something to drink there. So she had to mean the hotel and why in the hell was he even thinking about this shit—

Taking a deep breath, he joined her outside, telling himself he'd get her in the car, get this done, get home so he could die in peace. Or in agony, actually.

But she met him before he even made it halfway across the sidewalk, one hand coming up to cup his neck, the other hooking in the front of his jeans. She slid her fingertips inside the waistband and Law's eyes damned near crossed.

Her tongue slid out, dancing in a burning pattern along his neck and he swore, all but ready to beg for mercy and then he saw his car—finally—why in the *hell* was it parked over there?

Grabbing her wrists, he pulled her loose, liquid body away from his and nudged her across the parking lot to the car. "Get in," he grunted.

"Don't wanna," she whispered, staring at him from under her lashes.

Her eyes . . . they burned like molten gold as she stared at him in the dim light. Her tongue came out, slicking along her lower lip.

Law could have gone to his knees.

"Too far to walk to the hotel, sugar," he said, trying to keep his voice even. He sounded a little hoarse, maybe, but not bad. Good—he could do this. He could.

"Hmm. Hotel. That's a good reason." Then she slid up against him, pressed that body against his, all long and lean and lush.

He couldn't do this—

Swearing, he fisted a hand in her short hair, yanked her head back and slanted his mouth over hers. She opened for him, humming with delight and Law was cursing himself even as he gorged on her taste. Fuck, she was sweet—hot, sweet, and perfect. And drunk . . . had to remember that, had to . . .

Her tongue slid against his and she slid her hands under his shirt, skimmed them up his sides, then down. But then she reached between his legs, palmed him through his jeans, and Law groaned.

It took more strength than he thought he had to tear himself away from her.

"Car," he snarled, putting two feet between them. Then three. "Damn it, get in the fucking car."

She laughed. It was low, husky, and all too seductive. "Awww . . . you're no fun."

"Get in the car, Nia," he snapped. *Damn it, before I do something you'll hate me for—before I do something I'll* hate *me for.* She'd leave Ash sooner or later, and he'd never see her again, but damn it, he had to live with himself and he didn't want to take advantage of a drunken woman who was going through hell.

She smirked. "Fine. It's not like the hotel is *that* far away."

As he circled around the car, he grimaced. She wasn't joking. The hotel was only a mile away.

It wasn't as if she was very likely to sober up and as he slid into the driver's seat, she immediately laid a hand on his thigh, stroking up, then down . . . up. Down. Teasing. Taunting.

"Would you stop?" he finally begged.

She laughed again . . . and stopped.

It gave him a few precious moments to try to cool himself down. He could do this. He could. He just had to remind himself how she had looked earlier when he'd seen her talking to Ezra.

A few months back.

Yeah. He could do this. Really.

A soft sound came to his ears.

At first, he didn't quite catch it. Then, abruptly, he started to laugh.

Shit.

She'd fallen asleep.

Son of a bitch.

Looked like somebody had decided to cut him a break, after all.

# CHAPTER
# SEVEN

IF THERE WAS ONE THING NIA HATED ABOUT GETTING drunk, it was the fact that she remembered it all the next morning. In vivid, Technicolor detail.

She lay on her bed at the oh-so-cleverly named Ash Hotel, staring up at the ceiling, still wearing her jeans, her T-shirt, even her damned shoes, and replaying the entire night, from start to finish.

Seeing Law. Talking to Law. Kissing Law. *Groping* Law.

Groaning, she sat up and covered her face with her hands, tried to figure out just what in the hell she'd been thinking. Except that was the problem.

For the first time in months, she hadn't been thinking. She'd let herself just . . . relax. It had been, well . . . nice. Just sitting there. For a little while she'd been able to forget about things.

"You don't have a *right* to forget," she muttered, utterly disgusted with herself. No right—at all. Her cousin had been murdered, and everything inside her screamed that the guy who had killed her was *not* dead.

What right did she have to forget?

With tears pricking her eyes, she climbed out of the bed, stripping out of her clothes and leaving them in a

trail on her way to the bathroom. A hot shower. She
needed a hot shower. Then coffee. Then she'd continue
kicking her ass, while she figured out how to face Law
again . . . after she'd all but eaten him alive . . .

Guilt and embarrassment—a bad, bad combination.
But that wasn't enough—just the memory of last night
was enough to reignite the burn of hunger.

"Shit."

Heat hit her low and hard, square in the belly. So *not*
what she needed. She wasn't the type to ever really get
hangovers, and other than just a vague queasy feeling, a
whole lot of embarrassment, and plenty of guilt, she had
been feeling fine, until now.

Bracing her hands on the counter, she sucked in a deep
breath and muttered, "A long time. That's all. You were
drunk. It had been a long time. That is *all*."

She just needed a damned orgasm. That was why he'd
been so damned appealing. That was why she felt like
she could have eaten him alive. Why she was still inclined to do just that—

Swearing, she climbed into the shower and cranked
the heat up to high. As the hot water came pouring
down on her, she braced her back against the cool tile
wall. She had been alone too long. Just alone too long
and she needed a climax.

Nia could give herself a damn climax, and she'd damn
well do it, too.

She didn't need a guy.

Except even as she slid her hand down her belly, it was
*his* face she was seeing. When she tried to block it out, it
only got worse. Nia whispered, "The hell with it."

If she had to think of a guy, there were definitely worse
ones to be thinking of . . .

Law twirled the keys and studied the door, the coffee,
the door.

Then his car.

He should just leave. She was probably still sleeping. It was after nine, though. And why in the hell wouldn't she want caffeine? She'd probably need it. Hungover and all, right? Who wouldn't want caffeine, need caffeine under those circumstances?

Besides, he did need to return her keys, right? He'd even gotten up early just so he could go to Leon's, drive the bike over here, then get back to his car, all without making it look like he'd been rushing around to get all of that done, too.

Granted, it had *occurred* to him last night that when he kept her keys in his pocket that he would have to come back here today. He could have even used the keys as an excuse to see her again later, but that seemed too . . . contrived. Was a lot better to just run around like an idiot without her knowing instead of making a heavy-handed pass, right?

He pretended he was being responsible. Had even insisted that was the only thought in his mind when he carried her into her hotel room and laid her on the bed. Although responsibility had nothing to do with why he'd decided to brush his fingers down her face. She had the softest damn skin . . .

"Stop thinking about her skin," he snapped.

"Excuse me?"

With red creeping up his neck, Law looked up and realized he had an audience.

And it was Deb Sparks, of all the damned people. Son of a bitch. Setting his jaw, he gave her a tight smile and said, "Just talking to myself, Deb. You know me."

"I see." She sniffed and glanced at the coffee in his hand. "Are you . . . visiting somebody?"

"No. I'm just here to talk to myself and stare at a door all day. You?"

"You don't need to be so rude," she said, drawing in

a sharp breath through her nose and glaring at him. Then she smoothed a hand down the front of her butter-yellow skirt. "I'm here to talk to Sam . . . you might not know him, being new in town, but he's the owner. He's looking for an assistant manager and I was thinking it would just be the *perfect* job for my daughter-in-law. My son is . . ."

*New in town*—never mind that he'd been here for about a decade now. But she'd call him new in town after he'd lived here fifty years.

"Uh-huh. That's nice, Deb," he cut in and lifted a hand, banging on Nia's door with a lot more force than necessary. Okay, if he had to choose between humiliating himself in front of a beautiful woman, or even waking up a beautiful, potentially hungover woman and listening to Deb Sparks?

He'd take either option with the beautiful woman over Deb. Hell, he'd take having his eyes jabbed with red-hot needles over Deb. Dealing with Deb was akin to being in the ninth level of hell, he figured.

Feeling her censuring gaze on him, he glanced back at her.

"You are such a *rude* young man," she sniffed. "Your mother must be *appalled.*"

"I know." He bared his teeth at her. "I can't help it. If I'm going to be rude, though, at least I do it to a person's face instead of gossiping about them behind their backs. Got to give my mom credit, though—before she died, she got that through my head, at least. You know, if you're here to talk to Sam, don't you think you'd have more luck if you checked out the office?"

She opened her mouth to reply as he lifted his hand to bang on the door again.

That was when Nia opened it. Wearing . . . holy shit . . . a towel.

Law just about swallowed his tongue.

A towel. Droplets of water. Nothing else.

Suddenly, he realized that maybe dealing with Deb *wasn't* akin to the ninth level of hell. At all.

The ninth level of hell was staring at Nia Hollister, with all those little droplets of water clinging to that smooth, warm skin. Here he was dying of thirst and he already knew, even before he looked into her eyes, there was no way he'd be getting a taste.

"Ahhh . . . I brought you coffee," he croaked out. Shit. Now his voice was all but breaking on him like a horny teenager's. Clearing his throat, he held out the coffee and lifted her keys. "And your keys. Ah, your bike's here, too."

She glanced at him, then at the coffee, the keys, still blocking the door, that towel clinging to the sweet swell of her breasts.

Off to the side, Deb sniffed again—that prissy sound managing to convey shock, displeasure, and avid interest all at once.

Nia blinked, her lashes drooping slowly over her eyes and then she slanted a look at Deb.

Recognition flared in that golden gaze. A dull flush stained her cheeks red, but she said nothing. All she did was smirk and then step back, pushing the door open wider.

Law lifted a brow. As he stepped inside, he tried to figure out . . . had he just stepped completely into that ninth level of hell or was this maybe some hidden doorway to heaven?

He was pretty sure it was hell, though.

He wouldn't be lucky enough for anything else.

After she closed the door behind Law, Nia accepted the coffee and sauntered away hoping he wouldn't see the fact that her knees were all but shaking just from the sight of him. Damn it, what in the *hell* was it about him?

She heard her keys jangle as he laid them down.

Focusing on that, she grabbed her robe from the hanger near the sink and pulled it on, discreetly slipping out of the towel before tying the robe's belt around her waist. "Why do you have my keys?" she asked as she lifted the coffee to her lips.

"Ah, just forgot to give them to you. Tired, late. You know."

"Hmmm." She sipped. The caffeine hit her stomach like a sucker punch, strong and powerful. "Tired. Late. Right. Thanks."

She slipped him a look and tried not to think about the way it made her feel when she saw him staring at her. Too hot inside, like she'd all but bathed her insides with the steaming coffee he'd brought her. Too damned hot.

Swallowing a whimper, she looked away. "Well, thanks. Appreciate the coffee. You bringing my bike back." She paused and shot him a look. "You didn't wreck it, right?"

"Nah." He grinned at her. "I can handle a bike. She's a nice one, too."

"Hmm. Well, don't expect to ride her again. But still . . . thanks. For everything." *For not pawing me last night even though I was pawing you—oh wait, no, why didn't you paw me?*

She'd wanted him to paw her. Still wanted it. She was still aching, deep down low, aching and so damn needy it was almost pathetic. No. It was pathetic. She needed, wanted, and more than anything, she was dying to put the coffee down, go to him and wrap her arms around him, see if he really tasted as good as she thought he had. See if he felt the way she thought he did . . .

Maybe it was all just a drunken fog and he wasn't that special. She could find out and then move past it.

Easy.

Right?

So easy.

Even as she considered that idea, he jerked a shoulder in a shrug and said, "Yeah. Okay. Take it easy."

As he turned for the door, her heart leaped into her throat.

"Wait."

With his hand closed around the doorknob, he looked back over his shoulder at her. Tawny hair fell into those intense eyes as he paused, waiting expectantly.

Her mouth went dry. Wait—shit, what was she asking him to wait for?

Her hands were shaking as she set her coffee down. Best place for it—the way her hands were shaking, she didn't *need* to be holding the damn coffee. "Ahh, listen. About last night . . ."

"Don't worry about it," he said, his voice distant. Polite.

*Hell. And what if I want to worry about it? What if I can't stop thinking about it?*

"Um. Well, I just . . . I'd had a few too many beers, and just was . . . well . . ." Hell. *I acted like a damn tramp, and I don't care and why in the hell didn't you just give me what I wanted? What I still want?*

She swallowed, looking past him. "I . . ." She blew out a breath, but nothing was making this any easier. Nia didn't have these kinds of problems, damn it. She didn't. If she wanted a guy, she wanted a guy. Granted, she preferred to have some sort of connection first, a strong one—and she sure as hell felt one here, even if she didn't really know him.

When there wasn't a connection and she needed some sort of release, she could handle it herself—no guy required. She actually *preferred* it that way. It was easier, safer, just plain better.

But she'd already proved that wouldn't work right now. She wanted *him*. Needed *him*.

"Look," she said, clearing her throat. *I can do this. I know he wants me. This is easy. Hell, he probably was holding on to my keys* hoping *for something like this, right?* "About last night . . ."

"Nia, it's not a problem," Law said, his voice taking on a hard edge.

Narrowing her eyes, she snapped, "Well, it sure as hell is one for me!"

Law pulled his hand away from the doorknob and turned around, leaned back against the door. "Okay. Since you seem determined to lay into me about something, why don't you tell me what the problem is, then?"

"You didn't finish it."

*Oh. Fucking. Hell.*

She hadn't just said that . . . hadn't just blurted it out like that, had she?

Law stared at her.

His brows drew low over his eyes. His voice was a low rasp as he said, "I didn't . . ." He stopped, cleared his throat. "I didn't finish what?"

Nia wiped her hands down her robe, then reached for the belt on her waist. She was making a mess of this. She could talk to people. At least she could *usually* talk to people. Guys were easy for her; she could be glib and charming and if she needed sex, then she was okay *getting* sex, but damn it if she was okay with anything right now. Not her life, not how she felt, and certainly not anything that included Law.

Untying the belt, she shrugged out of the robe and then stepped toward him. Staring into his eyes, she said, "I might have been drunk, but I knew what I wanted."

"Shit." Law closed his eyes, slammed his head against the door at his back. "I don't make it a habit to have sex with drunk women—it's a rule of mine."

Nia leaned in and nuzzled his neck, breathing in the scent of him. Man, he really did smell that good. Wow. If he smelled that good, then maybe the other stuff was really that good, too. "It's a nice rule . . . I like it. But I'm not drunk now. And I still want you."

His hands came up, gripped her waist.

"Nia . . ."

Tipping her head, she stared into his tawny, hazel eyes, so intense, so burning-hot and all-consuming. Had she ever had a man look at her like that? Like she was all? Like she was everything? The center of his universe? Hell, screw the center . . . Law was looking at her like she *was* his universe.

Closing the minute distance between them, she pressed her mouth to his, lightly. "I want you." Against her belly, she could feel the burning, hot length of him. "I know you want me. And I'm perfectly sober. So . . ."

Law was certain he'd fallen into some alternate universe at some point in the past five minutes. Or maybe he'd hit his head and was hallucinating. Could be one of those fugue states, even—were there hallucinations in fugue states?

Nia pressed her lips to his and he groaned, opening his mouth.

*Slow down—think—*

Except he was pretty certain that wasn't possible. Thinking. Slowing down.

And what in the hell was there to think about, anyway? She wasn't drunk—she was clear-eyed, sober, and that long, coffee-and-cream body was pressed against his, warm and sweet and naked and he wanted her like he wanted his next breath.

It was more than a want—it was a blinding, desperate ache and what was there to think about?

Gliding his hands up over her sides, along the curve of her rib cage, up until he could cup her breasts in his hands, he plumped the warm, soft weight of her, stroked his thumbs over her nipples.

She whimpered into his mouth, then tore away, her head falling back on a ragged sigh.

"You sure about this, Nia?" he rasped, staring at her through slitted eyes. She needed to be damn sure because he was going to die if he stopped—yeah, it might not be logical for a man to die of sexual frustration, but he was pretty sure it could happen. After all, he'd been dreaming about *this* woman from the time he'd laid eyes on her. Even though he'd only seen her a few times— even though until last night he'd only touched her when he was trying to get a fucking gun away from her. Didn't matter, because the moment he'd looked into her golden eyes, he'd felt something—a click—something that went deeper than anything he'd ever felt.

"Sure?" She smiled at him.

That smile—damn it. That smile ought to be illegal. No woman should be able to smile at a man like that, because it did bad, bad things to a guy's sanity.

As that smile curled her lips upward, smug, female and so fucking sexy, she slid a hand down his chest, down to the waistband of his jeans. She paused to stroke him through the thick denim and he groaned, leaning into her touch.

"What do you think, Reilly? Am I sure?"

Law swore and shoved away from her, grabbing the back of his shirt and stripping it away. He came back to her, cupping her face in his hands. "Insane—you want to drive me insane, I can tell."

Nia chuckled against his lips. "Do I? I'm not trying to drive you insane, sugar, I promise."

"You don't have to try," he muttered, nibbling at her lower lip. "Open your mouth, damn it."

Not that he was waiting . . . he pushed his tongue inside her mouth, desperate for the taste of her. He slid his hands down her neck, along her shoulders, her collarbone, along the slope of her breasts, toying with the hard, puckered crests of her nipples. She gasped and arched into his hands. "Law . . ."

Fuck, she was responsive—hot, sleek, and responsive, reacting to each touch like it was the first, like everything he did drove her wild. It was so erotic, so mind-blowing, and he couldn't think, couldn't breathe. Sinking to his knees in front of her, he pressed a stinging series of kisses down the midline of her body, one arm wrapped around her middle, watching as she arched back, her hands resting on his shoulders, her nails biting into his skin. He pressed his mouth to the curve of her belly, stroking one hand up her thigh.

She parted her legs, rocked against him. "Bed," she panted. "Damn it, take me to bed."

"What's your hurry?" He licked her navel, bit her lightly. The mound of her sex was covered with a neatly trimmed patch of tight, black curls and he could already see the moisture gleaming there. Inching lower, he pressed another kiss just there, brushed the tips of his fingers across the curls. The heat of her . . . he hissed out a breath as he felt the heat, the moisture.

"My hurry?"

He looked at her from behind his lashes and smiled. "Yeah . . . what's your hurry? I want to touch you . . . taste you."

"And I'm dying," she groaned. "Spent five minutes in the shower trying to get myself off after last night and I'm still dying . . ."

The image of that blasted through his mind. Law's eyes just about crossed as he found himself picturing her, that long, sexy body . . . standing under the spray of water, her fingers moving in and out. Oh, hell . . .

His brain almost exploded on him. Swearing, he stood up and slanted his mouth over hers. Cupping the heat of her sex in his hand, he ground the heel of his palm lightly against her and pushed one finger inside her. As she closed around him, greedy, slick and tight, he shuddered.

She cried out against his mouth.

Desperate, dying, he pulled his hand away and wrapped his arm around her waist, hauling her against him. Couldn't let her go—he had the weirdest damn feeling that if he stopped touching her, even for a second, he'd wake up and realize this was a dream. Something. Couldn't stop touching, couldn't stop . . .

Those long, muscled legs wrapped around his hips as he boosted her up and turned, taking the three strides it took to get to the bed. He half-staggered, half-fell onto it, turning so that he went down first, with Nia sprawled atop him. Hot, sleek, and perfect. Her legs parted, settled on either side of his hips and she rocked against him. Both of them groaned. He could feel her, through the heavy, too-tight denim of his jeans. She sat up, reaching for his belt buckle, her fingers struggling to free him.

"You're wearing too many clothes," she said.

"Yeah." He rested a hand on her thigh, stroked it up to her hip. "You're not . . . fuck, you're gorgeous."

A slow smile curled her lips. "Thank you."

He might have said something else, but then she managed to get the zipper undone and she had her hand inside his jeans, shoving his boxers down quick as a wish and his ability to speak abruptly died. All he could manage was a ragged grunt as her fingers closed around him, pumped up and down once . . . oh, shit.

". . . a condom?"

Cracking one eye open, Law glanced up at her. What was she saying? Didn't she know he couldn't think, not when she was touching him? What was she talking about? *Why* was she talking?

"You got a condom?"

Oh. Shit.

Law groaned. "No."

Her jaw dropped. "You . . ." She closed her eyes. Then opened them, that golden gaze flashing. "You don't have a rubber?"

"No. I don't generally carry them around unless I'm planning on getting laid and that wasn't why I came." She was still touching him—shit. Grimacing, he reached down, closed his fingers around her wrist. She had to stop, or he was going to do something he hadn't done since high school. Tugging her hand away, he blew out a breath, tried to convince his burning, raging body that it needed to cool down—now.

"You . . ." she licked her lips, still sitting astride his thighs, a confused look on her face.

This wasn't making sense. Nia tried to get it to make sense and it wasn't happening. He'd come here, after last night—brought her coffee—and he hadn't brought a damn rubber.

Okay. It still wasn't making sense. Not a lick of sense. None. Taking a deep breath, she wet her lips with her tongue and tried again. "You seriously don't have anything?"

He eased her off, his hands—calloused in all the right places, just enough to feel good as he touched her—stroking up over her sensitized flesh and sending signals to her overheated brain. "No, Nia. I don't." He winced as he sat up, adjusting his jeans.

She swore, her body tight, hot, aching so bad. Drugstore—one of them could go to the fucking drugstore—

A phone rang.

Law grimaced. He gave her an apologetic look and stood, pulling it out of his back pocket. He cleared his throat before he answered it. She took a little bit of pleasure in hearing the harsh, unsteady rasp of his voice as he said, "Yeah?"

Listening to the one-sided conversation, it didn't take her long to figure out that she wouldn't be getting any relief after all. Apparently Law had someplace to be.

"Yeah . . . yeah, no. It's okay, sweetheart. I can be there in about a half hour. Uh-huh. It's okay." He disconnected a few seconds after that and proceeded to swear a blue streak.

She waited until he stopped and then asked, "So. I take it you don't have time to run to the drugstore and buy a box of rubbers real fast, do you?"

"Afraid not." He laughed, rubbing the heel of his hand over his chest. "That was Lena Ri— uh, King. Ezra's wife. She needs a ride into town and Ezra's stuck in court for the next little while. She's not feeling too good—has to go see the doc and . . ."

Nia climbed off the bed and slid her arms around his neck. "It's okay." Pressing a kiss to his chin, she murmured, "Well, not exactly. I'm dying here. But you wouldn't be worth much if you left a sick friend hanging just so you could get laid, now would you?"

He eased his chin down, slanting his mouth over hers. "Maybe we can take a rain check?"

"Bet your ass," she said. At least that's what she tried to say. The words were lost in a hungry, voracious kiss that stole the breath right out of her.

Law skimmed a hand down her side, along her ribs, the indentation at her waist, over her hip. She gasped as he slid it between her legs and cupped her. "Just how close are you to dying? Because I wouldn't be worth much if I left you in a dire situation either . . . Just how dire is it?"

"Pretty dire," she said, her voice hitching in the middle.

He pushed one finger inside her, rotated his wrist. She bucked against his hand and started to rock. Law wrapped his free arm around her waist, supporting her. Lifting his head, he stared down at her—he wanted to keep on kissing her, tasting her, feeling her moan and sigh against his lips, but more, he needed to see her, watch as he made her come. Because damn it, he was going to have that, at least.

"Pretty dire, huh," he teased. Her eyes darkened, shielded by the fringe of her lashes as she rode his hand, her hips pumping back and forth. "Then I have to take care of you . . . always have to help a woman out."

He dipped his head and raked his teeth along her neck.

Her head fell back on a gasp.

He pressed his thumb against her clit, circled it, teased it.

Nia cried out, a harsh, high sound. The walls of her sex tightened around him, snug and slick. He added a second finger and gritted his teeth as she squeezed tight and whimpered his name. Another slow stroke, another teasing circle around her clit.

The diamond-hard points of her nipples taunted him and he wanted, so bad, to stretch her back out on the bed and learn every inch of her body, first with his eyes, then with his hands, then with his mouth. But first he'd have to make love to her, hard and fast, easing this vicious ache before it killed him.

No time, though, no fucking time. All he could do was continue to pump his fingers, in . . . out. He nuzzled her neck again and felt a shudder run through her. He bit her lightly and felt her stiffen. With a twist of his wrist, he brought her to climax—the sound of her harsh, ragged moan was almost enough to have him coming in his jeans. He groaned, burying his face against her neck as she rocked against his hand, whimpering, her nails biting into his shoulders.

Hot . . . sweet, and so damned perfect. Erotic as hell.

Nia sagged against him, stunned, dazed. She . . . what . . . hell.

Tipping her head back, she stared at him. "I . . . wow."

Law grinned at her. Then he dipped his head and rubbed his mouth gently against hers. "I have to go."

"Go?" she repeated dumbly. Fifteen seconds later, she remembered. Shit. His friend. That, more effectively than anything else, served to cool the fire in her blood.

His friend. The one who looked eerily like Joely.

"Yeah," she said, forcing the words through her tight throat. "You go."

She swallowed and eased back, tried not to let anything show on her face.

But those eyes of his, they seemed to see everything— far below the surface. He brushed his knuckles down her cheek. "You okay?"

"Yeah." She gave him a tight smile and moved across the room on shaky legs. Need still pulsed inside her, making her head spin. Making it so hard to think, so hard to focus. "I just . . . um. Your friend, Lena. She . . ."

"I'm running her to the doctor's office," Law said quietly.

"Yeah." She scooped up her robe from the floor and tugged it on, wrapping it around her suddenly icy body, needing the warmth. She hadn't been cold until she'd stepped away from him. Hadn't been cold at all. But now . . . Suppressing a shiver, she gave him another smile, a little less forced, a little more real. "You need to go," she said quietly.

He crossed the room, paused by the sink and washed his hands. Then he turned to her, cupped her chin. "Rain check," he muttered, pressing a hard, hungry kiss to her mouth. "Man, you're doing bad, bad things to my head, Nia. Bad things."

For some reason, that made her smile. Only fair, she figured. She took one look at him and the ability to think clearly seemed to disappear.

Guys didn't affect her like that. They simply didn't.

But Law, she had already realized, wasn't just any guy.

# CHAPTER
# EIGHT

SHE DIDN'T TRACK HIM DOWN ANY TIME SOON.

She was tempted, though. That rain check was one she definitely wanted to redeem. Nia couldn't let herself get distracted by him, though. As appealing as he was, he wasn't her reason for coming.

Joely was, and damn it, she was going to find some answers.

She spent the next few days researching, combing through archives and newspapers at the library, although at the oddest times, thoughts of Law would creep into her mind and she'd find herself thinking about him. She'd find herself thinking about heading out to his place, wanting to see him.

A few times, she almost decided to go there. Almost. Something always stopped her, though.

First, she needed to do what she came here for. Joely—she was here for Joely. Although, damn it, she was just spinning her wheels, it seemed like. Spinning her wheels, existing on nothing but Diet Coke and cigarettes and cereal. She couldn't even find her much-needed Monster at the Circle K half the time.

The archives were proving to be useless. Very useless. Nothing useful there, but then again, she really didn't figure the killer had taken any victims from his hometown. Stupid that.

All sorts of women had gone missing, but without any bodies . . .

The names, they blurred together on her, ran together like smeared ink, making no sense, one big jumble on her mind, with nothing standing out. By Thursday, she was so tired of reading about missing women, so tired of this self-assigned quest and wondering why she couldn't do this from home. Instead of heading to the library, she went to the courthouse.

Not to talk to Ezra, though. She didn't have anything to talk to him *about*. She just needed something else to focus on—a starting point. Good thing she knew how to research like mad, because that *something* turned out to be going through the police reports in the weeks following Joely's disappearance, bits and pieces she picked up on when reading through the archives and such.

Had to love the open government thing—unless they played into open cases, nobody could tell her she couldn't look at police reports.

A lot of drunk and disorderlies. A lot of driving under the influences. More than a few reports that had something to do with spousal abuse. Nia sighed as she combed through them, figuring she was wasting time. After three hours, her head was pounding, her neck was stiff, and her eyes were gritty and dry.

Lunchtime—she'd go until lunchtime and then take a break. Or maybe stop for the day. She needed a smoke, anyway. "Need to quit," she muttered, although she was a little surprised she even cared. But she wasn't going to worry about that right now.

Five minutes before her self-imposed deadline, she came across a mention of a name that sounded very, very familiar.

Lena. Lena Riddle.

Lena . . . Yeah, they'd just gotten married. Was this Ezra's wife?

Getting that report took a few more minutes than she liked and she had an itch down her spine the entire time she waited. That itch only got worse once she had a copy of the report in her hands.

What she read was enough to make shivers run down her spine.

Especially when she got to the date. Just a few days after Joely was kidnapped. Before her body was found.

Nia squeezed her eyes closed, counted to ten.

*Subject reports hearing screaming in the woods:*

*"Somebody was in the woods. I could hear her screaming, screaming for help."*

*Subject described the voice as female. Heard the voice call out five times and claims the screams came from the woods to the east of subject's property.*

The subject. That would be Lena.

Shit. Lena heard somebody screaming . . . screaming in the woods by her house. After a few days of nothing but frustration and emptiness, Nia's headache was gone, replaced by the low-level burn of excitement, the hum of her instincts.

*This* was something. She didn't know how she knew it.

But it was something . . . She needed to check out those woods.

Of course, she suspected the sheriff wouldn't be too pleased if she was out there trespassing.

So she'd have to make sure she wasn't caught.

"I heard you were down here."

*Speak of the devil . . .*

Nia didn't flinch at the sound of Ezra King's voice, nor did she blush. She neatly gathered up her notes before she looked up at the sheriff.

"Hello, Sheriff."

He eyed those reports for a second, then shifted his gaze to her face. "Heard you've been spending a lot of time reading up on police reports, checking out the archives."

"Yes."

"Anything interesting?"

"The town has an awful lot of people with the last name of Jennings," she said dryly. "And more than a few people who can't hold their liquor."

"Ain't that the truth," he muttered, shoving a hand through his hair. "But somehow, I don't think that's the sort of thing keeping you from going back to Virginia, Miz Hollister."

"It's not." She slid her notes into her bag, then her laptop. "I'll go back when I'm ready."

"And when will that be?"

She shrugged. "Man, some of you are really interested in how long I'm hanging around. A girl might think she isn't welcome. Between you and Law . . ."

"Law." A grin tugged at Ezra's mouth. "Yeah, I heard you went out with him on Monday."

"We didn't go out. We just ended up at the same place."

"And then he took you back to your hotel," Ezra finished, still grinning. "Brought you coffee the next day and you answered the door all but wearing your birthday suit."

Nia narrowed her eyes.

"Small-town gossip. It's effective."

"That Sparks woman is a malicious bitch," she said.

"True. Although she's not the one who mentioned the fact that you two were seen leaving the Grill on Monday. I actually heard that one from a deputy of mine." He glanced back at her desk, but Nia had already cleared it of anything that might give him an inkling of what she'd been looking at, other than the police reports, and he'd known about that hours ago—he even knew which reports she'd asked to see. He'd be checking out those reports later, too.

"Well, I'm glad my personal life is so interesting to everybody," she drawled.

"Hey, you're not from around here and you've got something interesting attached to your name," Ezra said, shrugging. "If you thought people weren't going to pay attention, especially if you start hanging around somebody like Reilly . . . well, then you weren't thinking too clearly."

"And what's wrong with Reilly?" she demanded, only to snap her mouth shut the second the words left her mouth. *Damn it.* "You know what? Never mind. It's not like I'm looking to marry the guy. I got to go."

No, she didn't. Not really.

But she'd managed to keep Law Reilly out of her mind for the past few hours and she'd like to keep it that way. Except now, it was a little too late. Ezra had opened those gates back up and once more, thoughts of Law were dominating her thoughts.

"Shit." Ezra rubbed the back of his neck as Nia stormed off.

He'd handled that well.

"Hey, Sheriff."

Distracted, Ezra looked up, saw a familiar face—Jennings—one of the infinite Jenningses. Pleasant face, blue eyes, and wire-rim glasses, bald . . . the man was familiar, but Ezra couldn't place him.

The name escaped him for a minute, and just then, he was too aggravated with himself to worry about wracking his brain for a name.

He needed to catch up with Nia—talk to her, and forget her love life.

All the prying around she was doing, well, he wanted to know if she had seen anything that caught her eye, and he also wanted to make damn sure she was being careful.

Lately, he was feeling twitchy. He hadn't felt this twitchy since the day Lena had told him about the screams she'd heard. Something weird was going down and he needed to be ready for it.

So instead of slowing down to chat, he just nodded and kept on walking.

Of course, by the time he got outside, Nia was already pulling out of the parking lot.

Later that night, Nia told herself she wasn't going to the Grill just to look for him. At least not *just* to look for him. She needed to eat dinner, right? And if she decided to go to the Grill rather than out for fast food, so what?

He wasn't there, though.

She did bump into a city cop who seemed vaguely familiar—*very* vaguely. He kept his hair clipped short, so close to his skull she could see the scalp. He had nice eyes, eyes that briefly flicked over her body with an appreciative glance as she settled onto a stool at the bar.

She'd thought about leaving, but if she left, how would she know if Law came in or not? So she didn't leave.

"Hey."

She smiled at the cop with half a mind to dismiss him, but then she realized that maybe she could work him a little, get some information out of him that she hadn't been able to get from King earlier that day.

Not entirely likely, but possible.

"Hi." She gave him a less forced smile before signaling to the bartender—a Diet Coke, this time; after the beers she'd put away last time, she didn't need anything else.

"You're Nia Hollister."

She suppressed her wince—barely. Giving him a wry smile, she said, "Hell, I guess the stuff I've heard about small-town grapevines is all true, huh?"

"Yeah, pretty much." He smiled. "Kent Jennings."

"Another Jennings . . ." She shook the hand he offered.

He grinned at her. "You know, there's really not as many of us as it would appear. It just seems that way."

"Uh-huh." She lifted a hand and ticked off her fingers as she counted. "So far, I've met a deputy by the name of Jennings . . . family?"

"That's Keith." He grinned. "Third cousins, maybe fourth. I don't keep track."

"Okay. The mayor's a Jennings. I saw that in the paper. There's also a DA Jennings." She ticked off two more fingers.

"Yep. Brothers. That's Hank and Remy. We're also cousins. I'm a fairly watered-down Jennings, to be honest." Kent shrugged and said, "You get used to it, growing up around it. Remy and Hank, they're kind of the center, if that makes sense."

*The power base,* she supposed. Every dynasty had one. From all she'd been able to tell over the past week, the Jennings family had their own little miniature dynasty going here. A friendly one, but still. At least on the surface.

"I heard you been spending some time going through police reports and other public-type documents," Kent said.

Nia slid him a narrow look. "So just how does this small-town grapevine work? Word of mouth? Telephone? E-mail?"

"All of the above. It makes that grapevine even more efficient." He winked at her. "That's how I was able to keep up with everything, even working a few extra shifts. I've heard about your interest in our town's arrests and all, I've heard about your bike, I know what hotel you're staying at . . ." He flashed her a smile. "Other things, but my mom might smack me if I mentioned one or two of the details."

Nia didn't blush. She didn't give a damn if people were talking about the fact that she'd all but crawled all over a good-looking guy. She did wonder if it might bother Law, though. Wondered if it was going to cause him problems with Hope. Yeah, he'd said she wasn't his girlfriend, but she was something to him—Nia had seen that.

Smiling at the cop, she asked, "You always listen to gossip?"

"So it's gossip then?"

In the middle of lifting her drink to her mouth, she paused, thought about it. Shit. Blowing out a breath, she said, "No."

"Didn't think so." Then he sighed. "Reilly's good people. Not from around here, but he's good people. So. How come you're here then?"

"Because I am," she replied edgily. Geez, what was with these people, so fucking nosy.

Kent slid her a look, flashed her a smile that was so easy, so charming, it was hard to stay irritated. "Sorry, don't mean anything by it. I'm just curious. If you're looking for him, not likely to find him here. He doesn't come into town much on the weekend—we don't get too rowdy around here, but when we do . . . well, it happens on the weekend."

She flushed, shrugged. Was she that obvious?

Hell. Maybe.

"I'm here to get something to eat, to drink. It's not like they serve dinner at the hotel."

"Good point. If you're going to be in town awhile, you ought to hit up Roz over at the Inn. She sublets the cabins every now and then—and they got better food there. A few of the cabins even have kitchenettes. Quieter out there. A lot more private than anything you'll find in town." He slid her an amused smile. "It's only a few miles away from where Reilly lives, too."

"And that should make a difference, huh?"

"You going to tell me it doesn't?" He lifted a brow.

Shit.

Scowling, she focused on her drink and wished she'd ordered something stronger.

"The Inn, huh? So where is it?"

He laughed.


He knew she was still in town.

After all, this was Ash, and in Ash, anything different was a hot topic for discussion . . . Nia Hollister was different, and not only was she different, she was hot—in more ways than one.

He'd heard she all but closed down the Grill with Law Reilly earlier that week.

He'd heard she had been seen in the sheriff's department.

He kept hoping to hear she was leaving town, but so far, that hadn't happened.

As a matter of fact, as the days passed by, she'd spent them at the library, *researching* . . . going through the archives. And rumor had it she'd spent today going through police reports filed through the city and county.

As if it wasn't bad enough just having her in his town, where she didn't belong. Just having her here was bad. Troublesome. In a lot of ways. There was little question in his mind *why* she was here. She hadn't accepted what had happened to her cousin. She wanted more, was willing to dig to find it.

But how long would she stay . . . ? How deep would she dig? Why was she messing around in the archives at the library? Over at the courthouse, rummaging through public documents?

Slowing to a stop in front of the Ash Hotel, he glanced over—casual. He knew how to do casual. Knew how to go unnoticed, how to be unseen even when everybody was looking right at him.

Then he narrowed his eyes, hardly able to believe what he saw.

She was packing up. Loading her things onto her bike. Well, well. He hadn't seen this easy ending coming. Still smiling, he pulled on through the stop sign and finished the drive into town. He was in the mood for some coffee and breakfast. Maybe he'd hit the café.

She was leaving . . . good.

Damn good thing.

"You sure you're okay?"

Rolling onto her belly, Lena buried her face in her pillow and groaned. They'd only been married a few months and normally, Ezra just wasn't the type to hover.

Then again, normally, she didn't spend several days all but hugging the toilet. It had finally passed, but she was still so damned tired. All week, all she'd done was sleep, wake up, try to eat . . . then lose interest and go back to sleep.

"I'll be better after about another twenty-four hours of unconsciousness," she mumbled. "Go. Go to town, have coffee with the boys and talk about whatever you cop types talk about at these 'not-staff' meetings."

He sat on the edge of the bed and she could all but feel the reluctance rolling off of him. One roughened hand stroked her back, lingered low on her spine, his fingers digging into the tense muscles there. "If you're sure you'll be okay . . ."

"Well, I'm really anxious to get my boy toy over—so get out already." Then she sighed, rolled over. She reached out and her fingers brushed his leg. "Ezra, I'm not dying or anything. I'm even starting to feel better and just need some sleep. Go to town and while you're there, get me some Tylenol and some chicken noodle soup. I almost feel hungry."

He chuckled. "Now I *know* you're sick, if you want me buying you some sort of soup in a can."

"Hey, I'm sick . . . it's not like *I* can cook it. And I want to get better, which means I can't trust *you* to do it." She forced a smile for him, even though her eyes felt heavier by the second.

"Okay." He sighed and bent over, his lips brushing over her chin. "I'll call and check on you in a while."

"Umm."

She was asleep before he hit the doorway.

Ezra glanced back, saw Puck lying there, his head on his paws, a mournful look on his face. If Ezra didn't know better, he'd think the dog was having sympathy sickness or something. And as soon as that thought rolled through his mind, he found himself thinking—*morning sickness*.

It had been his first thought, but Lena had already shot that idea down. It was the first thing the doctor had checked when she'd been seen. He was fine with that, too. He wasn't exactly *opposed* to having kids. He just wasn't sure he wanted them *now*. They'd just gotten married. Still getting used to each other.

And here he was, getting used to a new job, doing one thing he hadn't thought he'd be doing again.

The weapon he wore at his side weighed on him. A lot.

It was a burden he hadn't planned on taking back up

again, but when he'd been approached about taking Dwight's place, for some reason, he'd been unable to say no.

Not that saying *No* was hard for him. Ezra was just fine saying no when it suited him. When it felt right.

This time, it hadn't felt right.

As a matter of fact, saying yes had felt about as right as anything he'd ever done—almost as right as when he'd asked Lena to marry him. Even though this was a burden he hadn't planned on carrying, it fit.

It was one he was suited to, one he was meant to carry, he supposed.

It was a hell of a lot more laid-back than anything he'd done before he'd been injured. The job with the State Police, the crime rings he'd dealt with, stolen property—chasing after leads, dead ends, all that shit, sometimes spinning his wheels for twelve, eighteen months at a time, all for nothing. No, this was better.

A lot better. And the "staff" meetings Lena had been ribbing him about were a lot easier to swallow. Not that this was a real staff meeting, although they had those, too. Every couple of weeks, he'd meet up with the rest of the staff and just talk.

It had started out informally—and it was still informal, but Dwight Nielson had cast a long shadow here; taking his place wasn't easy. There were more than a few deputies who felt they should have gotten the job that had been "given" to some outsider.

Trying to establish an environment where they could all work together wasn't easy and this was one way of moving forward. Trying to win them over one at a time.

Those who didn't like it, as far he was concerned, they could kiss his ass.

He wasn't going anywhere and he wasn't playing by the good ol' boy rules they seemed to think they could lay out, either. Ezra was in this for the long haul—they needed to deal with it.

Fortunately, the hard cases were the minority.

By the time he made it to the café, it was hopping. Along the back wall, he saw his men, and only two empty chairs. Keith was there, along with Ethan Sheffield, Walter Manning, his deputy sheriff Steven Mabry along with his brother Kyle, Kent Jennings, several of the guys from the night shift . . . Ezra smiled.

More than the last time. He had to make his way through the maze of tables—like most mornings, the café was packed.

The mayor was at a table with several of his cousins—Carter was there, Remy and Hope, Angie Shoffner and her husband Bill. She'd been a Jennings until she married him. Ezra assumed half of the people at the table were probably from the Jennings clan, too, but he couldn't be sure. He was still learning names.

Jennings—seemed like they owned most of the damn town.

Lucy Walbash was there, having breakfast with two of her grandsons—Ezra couldn't remember their names for the life of him. She beamed at him and he smiled, but was glad the crowd kept him from getting to her easily. Lucy had been one of his grandmother's best friends and he adored her, but she could talk like nothing he'd ever seen.

He dropped into one of the spare chairs and glanced back at the crowd. "Did you all have to threaten to arrest people to clear a table or what?"

"No." Keith smiled from behind his coffee cup.

Ethan smirked. "He's messing around with Natalie lately—she kept the table open for him."

"You and Natalie?" Ezra cocked a brow at his right-hand man and tried to wrap his mind around that picture—it wasn't quite coming together in his head. Keith had plenty of women who flirted with him—all but threw themselves in his path sometimes, but Keith was oblivious. Maybe that was why the picture didn't work. The guy just never seemed to notice women.

But now he had a red flush creeping up his neck and had developed a very strange obsession with his coffee cup. "You know, that takes balls," Ezra said, unable to resist teasing him. "I don't know if I'd want to go chasing after one of Miss Lucy's granddaughters. That lady terrifies me—hell, I'd almost rather go chasing after one of Miz Tuttle's girls than one of Miss Lucy's."

Keith gave him a dark look. At the same time, he smacked Ethan on the back of the head. "I'm not chasing after anybody," he said, his voice stiff and formal. "And don't we have things to talk about?"

Ezra laughed. "Sure. What do you want to talk about, loverboy?"

"Hey, I saw that woman—Nia, Nia Hollister—a few days ago. Up at the Grill," Ethan said, swiping his scrambled eggs through some ketchup before he popped them in his mouth.

"Your wife know you still go down there flirting?"

Ethan hunched his shoulders. "Ain't flirting. Just shooting pool, having a few drinks. She knows I wouldn't do anything." He shot Kent a narrow look. "I heard Kent had a few drinks with her last night."

Kent rolled his eyes. "I didn't have drinks with her. She was there and I was there. It's not like there are a whole lot of choices around here if you don't want frozen food. Plus, it's close to the hotel where she was staying."

At the other end of the table, one of the night deputies, Craig Dawson, glanced up, his eyes bleary, a heavy growth of stubble on his narrow face. "You talking about that Hollister lady? Shit, she's hot. I saw her out with Reilly the other night—they were . . ." His words trailed off, but the grin on his face did a pretty good job filling in the blanks. He paused long enough to take a drink of coffee and added, "I thought I might have to arrest them for indecent exposure—although it was one hell of a show."

"Pervert," Keith muttered, shaking his head.

Dawson smirked. "You're just jealous you don't get to see the good shit."

"Yeah, knocking on windows when kids start getting hot and heavy down at the park, that sounds like my idea of a good time," Keith muttered with a curl of his lip.

Kyle Mabry leaned forward. "Hell, I saw Hollister and she ain't no kid." Although he was only in his early forties, he was already bald, his body built solid as a brick wall, and his face was perpetually red, like he'd spent too much time in the sun. Good-natured and easygoing, Mabry also liked to take things apart, piece by piece, Ezra had learned.

He should have known Mabry would be the one to ask.

"So how come she's here, anyway, Sheriff?" Kyle asked. "What's she doing back in Ash? Not like there's any reason for her to be here, and you'd think she'd want to put this whole mess behind her."

Ezra made a noncommittal sound and shrugged. Yeah. One would think that. But Nia wasn't about to put this whole mess behind her. She couldn't.

"Her business here is her own," he said as more and more gazes swung his way. Ignoring the question would just draw more attention to it, he guessed, but for reasons he didn't completely understand, he was reluctant to voice Nia's reasons for being here to everybody. Keith knew. And Lena.

That was it.

There were a few in the department who had likely guessed, and more who *would* guess, the longer she hung around, but he wasn't going to confirm it. Not just yet.

"Doesn't much matter," Ethan said, scooping another bite of ketchup-drenched eggs into his mouth. "Leslie's sister, she works weekends at the hotel, and guess who checked out today?"

"Nia didn't leave town." Kent popped a piece of bacon into his mouth.

"She checked out of the hotel," Ethan pointed out.

Natalie appeared at the table just then. "Y'all talking about Nia?"

"Yeah. She's leaving, though."

"No, she's not," Natalie said, shaking her head. She glanced at Keith, brushed a hand along his shoulders as she refilled his coffee cup.

Keith reached up, returned the caress, all without looking at her.

Natalie continued to talk. "She's already checked in over at the Inn—subletting one of the cabins that Roz doesn't use much."

"Really?" Ethan's brows shot up.

Ezra glanced up at Natalie.

She grinned. "Hey, I hear things." Then she wagged her eyebrows. "You know one of my sisters helps Roz with the cleaning—she was out there when Nia checked in. Mentioned it when she called a few minutes ago to see if I wanted to go to Lexington with her later."

Natalie took his order and as she paused by another table, he heard somebody else asking about Nia—that poor girl, how awful it must be for her. Beth Caudill, one of Deb's cronies. No doubt everybody who *didn't* know about Nia's change in location, well, they'd know by lunchtime. Five o'clock at the latest.

The small-town grapevine, Ezra thought, amused. Nothing quite like it.

She hadn't left.

Outwardly, he chatted, made small talk, things he'd done all his life.

He ate his breakfast, even asked for a second helping of pancakes. He drank three cups of coffee, expressed his concern about the possibility of a super Walmart that might or might not be built over in Oakfield. He listened to the women gossip, the men complain, and did his own share, as well.

But all the while, on the inside, he brooded. Nia Hollister hadn't left.

And not only had she not *left,* she'd settled down at the Inn . . . in one of the cabins. Those cabins were a more long-term arrangement than a vacation-type stay.

If she was staying there . . .

Fuck.

This was not good.

The Inn was just a few miles from Law's place, just as the deputy had promised. Kent had given her directions, a phone number, even told her to use his name—*I'm a cousin, sort of.*

Nia was starting to think half the town was a Jennings, or a *cousin, sort of.*

By midmorning that Saturday, she had a better place to stay—a cabin, with a kitchenette, for roughly a little less than she'd be paying at home. That was going to kill her savings, if she didn't find somebody to sublet her place. Not that it was going to be an issue—finding somebody.

Settling in, though, as expected took awhile.

After all, she had to buy stuff. Especially since Nia didn't plan on going anywhere just yet—not until she found some of the answers she needed. She had to get food. Had to call back home, see about that subletting deal—yeah, she'd already gotten the ball rolling, but still, checking in never did hurt, right? She also needed to get a friend to go in and send her some more clothes and stuff.

And no, she wasn't procrastinating—why should she? It wasn't like she was *obligated* to go out and see Law.

Even though she wanted to. Even though she *needed* to, longed to . . .

There was just other stuff she needed to do. Other, important stuff, stuff that allowed her to . . . think. Think about the fact that she wasn't sure she was equipped to deal with him, or the fact that he made her brain shut down, even as he made her heart ache, like no other guy had ever managed to do.

Think about the fact that she was here for one reason—one reason alone, and it had nothing to do with him. Once that was done, she'd leave.

So did she really need to get involved with him?

Probably not.

Not that it kept her from thinking about him . . .

Law swiped the towel over his face as he came back inside.

Catching sight of a familiar head of hair in the office he'd set up in his living room, he scowled.

Waiting until he could say something without gasping, he just glared.

A minute passed before Hope lifted her head and smiled beatifically at him.

"Hi."

"It's Saturday," he said, pointedly.

"Yes. And tomorrow is Sunday. After that? Monday. Then Tuesday. Just think, they said we'd never use the stuff we learned in school, but here we are, using those basic skills we learned in kindergarten," she drawled, grinning at him so that a dimple flashed in her cheek.

"I don't pay you to work on weekends." Shit, he didn't exactly pay her an hourly wage, period. And it wasn't like he cared—he just wasn't in the mood to put up with anybody today. Except maybe . . . no. Wasn't thinking about that, about her. Wasn't thinking about that rain check he hadn't cashed in.

Hope smirked. "You pay me on salary—doesn't matter when I get the job done, as long as I get it done. And the work is piling up since you have a book coming out in a couple of weeks, and a deadline. Figured I'd get a jump on the e-mail and the stuff you need mailed."

Shit, the book. He'd all but forgotten it. What the hell?

Sweat trickled down his back, but the tension Law had hoped to burn off during the run remained, lurking just under his skin, an edgy, greedy beast. Setting his jaw, he studied the work Hope had already piled around her—settling in. "Don't you have plans with your hot-shot lawyer?"

She shrugged. "No. He got called in for something or other and I didn't feel like hanging around the apartment." Cocking a brow at him, she asked, "Is there a problem?"

*Shit.*

Law sighed and rubbed the back of his neck. "No. I just . . . no. Edgy. Pissed. Distracted."

"Grouchy?" she offered, helpfully.

He grunted. "I'm going to go shower, get some work done. You do whatever you feel like messing with."

"Hmmm." Hope had already shifted her attention to the stack of work in front of her. He barely knew what it was. He knew what she *did*—in theory. He'd done it for years, but ever since she'd taken over all the chores that went along with writing, his life had gotten a lot easier. She'd streamlined the process and he didn't even have to think about a lot of it anymore.

He was already dreading the day he lost her, and he was so worried it would happen—would Remy want her to quit? Not that it made any sense or anything, but still. And it was easier to think about that than the other shit crowding his mind.

Like Nia—the rain check.

Fuck.

He'd made up his mind yesterday he wasn't thinking about her. Wasn't going to go down that road right now. No. Not right now, because until he had some sort of handle on what he was feeling, how he was going to deal with it, the last thing he needed to do was think about her—especially when he was this on edge.

Because he was all too likely to storm back to the hotel and finish what they hadn't been able to finish. Damn it all. There came a point in time when cold showers, perseverance, and even a little old-fashioned self-service just didn't do the trick.

Law was well past that point.

The nightmare came.

In the pretty little cabin, in a bed far softer than anything a budget hotel, even a nice, privately owned budget hotel could provide, the nightmare found her.

Trapped in the woods.

Nia ran . . . but she was no longer Nia. She thought perhaps she was Joely.

But she wasn't sure. She only knew she was afraid. And desperate. So desperate. Desperate to live. Desperate to escape the nightmare that chased her. Desperate to escape that evil.

He laughed. He mocked her.

Pain tore through her.

Shuddering, biting, clawing—it flooded and surrounded, encompassing her entire being.

But worse than the pain was the fear. And the knowledge.

She wouldn't live through this.

She knew. He would kill her.

*"Fuck . . ."*

Nia jerked upright, all but sobbing for breath.

Tears burned her eyes and she fought free of the blankets. A cold sweat left her chilled, left her aching, left her burning. She could almost feel the sting of the branches on her flesh, smacking into her as she ran headlong through the woods.

*Shit, shit, shit, shit.*

Scrubbing her hands over her eyes, Nia swallowed the knot in her throat, tried to brush it off. A dream. Just a dream. Nothing more.

Determined to shrug it off, and knowing that she'd never sleep, Nia made her way to the dresser where she'd stored her meager supply of clothes. There sure as hell wasn't much to choose from, but she had what she needed—including workout clothes.

What she needed right now was a hard, driving run—something that would exhaust her and wipe that dream from her mind.

With that in mind, she changed. It took her less than five minutes to hit the door. She was halfway down the cobbled sidewalk that wrapped around the property when she ran into Roz—her temporary landlady.

Roz gave her a smile. "Wow. You're an early riser."

"Can't sleep," Nia replied, trying to keep the edge out of her voice. "Was going to try a run, see if it cleared my head."

"Running to clear the head? Oh, honey . . . just try coffee. Lots of it." She stood up, brushing the dirt from her knees and stretching her back. "Early mornings aren't meant for exercise."

"Well, I'd rather run than garden." Nia glanced at the tools spread around the other woman.

Roz laughed, stripping her gloves off. She tossed them down on the little green bench—it was a strange looking contraption, Nia thought, but what did she know?

"Gardening isn't so bad, once you get it going." Absently, she toyed with her necklace and shrugged. "It's just the getting it going that's a pain."

"And the weeding. Fertilizing . . . whatever you have to do." Nia made a face. "No, thanks." She gestured toward the main road and said, "You figure the road's okay for my run?"

"Should be, especially this early. We've got other crazy people who like to run and most of the people around here are courteous enough drivers." She tugged her phone out of her pocket and checked the time. "The kitchen doesn't open until lunchtime, but there's a continental breakfast every day. You're welcome to grab you some coffee or something if you need it. It's not included in your rent, but I imagine you haven't had time to stock up on basics or anything."

"Thanks." Nia forced herself to smile before she turned and headed for the road, determined to run that dream out of her head—to outrun that nasty, clinging evil, the fear.

The run didn't do it. Two cups of coffee and a shower didn't help much either. The dream clung like the nasty dregs of a hangover.

In desperation, Nia did something she hadn't done in years.

She went to church. Her parents had been devout believers. Nia, not so much. But there was a peace she often found within the walls of a church, and right then, more than anything, she needed that.

Something, *anything* to wipe those images from her mind.

Ash First Methodist stood on the square, pretty and quaint, the sun glinting off the stained glass windows, people gathered in little groups of twos and threes and more on the steps as she quietly slipped inside.

Or *tried*. Should have waited until the service started. A dozen people tried to say hello. Tried to welcome her.

She gave them a tight smile and pretended to be invisible. She didn't want a welcome. She just wanted peace.

Peace . . .

Hope and Remy slid into the back pew just before the sermon started. With her cheeks flushed and her body humming, she was almost certain that everybody knew why they were running late.

Remy just settled next to her, that easy, lazy smile on his face, his arm wrapped around her, staring toward the front like he didn't have a care in the world.

Not a one.

Hope knew they were staring—she knew it.

Remy leaned over, pressed a kiss to her brow. To anybody watching, it was just an absent kiss, soft and easy. But he lingered long enough to murmur, "Relax, angel."

*Relax*—

Damn it, they were supposed to have lunch with his mom. And she was . . .

"Nobody is looking at you," he murmured as she tugged on the hem of her skirt.

The skirt he'd pushed to her waist not that long ago. Man, they were in *church*. She had to get her mind where it belonged.

"*Relax*," he murmured again, catching her hand. "Nobody even noticed us."

But even as he said that, Hope stiffened, abruptly aware of somebody's gaze.

A very intent, interested gaze.

Just across the aisle.

Hope stiffened when she found herself staring into a pair of familiar golden eyes. The sight of that woman's face was enough to chase every last bit of embarrassed heat, embarrassed humor away. Her spine stiffened and the heat that flooded her had nothing to do with embarrassment now.

What in the hell was she doing here?

Next to her, Remy took notice—of course, he noticed everything. His hand came up, curling over her neck. "You okay?"

"I'm fine," she whispered, giving him a tight smile, one she didn't feel.

But she couldn't really go into it here.

"What's wrong?" he asked the second they cleared the crush of the crowd.

Lifting her eyes to his, Hope wondered what to say. Of course, she'd gone through a hundred possible options over the past hour, and she'd discarded all of them. "I . . ."

"Ms. Carson."

That low, husky voice caught her attention and she turned her head, found herself staring at Nia Hollister.

She set her jaw against the nerves, against an instinctive kick of fear. Remy's hand closed around hers.

Nia's eyes flicked from her face to Remy's, then back. "Can I have a moment? I . . . ah, I need to apologize to you."

Hope's gut response was to say no. Her second response was curiosity.

She wavered back to saying no—the fear weighing strong, along with a healthy dose of disgust and anger after what this woman had done, how she'd accused Law, and the wedge it had driven between her and her best friend, even if it had only lasted for a few days.

In the end, though, manners won out. Angling her head toward the square, she said, "Sure." But she held tight to Remy's hand. Hell, maybe this way, he'd work it out on his own and she wouldn't have to work to figure out how to explain—because if he didn't figure it out, she *would* have to explain.

Already a lead weight settled in her gut, just thinking about it, because it felt, once more, like she was being pulled in two—Law's strange fixation on this woman, and knowing that Remy would want to know—hell, *should* know . . .

A shiver danced along her skin as Remy rested his hand low on her spine. She could feel the weight of his gaze and from the corner of her eye, she saw him studying both her and Nia—could already tell that the wheels were spinning for him.

Those dark, dreamy blue eyes of his were narrowed and watchful, wondering. Already piecing things together, she realized. They came to a stop across the street in the town square under the shade of a towering oak and Nia didn't waste any time—Hope had to give her credit there.

"I owe you an apology," Nia said, her voice flat, her gaze direct and although there was a faint flush riding on her cheekbones, she looked as cool as a cucumber. Too cool, too collected. "What I did to you was unforgiveable, I know, but I still wanted to apologize. I'm sorry."

How in the hell was this the same woman who had been standing in Law's place months ago, all but ready to break as she held a gun on them?

Taking a slow, calming breath, Hope tucked her hair back behind her ear and said, "Okay."

"Just like that? Okay?"

Hope smirked. "Yeah. Okay. But I'm not looking to invite you out for a girl's night or anything." Then she scowled as a thought occurred to her. "Ah . . . you're not going to be around here a lot, are you?"

"Afraid I will be." Then she looked away and some of that cool, calm façade shattered. When she looked back at Hope, something else glimmered in her eyes—something real.

Something that Hope could almost relate to. "But don't worry. I don't plan on causing you any more trouble."

"And what about Law?"

Nia's lashes swept low over her eyes. "Law doesn't need to worry about that happening again, either. You have my word on it."

Hope wanted to tell Nia just what her word meant—it shouldn't mean jack, but Hope had a feeling it probably did mean something. There were still plenty of people in the world who meant it when they gave their word—she had a feeling this woman was one of them.

Still, there was a weight to Nia's words, a glint in her eyes . . . what was that . . .

"Okay, then." Nia nodded and glanced at Remy, then went to turn away.

"Nia," Remy said quietly. "Nia Hollister."

Hope rested a hand on his arm and squeezed, looked up at him.

Nia looked at him, a brow cocked expectantly. "Yes?"

Remy looked from Nia back to Hope.

And for some reason, she found herself echoing Law's thoughts—this woman wasn't going to be any sort of threat. At least not to her, not to Law. Trying to convey all of that, or even half of that, though, with just a look?

Remy sighed. Then looked back at Nia, shook his

head. "Nothing. Just recalled hearing the name. You enjoy your visit."

As he watched the woman walk away, Remy muttered, "I didn't just do that. Shit, tell me I didn't just do that."

"She's not going to come storming up on me and Law again, Remy," Hope said, absently stroking a hand up and down his arm.

He was inclined to agree. Still, once he'd figured out who she was, anger had surged, swelled inside him, threatening to spill out and choke him.

"It doesn't matter if she's likely to do it *again*—she shouldn't have done it *once*," he bit off.

"You're right," Hope said quietly. "But she went through something you and I don't want to even imagine. She didn't deal with it well. Although I'll admit, she reacted the way I'd probably *want* to."

"What . . . flip out on a couple of innocent people?"

"She took action," Hope replied, shaking her head. "And once she figured out it wasn't us, she walked away. She didn't let her anger or grief dictate everything. And more . . . she just apologized. Something tells me that wasn't easy. She wears her pride better than I wear my shoes." With a smirk, she glanced down at the cute silver sandals Remy had bought for her.

He sighed and stroked a hand up her back. "You wear your shoes just fine." Dipping his head, he nipped her lower lip and murmured, "More than fine. Those shoes were the reason we were late to church, remember?"

"I thought it was my skirt."

"Skirt. Shoes." Curling a hand around her hip, he kissed her, soft and slow. "You . . . always you."

She sighed into his kiss, opening for him.

He tore himself away, though, reminding himself—he had plans for the day. Important ones. And he wasn't about to let his aggravation at himself, his anger with Nia Hollister, or anything else interfere.

Sliding a hand down her arm, he made himself stop thinking about Nia Hollister. "Come on . . . we need to get over to my mom's house. Lunch and all of that."

It wasn't lunch that had him in a hurry. It was what he had planned after.

# CHAPTER
# NINE

SOME PEOPLE BITCHED ABOUT THE BLUE SCREEN OF
death—the computer locking up on them.

Law's current problem was the white screen of death.
It wasn't writer's block. He knew where he needed to be
going with the story and he was getting there—slowly,
but surely. His deadline was getting close, but he wasn't
worried about it. He'd get there, he always did.

The problem was every time he paused to think
through something—and that was often—he found his
thoughts drifting. Shit, screw *drifting*. That made it
seem aimless, like there was no destination.

His thoughts were on a zipline, drawn straight to one
place—to one person. Nia. And instead of the story,
he'd find himself thinking about her.

Thinking. Wanting. Craving. Twice, he even found
himself thinking about heading to the hotel. Once, he
even made it all the way to the door before he stopped
himself. He couldn't be doing that.

Not yet. What he needed to do was get his head on
straight—as far as Nia went, whenever he saw her, the
thought process stopped and he needed to get a grip on
that before this went any further.

It seemed like a good, simple, straightforward plan.

One he could stick to easily enough. After all, she wouldn't be in town forever, and it wasn't like he had to go into town, right?

At the sound of an engine rumbling down his drive, Law's body sprang to immediate reaction. Swearing, he shoved back from the desk he'd crammed along one wall and headed to the window, staring in disbelief as Nia came cruising down his drive.

"Nia," he muttered. "Fuck."

Oh, hell—that was a bad couple of words to use so close together, because that was exactly what he *thought* whenever he thought of *her*.

Mouth dry, he raked his nails over his stubbled jaw, glanced down at himself. He'd showered that morning—only way to wake up—but he hadn't shaved since Friday and the jeans he was wearing had seen better days. Hell.

This was stupid. He was not going to stand there and worry about his fucking jeans, any of that shit—he wasn't Remy, damn it. What in the hell did he care what clothes he was wearing, as long as they were clean? He'd showered, he was dressed, and that was all that counted, right?

He didn't even know why she was here, right?

But when she knocked, his body was already one tightly coiled spring and his blood boiled, burned. Walking was an agony, his cock aching, thick and ready, even before he opened the door. He could still taste her kisses, still feel how tight, how hot she was.

"Get a grip," he muttered as he reached out, opened the door.

Nia was staring off to the side, giving him another microsecond to get a grip, not that it helped much. As her head turned and her gaze settled on his, he was left standing there, floundering, burning . . . aching.

"Hey."

A smile curved her lips.

"Hey, yourself," she murmured, cocking her head. "You up to much today?"

Law jerked a shoulder. "Not much that has to be done, really."

She sauntered forward, closing the distance between them, and he tried to remind himself—he had just decided he really needed to figure out what was going on here, whether there even *was* something here . . . it was the smart thing to do. The logical thing. The adult thing.

But as he breathed in, her scent hit him, low and hard, spreading through him, heating his already overheated blood, fogging an already fogged brain. She lifted one hand, rested it on his chest. "Maybe I can come in for a while . . ."

"Maybe." The fog in his brain heated, turned to steam, melting brain cells, turning everything to mush, and it only got worse as she stroked her hand up, curled it around his neck, tugging him down for a kiss. "Depends on why you want to come in, though. Not looking to sell me anything, are you?"

Nia chuckled against his lips, then she pulled back and stared into his eyes. "I was thinking about settling up on that rain check." Then she pulled out a strip of condoms.

Shit. Screw logical. Screw mature. Screw adult.

Staring into Nia's eyes, he took the rubbers and slid an arm around her waist and hauled her close. Keeping her locked against him, he stumbled inside, unwilling to let go, not even for a second. He fell back against the door, using his body to shut it as he tangled a hand in her hair.

He didn't waste a single word as he slanted his mouth over hers—what was the point, anyway? They both knew what they needed to know. He wanted her—she wanted him or she wouldn't be here, right?

She opened for him, but when she would have taken

control of the kiss, he refused, wouldn't let her. This hunger, it was killing him.

Eating him alive and had been ever since he'd walked away from her. Jerking her head back farther, he groaned, feasting at her mouth like a man starved. Her hands slid up his back, her nails raking lightly over his flesh.

The way he touched her—hell, there was something so unbelievably erotic, so mind-blowing. His fingers skimmed along her sides, then one hand came around, gripped the back of her shirt, dragging it up. Nia shivered as he slowly bared one inch after another.

She leaned back to let him strip it away and when his eyes went wide at the sight of the red satin bra, a thrill rushed through her. A harsh breath escaped him and he settled back against the door, spread his legs wide, drawing her into the vee of them.

"You're out to drive me nuts," he muttered, cupping her breasts in his hands. "I know it."

She might have said something—anything, but then he pressed his mouth to her flesh, to the sensitive valley between her breasts, nuzzling her, then blowing a puff of air over her skin and watching as she shivered.

Hell—even if she'd *planned* to drive him nuts, it wouldn't matter. Any plans she might have tried to make, they would all fall apart—plans required thought, further planning . . . execution . . .

She wasn't able to think enough to do that, not when he was touching her, not while he had those long-fingered, agile hands gliding over her body, stripping her clothes away. And not with his mouth cruising southward down her neck and lower.

As he nibbled his way along the slope of one breast, Nia curled an arm around his shoulders, struggling just to maintain her balance. The other hand, she slid up, then down one of his arms, tracing the hollows and swells, learning the feel of his skin, his muscles. Long, rangy, and lean—so nice.

When he went to his knees in front of her, she just about went to hers—hard to think, hard to breathe—could barely manage to keep her eyes open as he pressed his mouth to her pubic bone, his breath stirring the curls between her legs.

The first light brush of his tongue against her clit had her shuddering.

The second touch had her groaning and she braced both hands against his shoulders, tried to stand despite the fact that her legs seemed to have turned to water.

Then he curled his tongue around her clit and Nia could have sworn she saw lights exploding. Her breath caught in her lungs, the muscles in her body went rigid. Nothing, absolutely *nothing* seemed to exist except for the way that man was teasing her closer and closer to climax, using his tongue in a way that was nothing short of diabolical.

One hand stroked up her calf, pausing just long enough to nudge her legs farther apart and she wobbled, almost fell, so focused on his mouth and what he was doing. Law steadied her with his free hand, muttered something against her flesh, but she didn't know what, nor did she care, holy hell, that mouth . . .

Then it wasn't just his mouth—he pushed two fingers inside her and twisted his wrist, screwed them in, out . . .

Nia sobbed out his name and all but collapsed.

Law caught her, turned and eased her to the floor, barely breaking his rhythm. He tongued her clit, sucked it into his mouth and pulled oh, so carefully, before releasing it. And still, he pumped two wicked, clever fingers in—out—

"Don't stop," she begged, fisting her hands in his hair, desperate, so focused, so fixed on it—so close, so close.

"Not on my life," he muttered. Another stroke of his fingers, another light, gentle tug with his teeth.

Nia shattered, shuddering, shaking, sobbing his name as she came. The orgasm wrenched through her, drawing tighter, tighter . . .

And then Law was gone.

Holy fuck—

Law shoved back on his heels, his head full of the taste of her, the feel of her, the sight. With a shaking hand, he fumbled for the rubbers she'd brought with her. It took two tries to tear the damn thing off the strip, another two tries before he managed to get it open.

Her eyes, golden and blistering hot, stared up at him.

Her hips were rocking—frenzied, small movements, like she still was trying to feel his fingers inside her.

Not enough—*he* needed to be inside her. All of him.

His fingers didn't want to work and the damn rubber didn't want to cooperate and by the time he had it rolled down over his aching flesh, the fog in Nia's eyes had cleared. She had one elbow behind her like she was about to sit up.

He came over her, catching her face in his hands. She opened for him and he shuddered as her tongue came out, stroked over his, sucking it into her mouth. Her hands raced down his back, caught his hips, tugged him close.

That was all the invitation he needed.

Hardly able to breathe for want of her, he drove inside, his groan mingling with her cry.

She was tight, clenching down around him, squeezing him, milking him, drawing him deeper and deeper . . .

"Oh, hell, yeah," he muttered against her lips. "You feel so damn good."

Nia smiled against his lips. "You feel pretty damn good yourself." Bringing one leg up, she arched her hips and groaned.

He echoed the sound as she clenched tighter around him, the silken, snug walls of her pussy gripping him through the thin shield of latex. Bracing his weight on his elbows, he rocked against her, slow . . . easy—even though every last thing inside him screamed, *Harder . . . faster . . .*

Months of dreaming of this, damn it, it was going to last longer than a hundred and twenty seconds.

Then Nia hooked her leg over his hip and slid a palm to grip down his back, her hand on his ass, her nails biting into his skin. She arched up, meeting each thrust, moving faster, demanding, driving him—

Tearing his mouth away, he snarled, "Fuck."

He shoved upright—distance, needed distance, needed to get away from her mouth, needed to slow down and think . . . But now, his position drove him even deeper and he stared down at her as she whimpered, her eyes wide, almost glassy. A broken plea on her lips.

Hell . . .

Shifting his weight, he reached between them, circled his thumb over her clit, teeth clenched as she tightened around him—when she came, he bit down on the inside of his cheek and hoped the pain might clear his head, because damn it, he was dying.

Her breathing ragged, her body went lax under his. "We're not done," he rasped, fisting a hand in her dark, short hair. Law greedily took her mouth as he started to ride her again—deep, hard. So damned hungry, so damned hungry . . .

If she'd had the breath, she might have told him to give her a minute.

But even if she *had* had the breath? He would have stolen it away again.

Even as she was drifting back down, Law had his mouth on hers, one of those deep, demanding kisses that drove every sane, logical thought from her brain. And he was moving, his body hard and hungry and hot, his cock thrusting deep. If that wasn't enough to drive her to insanity, he had his hand between them, his thumb stroking over her clit, toying with it, stroking in fast, hard circles and every damn time she thought she'd get her breath, he stole it back away.

Dying.

Nia was dying—couldn't live this long without breathing, take this kind of pleasure and still survive.

She knew it.

Then his mouth was gone, stroking along her cheek, down her neck. His teeth raked along her skin and she shuddered, shivered. "Hell, Nia," he muttered. "What are you doing to me? What the hell . . ."

He bit her neck, licked the small hurt, kissed it, repeating that over and over as he moved down her neck, along her collarbone down to her breast. By the time he reached her nipple, she was desperate, so desperate to have him kissing her there.

But he didn't.

Instead he reversed his path, kissing back up the way he came, and starting that same trail down her left side.

She groaned as his chin nudged her nipple this time and she fisted a hand in his hair. "Stop teasing," she muttered.

"You don't like teasing?" he whispered, his breath blowing a warm puff of air along her skin.

"Law . . ."

He chuckled . . . then caught her breast in his hand, plumped it, stroking his thumb over the nipple.

That was . . . nice—but not enough.

Tugging him closer, she whimpered and arched up, pressed tight—damn it, she was dying, her nipples burning hot points and if he didn't . . .

Then he did, his mouth closing around one aching tip. Nia slammed her head back against the floor as the pleasure blistered through her head, molten hot, thick and mind-blowing.

Mind-*shattering* . . .

Another climax loomed—massively powerful, too massive. Instinctively, she tried to pull back, without even realizing.

"No," Law muttered, slanting his mouth over hers, his voice gruff, kisses hungry. "Stay with me . . ."

*Stay with me* . . . Self-preservation insisted she pull back. But she couldn't—she just couldn't. Greedy, desperate for him, she clutched him close, opened for each bruising, hungry kiss. Reveled in each deep, driving thrust.

*Stay with me* . . . Nia was starting to realize it would take a hell of a lot to pull her away.

He groaned out her name, a harsh, ragged growl. Deep inside, she felt his cock jerk and swell, felt him throb and rasp over already swollen and sensitive tissues.

It was too much—way too much. Tearing her mouth away from his, she sank her teeth into his shoulder, shuddering as her orgasm slammed into her.

He braced his free arm at her shoulders, held her steady—held her together because she thought she might be flying apart.

. . . *hell*.

Coherent thought escaped him.

The ability to *move* completely evaded him.

He lay sprawled over Nia, dimly aware that he *needed* to move, but unable to manage it. She laid a hand up his side, let it linger there for just a second before it fell limply to the side.

He might have smiled at the sound of it hitting the

floor, but that was kind of how he felt. Boneless. Drained.

And he needed to *move* . . .

Groaning, he stiffened his arms and managed to roll away, ending up flat on his back next to her. In the middle of his foyer. He stared up at the dark ironwork of his light fixture, his mind slowly trying to come back to life.

He had just had the best sex of his life with a woman he had met all of five times. Including today. On the floor of his foyer.

Next to him, Nia snickered.

Lifting his head took something of an effort, but he managed. Barely. Cocking a brow, he waited.

She rolled onto her side and snuggled up against him, grinning at him. Her golden eyes were mischievous, full of smug, female satisfaction. "You know, I'd planned on jumping you when I got here, but I thought maybe we could make it to your bedroom," she said, resting her chin on his chest. "I don't know what came over me."

Law smiled. "I don't think you were on your own in this." He grimaced and eased away, slowly sitting up and surveying the floor. His jeans were lying by the door, his boxers a few inches away. He didn't even remember taking them off.

Her clothes were everywhere—her jeans in a heap by the stairs, her shirt by the arched opening to the living room, her bra and panties somewhere in the middle. Law scooped up the lacy tangle of her underwear, eyeing it. "I think we did some damage here," he mused.

"We?" She sat up and snagged the panties from him, eyeing the torn lace and silk. "I think I was busy tearing your clothes off, not mine. You tore them, pal."

He thought back, trying to remember just when he'd peeled that red lace and silk away from her—peeled, torn, whatever. "Good point. Okay, I tore them. Maybe I owe you a new pair."

"Maybe?" She rested her chin on her knee, dropping the torn lace on the floor. "Maybe you do." She snickered again as she looked around the foyer. "The floor. I can't believe I jumped you on the floor."

Just staring at her was enough to make his mouth go dry, he thought. And his heart ache, in the weirdest damn way. "It was a mutual jumping, I think. Besides, unless you're in a rush, we can always aim for the bedroom." He scrubbed his hands over his face, realized he could smell her on him—realized he really liked it, too. A lot.

"Hmmm. No rush. You know, I haven't done anything that crazy in years." She came to her knees and settled behind him, her arms draped around him. The soft, warm weight of her breasts pressed against his back was enough to have his dick twitching in interest already.

*Down, boy,* he thought ruefully. Going at it on the floor again was *not* what he needed to do. Finesse— some finesse here. He knew the meaning of the word, thought he could manage it. Under normal circumstances, he usually did just fine, too.

Glancing back at her, he brushed a hand down her arm. "Have to admit, I haven't either." Her mouth drew him and before he realized it, he was kissing her, bringing his hand up and holding the back of her head, in case she tried to pull away.

Not that she did.

Hell.

He could get used to this. Way too used to this.

Easing back, he made himself pull away, forced himself to stand, put some distance between them. Although he didn't feel the levity at all, he said, "I don't know about you, but I could stand a shower."

Her lashes low over her eyes, she stretched. Then she

stood and smiled at him, closing the distance between them and stroking a finger down the front of his chest.

"Is that an invitation, Reilly?"

"Sounded that way to me." His heart stuttered as she pressed against him and the flicker of interest became a slow, inexorable rise, one he couldn't have fought for anything. "You're going to be trouble, Nia Hollister," he muttered. "All sorts of it, I can tell."

"I've always been trouble."

He came through the woods.

Before he made plans, before he considered what plans he might need to make, he needed to know *why* she was here.

After all, Nia Hollister's visit to town could be mundane.

He didn't believe that, though. Visits to the sheriff, nosing around through public records. No. It wasn't mundane. But he couldn't decide how to handle it until he *knew*.

There was a reason, and he needed to know what it was, needed to know more about her. He already knew a disturbing amount—enough to know that if she just disappeared, it would be noticed.

She wasn't just a photojournalist—fancy name for a photographer, he figured. She was actually fairly famous in her field. Had enough of a name that she'd be missed. People would notice. He couldn't risk that.

If this was a bigger city, he could think she was here to take pictures. If she was a reporter, he could almost imagine she was here to do some sort of story about her cousin's death. And still, that wasn't an idea he could discard. Definitely not. A story about that wouldn't be good. Too much focus on it would be . . . unpleasant. For him to allow it would be unwise.

And that was why he was proceeding with caution, because he wasn't going to do anything that would draw attention back to things *now*.

Photojournalists weren't exactly the biggest names out there from what he could tell, but she *was* a name—a known one.

She couldn't just disappear. Should she die and the circumstances were even remotely suspicious . . . no. That would be bad. Very bad. He had to be careful here, had to decide if he needed to do anything at all—and unless something *had* to be done, he'd do nothing. He'd screwed up, and now he had to wait until things settled, had to be cautious. And no more mistakes.

From the woods, he watched Law Reilly's house, waited. He didn't like approaching in the daylight, even from this angle, although he knew nobody would see him, unless they were watching from somewhere in the back of the house.

Which Reilly could very well be doing.

Except Nia's bike was out front. He'd seen her turn in. Had been following her, watching her.

Finally, he made a decision. He couldn't keep waiting where he was, in the shade and safety of the trees. He'd come here to evaluate. He needed to do that, or leave.

Slipping out of the woods, he started for the house, keeping to the corner where he wasn't as likely to be seen. He also kept at a slow, casual pace, hands tucked in his pockets. Harmless . . . he was just harmless, and wasn't out there to cause trouble . . .

# CHAPTER

# TEN

IT WAS NEARLY AN HOUR BEFORE THEY MADE IT OUT of the shower and downstairs to the kitchen, where Law put Nia at the island. When she would have climbed off the stool, he pointed and said, "Damn it, stay there. I need food."

"You're cranky." She smirked at him and slid off anyway. "I was just thinking about getting my clothes. I need a cigarette."

He frowned. "Those aren't good for you."

"Gee, really?" She made a face at him. "I know. I just . . . hell, I stopped years ago. Going to stop again, sooner or later. It's just this mess with Joely . . ."

Law paused and closed the distance between them. He pushed his fingers through her hair. "If you stopped once, you can do it again, then. But do you really think she'd want you poisoning yourself? Not just with the worry, but with the cigarettes, too?"

"Stop." She sighed and rubbed her neck. "We've had sex a few times—doesn't mean you get to dictate to me about my health. And I already *know* this. Now are you making us food or what?"

"Making food." He dipped his head and pressed his mouth to hers. "And I'm not trying to dictate. I can't help that I'm already stupid with how much I think about you. That's your fault."

"Is not." She scowled at him.

"Yeah, it is. Has to be. Haven't ever had anybody else tangle up my head the way you do. So that means it's your fault." He nipped her lower lip and moved away, heading back to the fridge. "Now be a good girl and I'll make us some lunch."

"A good girl," she echoed, chuckling. Then she sighed. "What the hell. I'm hungry, anyway. Didn't get much in the way of breakfast."

"Hard to get a decent breakfast staying at a hotel. And eating at the café every day will get old," he said, rooting around for the bacon he'd picked up, some tomatoes. He could cook well enough but he hadn't exactly planned on company—the most he could do was BLTs and some soup. Hopefully that would work.

If she came back, though, Lena had taught him a few easy things that just might wow a woman. He found himself thinking about making Nia dinner—candlelight. Wine. Yeah, he liked that idea. Liked it a lot.

". . . at the hotel now."

"Huh?" He glanced up, realized she'd been talking and he'd been off in his own world. That wasn't anything new, but it wasn't like Nia was used to that. Frowning, he dumped the stuff he held onto the counter and said, "Sorry. Got to thinking about something else, didn't hear you."

She lifted a brow and although she didn't say anything, he could tell she was a little put off.

"I wasn't ignoring you," he said, trying to keep the defensive tone out of his voice. "I was just . . ."

"I didn't say anything," she said, her voice cool.

"I know, I was just . . ." He felt the slow creep of red climbing up his neck and realized with no small amount of humiliation that he was blushing. Ah, hell. Turning around, he started rooting through the cabinets even though it didn't take five seconds to find what he needed, not with Hope's meticulous organization. "I . . . ah, well, all I plan on doing is soup and sandwiches. My mind kind of wanders, and I got to thinking about making you dinner one night. If you'd want to come back out, that is. Started thinking about . . . I dunno, a date."

As soon as the words left his mouth, he felt like the world's biggest jackass.

Shit. Grabbing a can of soup, he slammed the cabinet door with a little more force than needed.

"A date, huh?"

Her voice came from just an inch or two away.

Turning around, he leaned against the counter and tried to pretend he was a lot more relaxed than he felt. "Yeah. You know, if you wanted."

She'd slipped off the stool and stood close, too close. She was smiling, he realized. A soft smile that hit him straight in the gut, straight in the heart.

"A date . . . where you make me dinner."

He glanced off past her shoulder, jerked a shoulder in a shrug. "Yeah. I'm no Emeril or anything, but I can cook okay. Lena . . . ah, Ezra's wife? She's a pretty good friend of mine and she's a chef, taught me a thing or two after she figured out about all I could do was macaroni out of a box and . . ."

That was all he managed to get out before she pressed her lips to his.

It was a quick, easy kiss and then she backed away, leaning against the island and staring at him, still smiling that slow, easy smile.

"Law, I've got to say, that's probably the sweetest invitation I think I've ever had. I've never once had a guy offer to make me dinner. Just tell me when—I'm there."

*Sweet*—his blush only got worse and he turned away, hands feeling too big, his throat dry and tight. Hell, she made him feel like he was back in high school. Shit, middle school, when he had a crush on the cute teacher's assistant—some blond bombshell who wore her sweaters just a little bit too tight. Only this was worse. So much worse.

This wasn't just hormone-driven, adolescent-crazed lust. He might wish it was, but . . .

Clearing his throat, he busied himself with ripping open the bacon. "So what were you saying about the hotel?"

"I checked out. Some city cop, Kent Jennings, mentioned that there was a bed-and-breakfast not too far from here and the owner sometimes sublets the cabins. By the way, just how many Jenningses *live* around here, anyway?"

Absently, he said, "A lot."

The Inn. She was staying at the Inn.

Once he had the bacon sizzling on the stove and his hands washed, he turned back and studied her, an uneasy feeling stirring inside his chest. "You're staying at the Inn."

"Yep."

"I take it that means you'll be around awhile? Roz only uses the cabins for long-term stuff, a month or longer, at least."

"Yeah, I know. She gave me a sweet deal—three months for the price of two if I paid it all up front." She grimaced and said, "I went ahead and did it, figured I might as well."

Law was quiet, thinking it through. Roz probably had her sign some sort of short-term rental agreement. But she was a fair woman—compassionate. She'd let Nia out of the deal, and Law could help her find someplace else. Blowing out a breath, he met her eyes. "You sure you want to stay there?"

She blinked. "Why wouldn't I?"

"Nia . . . Lena works there."

Something moved through those golden eyes, but before he could interpret it, she looked down. When she looked back up, just a minute later, the look was gone and her gaze was unreadable. "And your point would be . . . ?"

"How easy is that going to be for you?" he asked, shoving away from the counter and moving to stand in front of her, reaching up to trace a finger down her cheek.

"It won't," she said flatly. "But *nothing* has been easy for me for almost a year and I don't expect that to change now." Then abruptly, she smiled, a sly smile, as she reached out and hooked her fingers in the front of his jeans, tugged him closer. "Although, actually, I can think of *one* thing that was remarkably easy . . ."

"You calling me a thing?" He wasn't so sure he wanted to let it go as simple as that, but that was her pain and if this was how she wanted to deal with it . . . although he wished he could offer her something more, some sort of comfort, something to take the darkness and the sadness from her.

"Hmmm. I don't know. Nah, you're not a thing. Maybe you're a fling. Yeah, that's more like it. Is that what we've got going here? A fling?"

She nibbled her way along his bare chest and Law hissed as she bit lightly at his nipple. "A fling? Hell if I know. Can't say I've ever been anybody's fling before." He was tempted to reach down, cup her hips under the hem of the T-shirt she wore.

But the scent of frying bacon hung in the air. Instead, he eased away, bussed her lips lightly.

"Maybe before we figure out what to call it, we should figure out what it is," he decided, keeping his voice light, easy. Even though he definitely wasn't feeling light or easy right now. "By definition, flings are general short-term, right? But you're not ditching town in a few days. You planning on trading me out for somebody else in a few weeks, Nia?"

She snorted. "Trading you out? You're not a car, Law."

Flipping the bacon, he shrugged. "Well, it's a fair question. Otherwise, how can I figure out if this is a fling or not?"

"Call it whatever you want. Just feed me. And don't worry . . . I'm not much for flings myself."

He glanced over his shoulder at her, a smile tugging at his lips.

The sight of that smile had her heart skipping a beat or five. Waiting until it leveled out, she tucked her hands in her lap, discreetly wiped her sweating palms on the T-shirt she'd swiped from him. It smelled of him and she knew she'd be smelling him on her all day.

"Don't see that it matters what we call it, anyway," she said, striving for casual. "They are just words anyway, you know."

"Words." He turned around, once more leaned against the counter, hands braced on it. "Words can do a lot of things—as much as you want, or as little as you want, if you think about it."

Nia arched a brow. "Sounds like you spend a lot of time thinking about words."

He shrugged and shoved off the counter, ambled over toward her. Her heart did that weird little skip, but all he did was reach over her head, pull a small saucepan down from the rack hanging over the island. "You okay with soup?"

"As long as it's nothing gross like split pea or something like that."

He laughed. "Nah, you're safe. I can't touch split pea without thinking of *The Exorcist*."

Nia groaned and squeezed her eyes closed. "Oh, thanks so much for that image . . ."

"You're welcome," he said cheerfully. "I always feel better when I share an image like that. Helps lessen my mental agony."

Popping one eye open, she stared at him as he opened the red-and-white can. "Your mental agony. You're a strange character, Law."

"Yeah. I've heard that a time or two."

She shuddered and tried to scrub her mind of that image—thankfully it had been years since she'd tried split pea soup, so she wasn't inclined to gag, and she had a pretty strong stomach anyway. The shit she saw in her job . . . well, it wasn't for the faint of heart.

"Since we're not going to define just what we're doing here, I've got another question for you."

"Yeah?" She was almost afraid to hear, seeing as how his humor obviously ran to the twisted.

But when she glanced at him, his expression was serious.

Heavy, even.

He took his time, putting the soup on the stove, flipping the bacon again. Her belly rumbled at the scent and she thought about getting up to try to steal a piece.

Then he pinned her with that intense hazel gaze. How those eyes could look so dark and brooding, she didn't know, but he managed it. Her knees felt a little wobbly and all of a sudden, her heart was racing.

"Just why are you back in Ash, Nia?" he asked softly.

"Pardon?" Even as she forced the word out, she wanted to kick herself. Playing dumb wasn't going to work with him. But she didn't know how to answer that question.

*Tell him the truth*, a small voice inside her heart whispered.

Her head screeched, *No*.

Everything else demanded she do just that.

The truth—give him the truth.

But what if he laughed? What if he didn't believe her?

What if—God forbid—he pitied her and patted her back and sent her on her way?

Swallowing, she swiped her hands on the overlong hem of the shirt again, staring past his shoulder at the window. The blinds were down, but the window was open and occasionally, the blinds would move, pushed in by a small breeze. She focused on the small undulation, tried to get her thoughts in order.

Where to start . . . hell, where did she start?

Did she tell him the truth?

"Nia?"

She swallowed, jerked her eyes back to his.

Abruptly, she knew.

Yeah. She would tell him the truth. Somehow, she knew he wasn't going to laugh. Wouldn't pat her on the head and send her on her way. Whether he'd believe her or not, she didn't know, but he wouldn't dismiss it, either.

"My cousin," she said.

Law nodded. "I had a feeling it was about her. No other reason for you to come back here, is there?"

She swallowed again—there was a knot in her throat, huge and awful, and she could hardly breathe around it. But swallowing almost made her feel like she'd choke— choke on the tears, the pain. "You'd think it would get easier, right? I mean, according to the investigation, they found the guy who killed her. That's the closure I should need, right? What makes it easier for me to move on?"

For a long time he was quiet, nothing breaking the silence but a quiet sigh and the sizzle of bacon. Then he turned around, switched the soup to low, used the fork to transfer bacon from the skillet to a plate he'd lined with a couple of paper towels.

"You're trying to make it a process, sounds like, Nia. You can't. There's no right or wrong way to go about healing that sort of pain, to get over that kind of loss. You have to cope with it in your own time," he said as he turned back, coming to stand in front of her. He cupped her face in a gentle hand, stroked a thumb over her lip.

The gentleness of the touch, the compassion in his eyes, it all but broke her.

But the fiery burn of anger had settled in her heart . . . *finally.* And it gave her the strength she needed. Reaching up, she curled her fingers around his wrist, not to push him away, but to squeeze, to hold tight. Whether it was for support, to get his attention, she just didn't know.

"I can't *cope,* Law. Not right now. Not yet." She blew out a breath, focused on the middle of his chest— breathed in, breathed out. "I can't. Because I don't think Joe Carson is the one who killed my cousin."

Hope couldn't remember the last time she'd been on a picnic.

Not that this was a for-real picnic.

They'd eaten lunch with Remy's mom, Elizabeth.

Something about the way the woman had all but hovered over Hope had made her feel so self-conscious— and *that* made her feel guilty because Elizabeth was a sweetheart. They'd gotten to be friends over the past few months and Elizabeth hadn't ever acted like that before—staring at Hope with that shining, wide-eyed gaze and all but tripping over her feet as she followed them to the door.

She'd been acting weird enough that Hope had almost

asked Remy about it, but decided against it, especially seeing as how Remy was acting kind of weird, too.

Not mad or anything. Just quiet. And it made her nervous.

This was nice, though. Being here with him—some piece of land somebody in his family owned—Hope had no idea who. The Jennings clan seemed to multiply every time she turned around.

He had a basket with wine, more of that lovely local wine she liked so much, some strawberries, a blanket. Her heart all but melted at the romance of it. Hoping the smile on her face didn't look too goofy, she sat and combed her fingers through Remy's golden hair and stared at him.

Hell.

He was so pretty.

Too pretty.

And hers—he loved her.

Really loved her.

As if he'd been reading her mind, he opened his eyes and looked up at her—that amazing blue capturing her gaze, holding her. "I love you," he said softly.

Her heart danced in her chest. As her heart sighed, she laid her hand on his cheek and murmured, "I love you, too."

In an easy, lazy movement, he rolled to his knees and settled in front of her. "That's a good thing to know." A smile tugged at his lips. He caught her hand in his, lifted it to his lips. "Because I need to ask you something."

"Hmm. Okay." She swayed forward, pressed her lips to his. Hmmmm . . . he tasted like wine and strawberries. Hope slid her tongue along his lower lip and then eased back, smiling at him. "What did you want to ask?"

He didn't say anything right away. Still holding her

hand, he rubbed his thumb along the back of it—pushed something . . . oh, hell.

Hope froze. Looked down.

Her eyes widened as she watched Remy push a golden band, set with diamonds and an emerald, onto her left hand. Her ring finger. Oh. Oh, man. Her heart banged against her ribs.

"Will you marry me?"

*I can't cope, Law. Not right now. Not yet . . . I can't. Because I don't think Joe Carson is the one who killed my cousin.*

Nia Hollister's words echoed through his mind and although he tried to tell himself to be calm, he was having a hard time of it. She knew. Somehow she knew.

"That fucking *bitch.*"

He moved through the woods easily, moving on autopilot. He'd been here so many times, roamed these paths for so many years. They were like home to him.

It freed his mind to think—to brood. To fume. How? Shit. How did she know? He hadn't left any clues for anybody to figure it out—he knew he hadn't because if he had, the cops would already be all over his damn ass.

So how did *she* know? Bitch. Fucking bitch.

He wanted her dead—that's what he wanted.

But he knew better than to act rashly.

Couldn't do that. He'd done that before and it had brought hell down on him. Leaving Hollister's cousin here—*that* had been rash, although it had seemed to be a clever move at the time, a move that would solve his problems. He'd been arrogant, foolish, and it had damn near ended everything.

He hadn't been as careful as he needed to be in Chicago, either. Hadn't been careful with Mara.

Too many mistakes—and all it took was one for him to be caught.

Couldn't afford to screw up now. Not with her. *Fuck.* Careful—he'd be careful now if it killed him. Still . . . he had to watch her. Had to figure out his next move.

And he couldn't do that without knowing her. Always wise to know his prey. Always wise.

He needed her gone.

More than anything, he needed her gone and perhaps, if he could get to know his prey well enough, he could figure out a way to make that happen that wouldn't involve killing her, hurting her . . . anything that might spin things back around so that they took a closer look at her cousin's murder.

Something.

Anything.

Know your prey . . . always good advice.

Her soft, golden skin had a grayish undertone and her eyes glittered hard as glass as she stared at him—waiting, Law realized.

Waiting for him to either dismiss her or brush her fears aside.

He hid a cynical smile. If she knew him at all, she wouldn't look so worried—Law thrived on conspiracy theories, paranoid crap. What she was thinking didn't even come close to some of his crazier ideas.

She looked ready to break, he thought. It did the damnedest thing to his heart.

"If you're expecting me to look shocked or something, sweetheart, I'm going to disappoint you," he finally said. "Carson was a first-class bastard, but that doesn't mean I'll buy whatever story I'm handed by the police."

Startled, Nia blinked. "What?"

"You heard me. I'm not saying I don't believe he didn't do it, but that doesn't mean I won't rule out other stuff, either." He rotated his neck, grimacing as it popped. Absently, he reached up and rubbed at muscles gone tight.

"There wasn't any reason for him to hurt your cousin, Nia. Joe was a sick son of a bitch, but he had a method to his madness and I'm not seeing a method here. So while that doesn't mean I can't see it happening the way the sheriff's office says it happened . . . well, the same goes for the opposite."

Nia scowled. "That's about as vague as you can get. You like sitting on fences, Law?"

"No. I like being objective. I like proof. And yeah, they might have proof against Joseph Carson, but they didn't know him." He looked at her, felt the hate and rage tear through his heart, through his gut and soul, hoped it didn't show on his face. "I did. He was capable of all kinds of madness and cruelty and brutality like you can't imagine. But it was never random—your cousin was random. That doesn't fit the man I knew. Since the pieces don't fit, I don't believe in closing my mind to other options. This could mean there's still a killer out there."

"So . . . you don't think I'm crazy. Overreacting?"

Reaching up, he cupped Nia's cheek. "I think you're listening to your gut. People don't always do that enough." Then he stroked his thumb over her lip and added, "But do me a favor . . . don't go striking off on your own with a gun again. Especially an unregistered one."

Nia flushed, the mellow golden skin of her cheeks going pink. "I wasn't thinking then. At least not clearly."

"Speaking hypothetically—say you're right, and the killer is still out there. You think you'll be thinking clearly if you happen upon a roadmap and evidence that points the way to him?" Law asked sardonically. He shook his head. "If there *is* somebody else out there, he's dangerous, dangerous in a way Joe Carson never could be, because this guy is a thinker—a predator. Chances are he's from around here, and he's watching everything you do."

Those words left her shivering.

Nia swallowed and looked away, tried to pretend she wasn't terrified.

It wasn't happening.

"Fuck." She rubbed the back of her hand over her mouth. "Okay, now I really need a cigarette."

Yeah, she'd figured the killer was local, figured he would take note of her. But for reasons she couldn't entirely think about, she hadn't thought so far ahead as to think about whether or not he'd be *watching* her.

Was he?

Had he been?

A tremor wracked her body, and a second later, Law's arms came around her. One hand stroked the back of her neck, a light soothing touch. The other rubbed along her spine, steady and strong, warming her. "You okay?"

"Yeah." She swallowed and scowled, feeling very much the fool. "Just feeling a little freaked by that idea—freaked and foolish. I mean, I figured he was local, figured he'd know who I was, might see me. Why didn't I go beyond that?"

"Maybe because it would have made it too easy to talk yourself out of this," he offered. Then he tipped her chin up, stared into her eyes. "And you need to be here, I think. Otherwise, you wouldn't be."

"Yeah." Nodding, Nia closed her eyes, then leaned back in and snuggled close. "I do."

"The mind has a way of protecting us—we see what we need to see and when we're ready for more, we get more. You weren't ready to think that next step, so your mind just processed what you were ready to deal with."

Despite herself, she smirked.

"You know, I've never once asked you what you do for a living," she murmured. "What are you, a shrink?"

"Shit, no." He barked out a laugh. "Absolutely no."

He considered telling her, then ruled it out. Not yet. "You know . . . I could tell you, but well . . . I only tell women once I'm sure it's moved beyond the flinging stage."

She laughed weakly. "Okay, then. I'll keep that in mind." She pushed against his arms. "I need a cigarette, Law. Bad."

"I've got a better idea . . ." He dipped his head and covered her mouth with his. "You just need something else to think about. I'll give you something . . ."

# CHAPTER
# ELEVEN

LAW ACTUALLY WORKED MUCH BETTER THAN A CIGA-rette, for the most part, she decided. Although she did slip out eventually to catch one on the porch. He sat on the porch swing, wearing nothing but low-riding jeans and making her think dark and delicious thoughts—*much* better than a cigarette, even if she was craving the nicotine.

Damn it. Okay, it really was time to start thinking about quitting . . .

She spent a couple of hours with him curled up on the couch, watching a bad movie, using up the last condom, and just before she could consider having a polite little tantrum, Law saved the day by disappearing down the hall to his bedroom. When he returned, he had another box of rubbers, unopened.

It was edging up on six and she was thinking about test-driving the new supply when she heard an engine.

Puzzled, she looked at Law, but the expression on his face was one of resignation.

"You expecting company?"

"No." He glanced at her. "It's Hope."

She saw the nerves in his eyes, the worry. Reaching

out, she laid a hand on his arm. "I can go." She wasn't sure what sort of relationship they had—especially after seeing Hope with the guy that morning, but she knew there was a deep connection between Law and Hope.

Law pressed his mouth to her forehead, then, quick as a wish, he stood up. "You're not leaving," he tossed over his shoulder.

"I'm not, huh?" She stood up and sauntered after him.

"No." Pausing in the doorway, he turned and bent down, brushed his mouth against hers, a long, lingering kiss. "At least I hope you're not. If you plan on hanging around town . . . well, Hope's a friend—one of my best, and . . ."

It was sweet, she realized. He looked uncomfortable, like he was fighting for the words. But she understood. He didn't want them at odds. It was weird, it was awkward as hell, considering she already knew Hope Carson had about as much use for her as she'd have for a scorching case of herpes.

But Hope mattered to him, and because he seemed to want Nia to matter, he wanted them to at least not dislike each other.

She wondered how many guys would care.

Sighing, she skimmed a hand back through his hair and pressed her brow to his. "Mind if I at least put some jeans on?"

"Actually, yeah. It's almost a crime to cover that ass of yours." He cupped her butt in his hands and squeezed. "But I can see why that might make you more comfortable."

Smirking, she eased away and had just barely managed to get the jeans in her hands before the door opened.

The awkward smile she had plastered on her face froze.

Hope wasn't alone.

Law sauntered into the foyer, caught sight of the other man and promptly placed his body in front of Nia. "Hell, Hope, if you were bringing him, you coulda warned me," he drawled.

Hope pursed her lips as she peered around Law, watching as Nia struggled into her jeans.

Her fingers suddenly felt a lot more awkward, fumbling with the zipper, the button. She was acutely aware of the bra she wasn't wearing, of her rather disheveled hair.

But she knew how to brazen her way through anything. Almost anything.

Moving out from behind Law, she tucked her hands into her pockets and smiled at Hope. It felt fake as hell, but at least she wasn't holding a gun—that was an improvement over the last time she'd been in the house with this lady, right?

"Hello, again, Ms. Carson."

"Ah . . . maybe you should call me Hope." She pressed her lips together, a smile tugging at the corners as she looked from Law to Nia. "I . . . well, I guess that's your bike out front. I didn't recognize it. I'm not too good at that sort of thing."

"Yeah." Nia fought the urge to hunch her shoulders. Damn it, she wasn't going to feel uncomfortable here— Law wanted her here, right? If he didn't, he would have made that clear.

An awkward silence stretched out. Nia shuffled her feet and was just about ready to tell Law she'd call him—come back later, *something,* and then Hope reached up, tucking her hair back.

Nia noticed something.

Something glittery, bright and gold.

A ring—one Hope hadn't been wearing earlier, she was pretty sure. Without thinking twice, she blurted out, "Nice rock."

Law glanced at her, a puzzled look on his face.

Then he looked at Hope. Two seconds, a grin split his face and he was across the foyer, whooping as he caught Hope in his arms, spinning her around.

Despite herself, Nia smiled.

The love between the two of them was obvious.

Obvious, strong . . . and it broke Nia's heart to look at them. Not because she was jealous. What she saw between them wasn't anything more than the sort of love a brother and sister would share, she imagined—a lot like the love she'd shared with Joely, really. That's what it was . . . she realized. That was their bond.

And that was why it hurt so damn bad.

Swallowing the knot in her throat, she backed away, leaving them and ducking back into the living room. Her bra and her torn panties were still in a neat little pile by the door and she managed to gather them up without Law noticing, but as she headed down the hallway for the bathroom, the excited chatter behind her went oddly quiet.

She didn't hear him behind her, but nonetheless, knew he was back there.

Swearing under her breath, she tried to plaster a smile on her face as she turned to look at him.

"You said you weren't leaving."

Glancing past him, she looked at Hope who had already turned to her apparently new fiancé. Hope was gazing up at him, and he was smiling down at her, toying with her hair.

It was a look that seemed too intimate to be shared, even though Nia was the only one who could see them.

It was a look that made her heart sigh in wistful envy.

Swallowing, she tore her eyes away and looked back up at Law. "I hadn't planned on it. But this . . ." She blew out a breath and said softly, "This is something special and I don't need to be a part of it."

"And what if I want you to be a part of it?"

The look on his face, in his eyes, made her melt. Reaching up, she laid a hand on his cheek and murmured, "Then I have to say, as sweet as you are . . . it's selfish." She flicked a quick look at Hope, then back. "This is about her, and Law, she's not comfortable around me, nor *should* she be. Don't force me on her . . . don't mess this up for her."

He caught her chin in his hand and dipped his head, pressed his brow to hers. "You don't need to be getting all logical on me."

"Ha-ha." She rubbed her mouth against his and then eased back. "Maybe I can leave you my cell number. You could call me."

"Hmmm. Yeah. Maybe I can do that."

She gave him another weak smile and disappeared into the bathroom while the crack in her heart widened.

Widened . . . and now it was spilling out black, bitter poison.

Just seeing Law and Hope together had reminded her. Reminded her, once more, why she was here.

When she was with Law, it was easy to forget . . . easy to let herself forget.

She couldn't keep doing that. She needed to be doing *something*.

Nia didn't even know what, but she needed to be doing something.

Law wasn't too happy about her leaving, but he did get Nia's number.

If he had his way about it, he'd either be joining her

that night, or she'd be back at his place. Although maybe that was rushing things.

Maybe they could just have sex again . . .

Shit. As she told Remy and Hope good-bye, he bit his tongue on trying to talk her into hanging around.

She was right.

The air was already too damn tense, and things between Nia and Hope needed to ease up on their own. He could see that.

Didn't mean he had to like it, right?

As long as Hope, and most especially Remy, didn't give her grief when she left, maybe things could start to settle a little.

Hell, he never would have thought he was an optimist.

To their credit, neither Hope nor Remy said a thing while Nia was in the house. And they didn't even say anything the minute the door closed. It wasn't until the sounds of her bike's powerful engine had faded that Hope looked at him, her brows arched over green eyes.

Somehow, she managed to look amused, concerned, and irritated, all at once.

"Well. That was unexpected," she said slowly.

"Was it?" He scratched his chest, wished he wasn't already missing Nia like hell. "Why don't I take the two of you out to eat? We could go to the Inn. A congratulations sort of thing."

"Actually—" Remy said.

"That's a great idea," Hope interjected, narrowing her eyes and giving Remy a look that all but dared him to say anything. "And you can tell me all about your weekend."

Law lifted a brow. "Hope, my weekend is none of your business."

"Did you forget the last time she was here?"

"Nope." He gestured toward the living room. "I need to go change. I'll be down in a few."

"Damn it, Law . . ."

He tuned everything else out, told himself he'd figure out some way to calm her down, level things out while he changed. But his mind was straying . . . wandering back to Nia, and the sudden grief he'd seen in her eyes.

Her cousin. She hadn't said anything, but something had her thinking about her cousin again.

"Whoa . . . sparkly . . ."

Hope flushed as Roz shot her a look and waggled her eyebrows, then nudged Remy with her elbow. "You did good, man. Lena, this ring is gorgeous, emerald and diamonds. Classy, unique . . . lovely."

"You'd know jewelry," Lena said dryly, making her way over to the private table with a bottle of champagne.

"Well." Roz chuckled, toying with the golden chain around her neck. "I do love my shiny stuff."

From behind, Carter hugged her. "We know that, baby."

Hope smiled up at the two of them as Carter rubbed his cheek against his wife's, his darker blond hair mingling with Roz's pale, almost platinum blond. He kissed her gently and then eased back, grinning at his cousin. "So. You're getting married. I would have had a hard time believing it a few months ago, you know. But ever since Hope showed up . . . well, I guess things change. Congratulations."

"Thanks."

"I called Ezra," Lena said. "He's coming out, too. An impromptu party . . ." She grinned wryly and added, "Although I won't be in attendance much. We're packed out there."

"We'll do a for-real thing in a few weeks, maybe," Law said. "Casual, though. Maybe at my place."

Hope glanced down, hoping he wouldn't see the worry in her eyes. His place . . . so he could invite Nia? Immediately, though, she wanted to kick herself. If he cared for the lady, she needed to get over this, right? Besides, it wasn't like it would last that long. Nia was here for . . .

Abruptly, Hope scowled. Just why *was* Nia here?

She couldn't stay in the cabin, Nia realized.

She'd planned to just get some more research done— her contacts had e-mailed her a veritable mountain of data and there was so much to comb through, plus she'd thought about trying to narrow things to *this* area.

But she couldn't stay in the house.

Couldn't.

In the end, she left, thinking maybe she'd ramble around the Inn, but halfway down the path, she froze, watching as a big, old white truck came rumbling down the drive.

It wasn't the truck that froze her in place. It was the woman waiting out in front of the Inn. Sitting patiently at her side was the dog. Both were gazing at the truck and that told Nia who was probably inside it, especially as the dog's tail started to wag.

Ezra.

Nibbling on her lip, she watched as he parked. He climbed out and saw her, gave her a half-wave, but he was focused on his wife. As they disappeared into the house, an idea started to burn in the back of her mind.

Lena was here.

Probably working.

Now Ezra was here. Would he be here for a while?

Hmmm.

Glancing down at her clothes, she decided it would do for a quick drink. After all, Roz had told her she could grab food in the Inn, either at the bar or take-out from the restaurant, eat in there and run a tab . . . whatever.

She shouldn't be thinking along these lines.

Not at all.

But she kept thinking to herself that she needed to do something.

And now she just might have a shot. Ezra was eating there at the Inn. As was Law, Hope, and her fiancé—Remy, Nia thought was his name. All of them, tucked into what looked like a private dining room. She recognized Law's voice, although she hadn't seen him.

And the idea that had just been a mere whisper was now a roar.

Ezra and Lena were both here. Lena—

Seeing the woman who looked so much like Joely pulled Nia's thoughts back to her focus, back to her purpose for being here.

Nia hadn't been completely sitting on her hands. Or on Law's lap . . . under him. She'd talked to people, done some investigating on her own—all public records stuff.

And now she was thinking of the screams. The screaming . . . out in the woods.

Lena had reported hearing a woman screaming.

Without bothering to get a drink, Nia slipped out of the Inn and hurried back to her cabin. It was daylight—for a little while, at least. Lena and Ezra were occupied. She might as well poke around. And although she hadn't taken it with her to Law's, she *did* have another unregistered gun. One she'd be more than happy to use.

Yeah, it was stupid—very damn stupid, she knew it. Dangerous.

But Nia was going to take a chance on being stupid,

on doing something dangerous, because she couldn't live with this uncertainty in her gut, and unless she *found* something, nothing would change.

Ezra King might have some doubts of his own—she wouldn't be surprised.

Law Reilly might suspect that not everything was exactly as it was reported in the official files. But suspicions wouldn't do a damn bit of good if nobody ever bothered to look any deeper.

Or look *at all.*

That's all she wanted to do right now—look. Look around some, see if she'd see anything, notice anything . . . or anybody.

She parked her bike just inside the woods. It wouldn't be a good thing if somebody saw and then called it in, reported it. Nia had no doubt Ezra would hear about it, and she didn't want him rushing out here.

He wouldn't have any trouble figuring out what she was doing.

So it was better she just not be caught. She kept the gun tucked into a holster just under her left arm—easy to draw, hidden by the light jacket she wore. Although it was hotter than hell, even under the trees. She'd rather be hot and alive than cool and dead.

She also had a compass, used her phone to mark the position of her bike with the GPS—yeah, she'd done a few hikes before. She had bars on the phone, so hopefully she wouldn't get too lost. Hopefully, she wouldn't get lost at all.

Moving into the perpetual twilight of the trees, she paused a moment, let her eyes adjust. She'd deliberately picked a spot close to Lena King's place to enter the trees. From here, she could just barely make out the gap where Lena's property started, although she couldn't see the house, yet. It was back from the road just a bit and as Nia walked, she started to catch glimpses of the white-painted wood, the russet-red shutters, bright blooms of flowers.

For reasons she couldn't explain, seeing that house left her chest aching. Had tears stinging her eyes.

She could almost see Joely struggling through the underbrush, struggling to reach the house.

Could hear the footsteps behind her—

A breath hissed out of her and she threw herself to the side, drawing the gun from her holster, staring around the woods, her back pressed to a tall oak. Listening— was there somebody following her?

No.

There was nothing.

*You're going crazy, Nia.*

Blowing out a breath, she closed her eyes, sent a look skyward. Over the next thirty seconds, her breathing calmed, her heart rate leveled out. Once she thought she might be able to speak without dissolving into the screaming meemies, she stared out over the trees . . . waited another minute.

Nothing. No sound.

Not even the breath of sound. Not even the suggestion of it.

Okay.

She took another slow step, and another . . . trying not to let thoughts of Joely crowd her mind. It was hard, though; she felt like there was nothing but the other woman's memories, her thoughts, her losses, her aches, her sorrows, storming inside her.

*Focus on why you're here. Not on Joely,* she told herself.

But Joely *was* why she was here.

Joely's life . . . ended. Her wedding—the one that would never happen.

Echoes of those dreams.

Why?

If Lena had heard screaming, if it had been Joely, *why* had she been *here*?

Was there a house? Some place for him to hide her? To hide *them*?

"No," she muttered, shaking her head. Didn't make sense.

If there was a house here, Sheriff Nielson would have known—they would have checked things out. Investigated. A shiver raced down her spine as she took one step, then another, her footfalls crunching on the damp bed of twigs and leaves.

Something—there had to be something out here.

Moving deeper into the woods, her eyes running along the trees, she started down a slope. The trail abruptly veered to the north, away from the lip of a cliff. Cautiously, with a quick glance around, Nia edged off the trail toward that precipice.

Something . . . had to be something.

"No," she muttered, shaking her head. "Not *something*. Some*place*. Someplace hidden."

She kicked at the rocky ground under her feet, an idea brewing in her head. A cave, maybe?

"A cave," Nia muttered. Abruptly, she passed a hand over her face and realized she was talking to herself, realized she was standing in the middle of the woods, one hand gripping her gun, and she was talking to herself. "Hidden."

She closed her eyes as she ran that idea through her mind.

And then abruptly, an icy cold chill gripped her. Someplace dark. Hidden. Where he could have kept her alone, trapped, at his mercy.

In her gut, Nia knew, it had been here. Or someplace close . . . *very* close.

"Where is it, Joely?" she whispered, turning away from the cliff and looking around, her gaze searching, although she didn't know what she searched for. What . . . where . . .

She squinted, trying to make things out as she started back up the trail.

And that was when she realized how dark it had gotten. Swearing, she jerked her phone out of her pocket, checked the time.

Shit.

She'd been in here for almost two hours—how in the *hell* had that happened? Fuck. Needed to get out of here. This was *not* where she wanted to be once the sun went down. She stumbled along the trail, half-tripping in her haste to get out of there.

She'd be back, though. At some point. She'd be back. And she'd keep looking, too, because there was *something* here. She knew it . . . and even as fear pushed her to move faster and faster, she felt like she had *finally* accomplished something. Even if all she'd mostly done was freak herself out.

He didn't go to his place often.

He wasn't planning to go there now, but every now and then, he just drove by it . . . thought about going inside, reliving things.

Reliving *that* night.

When Jolene Hollister had gotten away—

"What the fuck?" he snarled.

He came around the corner just in time to see Nia Hollister emerging from the woods. Under the smooth, café au lait brown of her skin she was pale, and even from here he could see how her steps stumbled as she tried to shove her bike closer to the side of the road.

What in the hell was she doing? His hands started to

sweat. He pressed on the gas, thought about pointing the van at her—gunning it. She wouldn't stand a chance—

Fuck, what was she doing in the woods?

A car came blasting down the road, honking at Nia. She flinched, cringed.

As the driver waved at him, he automatically waved back, a smile plastered on his face. And because he'd been seen, he couldn't think about doing anything else.

"Careful," he reminded himself. "Have to be careful . . ."

Swallowing his snarl, he slowed down as she threw a leg over the bike. "Hey there. Ms. Hollister, right?" He rested his arm on the door as he stared at her from inside his van, gave her a friendly smile—the same smile he'd given her cousin, the same smile he'd given Kathleen Hughes, the same smile he'd given Carly Watson and more than a dozen other women . . . right before he'd lured them to their deaths.

She just stared at him, her eyes lost in her wan face.

"You okay?"

"I'm fine," she said, her voice hollow.

"You sure? Look kind of pale. Like you seen a ghost."

She flinched. Then, looking away, she took a deep breath, squared her shoulders before she looked back at him. "I'm fine, sir. Just having some bad moments, that's all. Got a little too hot, I think."

He nodded in understanding. Then, as his rage and worry began to boil out of control, he pressed on the gas. He needed to get out of there now. As he drove away, he kept an eye on his mirrors, watched as she sat there on her bike.

Just sat there.

He needed to think . . . She was prying around just a little too much now. What was she doing in there? Had she found his place? Setting his jaw, he turned on the police scanner and listened, half-expecting to hear a call going out.

There wasn't one. Didn't necessarily mean anything, though. He needed to get out of there. Check and make sure his traps hadn't been disturbed—he'd know if somebody had been too close.

He couldn't have her doing this. She needed to get out of his town. Preferably on her own. Because if she didn't leave, he'd have to *make* her leave.

# CHAPTER
# TWELVE

No.

Nothing had been disturbed. Although he could see where she'd been . . . she'd come within thirty yards of the first trap he'd set up. Not a trap that would have harmed anybody, just enough to let him know somebody had been close.

This was close, though, far too close. Something had to be done about her, and now. Before she got any fucking nosier. Damn her. Damn that bitch.

It was almost nightfall by the time he emerged from the woods.

Full dark by the time he got home. Alone in the silence there, he started to plan. He'd kill her in a heartbeat if he thought he could do it and not bring suspicion back onto her cousin's death. But it would—that was why she was *here*.

Worse, Ezra Fucking King knew it, Law Fucking Reilly knew it. He couldn't kill her without alerting them.

So he had to find another plan.

Needed to get her *away* from here . . .

\* \* \*

To her surprise, nightmares didn't plague her sleep. Although Nia would have thought after the day she'd had, she'd have so many nightmares—she even feared going to sleep. But after two A.M., she couldn't fight it any longer and her body crashed. She slept deep, dreamless . . .

But then, something jerked her awake.

She lay there, heart racing, adrenaline crashing through her, and terror was a living breathing beast in her gut.

She didn't even know *what* woke her. She only knew something was *wrong*.

The room was dark—too dark—and quiet. So quiet.

A strange, skittering sound came from by the window.

She swallowed, staring at it.

The lights—last night, there had been light outside the cabin—just those silly decorative lights that did no good at all, but it was better than nothing, right?

But they weren't there now and *nothing* was all she had, nothing but the silvery moonlight, shining around a . . . hand.

Nia's breath froze inside her lungs.

Hissing out a breath, she jerked up in the bed. Automatically, she went to turn on the light. But then the hand moved, and she swallowed the whimper in her throat. A shadow eased in—tall, at least he *seemed* tall . . . distorted by the window, by the light of the moon.

Oh, hell—

Swinging her legs out of the bed, she stood, still staring at that hand, at the silhouette of the man she could see. Her heart banged against her ribs and she would have *sworn* he was staring in at her, staring in at her through the curtains. Like he knew she was in there—like he knew who she was—like he knew she was awake.

Refusing to take her eyes from that shadow, she

grabbed her duffel from the floor. The gun was stashed inside it. She pulled it out slowly, her hand steady. Just as slowly, just as steadily, she eased the safety off and backed away over to the bed. With the gun in one hand, she reached for the landline phone on the bedside table with the other.

She thought about calling Law—damn, but she wanted him there.

But his number was programmed into her cell, and she wasn't about to risk letting this guy know for certain she was awake by calling for help on her iPhone and letting that bright little light act as a beacon.

Not while he continued to stand there . . . continued to watch. So instead, she pressed *9-1-1*.

It wasn't until she opened her mouth to speak that he turned away.


"You're certain."

Staring into Ezra King's tired eyes, Nia swore and buried her face in her hands. "Damn it, you think I called you out here for fun, hotshot? Yeah, I'm certain. More, he left footprints, damn it. They aren't *my* footprints—I might not wear Cinderella's glass slipper, but my feet aren't *that* big."

Ezra nodded.

He'd already had one of his deputies taking notes, pictures, measurements—she'd watched, glad he was at least *pretending* to pay attention. And she didn't think it was a pretense, either.

Ezra nodded again and looked back at the notebook he held. "You got anybody from back home that might have followed you? You got a high-profile sort of job. Any stalkers?"

"Stalkers?" Nia laughed humorlessly. She wrapped her arms around her middle, but it did nothing to ease the ache inside—she was cold, she was miserable, and scared.

Damn it, she should have called Law—almost had, several times. But what would she have said? *Hey, I know we've had some great sex and all, and I know we're not exactly sure what we're doing here, but I'm kind of freaked out. Could you maybe come over? I know it's late, but I'm scared . . . I want you to hold my hand.*

Hell, no. She wasn't about to risk being that vulnerable. Not right now. Not yet.

"Nia?"

Looking back at him, she scowled. "No, Sheriff. I don't have any stalkers. And my job's not that high profile. I won't ever count as high profile unless I just luck out and hit a major story. A few people know my name. And most of them are people who've worked with me. But I don't have any crazed fans stalking me, nothing like that."

Another slow nod. But she had the feeling he didn't like what she'd told him.

Nia wasn't all that delighted with it, either, because she knew what it meant. The only logical answer—somebody knew she was asking questions. And there was only *one* person who knew for sure that she had every reason to ask those questions.

Joely's killer.

Fear punched through her, but she didn't let it control her, didn't let it take her over. She wouldn't. Setting her jaw, she held Ezra's gaze, saw the knowledge in his eyes.

She opened her mouth, but he gave a tiny shake of his head. For just a moment, he shifted his gaze over her shoulder, all without moving his head.

Nia snapped her jaw shut, not certain just *what* he was trying to say. But right now, she was freaked enough that she'd listen. Listen to somebody who seemed to believe her.

So she waited.

Waited while the deputies did their thing, while they came up and muttered in their cop-speak to the sheriff, waited, and waited, and waited—gritty-eyed and chugging coffee like there was no tomorrow. She'd just put the second pot on when the last of the deputies disappeared out the door.

Turning around, she saw Ezra standing by the door.

"I'm leaving two of my deputies here," he said flatly. "And if so much as a jackrabbit pokes an ear out of place, I'm to be called."

"I didn't see a rabbit, King," she snapped.

"That's what I'm worried about." He rubbed a hand over his face, looking tired and pissed off. "How many people know *why* you're here, Nia?"

She shrugged, staring down into her coffee cup. "Beats the hell out of me."

"How many?" he demanded, an edge to his voice.

"Shit, how in the hell am I supposed to know? It's not like I went and took out an ad, damn it. I told you. That's it."

"Me. Just me. You didn't tell Law?"

"Hell." Scowling, she rubbed her eyes. "Yeah. I told Law. But I'm pretty damn sure he wasn't lurking outside my door."

"I'm pretty sure he wasn't either. I'm just covering the bases. So Law knows. Who else?"

"Nobody."

He lifted a brow.

"Damn it, I haven't exactly been making friends, you know. Yeah, Law knows, but other than that, I didn't *tell* anybody."

"Think anybody has guessed? Anybody asking a lot of questions? Like the librarians while you were digging through the archives, anybody at the courthouse? Anybody, Nia. I need to know just *who* could know you're here because you don't think your cousin's killer is dead."

She gave him a sharp-edged smile. "Well, if you put it like that—three people, for sure. Yeah, I did tell Law. But it wasn't him. So besides Law. You . . . and her killer. I'm pretty damn sure *he* knows why I'm here."

Ezra closed his eyes and pinched the bridge of his nose. "Fuck." Then he opened them and pointed a finger at her. "Stop. Whatever you're doing . . . *stop*. Maybe even go *home*. I'm doing what I can, but damn it, I don't want another dead woman on my hands."

"And I don't want my cousin's killer going unpunished!" she shouted, the words ripping out of her. Spinning around, she slammed the coffee cup down. She braced her hands on the counter and swore as the fear of the night hit her hard and fast. "Wait . . . what, you're doing what you can?"

Ezra sighed and rubbed his eyes. "Yes. Quietly. Which is the way it *has* to be, Nia. Whoever in the hell is behind this *knows* this town, knows the people. I can't run the risk of him catching on to what I'm doing, so quiet is how I have to handle this. And it would be a hell of a lot easier for me if you would just *go* home—where you'll be safe."

She snorted and shook her head. "Damn it, you think I *wanted* something freaky like this happening? But I can't just leave, Ezra. I can't."

"What if you're right, Nia?" he asked quietly. "What if you're right . . . say the guy who killed her set everything up, is walking around this town, scot-free, and he sees you. He *knows* why you're here, what you're up to. Now he's got a new focus. You want to be that focus, lady? You got any idea what he did to your cousin? He didn't just *kill* her."

"I know what he did to her." She swallowed the bile, set her jaw against the grief and fury. Then she turned around. On legs that trembled, she made her way to her bag and reached inside, pulled out the file. Joely's autopsy report was in there. Reading it had been one of the hardest things she'd ever done. "I know people, King. I know what he did to her—in detail."

She held it out to him.

A heavy sigh escaped him as he accepted it. "How did you get a copy of this?"

"I know people," she repeated, shrugging. "And with some of them, I know things they'd rather I not know. I called in favors, I bribed, threatened. Whatever. Does it matter?"

Ezra frowned. "I didn't hear that. I swear, I didn't hear that." Then he gave the report back. "I don't need to read it. I've already done that. And you shouldn't have."

"I had to."

"You had to see that," he muttered. Then he shook his head. "Okay. If it was me, I would have done the same thing. Maybe you were a cop in your past life."

"Please. There's no need for insults," she said, summoning up a weak smile. Then, weary to the very bone, she sank down into the overstuffed armchair. There was a throw artfully draped over the arm and she caught one end, dragged it across her knees. "I can't go home. I can't. In my gut, I know there's something more to what happened. I know it. And I'm going crazy just sitting at home—I can't work. I can't sleep. I can barely eat. This is dominating my mind and unless I do *something,* it's going to drive me crazy."

"I think it already has," Ezra muttered. "You realize that if you get involved in any way, do anything that I perceive as interfering in a case, or as dangerous—to you, to others—I'll lock your butt up. And that's not an empty threat."

She gave him a ghost of a smile. "Hey, how can I be doing anything that's getting *involved*? The case is officially closed, right?"

Ezra just grunted. "I meant what I said."

He headed for the door.

"Remember—you see even a jackrabbit, you call."


She'd seen him. He'd thought she had—had heard the movement.

But the police sirens confirmed it.

Smirking, he wondered what she'd been thinking as he had stood there outside her window.

Would she leave now?

He thought about it for a minute and then decided. No. She wouldn't leave. Not that easily. It would have to be a slow thing, he suspected.

Terror coming at her in the dead of the night, gradually.

He'd have to be more subtle next time, though. He shouldn't have left the footprints. But he'd wanted to see how she would react when she saw him—know thy enemy.

And his enemy had balls of brass, even if she was a woman.

It would take a lot to really throw her off. To make her leave. It was a waste really. What he *wanted* was to *take* her. Not chase her away, but to take her, break her. But that would be too risky.

The sheriff had already left deputies watching her cabin.

Anything that happened to her now would cause him problems, and he already had enough problems, just having her here.

Later, though . . . Yes. Perhaps later. Years later. Down the road.

Smiling, he tucked that thought into the back of his

mind as he climbed out of the shower. He needed to get ready to face the day. He had a present to give to a lovely lady. He had work to do. He had planning to do.

Busy, busy . . .

*"What?"*

Ethan lowered the cup of coffee and stared at Law's furious face. "Ah, well. She saw somebody outside her window. Me and Kyle Mabry had to spend the rest of the night out there—I was covering for Keith, needed the money and—"

"Forget that, don't care—what do you mean she saw somebody out her window?" Law demanded.

"Just that." Ethan shrugged and took another sip of his coffee.

Law was about ready to shove the coffee cup down the deputy's throat if he didn't start talking. Right before he opened his mouth to make the threat, Ethan said, "Call came in about two this morning. We went out there and I put in a call to the sheriff."

"Why call Ezra?"

"Because he expects us to—just like Nielson did. Weird stuff, he wants to be told. This is weird, you know? I mean, she's not local, plus she's related to the woman who died. And . . ." His voice trailed off.

"And what?"

Ethan shook his head. "Shit, I keep talking about this, the sheriff is going to have my ass."

"I'm tempted to beat your ass if you don't talk."

"Yeah, but you can't fire me."

"Fine." Law slammed his mug down on the counter. "I'll just head over to the sheriff's office, talk to Ezra."

"He's coming in late today."

"Then I'll head to his house. I know where he lives."

Although he was tempted to go to Nia's. And he would—right after he cooled off.

Why hadn't she called him? What the hell was going on?

Abruptly, he found himself thinking about what she'd told him. Her fears that Joe Carson hadn't killed her cousin. An icy sweat broke out over his spine and all of a sudden, he didn't give a shit about cooling off. He took off for his car at a jog. Blind fear grabbed him—almost choked him. Would have choked him, if he hadn't throttled it down.

It wouldn't be smart for somebody to grab her, he told himself. Not if the killer really was still alive. *If* the killer was alive, then there was some sort of connection, or something—something that Nia had stumbled on to, knowingly or otherwise.

Killing her was stupid now. If the killer *was* alive, then he was smart.

Wouldn't risk killing her . . . yet.

Law didn't think.


Sleep evaded her, but she didn't want to sleep anyway.

Nia was happy to stay in that chair, floating along in that little twilight place between sleep and wakefulness. Zoning out. That's what she was doing. Zoning out.

But when a fist started pounding on the door, it damn near scared her to death and she shrieked, struggling free of the blanket, ending up in a tangle on the floor.

Something crashed against the door.

She heard somebody call her name.

Confused, her butt hurting, she looked up and stared at the door, shuddering in its casement. *Law*—?

Another crash against the door. Damn it, he was going to tear the damn door off the hinges! Swearing, she shoved to her feet and rushed to the door, throwing it open just as he was about to throw himself against it a fourth time.

"Damn it, are you insane?" she snapped.

He caught her around the waist, jerking her against him.

Stunned, her head spinning, she stood there, her face pressed against his neck, the scent of him flooding her head. Right when she'd almost caught her breath, he pushed her away and stared down at her. "Are you okay? Why in the hell did you scream?"

Then he was turning her head this way, that way.

The concern in his eyes was doing weird little things to her heart—as was the fact that he'd all but busted the door down because he'd been worried, but still. Scowling, she pulled away from him and smoothed her shirt down, noticing that she was still wearing the wrinkled T-shirt she'd pulled on when she'd called the sheriff's department.

"I'd been sleeping," she said. "I . . . well, I fell out of the chair when you knocked. Guess that's what you heard."

"I . . . oh." He frowned, shoved a hand through his hair. It was standing up in spikes and tufts, like he'd been doing that a lot lately. He had the grace to look a little abashed, but that faded about three seconds later, replaced by an annoyed look. "I heard you had some company last night."

She cocked a brow. "Well. That small-town gossip really does get around, huh?"

"Why didn't you call me?"

"I called the sheriff's department," she pointed out, gesturing to the rapidly approaching deputies who'd been sitting in their car.

"Yeah. I'm glad you did. But you could have called me, too."

Something flashed in his hazel eyes . . . something that looked like hurt. It made her uncomfortable, she realized. And it made her wish even more that she *had* called him.

"I wanted to," she said quietly, unaware she'd been planning to say it until the words were already there, hanging between them. Sighing, she waved the deputies off and retreated back into the cabin, leaving Law to deal with the door. "But I . . . hell."

Tired, she sat on the side of the bed, clasped her hands between her knees. "We still don't even know what we're doing together, do we, Law? Other than sex and me waving a gun at you and you trouncing my ass, we have no history."

"Do we need a history for me to worry about you?"

She looked up, watched as he crossed the floor. He crouched down in front of her, reached up. He cupped her cheek and rubbed his thumb over her lips. "Do we, Nia?"

"No . . . I don't guess we do." He was melting her. Working his way so deep inside her already. How did she handle it? How? Blowing out a shaky breath, she reached up and covered his hand with hers. "I wanted to call, almost did several times. But I . . . well, I needed it too much. I don't like needing people, needing anybody. Especially when I'm already freaked out."

A faint smile tugged at his lips. "Well, I think I can get that." He eased up, rubbed his lips over hers. "Maybe you can tell me what happened, then. So I don't have to go beat it out of the sheriff."

That startled a laugh out of her. "Beat it out of the sheriff?"

"Yeah. Although sometimes I think about beating him up just for the hell of it."

"Hmm. Yeah, I heard you have a thing for his wife."

"Had—it's a past thing." Law scowled. Then he settled down on the bed next to her, slid her a sly grin. As he laid a hand on her thigh, he murmured, "I got a thing for you, if you want the truth."

That grin of his made her heart race. Or maybe it was the fact that he had his hand resting so high on her thigh. Both, perhaps. "Do you, now?"

"Hmmm. But you're not talking."

"No. I guess I should. Would hate to see you get arrested for assaulting the sheriff." The lighthearted moment passed as she looked at the window. The terror of the past night rushed up, grabbed her. "I was sleeping. Something woke me. I don't know what. I don't remember hearing anything. When I opened my eyes, it was too dark in here—earlier there had been lights, and last night. From outside. But not then. The only light was from the moon. I saw . . ." She broke off, took a deep breath. "I saw something out the window—a hand. It moved, closer. *He* moved. He was standing right outside the window. Staring inside."

"He . . . you're sure it was a man."

"Yes."

"Did you see him? I mean, his face? Any idea what he looked like?"

"No, just a silhouette. But it was a man, I'm sure of that." She turned her head, met his gaze. "I didn't turn on the lights—didn't want to look. I had a feeling he *knew* I was there, watching him. But I didn't want to see if I was right. I grabbed my gun, called nine-one-one. Right before I started to talk, he turned around, left. Just like that. Almost like all he wanted to do was make sure I *saw* him."

For a long time, Law was quiet, his face grim, eyes staring off into the distance. Finally, he looked back at her. "You know this could just be some kid trying to freak you out, right?"

"Please." Nia sneered.

He shrugged. "I don't entirely believe it either, but I don't dismiss any possibility. Speaking of which . . . any chance it could be an ex-boyfriend? Ex-husband?"

"There are no ex-husbands and the possibility of it being an ex-boyfriend is so slim, it might as well not exist." She eased away from him, pushing a hand through her hair as she stood and started to pace. "Look, Law, I appreciate you not just laughing the idea away, but I already know who this is—there's only one thing that makes sense to me. It's the bastard who killed my cousin . . . and it wasn't Joe Carson."

Golden eyes shouldn't burn that hot, he thought. Molten gold. Fiery. Full of fury, despite the fear.

Rising from the bed, he cupped her cheek in his hand and rubbed a thumb over the curve of her lip.

"I'm really starting to suspect you're right," he said, his gut going tight with both fear and rage. As he stared at her face, images of the girl who'd been killed, dumped on his land like so much garbage—her cousin, her family—flashed through his mind. That could be her.

If the killer wasn't Joe, if he wasn't dead, then he was out looking to terrify her.

Nia's brows drooped low over her eyes. "You . . . wait. What, you believe me?"

He stroked a hand through her hair, curled it over the back of her neck. "Nia, you don't strike me as a woman who is going to jump at imaginary shadows." He smirked and added, "I might. But I'm a paranoid bastard. If you're positive it's not an ex, and you're probably right it's not some kid looking to freak you out . . . what else is the logical conclusion?"

"You know, not too many people would come to the logical conclusion that the killer isn't the dead guy everybody thought."

The suspicion in her eyes, for some reason, appealed to him. Grinning, he dipped his head and nipped her lower lip. Against her mouth, he murmured, "Well, I don't tend to think like most people, maybe."

Then, because her mouth was still so handy, and because she tasted so fucking good, he kissed her.

She opened for him with a sigh, arching against him as she slid her arms around his neck. Wrapping one arm around her waist, he kept the other curved over her nape, angling her head to deepen the kiss.

Her hands stroked down his chest, slid under his shirt. Short, neat nails bit teasingly into his skin, raking lightly over his flesh. But when she went to stroke him through his jeans, he groaned and pulled away, catching her wrists. With his breath coming in hard, ragged pants, he pressed his brow to hers. "Didn't come here for this," he muttered.

"So? Does that mean we absolutely can't?"

Opening his eyes, he stared at her. Lost himself in her . . . it could be so easy to do that . . . so easy.

"No." Boosting her up into his arms, he whispered, "It doesn't mean that at all."

# THIRTEEN

"So what all have you done?"

Nia forced one eye to open, staring at Law. "Pal, if I need to explain it, then I must not have been doing it right," she said dryly.

He grinned.

"Funny." With one palm cupping her breast, he lightly pinched her nipple. "I promise, you did all of *that* right, absolutely. But I wasn't talking about us. I'm talking about whatever you've done that's caught his eye. If we're going forward on the assumption that it's him, then something you've done must have freaked him out if he ran the risk of coming out here where he could be seen."

She scowled. "Hell, he's a sick fuck and sick fucks get off on scaring people—that's their pleasure in life. Does he need a reason to come out here and scare me?"

"Actually, yeah. Because sick fucks usually like to continue their mission of being sick fucks," Law said. Absently, he stroked his thumb along the silken curve of her breast. "And if he gets caught, that interferes with his mission. He's gone to a lot of trouble already to avoid getting caught. That's what Joe was about—throwing people off the trail. That's what leaving your cousin on my land was about, too, I bet. Throwing people off the trail."

He frowned and sat up, raking his fingers through his hair.

"Lena," he muttered and shook his head.

"What?"

He looked over at her and said, "I just thought of something."

"The night she reported the screams."

He cocked a brow at her. "How did you know about that?"

"I started going through some of the public records and archives, that sort of thing." Shivering, she sat up and dragged the blankets around her. Her golden eyes were tormented, sad, and it only took a moment to figure out why.

"I think it was Joely she heard screaming," Nia said quietly, staring at him. She swallowed and closed her eyes. When she looked back at him, her eyes were damp, but she didn't let the tears fall. "I think Joely almost escaped, but he caught her. Lena must have heard her."

Law nodded. "That makes sense. They looked around some, but it was late, dark. They came back out, did another go through the woods, I know that. There just wasn't anything for them to find."

"I was out there. Looking around."

"Out where? In the woods?" Law demanded.

"Yes."

Law closed his eyes. Told himself to count to ten—but he reached thirty and still hadn't calmed down.

"Let me get this straight—you go into the woods where you're pretty sure your cousin was killed, and you're just merrily hiking along. Am I getting this right?"

She cocked a brow. "Yes. That's about right."

Long, tense seconds of silence stretched out between

them before he shattered it as he demanded, "Why? What in the *fuck* were you thinking?"

"I was thinking that he has someplace out there where he had her," she snapped, shoving to her feet. She planted her hands on her hips and glared at him. "And right now I'm thinking I don't care for your attitude, damn it."

"Too fucking bad, because I don't care for the thought of something happening to you!"

Swearing, he turned around and started to pace, images of what could have happened running through his mind even as other thoughts swamped him, turning everything into a jumble. *Shit, shit, shit—*

"What were you hoping to find?" he snapped. "A little treehouse with a sign reading *Serial Killer's Hangout, please come in?*"

Well, one thing about that tone of his, it did a damn fine job of turning her uncertainty and fear into anger.

She sneered at him, torn between kicking him out and railing at him. The only thing that kept her from doing so was the fact that she had *known* going out there wasn't all that smart—and she didn't give a damn. She'd do it again.

"Look, hotshot," she said, struggling to keep her voice level. "I know it wasn't the smartest damn thing in the world, but I can't just keep waiting around and doing *nothing.*"

"And what in the hell did you think you'd accomplish going out there?"

"Well . . . I certainly made somebody uncomfortable, didn't I?" She glanced toward the window and suppressed a shiver. Wrapping her arms around herself, she retreated to the bed. She settled on it with her back pressed against the carved wooden headboard, knees drawn up to her chest.

"What am I supposed to do, Law?" She stared at him. "Just wait around forever when I know, in my gut, that the bastard who killed her isn't dead? Because the sheriff can't do shit unless he finds some kind of proof."

"Damn it, Nia." He swore and looked away, a heavy sigh leaving him. He dropped down onto the couch, staring at her with dark, worried eyes. The anger had drained away, as quickly as it had come, it seemed.

But he was still worried. She could see that.

"What am I supposed to do?" she asked again. "I *can't* go back to my life until something happens here. I can't. I tried. I'm too hung up on this, and if that makes me obsessed, then fine, I'm obsessed. If I run headlong into something and that makes me a fool, then fine . . . I'm a fool. But at least I'm doing something. I can't *not* do something. Joely's killer isn't dead. And I can't pretend like he is."

*Fuck.*
The longer he stared into her golden eyes, the harder it was to hold on to his anger—not that he was letting it go. He was still madder than hell about that—mad, terrified—shit, he couldn't remember the last time he'd been that scared.

Unless maybe it was when he'd been tearing through the woods after Remy, trying to track down Hope all those months ago.

This, though, something about it felt maybe worse. The thought of Nia going through the woods . . .

*Stop. She's fine. Focus on what in the hell she hoped to find—and next time, make sure she thinks to take you with her.*

Blowing out a breath, he locked his eyes on her face, tried to block the worry, the fear, all of that out. He needed to think now—needed to listen. "What were you hoping to find, Nia?"

"I don't *know,*" she said again, groaning. She smacked her head back against the headboard, closing her eyes. "And hell, once I was out there, I started walking around, wondering . . . the cliffs. Made me think . . ."

Her voice trailed off and she looked away.

"What?"

Nia shook her head. "Nothing."

"Nia . . ." Scowling, he shoved off the couch and crossed the floor, settled down on the bed, just in front of her. Pulling on her ankles, he eased her legs down, one on either side of his hips, then he curled his hands around her butt, tugging her into his lap. "What is it, Nia?"

When she remained silent, he nipped her chin. "Come on, baby. I haven't thought anything you've said was crazy yet, have I? Other than you trampling around by yourself when you're pretty damn certain there's a killer's hangout somewhere close by, that is."

Cupping her cheek in his hand, he guided her face around until she was looking at him. Her eyes, darker with worry, fear, met his. Sighing, she dropped her head forward, resting it on his shoulder. "I don't know how to explain it, but I think she died there, Law. Somewhere in those woods. I . . ."

She stopped, licked her lips. "I think she died there—was killed there. Somewhere close. I think he has a place in there." She swallowed and lifted her head, stared at him. "I . . . you asked what I was looking for. I think . . . well, I think there might be a cave or something like that out there. There has to be *something,* you know. If she did die out there, it has to be someplace he can hide, because if there was a house, people around here would know, right? So underground, a cave, that sort of thing, it makes sense. I think he's got a place, someplace where he kept her, held her prisoner."

A cave—
A *cave*—

Law looked like she had smacked him across the side of his head with a two-by-four, Nia thought, staring at his face. His eyes were dazed, distracted, staring off into the distance. He muttered something, shook his head.

"What?"

He didn't answer, though, just kept muttering.

She didn't really get irritated, though, until he rather unceremoniously moved her off his lap onto the bed. He reached into his pocket and pulled out his phone while Nia stared at him, trying to figure out just what in the world he was mumbling about.

"Law?"

He didn't answer, still fiddling with his phone. Irritated, she clambered off the bed and stood up, getting pissed off. What in the world had she said?

"Damn it," he snapped behind her.

Turning around, she looked at him as he stood up and shoved his phone into his pocket.

"What in the world are you mumbling and shaking your head and scowling about?"

"I'm not sure. Come on. We need to go back to my place—I need to check something out." He grabbed his jeans, pulling them on without bothering to look for his boxers.

She stood there admiring the view, a little too distracted by said view for a moment to even realize what he'd said. Then she jerked herself back to attention. "Huh? Go where? Check what out?"

"Something. I'm not sure," he said, that distracted look still on his face—distracted, kind of sexy, brooding. He had a faint line between his brows like he was thinking damn hard about something and despite her irritation over his suddenly strange behavior, she found herself thinking about how damn gorgeous he was—and then she wanted to kick herself.

Crossing her arms over her naked breasts, she glared at him. "You're not sure what we're checking out?"

"No. That's why we need to go home. It's been a few years since I looked at all that shit." He stared at her, frowned. "You're not dressed."

"No. I'm not. You haven't told me why we're supposed to be leaving or what we're looking for." Fucking strange—why hadn't she noticed how easily his mind moved from one topic to another before now?

"Caves—you said something about caves," he said patiently, like he was talking to a child. Like she could follow whatever very strange path his brain was obviously taking—the one she was having a very hard time following. "I need to look at my maps."

"Maps?" She stiffened. Inside her chest, her heart skipped a beat.

"Yeah." He looked around. "You need clothes."

"Damn it, Law, what *maps*?"

Rummaging through Nia's closet, he pulled out a black shirt. He tossed it at her, along with the bra that was draped over the foot of the bed. "The maps that aren't here," he said, trying to guide his brain back to the present, although it was racing just then—racing as a picture suddenly started to come into focus.

It wasn't *caves* Nia needed to be looking for—although she didn't need to be looking for a damn thing, and shit, he couldn't exactly leave her alone, either. He saw a pair of jeans in a tangle on the floor and he scooped them up, dumped them in her arms. She was glaring at him, giving him the same irritated look a hundred other people had given him when his brain took a little side trip, but he wasn't about to try to explain anything to her just yet.

Ezra needed to know this first. And Law wasn't about

to tell Nia what he was thinking and then *leave* her here. So she needed to go with him, so she'd be kind of stuck with him—stuck, and safe.

While she stood there, *still* not getting dressed, and fuming, he gave her the smile that he used with others—sheepish, self-deprecating. "Look, I just need to look at a few things—you made me think of something, but I can't entirely remember it, okay?"

Not a lie. He *didn't* remember entirely . . . *where*.

"So the sooner we get to my place and I look at the maps and stuff, the better, right?"

Her eyes full of suspicion, she turned away and headed to the bathroom.

Five minutes later, she emerged, dressed, silent, and still watching him like she didn't entirely trust him.

# FOURTEEN

THE DEPUTIES FOLLOWED THEM.

Law wasn't too sure how he felt about that, but he wasn't going to throw a fit about it, either.

Right then, his brain was too occupied just trying to figure out what in the hell he was going to do once he told Nia what *was* in the woods. Not *caves* . . . but yeah, there was something underground. Or at least there had been. A long time ago.

Stands to reason it could still *be* there, right?

And if it was, what then? What then? Short of locking her up and throwing away the key, he suspected he didn't have a chance at keeping her out of those woods.

But if the incident from last night had *anything* to do with what she was doing in the woods yesterday . . .

*Shit.*

The drive home took too long, and yet, not long enough. He was still wracking his brain, trying to come up with ideas, plans, scenarios—things that normally never failed him.

For once, though, his mind was blank.

The silence between them was tense, heavy, as he parked behind the house, not bothering to put the car in the garage. He had a feeling they'd be heading over to see Ezra sometime that afternoon, so what was the point?

He tucked the keys in his pocket after he unlocked the back door, automatically reprogramming the alarm system he'd had installed after what had happened months ago with him and Hope. Nia came in behind him, sauntering into the house with her hands tucked into her back pockets. As she moved over to the island, he shot a glance at the key rack where he kept the keys to the other cars.

Shit.

He grabbed them, tucked them into his pocket, too—he always kept the two spare keys there even though Hope had a set herself. Couldn't make it that easy for Nia to take off running if she got pissed, right? Not that she'd ever do anything that impulsive, he thought sardonically.

She gave him a quizzical glance, which he ignored in favor of the liquor cabinet.

He needed a drink. A strong one. Screw heading over to Ezra's—Ezra could come here.

"Want a drink?" he asked as he pulled the whiskey out of the cabinet.

"Sure." She grimaced and said, "I'll take the whiskey with some Coke, if you've got it. Whatever has your boxers in a twist probably isn't going to improve my mood."

He sighed. "Sorry. I . . . shit, my brain doesn't track too well when I'm distracted. Gets worse when I'm worried or pissed. Right now, it's both." He fell silent as he made her drink, then his own. She got Coke and ice for hers—he drank his straight. It burned a line down his throat, but it didn't do a damn thing to ease the knots in his belly.

"Come on," he said after he topped his drink off. "Some of the shit is going to take me a few minutes to find."

*   *   *

A few minutes?

Hell, Nia thought, two hours later, while she listened to a one-sided conversation—how about a few *hours*?

"You sure? Damn it, I thought I'd checked there— yeah, yeah, okay."

He hung up the phone and sighed. "Hope rearranged everything, has my maps filed up in the attic."

"We just spent an hour in the attic."

He scowled. "Yeah, but I wasn't looking in a file. Was going through the boxes where I'd dumped it all."

Nia shoved off the doorjamb, eyeing the office with no small level of curiosity as Law headed toward her. "So what's the office used for? You don't seem to use it."

He stopped dead in his tracks, and unless she was mistaken, his face went a little pale and his eyes went dark and flat. Then he gave her a grim smile. "No. No, I don't use it. Not anymore."

"Why not?"

He turned his head. Automatically, she followed the direction of his gaze with her eyes, but she didn't know what he was seeing.

"Just how far back did you go when you were reading about Joe Carson, Nia?" he asked quietly.

"Pretty far," she said, shrugging. Abruptly, it hit her. Shock stiffened her body and although she couldn't see whatever Law saw in his memories, she knew what he was looking at.

That empty space on the floor—it was where the deputy had died. He'd been murdered . . . in this room.

Wincing, she said, "This is where the deputy died, isn't it?"

"Yeah." Law was rubbing his forearm.

She wondered if he even noticed. Unable to take the dark, tormented look on his face, she made herself take the first step into the room—it hadn't bothered her just a few minutes ago, but now, well, she didn't want to be in there. She did it, though. One step in front of the other, until she was close to him, close enough to reach out, offering her hand. "Come on. You still need to show me these maps that have you so worked up."

He gave her a tight smile. "Worked up?"

"Yeah. Worked up, stressed, boxers in a twist."

"I think I left the boxers at your place," he murmured.

"Damn, I think you're right. You're commando under those jeans." She winked at him. "Now how am I supposed to focus on anything?"

When she tugged on his hand, he followed along, shutting the door snugly behind him.

"So I guess you don't much like being in there, huh?"

"No." He sighed, absently rotated his neck, reaching up to rub it. "I've thought about locking the door and then just throwing the key away, but that seems a little extreme. It's just a damn room."

He shoved a hand through his hair. "Come on. We're going back up to the attic."

"Fun, fun . . ." She stepped aside and gestured to him. "I'll let you lead the way. And I'll think about you being commando under those jeans."

Once they were back up in the attic, it took exactly four minutes to locate the maps.

They all but overflowed the top two drawers of one filing cabinet. He had six of them, all lined up against the far wall. Eyeing them with a curious gaze, she looked at Law. "You a packrat or what?" she asked as he handed her a thick binder. He grabbed another one before sliding the cabinet closed.

"Nah. Well, not exactly. This is just stuff I either need to keep for a while or stuff I'll end up using."

Nia snorted and looked pointedly at the six filing cabinets. "Exactly what would you need to keep that could fill six file cabinets? It sure as hell can't be your taxes."

"You haven't seen my damn tax return," he muttered. Then he sneezed. "Come on. We'll look at these downstairs. Too much dust up here."

Trailing along behind him, she flipped open the binder, eyeing the plastic page holders, labeled and stuffed with maps. "Somehow I don't think you're the one behind this organization here," she said.

Law just grunted.

"You had Hope do all of this? Hell, Law, how lazy are you? And why is Hope the one organizing this shit for you?"

"Because that's what I pay her for," he replied.

"You *pay* her to organize your junk? Why don't you just throw it out?"

"I pay her because that's her job." He shot her a narrow look over his shoulder. "I can't toss it out—I'll probably need it at some point, or I *could* need it."

"What do you mean you could need it?" She studied one of the maps—she knew this one pretty well, actually. It was a map of Colonial Williamsburg. "Just what use could you have for a map of Colonial Williamsburg?"

He headed into the living room and flopped onto the couch, hunching his shoulders a little as he muttered something too low for her to hear.

"What?"

"Research." He snapped the binder closed and dumped it on the table. Leaning forward, he looked at her, his mouth twisted in something not really a scowl, but not a smile, either.

If Nia didn't know better, she'd think he looked uncomfortable.

"Research?" she echoed. She flipped through the binder. It looked like she had the back half of the alphabet, as far as states went. There were maps for Texas, North Dakota, South Dakota, New Mexico, West Vir-

ginia, Virginia, Washington—state and the District of
Columbia. "Okay, so are you a travel agent in training
or what?"

The look in his eyes was flat, emotionless, but she still
had the weirdest feeling he was uncomfortable. *Very* uncomfortable. "No, I'm not a travel agent," he said.

"Okay. So what are you?"

He grimaced. "I'm a writer."

"A writer."

"Yeah. Books. I write books. I pick up things like
maps and stuff when I travel in case I decide to base a
book somewhere, because I can't remember the details
when I need to remember the details." He shifted again,
still with that vaguely uncomfortable look on his face.
"Okay?"

"A writer."

"Yeah." He reached for the binder again, focusing on
it like it held the answers to the universe and beyond.

Nia looked around the cluttered living room/office,
eyeing the haphazard pile of new books stacked against
one wall. New books. All by the same author. She'd noticed it the other day, vaguely, but she'd been so focused
on Law, she hadn't paid it that much attention.

Now her eyes zeroed in on the name and she looked
back at Law, then at the books.

"Law Reilly," she muttered, shaking her head.

The books had a different name on them . . . but not
so different from his legal name, which she'd looked up
back when she was still checking out details on everybody she could think of who might have a connection to
her cousin.

Law . . . short for Lawson.

*Edward Lawson Reilly.*

*Ed O'Reilly.*

"Holy shit—you're Ed O'Reilly?"

Those lean shoulders hunched even more and if she

wasn't mistaken, the tops of his ears were brilliant red. She couldn't see his face, hidden by the shaggy fall of his bangs.

"Law?"

"What?"

She waited for him to look up, but he was still looking at the binder. Looking at it—but not much of anything else. She had the feeling it was there just to keep him from staring at his lap.

Sighing, she dumped her binder on the table and grabbed his away, set it aside as well. "Will you *look* at me?"

He blew out a breath and shot her a narrow look. "You know, you were all but breathing down my neck for the past two hours while I looked for these. Now you want to chat?"

"I just want an answer," she said, feeling oddly charmed. He was embarrassed, she realized.

"An answer to what?"

"Are you Ed O'Reilly?"

He rolled his eyes. "Yeah. Now . . . the maps?"

Pursing her lips, unable to resist, she skimmed a hand through his hair. The thick strands, golden-brown mixed with strands of lighter blond, darker brown, were cool against her fingers, and soft. "You know, I've read a few of Ed's books. I always pictured him the older sort—in his fifties, maybe. Balding. With a paunch."

Law lifted a brow. "Your point?"

"You don't look like an Ed." She leaned in and kissed him, lingering long enough to nip his lower lip. "That's my point. You just don't look like an Ed. And it's kind of cool. I didn't know I was sleeping with some hotshot crime writer."

He snorted. Then, with a sly smile curling his lips, he reached over and laid a hand on her inner thigh, stroking higher and higher until his fingers brushed against her crotch. "Well, I need to do something to keep up with the sexy photojournalist, right? Hey, you got your camera? Maybe we could set it up and you could take some pictures . . ."

He stifled her laugh as he slanted his mouth over hers.

By the time he lifted his head, she was breathless and he looked pleased with himself. Having successfully distracted her, she figured.

"So . . . can we look at those maps?"

It wasn't one of the many maps he'd picked up at stores or gas stations.

This one was older—one that had been hand-drawn, something he'd found at an old rummage sale. It was so fragile the paper felt like it was going to disintegrate just at his touch and he could have kicked himself for not doing something to protect it.

But it had been years since he'd picked it up and he'd been focused on another project at the time—just hadn't been thinking.

Law unfolded it carefully, all but holding his breath until he had it spread open over his coffee table.

"A few hundred years ago, most of this land around here all belonged to one of two families," he said absently.

"Let me guess . . . one of them had the last name of *Jennings*," she quipped as she bent over, peering at the faded print on the map.

"Yeah. The other one was Ohlman. Lena lives right about where the line was drawn between their property." He traced a line down between it, not quite touching the paper. "The house used to be right about here . . ."

He indicated an area on the map. It didn't mean jack to Nia. Then he circled the area around it, a pensive look on his face.

"The Ohlman family had a lot of people who sympathized with the Northern states during the Civil War—helped hide runaway slaves. I was thinking about doing an alternate history story once, basing it here. Did some research—apparently the old Ohlman place had some underground areas—cellars, that sort of thing, where they'd hide the runaway slaves."

*Cellars . . .*

Nia hissed out a breath and shot up off the couch.

Good thing he'd been prepared for that. She wasn't the type to sit and wait around, was she? But before she could take even two steps, he caught her, his hand snagging the waistband of her jeans. He set the map aside with his free hand.

She craned her head around, glaring at him. "Let go."

"No." The distant, distracted look on his face was gone, replaced by one of flat and focused determination.

"*Let* go," she repeated, jerking against his hold. "Don't you get it? That could be where he did it. If I can find something—"

"I *do* get it. And that's why I'm not letting go." He jerked against her jeans—jerked hard until she ended up on his lap and then he wrapped an arm around her. "If he had a place there, he's too likely to be watching for you and you are *not* taking off into those woods by yourself, sweetheart. Not happening."

She narrowed her eyes at him. That was all the warning he got—and fortunately, it was about all the warning he needed.

She ended up stretched out under him on the floor, their bodies wedged between the coffee table and the couch. Her eyes snapping, her mouth twisted in a snarl, she glared at him. "Get *off*," she ordered, bucking against him.

"Why, so you can take off into the woods again and

maybe this time do something that really pisses the killer off so he comes after *you*?"

She bucked under him once more.

He pressed his hips against her, used his weight to keep her trapped.

"You son of a bitch." She twisted against his hold and the fury in her eyes gave way to heartbreak. "Damn it, I can't *not* do something."

His own heart ached—damn near shattered as tears glittered in her eyes. Lowering his head, he pressed his lips to her cheek, caught a tear. "I'm not asking you to not do anything . . . I just don't want you running off blind. I want you *safe*, Nia. Hell, I *need* that. I need you . . ."

*I need you . . .*

The words hung between them, but he didn't take them back. Didn't try to explain them away. He did need her. He couldn't explain how it had happened this fast for him, couldn't explain just what *this* was . . . he just knew from the time he'd laid eyes on her, he'd felt something, and it had been growing ever since then.

"You can't need me," Nia said, her voice quiet, sad. "You don't even know me."

His mouth twisted in a bittersweet smile. "You can't tell me what I need, what I don't need, baby. That's kind of up to me." He eased the grip he held on her wrists, fully prepared for her to try to slip away.

But all she did was ball up her fists, press them against his chest. Her head turned to the side and she blew out a breath.

"What do you want from me, damn it? I can't just ignore this," she said, closing her eyes.

"Not asking you to." He caught one wrist, lifted it to his mouth and pressed his lips to the reddened flesh there. "I'm sorry."

"You haven't answered me."

"I'm going to call Ezra, have him come over. We talk to him, see what he says." He kissed her other wrist, wincing as he saw the angry red marks left by his grip. Damn it. He wasn't sorry he hadn't let her take off blindly, but he didn't like seeing that he'd left marks on her either.

Easing back, he watched her face, wondered if he'd torn what he was just now realizing he needed from her.

She sat up and he reached up, stroked a hand down her face. She stared at him, scowling. "I ought to deck you," she muttered. But she turned her face into his hand, rubbed her cheek against him. "Jerk. Most of the guys I know can't take me down that fast."

Law grimaced. "I . . . shit. I can't even say I'm sorry straight up, because if you try to make for the door, I'll do it again. But I didn't mean to leave a mark on you. I didn't mean to hurt you."

"You didn't." Nia sighed and glanced at her wrists, flexed her fingers. "I just bruise easy. Only thing hurt is my pride. And I still ought to deck you. But I suspect you could stop me pretty damn easy."

"I won't."

She rolled her eyes. "It's no fun if you *let* me." Then she scooted back and stood.

Law remained alert, ready to grab her again. She wasn't running off on him, damn it. He didn't care if he had to tie her to a damn chair. But all she did was settle down on the couch, eyeing the map with a sidelong look. "Fine. Call Ezra."

"Ah . . . okay." He tugged his phone from his pocket. "Wait."

Lifting his gaze, he looked at Nia. Her golden eyes rested on his face, direct and serious. "If he brushes this off, I'm going back out there. I don't care if you go with me or not, but you can't stop me. You know that."

"Yeah." Law grimaced. "I know that. And you can bet your ass I'm going."

"I said, *not* today," Ezra repeated over Law's insistent voice.

"Damn it, Ezra, would you just listen—"

"You need to listen," Ezra snapped. "Look, it's getting late and it gets dark damn early in those trees. Plus, I don't plan on traipsing around in there and leaving Lena alone. *Not* today. Come over tomorrow—I'll take a fucking personal day. I'll call Remy, see if he can do the same—he's one person I know *isn't* involved in anything like this. He can stay with Lena. He and Hope can come over. You come over. Remy can stay here with Lena and Hope, we'll go into the woods with Nia and look around, see if we can find anything."

Law blew out a breath and slid his gaze to Nia. She stood there, arms crossed over her chest, legs planted wide, a mutinous look in her eyes.

"Fuck."

He could see the sense in Ezra's plans. Could see it rather well.

But seeing it, and talking that sense into Nia? Two different things.

He disconnected without saying anything else and looked at Nia. She was already shaking her head. "Don't even try to talk me out of going out there, Reilly. It ain't happening."

"I'm not going to try to talk you out of going—I just want you to *wait*," he said. "Until tomorrow."

"Wait." Still shaking her head, she backed away from him, wisely keeping some distance between them. "You want me to wait. How long am I supposed to keep waiting, damn it?"

"Twenty-four fucking hours," he snapped. "Less. Look, it's already close to five. In another few hours, it will be getting dark and it gets darker earlier in the woods. We'd have a couple of hours—that's not much and those woods cover several hundred acres."

"You've got a damn map!" she shouted.

"Yeah, one that's older than dirt and it's not like they were exactly using GPS back when it was drawn." Softening his voice, he shook his head and said, "Nia, it's one day. Less. Plus, this way, Ezra is with us, and he'll be able to have somebody there with Lena, too. Assuming there *is* somebody out there who we need to worry about, and I think there is, he can't leave her unprotected."

Nia opened her mouth, only to snap it closed. She groaned and covered her eyes, leaning back against the wall. "Why would he think she'd be in trouble?"

"Everything here all goes back to her," Law said quietly. "I know, for you, it started with your cousin, but the crazy shit that started in this town, everything went insane the night she made that call about the screams. If it *was* your cousin, and if the killer is still alive . . . hell, Lena is the one who started the ball rolling on him—his problems started with *her*. He wouldn't have to be insane to get pissed off at her and we already know he's a sick fuck, right?"

He stared past her, toward the wall, but it wasn't the wall he was seeing.

He was remembering a night. Hell, he still didn't have his memories of that night. Not much more than seeing Hope's face—the fear in her eyes right before he'd turned around . . . then nothing. His next memory was the agony, then waking in the hospital.

They'd all assumed it had been Joe.

But lately, Law was starting to wonder. Starting to wonder about *everything*. Had it been Joe? Somebody else?

Shit.

He didn't know what crimes he could pin at the dead bastard's feet and what crimes were actually the handiwork of a different, and possibly more dangerous, bastard.

Absently he flexed his arm, the remembered pain sneaking up out of nowhere, even though the actual pain had long since faded. Hearing the floorboards creak, he shifted his gaze to Nia's face. For a second, he thought about keeping his admittedly paranoid thoughts to himself. But then he decided against it. If it made her think twice? Great. Of course, not that it mattered. He really didn't give a flying fuck if it pissed her off. She wasn't going gallivanting off into those woods tonight. He didn't care if he had to have Ezra arrest her cute ass.

"You know, lately, you're making me question all sorts of things," he said, spreading the fingers of his right hand wide, rotating his wrist and listening to the bones pop. He didn't look at her as he spoke—he studied his arm, the scars from the surgery that had been done to set the bones. "Shit like what really happened the night my arm was busted up—the night Hope was attacked. At first, people were thinking *she* did it."

He looked up at Nia's harsh intake of breath, smirking at the disbelieving look in her eyes. "I guess you didn't find that bit of information while you were digging around, huh? Yeah, that was the story first floating around. People were assuming she'd lost her mind, attacked me, then slit her wrists."

"That's bullshit," Nia said, her voice flat. "Who in the hell would think that?"

Law shrugged. "Well, at first, a lot of people. Even Remy had to consider it because it had been set up to look just that way. Her fingerprints were all over the bat that had been used on me. But then other evidence came up and I came out of the coma . . ."

"Coma—" Nia snapped her mouth closed, passed a hand over her face.

"Yeah." He crooked a grin at her. "You said you'd done some digging around . . . didn't you read up on that night?"

She looked away. "Not so much about that night. I skimmed some things, but reading about you and Hope . . . well, not exactly what I wanted to do."

"Shit. There *is* no me and Hope."

"Yeah. I get that." She glanced back at him. "What exactly are you getting at? Other than trying to distract me?"

"Like I said, I'm wondering now. About everything. First people thought it was Hope. Then we started wondering if it was whoever had put your cousin's body here. But then Joe Carson shows up and it looks like it was him—everything circled back to him, and it was like people almost forgot about the weird shit going on *before*. The screams Lena heard. What happened out there. Everybody just assumes Joe was the problem."

"And you're thinking otherwise." Nia tilted her head to the side, studying him.

He jerked a shoulder in a shrug. "I'm thinking it's a damn clever way to distract everybody."

She was no longer shooting glances at the front door—no longer measuring the distance between them, like she was trying to figure out if she could get to the door before he got to her. Although she didn't have a car. And she hadn't grabbed any of his keys—he'd made sure of that.

Hoping that meant she was cooling down, he took a few steps closer, watching her face, staring into pale gold eyes. "What's it going to hurt to wait another day, baby?" he asked softly. "This way, you got the sheriff with you, and he's not worrying about his wife. Plus we can let Remy know what's going on, too."

She sighed, shoved her fingers through her hair. "I hate waiting," she muttered.

"I get that. But a day . . . ? And I know this is killing you, but whether you like it or not, if all this shit really is happening the way you think, this is tied to all of us now. This bastard pulled all of us into it—Lena could be in danger, Hope could, *you* could."

"Just the women, naturally," she said, rolling her eyes. "Or have you forgotten somebody beat the shit out of you?"

Law scowled. "Beat the shit out of me, busted up my arm—and tried to kill my best friend? No. Haven't forgotten that. But on a scale of one to ten? What happened to me is a zero compared to what happened to Hope. What *could* have happened to you the other night. And hell, Lena would kick my ass, but if she's left alone? She's too vulnerable. All it takes to get to her is getting Puck out of the way."

The look in his eyes tore Nia's heart up. And then she realized just *why* he was so worried about Lena being alone.

"Oh. Oh, shit . . ." Rubbing the back of her hand over her mouth, she wanted to kick herself. "Yeah, no wonder Ezra doesn't want her alone. Damnit, does she even know what's going on?"

Law shrugged. "I don't know what he's told her. I figure he's probably told her some stuff, but how much? I don't know."

She saw him reaching for her and while a huge part of her still wanted to tear out of there and find what she'd come here for, she held still. As his fingers laced with hers and tugged her close, she stared into his eyes, waiting. Yeah. One day didn't matter much . . . and it was getting late. It had been about this time, maybe a little later when she'd gone into the woods the other day. If they really wanted to do some digging around, they needed more daylight.

He cuddled her close. "Will you wait?"

"You're bossy," she said on a sigh. But she slid her hands around his waist and tucked her body against his. "Why am I even putting up with this?"

"Hmmm." He skimmed a kiss down along her neck, murmured in her ear. "Maybe because you know I'm right. Because you agree. You just don't feel like you should?"

Scowling, she poked him in the ribs.

He laughed. Then he caught her wrists, loosely braceleted them with his fingers. "Well, would it help if I told you I'm not letting you out of this house? You could pretend you had no choice?"

Nia rolled her eyes and lifted her head from his shoulder. "Yeah, the Neanderthal act will really help."

She went to pull away but there was a look in his eyes, one that was dark, troubled. He rubbed a thumb over the bruise on her inner wrist, lifted it to his lips. "I don't want to pull a Neanderthal act or anything. But I really don't want you leaving . . . not when we don't know if it's safe," he said.

Goosebumps broke out over her flesh at the feel of his mouth on her skin.

And as he stared at her from under his lashes, her heart bumped against her ribs, did a crazy little dance. "If I ask you to stay, will you?" he said quietly.

"Depends on why you're asking." Oh, hell . . . was that her voice? That breathless little gasping voice?

"I'm asking because I want you safe," he said, pulling her close again. Then he dipped his head and nipped her lower lip. "And I'm asking because I'd also like you to spend the night with me . . . all night."

"Hm. Like a sleepover? Popcorn and movies?"

His grin was quick and hot. "No. Like you in my bed,

under me, while I taste every last inch of you . . . and then you do the same to me. Or you can go first . . . I'm a gentleman, you know."

Heat, hot and fast, hit her low in the belly even as her heart skipped a few dozen beats. Feeling more than a little breathless, she curled her arms up around his shoulders, rose onto her toes so that they stood eye to eye, mouth to mouth. "Well, that sounds like my kind of sleepover. Yeah. I guess I can spend the night. In the name of safety and all."

"Sure. In the name of safety." His hands stroked down her back, cupped her butt.

As they got busy on her ass, she nipped his lip. "And sex. The sex is important, too."

# CHAPTER
# FIFTEEN

THERE WERE SOME THINGS A GUY JUST DIDN'T WANT to tell his wife.

Now Ezra was perfectly fine telling Lena almost everything . . . even the fact that he'd been speaking with a beautiful woman on the job. After all, it was related to the job.

The one thing he *didn't* want to tell her, though, was how this beautiful woman was somehow connected to her. It was, he knew, something he should have already told her. He hadn't, though. For months, it hadn't been much of an issue. After all, the case had been closed.

But then, Nia Hollister had shown up in town and as much as he would have *liked* to brush her off, he hadn't been able to. Every instinct inside him had started to scream when she told him why she was there.

Joe Carson had been too easy. Part of him had suspected it all along. Which was why he'd quietly been poking into things on his own. Although he hadn't let anybody know, he'd been doing just that for months.

But granted, there wasn't much he could do when no crimes were being committed, when there wasn't really any evidence, no reason to *open* a case that had been closed.

Not until Nia Hollister had shown back up. The hair thing—that was something, but not enough. The jewelry thing, too. Then her little nighttime visitor. Yeah, things were adding up.

And he needed to talk to Lena. But hell, he wasn't looking forward to it.

As he made his way into the kitchen at the Inn, he saw Roz Jennings in the hallway, talking animatedly on the phone, her blue eyes bright with either amusement or irritation—sometimes with her it was hard to say. She saw him and gave him a distracted wave. He smiled back and kept walking. His leg was hurting like a bitch, but he ignored it, knowing it was more stress than anything else.

A way for his brain to focus on something else.

Like the fact that after he'd hung up the phone, he hadn't been able to hang around the house and wait for Lena to get off work.

Of course, he could have waited outside the Inn, but if he'd done that, somebody would have said something and it would have gotten back to Lena, and she would have come looking for him. So he might as well get it over with and let her know he was here, that he'd drive her home.

And when she asked why he was doing that, he'd just tell her he was a paranoid son of a bitch and he didn't plan on letting her out of his sight for the foreseeable future . . .

"Yeah, that's going to go well," he muttered just before he pushed open the door to the kitchen.

Puck was lying in front of the island, his head resting on his paws, but as though he'd known Ezra was coming, the retriever's tail was already wagging. Lena's head turned to the door. Black lenses shielded her sightless eyes. She always wore them when she wasn't home.

"Hey, beautiful," he said.

A grin curled her lips. "Hi, gorgeous."

It hit him, even after all these months, a punch in the gut—love, lust, need, amazement. She was his. He was hers. She loved him . . . he'd found her. The woman meant for him, only him . . .

Shaking his head at the direction of his thoughts, he made his way to her.

Her mouth tightened, a concerned frown. "Your leg's bothering you."

"Nah," he muttered, reaching up to pull her glasses off. "It's fine."

She might have said something else—*would* have said something else, but he didn't want to hear it. Before she could, he kissed her, tilting her face back and covering her mouth with his, listening as she sighed, satisfaction rolling through him as she opened for him.

He pulled back a minute later, his heart pounding heavy in his chest, lust a pleasant, heavy ache in his groin. Lena hummed and licked her lips.

Then she sighed and said, "Nice distraction . . . but your leg is still bothering you."

"Not so much now." Sliding a hand around her waist, he tugged her closer, tucked her hips against his. "Something else is bothering me now."

"Pervert." She grinned at him and then eased back. "I'm on the clock."

"Then take a break. We can slip into the pantry."

"Pervert. And I think that violates health codes." She snorted. "Give me my glasses."

Sighing, he pushed them into her hands and watched as she slid them back on. Leaning a hip against the counter, he studied the island. It was mostly quiet in the kitchen for now, but it wouldn't be for long. The rest of the help would be showing up any minute now. If he could just stall . . .

"So, what are you doing out here?"

Shit.

"Maybe I missed you. You usually don't work on Mondays."

She rolled her eyes. "Nice try."

"What . . . you saying I can't be missing you?"

She just waited expectantly.

"Okay. Things are just running a little slow, so I left work early. Now I'm just killing time," he hedged. "I'm going to take you home tonight."

Dark red brows arched high. Her mouth firmed out. "Oh, really."

She'd been in the process of getting back to work, but now she faced him again, crossing her arms over her chest. "And just why would that be, Sheriff?"

He popped his neck, staring out the window. "I just felt like driving my wife home. There a problem with that?"

"Not unless you spend the entire day loitering around my place of employment," she replied, her voice dry. She moved closer, lifted a hand.

Reaching out, he caught it. Pressing a kiss to her palm, he stared at her face.

He couldn't talk about this with her here, not now. Not here.

"What's going on, Ezra?" she asked quietly. Then she stiffened and sighed.

He heard it a second later—the buzz of voices and laughter. The rest of the kitchen staff.

"Well, you just lucked out, I think, didn't you?" she muttered.

Dipping his head, he pressed a kiss to the corner of her mouth. "We'll talk about it later."

"Is everything okay?" she asked quietly, ignoring the noise as the door opened and several of the employees joined them.

"Yeah."

He'd damn well make sure of that.

Her bike was there, parked in front of Nia's cabin. But she wasn't.

He knew, because he'd seen her over at Reilly's, along with her cop escorts.

Breaking in during the day was a risky move, but he wanted to act now while he knew she was still shaken. He went through the place from top to bottom, dumping her clothes in a heap on the floor, cutting them to ribbons as he went. Then using a bottle of black spray paint—the generic kind anybody could buy at Walmart—he sprayed a huge X over the mirrors in the bathroom and over the bureau, as well as the TV and along the walls.

He used his knife to slash up the bed.

He was in and out in under five minutes, going through the back door.

It opened up onto a lovely, rather private little balcony—made it so much more convenient for him. He'd been able to muffle the sound of the glass he'd broken on the back door simply by wrapping a rock in the small towel he'd stashed in his pocket.

He left the glass alone, his only concern now to get as far away from the little cabin as he could. Perhaps he'd pop into the Inn's lounge, have a drink. Talk to people. It was close to dinnertime. It wasn't unusual for him to be seen there. The Inn was a popular place, much like the bar where he'd seen Nia Hollister that first night.

He didn't want to deviate from his regular routine or anything.

As he circled around the property, he was smiling, rather pleased with himself.

She'd be freaked out. Probably pissed. She wasn't a coward, he knew that.

But this would upset her.

How much before she got too unsettled?

That alone might be enough to help him out. If he got her unsettled, made her look a little less . . . steady . . . then if she *did* go to the sheriff, he'd be less likely to pay her any attention, and that could buy him the time he'd need to plan better.

Yes. He thought that could work.

Rounding the bend, turning that around in his head, he was only half paying attention to the cars in the parking lot. The sight of a familiar truck almost had him tripping on his feet.

*That* truck hadn't been here earlier—he hadn't seen it.

Ezra's truck.

Fuck.

What was the sheriff doing out here?

Then he took a deep breath. It didn't matter. Hell, his wife worked here. Maybe he was there to see her? Uneasy, he slowed a little as he circled the parking lot, still heading for the Inn.

He didn't understand why, but the muscles in his neck and shoulders were damn tight now. Damn tight. The sight of Ezra's truck had him uneasy. Fucking uneasy . . .

A drink.

He needed to get a drink. Get home. Get fucked.

Relax.

He was so worried he was going to screw up, if he wasn't careful, he'd make his own self-fulfilling prophecy.

"*What?*"

Ezra stared into his glass of whiskey, debated on whether he should say it again.

But just when he was getting ready to, Lena shot up off the couch. Her face was cold and tight, her skin so pale. "Why didn't you tell me this before?"

"I didn't want to freak you out—I know I should have

said something sooner, baby." He stared at her, his heart aching. "I just . . . hell. I was just trying to figure out the right way. Then Carson died, and it looked like the case was closed and it was just a freak accident. Now . . ."

He sighed, lifted his whiskey up, tossed it back. As it burned a path down to his stomach, he grimaced and set the glass aside.

"And now?" Lena echoed, her voice stiff.

"Now, I don't know."

She snorted. "Yeah, nice try. *Now* it looks like maybe some psychopath is out there targeting women who look like me and you're deciding to tell me because maybe the killer isn't dead—"

"Lena."

She ignored him, talking over him, the words coming out so fast she was practically tripping over herself as she spoke.

Rising, he moved to her, catching her in his arms. "Lena. We don't know that. At all. Hell, it's not even *pointing* to that. It was *one* woman and trust me, I've been following up on any incident involving a woman who bears even a *resemblance* to you. I'm not finding any other connections here."

He reached up, touched her cheek.

She turned her face away. "Damn it, Ezra."

"Lena . . ."

A ragged breath escaped. It was followed by a sob. "Damn you. This was supposed to be *over,*" she whispered. She leaned against him, pressed her face against his chest.

"I know." Cradling the back of her neck, he wrapped his other arm around her waist, cuddling her close. "I know. But I'm not going to let anything happen to you. I swear it."

"You can't be with me all the time, though, can you?

And shit, neither of us can stop speeding bullets or crazy shit like that . . ."

"Shhhh." Capturing her chin in his hand, he tipped her head back, rubbed his lips over hers. "Stop thinking like that. And stop thinking I can't take care of you—and hell, stop thinking *you* can't take care of you. You've got better instincts than almost anybody I know. Just listen to them."

Tucking her against his chest, he eyed the dog lying under the window. Puck stared at him, his eyes bright, intelligent.

Yeah. She had good instincts. She'd also have him watching her. As well as one big, mean dog who was already crazy protective of her. Besides, Ezra didn't really see any reason why he couldn't be with her all the time. Or practically. If he had to all but live in her back pocket, have Reilly or Hope here when he couldn't be, or keep her at the Inn. As long as she wasn't alone.

He could make that happen.

At least for a while . . .


"What do you mean, they don't think Joe did it?"

Pinching the bridge of his nose, Remy wished he'd poured himself a drink before he'd sat down to talk to Hope about this. Shit. He didn't even know exactly *what* he was talking about, either.

He'd understood the urgency in King's voice, though, and that was enough.

Blowing out a breath, he reached out and caught Hope's hand in his. Her engagement ring flashed in the light. "Angel, I don't know exactly what's going on just yet. Ezra said he'd explain more tomorrow. But apparently there are some things that aren't adding up. He's worried about Lena. So we're going over there."

"But what does this have to do with Joe?" she asked,

her voice shaking. Her green eyes were overbright and she had bitten her lip so hard, it looked bruised.

Pushing back from the table, he came around to kneel beside her. He captured her face in his hands, rubbed one thumb over her lip. "Hope, I just don't know. We'll have to go over. Talk to them. See what's going on." Then he kissed her, softly, slowly. "But stop looking so terrified . . . regardless, Carson's *gone. He* can't hurt you now."

Tears welled in her eyes.

"I know that. But if *he* didn't do all that crazy, awful stuff . . . if he wasn't the one who killed that girl, then maybe . . ." Her voice broke and she looked down.

He followed her gaze, found himself staring at the fading scars that lined one soft, pale wrist.

"If Joe didn't do that, maybe he didn't do *this,* either," she whispered.

He kept his eyes down until he knew the fury he felt wouldn't show on his face. Gently, he lifted her hand up, kissed the faded scars. Then he looked at her.

"If it wasn't Joe, then we'll find who is responsible. And whoever it was? We'll get them. You were strong enough to face Joe, you're strong enough for this," he said flatly. "And I'm not going to let *anybody* hurt you."

Not again, he swore as he pulled her against him. Never, ever again.


"Not that one," he said softly, watching as she reached for a necklace.

He knew she liked it. He liked seeing it on her . . . and remembering.

But he didn't want her wearing it. She pouted, her lip sticking out.

Climbing out of the bed, he came up to her and nipped her lip. "Wear the gold one . . . it looks better on you, especially with the blue. And you know I love you in blue."

Tugging the hem of her skirt up, he spread her thighs and nudged her with his cock. "I really love you in blue," he teased.

As he'd expected, she stopped pouting . . . smiled. As she spread her thighs for him, she tossed the silver necklace down onto her dresser.

He needed to get rid of it. Hide it for now. Something. But first . . . tugging her thong aside, he opened her, pushed inside, watched her as they fucked.

"I love you," she whispered to him.

"Hmmm . . . love you, too . . ."

Later, as she slipped out of the room, after a hurried shower, he tucked the necklace into his pocket. He'd just put it out of sight for now. She'd think she'd lost it, especially after this morning. He loved her, but she was a fucking ditz. Of course, that was part of why he loved her.

So much easier to do the things he did when she saw only what he wanted her to see. But she was a sweetheart, too. He liked that. It appealed to him, always had.

Sooner or later, this mess would blow over and he'd miraculously "find" her necklace for her. But until then, it was just best it stay out of sight. With that resolved, he started planning his day. He had errands to do, work he needed to get done—he was behind, but he'd been so distracted he hadn't been able to think lately. He was *still* distracted.

So far he hadn't heard anything about Nia Hollister's latest visitor. But that could be because she hadn't yet gone back to her cabin. If she was spending the night with Reilly . . . Well, that was the first order of the day. Figure that out.

Then he needed to get his own work done. He could

check out things with Nia on the way to get some coffee, though. Wouldn't take too much time. And while he was working, he could try to figure out the next step. Because he suspected he hadn't done enough. Not yet.

He didn't know just what it would take with her. Oddly, though . . . for some reason, he found the idea sort of intriguing. Providing he didn't get too involved . . . too close.

It was dangerous, he knew, even thinking about getting any more involved than he had. The only rational explanation was that it had just been too long since he'd had a decent challenge. Months since Chicago and he couldn't even consider that a challenge. It had been a fuck, and a fuck-*up*, but not a challenge.

He needed one, needed the challenge, the thrill.

*Think,* he told himself. He needed to think. And as much as he'd like to get more personally involved in removing Nia Hollister from the scene, he just couldn't risk it, he knew.

Keeping his distance was crucial. It wasn't like she was getting close to anything, really. Yeah, she'd been in the woods, but finding his place without knowing where it was would be like searching for a needle in a haystack. Nobody could find those spots by accident—just wasn't possible.

He couldn't panic, couldn't take any more stupid chances.

With that thought in mind, he headed into town.

"She doesn't look happy to be here," Remy said, pushing his sunglasses up on his head and studying Nia. "Matter of fact, she looks pissed. Reilly, I got to tell you, that woman in a pissed-off mood doesn't do my state of mind much good."

Law looked at Nia. She was out pacing by the truck, her hands jammed in her pockets, staring off into nothing. She wore one of his shirts and under it her shoulders were rigid.

Yeah. Somebody who didn't know her would definitely look at her and see somebody who looked pissed off.

Law looked at her and saw somebody who looked terribly alone.

But he didn't say that. He suspected Nia wouldn't appreciate it and he doubted Remy would believe it anyway. "Well, if she's right, and I think she might be, wouldn't *you* be pissed off in her shoes?"

Remy scowled and pushed his sunglasses back down over his eyes.

"Don't worry," Ezra said, giving Remy a wry smile. "If she gets testy, Law and I are going to be the ones out there with her."

Remy snorted. "And that is supposed to make me feel better? You know what your wife would do to me if something happens to you? Any idea what Hope will do to me if something happens to Law?"

"Stop it," Law bit off. "She's not looking to get us out in the woods just to shoot us in the back, okay? So stop."

"No, she wants to go out there because she thinks that somebody other than Carson killed her cousin and the proof is . . . where exactly?"

"Look, we're just taking some time to walk around, okay?" Ezra said, his voice edgy. "Now are you going to keep bitching and whining or what?"

"Don't you think if there's something out there to find, you should have your men out here instead of her and the Grisham wannabe here?"

Law curled a lip at him.

Ezra, his face blank, said, "And what do I say when I call them out here? I'm looking for . . . something? I don't know what? And I'm looking because this woman's gut instinct says something more is going on?"

"Damn it, Ezra. You're walking awful damn close to a line here. If you fall, you're fucked."

With a thin-lipped smile, Ezra said, "Don't worry. I got good balance." Then he shifted his gaze to the house. "Besides, if she's right . . . this is a risk worth taking."

They might have said more, but Nia apparently had run out of patience. She turned on her heel and came stalking their way. "Are we heading in any time soon?" she demanded, ignoring Ezra, ignoring Remy, focusing only on Law.

"Yeah." He smiled at her, reached up and curled a hand around her neck, his fingers digging into the tight muscles there. "You sure you're up for this?"

She bared her teeth at him in a mockery of a smile. "I didn't come here to sit around and twiddle my thumbs."

"I know." Looking past her shoulder, he focused on Remy. "You're staying with the other two until we're back."

A muscle twitched in Remy's jaw but he gave a terse nod.

"And nobody comes in," Ezra added.

Remy's brows arched. In a voice heavy with sarcasm, he said, "I'll be sure not to have parties while you're out, Dad." Without waiting another second, he stormed to the house.

"He's pissy," Nia said.

"He's in a mood." Law gave her neck one last stroke and then let his hand drop, focusing on the woods. "From the best I can tell, we're roughly a straight mile from the first one. After that, there are a couple of others scattered around, one about a half mile west, but we have to hike down the cliffs to get to that one. This could take a while."

"Then let's get to it."

\* \* \*

It wasn't exactly a straight mile to the first. More like a mile and a half, and it was a waste of time. It had long since caved in. The second one wasn't in much better shape.

It was a harder hike to get to the third, although distance-wise, it wasn't as far from Lena's house—it was a hike down the cliff, and by the time they got down to the base, Ezra looked ready to bite something in two.

Law didn't blame him. They'd been out there for more than two hours and the way their luck was going, they'd be out there another three hours before they hit all the areas. This third one wasn't proving as easy to find as it should be, either. They'd been in the area for thirty minutes and still, nothing.

Swearing, he stopped and studied the map, aware that Nia was all but mindless with impatience. He wished he could do something, say something to help, but he had nothing for her.

He checked the compass once more, then the map. "Okay, we need to leave the trail," he said. "The trails aren't going to take us where we need to go anyway."

Ezra nodded, his face grim, mouth set in a firm, flat line.

Nia all but took off running—or would have if Law hadn't caught her arm. "Together," he said softly. "We need to stick together, and slow down now. We shouldn't be too far off."

She rolled her eyes but remained at his side. "Just what are we looking for, anyway?"

"I'm not too sure," he said, sighing. "This is farther in than I usually come. I've done some walks with Lena, but she doesn't come near the cliffs and she knows I'm not fond of hiking, so we don't generally come this far back. I'm out of my depth here. The big, bad sheriff over there doesn't do much hiking, either, I don't think."

Ezra grimaced. "Shove it, Reilly." His limp had become more noticeable over the past hour and harsh lines bracketed his mouth.

With a faint smile, Law kept walking, easing deeper into the undergrowth.

"There," he muttered. "Shit, I bet it's in there."

There was an odd growth of greenery there—something that didn't quite match with the rest of the forest. If he hadn't been *looking* for something out of place, he wouldn't have noticed, not in a million years.

"What?" Nia asked.

"I'm not sure yet." He drew closer and his paranoid mind had him going slower, slower . . . nothing. But his skin was prickling, all over.

"Damn it, are you part snail?" Nia hissed behind him. He shook his head.

Ezra muttered, "Keep your eyes peeled, Reilly."

He grunted, still inching forward. As he placed his right foot down, something creaked.

Wood—

Carefully, he lifted his foot. Narrowing his eyes, he used his foot to sweep it back and forth over the forest floor—or what *should* have been the forest floor.

But it was cloth—durable, thick cloth, the same indistinguishable shade of brown as the ground, covered with leaves and dirt. He backed up and crouched down, searching for the edge of it. Once he'd found it, he started to lift it. Nia gasped and lunged, but Ezra caught her. "Slow down," he said brusquely. "We don't know what we're looking at yet."

"But . . ."

"I said *slow down*. Reilly, come on. We need to mark the area—I'm going to call some favors in, have some friends come in and help me . . ."

Law tuned them out. Yeah, he knew what Ezra was

thinking. He suspected the sheriff hadn't entirely expected to *find* anything but more of what they'd already found.

This . . . well, it was unexpected. Somebody had gone to the effort to hide this, and that was already an oddity. The cop's mind was probably in overdrive now, whirling and spinning, either thinking about a compromised case, or maybe down the same direction Law's had gone—Law was a paranoid bastard. Maybe this guy was, too. Maybe there were traps . . .

But he got the cloth up without incident and found himself staring at a door, set in the earth.

He reached for the iron handle.

"Damn it, Reilly."

Lifting his head, he glanced at Ezra over his shoulder. "You want to call them and say, *Hey, I found a cellar. Come out here and help me make sure nobody died in it*. Or would you want something that looks . . . nefarious?"

Ezra opened his mouth, then snapped it shut. Finally, he snapped, "I can't *use* anything that I find down there. Not a damn thing."

"No. *You* can't. If *you* go in right now, into this place that's not on *your* territory, and *you* find something that could become part of a case, it could compromise a case, right?" Law gave him a thin smile. "But me? Being a nosy bastard who was just checking something out while you two caught up with me? If I find something and tell you about it, that's a different story, isn't it?"

Ezra glared at him.

"I'm going. Just me," Law said softly.

"No fucking way," Nia snarled, twisting her arm and breaking free from Ezra. She shot forward, but Law blocked her.

"Wait here," he said. "For now, just wait. There might not be anything down there, and even if there is . . ."

His voice trailed off.

Ezra stepped up. Curling a hand over Nia's shoulder, he said, "If there is anything down there, the fewer people inside the better—*you* being in there is going to make it even more complicated. It's bad enough with Reilly, but at least he's local and I can use his nosy ass and those maps as a reason why he was out there. People are used to him doing crazy things. But if you want justice for your cousin, you need to back away from this now."

*Justice*—

"Back away?" she said softly, arching a brow. She looked between Law and Ezra. Then she shook her head. "Damn it, neither of you would have even bothered trying to *look* for anything if it wasn't for me and now you want me to back away? Fine. You know what? Go fuck yourself."

Jerkily, she pulled away and stormed off. She was tempted to take off, but if she did, either Law or Ezra or both would come after her, she suspected. And even if she was pissed about this, she wanted to know if there was anything beyond that door—

There was a faint screech as metal protested. Swinging her head around, she stared, watched as Law peered down inside. He pulled a flashlight from the backpack he'd brought along and flipped it on, peering down inside. Then, just like that, he was gone, leaping down into that maw of darkness.

Her breath lodged in her throat until she heard his voice floating up.

"One big room—a cot, an area that looks like somebody could shower or something. Lights on the wall . . . don't work. Gas, maybe."

There was silence, for the longest time.

Then, he spoke again, his voice strained. "I'm coming back up—there's a ladder."

The first thing she saw was his face, pale and gleaming under a fine sheen of sweat. His eyes too dark, almost glassy. He climbed out of that hole but before he could say anything, he shoved past them.

She watched, stupefied as he stormed away and bent over, hands braced on his knees, like he was fighting the urge to be sick.

"Law?"

He straightened slowly, shaking his head.

"Damn it, Law, what is it? Did . . . was there something of Joely's down there?" she demanded.

He shook his head again. Then he held out his phone, but not to her. Ezra took it.

Whatever the sheriff saw caused little reaction. Tucking the phone into his pocket, he looked at Law. "It might not be for what you think," he said quietly.

"Fuck that," he muttered. He looked a little less pale.

Good, because Nia was about to kick his ass. "What did you see?" Storming up to him, she drilled a finger into his chest, about ready to pummel him.

He caught her fist, his grip tight, almost too tight. Eyes half wild, he stared at her. "I'm not telling you, damn it," he growled. "I don't want to live with that in *my* head. I'm sure as hell not putting it in yours."

She jerked away. Fine. Fuck this—she'd go look—

And he caught her by the waistband of her jeans before she took two steps.

Shrieking in frustration, she rounded on him and hit him, full force, her fist plowing into his jaw.

His head snapped back. When he looked back at her, there was next to no emotion in his eyes. "Go ahead and do it again if it will help," he said. "But I'm still not telling you and you are *not* going down there."

"Kids." Ezra stepped up, pushed between them. "I hate to break up this lovely scene . . . but we need to get back. Law, we need to figure out how we're going to spin this. For now, we've got lousy reception so that plays into our favor. If you want to try that shit, we were hiking and you got ahead of us, ended up finding that spot while you waited . . . ? I need you to e-mail me that photo . . ."

Staring at Law, she backed away, shooting another look at that dark hole.

Answers . . . so close.

"There aren't any immediate answers down there, Nia," Law said quietly. "If you go there, all you'll get is more nightmares. You don't need that."

She looked at him. "Isn't it up to me to make that decision?"

"You can't undo the damage once it's there. You can't take those nightmares away." He shook his head. "I'm not letting you do it." Then he moved around her and sealed that nightmare back up.

# CHAPTER
# SIXTEEN

Tools. Ropes stained with blood. Chains.

Those were bad enough. But the other things . . .

Law's gut clenched each time the image of the saw blade danced through his mind. The serrated teeth stained with blood. His gut clenched each time. He hadn't gotten sick, but it had been damn close.

Fuck. Fuck. Fuck. And Nia wanted that image in her head.

Shit, no. He had to watch her like a hawk, too, because for most of the afternoon, she'd been ready to take off running. He'd made his call, not necessarily fudging anything. Just leaving out one or two minor details.

Like that they had been *looking* for the cellar they'd found.

They'd just gone hiking.

Remy hadn't been pleased—Law could tell, but at one point, the lawyer had cornered both of them and snarled, "What are you two trying to do? Get all of us fucked?"

"Now, Remy . . . I never outright told you what we were doing," Ezra said easily. "Just mentioned Nia's concerns . . . then that we were going out for a hike.

And, to be honest, I didn't expect to really *find* anything."

Remy looked about ready to bust a vein. "You expect me to buy that?"

"Doesn't matter if you buy it or not. I can tell you, honestly, I didn't *think* we'd find anything. I figured our chances of finding anything out there were slim to none." Ezra shrugged, his green eyes direct. "Reilly and I have been out there before—never saw a damn thing. Didn't see why we'd expect it to be any different this time."

"But you did. And damn it, now what in the fuck happens?" he snarled. "You're the damn sheriff and you had civilians on what might be a murder scene!"

"Actually, only one civilian," Law corrected. "And we were just walking around—researching some old maps of mine. The cellar was on one of them and I wanted to take a look. I moved ahead and was wandering around while I waited for Ezra and Nia to catch up, that's when I found it."

Remy snorted. "Like anybody is going to buy that."

Law looked down at his maps, then back at Remy. "Well, I do have the maps. And come on, Remy, look at it logically. If Ezra had thought he'd be finding a murder scene, he'd have his men with him. Right? So logic tells us he wasn't expecting to find anything of the sort."

"Nah, he was just out there because he's into recreation," Remy muttered. "And that's why I had to take a day off of work . . . without telling anybody why. That's why *he* took a day off of work. Without telling anybody why. Like that isn't going to make people suspicious as hell. And by the way . . . why the big fucking secret?"

"Because the sheriff isn't sure just which of the townspeople are involved," Ezra said, his voice flat. Hard.

Remy stared at Ezra blankly, not comprehending.

Law realized the lawyer hadn't quite arrived at that

conclusion yet, that he hadn't connected those dots. Too close to it, he guessed—hell, Law hadn't lived here all his life, wasn't connected by blood or marriage to nearly thirty percent of the county. Remy was. His roots here, they went deep. More than likely, he would know whoever was behind this—more than likely, he had met the killer—might even be friends with him.

Shit, wasn't that a thought to have in your head?

"You know, for a sharp lawyer, you're not thinking very clearly here," he pointed out.

"Reilly. Shut the fuck up." Ezra focused on Remy. "Think it through, Jennings. If he's right, whoever did this is local. It's the only thing that makes sense. Whoever did it is local . . . and you know him."

"No." Remy shook his head, spit the word out like it tasted bad. "*Fuck,* no."

"Yeah. Which is why I wanted it quiet while I was out there. We couldn't put it off—Nia was out there yesterday and she's had some weird shit happen, which tells me somebody is paying too much attention to her. I couldn't risk *not* taking a look around, don't you get that?"

"You're nuts," Remy snarled. "There's no way—"

"Nothing else makes sense," Law said softly. "If she's right, then whoever did it put her cousin at my place to throw attention off Lena when she reported hearing the screaming that first night. That means either they knew we were close, or that the people in town already figured I was mostly still an outsider . . . or both. That cellar? Nobody *but* a local with pretty deep roots would know about it. It can't be anybody *but* a local."

"You're not a local." Remy glared at him. "But *you* know about those underground areas. Hell, *I* didn't know about them. Yet you did. Explain that."

"Sheer luck—I found the maps at a yard sale. If it wasn't for those . . ." He shrugged.

"This is bullshit," Remy spat.

"Look, I know this isn't—"

"Enough." Ezra pushed between them. "I've got work to do—in all likelihood, there's a crime scene to be processed. Remy, you're probably going to want to find a way to pass on this. Instead of hassling Law, why don't you think about how to do that? Law—get Nia the hell out of here."

Nia shot a look at the darkness of the trees.

She wanted—*needed* to get back there. But how could she possibly hope to, now? Assuming she even *could*. As though he'd been purposely intent on throwing her off, Law had led them on a winding, confusing trail back to the house and she hadn't been thinking clearly enough to pay attention on the way in to note details.

And of course, lousy reception meant she couldn't really mark the area either.

Out of the corner of her eye, she saw Law and she stiffened her spine, kept her gaze focused straight ahead. It was a stab of betrayal, even looking at him. He'd locked her out.

Kept her on the outside when she'd been the one to push him into finding this. The bastard.

"How long are you going to stay pissed at me?"

She set her jaw. Damned if she'd speak to him right now. Son of a bitch.

He sighed. "I'm not doing this to cut you out, Nia. Whether you believe it or not, I'm doing you a favor here."

Her resolution to remain silent splintered under her fury. Wheeling around, she glared at him. "I don't *want* your damn favors," she snarled. "I don't need your coddling, your protection, your fucking knight in shining armor routine. Maybe you needed to ride in and save the day with Tinkerbell in there, but I don't need a hero, damn it. Y'all never would have even bothered to *look* for anything if it wasn't for me. How could you cut me out like that?"

"Because I'm going to have fucking *nightmares* after what I saw," he snapped. "I'd rather it not be in your head."

Then he stopped, took a deep breath. "You want to be pissed off, you be pissed off. I'm sorry if I hurt you—that wasn't my intention. But if I had to make the same call, I'd do it again. And I'm not sorry for that."

He turned around and headed back into the house.

She waited until she heard the creaking of the door as it opened. Then, because she couldn't keep the question silent any longer, she blurted out, "What in the hell did you see?"

Law just shook his head. "Aren't your nightmares bad enough right now?"

He'd have to tell her, he figured. Sooner or later, if the cellar turned out to be what he thought it was, details would slip. He'd have to tell her. But until Law knew for certain, he wasn't going to put those images in her mind. If she hated him for it, then she hated him.

Feeling somebody's eyes on him, he looked up and saw Hope watching him. She was perched on the stairs, her elbows resting on her knees, her misty green eyes full of sympathy and sadness.

"Hey."

He gave her a tight smile and shoved his hands in his pockets.

"I guess you won't tell me, either, huh?"

Law lifted a brow.

Hope smirked. "Didn't think so." She shifted her gaze past his shoulder, staring toward the door. "You know, I really wish she'd drop the 'Tinkerbell' comments."

"She doesn't mean anything mean by it," he said wearily.

"I know." Hope lifted up a hand, propped her chin on it. "You know, she's probably not really angry at you. Just upset. Scared. Frustrated. Once she cools down . . ."

Law snorted. "No. She's angry. Really angry. At me. And it's too fucking bad, because I wouldn't do it any other way."

"Is it that bad?"

He stared at her. Then he looked down at the floor. "I don't want to sleep tonight, sweetheart. Because I'm afraid of what I'm going to see."

"So it is that bad."

"Worse," he muttered. He shoved a hand through his hair. He fucking needed a drink, but couldn't. Not yet. Probably wouldn't be wise to have one later, either. Not until he'd figured out how Nia was going to react. If she had any plans on slipping away, he had to be ready, had to watch her . . .

This was probably all over town by now.

"Did you hear?"

He held the coffee cup loosely, focused on doing just that because he wanted to crush it. Wanted to hurl the steaming liquid in Natalie Walbash's pretty face. Instead of doing that, he gave her a puzzled smile. "Heard what?"

Of course he'd fucking heard—

Everybody in the whole damn town knew. The sheriff's department was crawling all over the woods. His place. They knew about his fucking place.

*Nia*—

"Something weird is going on down in the woods between where Lena and Ezra live and the Ohlman property. I don't know what—I've heard everything, too. Somebody said they found where a cult worships, and somebody else said they found a serial killer's hangout, and somebody else said it's where they stashed money from a bank robbery. But something is *weird.*"

He forced a wry note into his voice and asked, "I wonder if the next story is going to involve little green men from Mars. Or maybe it's the secret hideout for a vampire . . . ?"

Natalie rolled her eyes. "Please. Not vampires. I'm so tired of them. Grandma is getting hooked on them. She likes the ones that sparkle." She topped off his coffee and looked up as the bell over the door jangled. The café was already packed, but it was only going to get worse.

Which was why he was there. The best place to hear news. Gossip.

Everything.

"I'll be by in a few minutes," she said, smiling at him. Then she was gone.

Leaving him alone. He stared down into the dark, steaming brew, but he didn't see it. Didn't see the cup, or the table . . . it wasn't Natalie's voice he heard, or anybody else.

He saw Nia, as she'd looked coming out of the forest. And he was imagining how she would have sounded if he had just aimed his van for her, run her down.

It would have been too quick. Too easy. And *over.* His secrets would have been safe. His hands trembled, the coffee splattering out, but he barely noticed.

Damn that fucking whore. He shouldn't have left his things there. Not after last night. But how could he have risked moving them *then?* With her poking her nose into everybody's business and showing up exactly where she shouldn't be . . .

Damn her.

". . . wasn't that Carson guy."

He stiffened. Without turning his head, he slid his eyes to the side, trying to find the speaker.

Female—ahhhh . . . bingo. He knew her. Married to one of the deputies, too. Ethan's wife. Oh, this was priceless. *Exactly* why he was hanging around here.

"What do you mean?"

She shook her head, her mouth drawn tight in a frown. "I don't know. He wouldn't say anything else. I get a feeling I might not be seeing much of him for the next few days."

"Shit. I don't want to think that we might have another crazy fuck running through our town. What in the hell is going on around here lately? The Carson guy, all the insanity last summer . . . ."

Idly, he reached down and stroked the knife he'd used to cut up the steak he'd ordered for lunch. He imagined taking it, standing and moving to stand behind the gossiping bitch just behind him, a little to the right. Grabbing her hair and jerking her head back, exposing her neck. The spray of blood as he dragged the blade over her flesh.

She'd be dead before anybody realized what he'd done, most likely.

Everybody would be so shocked—

*You're slipping.*

Because the image was so enticing, so rich and intriguing, he pushed the knife away, folded his hands around his cup of coffee. Too enticing, too intriguing.

He was slipping . . .

*No. No, you're not. You're in control.* He was in control. He'd always been in control. He didn't notice that as he set his coffee down, his hands continued to tremble.

Nia stared through the windshield. "I don't give a flying fuck if you want me alone or not. I said, *take me back to my cabin.*"

"Damn it, Nia." He slammed a fist into the steering wheel. "Don't you get it? You were right, okay? Something fucked up is going on, all the more reason for you to be careful and you want to go back there?"

"Not especially." She slid him a thin-lipped smile. "I just refuse to stay at your place and there really isn't anyplace else. I figure the cabin is more secure than the hotel room, at least."

She glanced in the rearview mirror at the car following along. "Besides, sugar, it's not like I'm on my lonesome. I've got my nice escort, remember?"

Law said nothing, a muscle jerking in his jaw.

She slumped down in the seat, arms folded over her chest. Misery sat in her chest, a tight, cold lump. Beneath it lurked the twin shadows of rage and guilt.

There was something monstrous and dark in Law's eyes.

She'd seen it lurking there all day—the echo of something haunting him, something he wouldn't share with her. What was it, this thing he wouldn't share with her? She had to know, damn it.

*You can't undo the damage—*

Tense moments of silence passed before he finally turned into the small parking area in front of her cabin. She half expected him to peel off in a fit of sulking fury.

But that wasn't Law's style, apparently. He was just a few inches away as she headed up, and behind him, the deputies.

"I don't recall inviting you in," she said, her voice bitchy. And she wasn't even sure *why*—she was pissed, but damn it, she didn't entirely understand just *why*. Did she really want whatever horror he'd seen inside her head?

*He isn't giving me the choice to decide for myself, damn it,* she thought. That was the problem.

"I don't care if you invited me in or not." He stared at her, his gaze level, flat. "I'm making sure everything is okay before I leave."

Nia glared at his back as he shoved around her, plucking the keys out of her hand. Then she gave one of the deputies a considering glance. "I didn't invite him in here. Can't you make him leave?"

Ethan shifted from one foot to the other, then gave Law a worried look. "Well, Ms. Hollister, I . . . uh . . . he already said he isn't staying . . ."

"Not the point." She had to grit her teeth to keep from yelling. "Fine. Screw it. I don't want him in, but he goes in anyway."

Stalking inside, she decided she was going to change, then go to the Inn, and get shitfaced drunk—

Law's arm came up, barring her way. She went to shove it aside, but then she focused on the room. She blinked, rubbed her eyes. But the image didn't change.

"What the hell . . . ?" she whispered.

Her room was destroyed. Completely destroyed. Clothes were everywhere. Black paint marred the TV, mirror, and walls. And the bed . . . she stared at it, trying to figure out what was wrong, but her mind wasn't processing it.

"It looks slashed," she murmured. "Somebody slashed up the bed."

"Ethan." Law—that was Law's voice. Coming from too far off.

Hands, gentle but insistent, tugged her aside. She didn't fight them.

For some reason, the fight was suddenly gone. Her head was spinning. Black dots danced in front of her eyes. A hand gripped the back of her neck and she realized somebody was pushing her, forcing her away from the open doorway, then into a chair on the porch. Her head was shoved down, between her legs.

Not helping . . .

Her bed.

Somebody had slashed her bed.

* * *

"Breathe, Nia," Law said. "You need to breathe so you can yell at me and threaten to kick my ass more, okay?"

Finally, she stirred under his hand and when she tried to sit up, he let her, staring into glassy eyes. Her pupils were too big, her normally warm skin almost ashen. "He cut my bed up," she said softly.

Law blew out a breath. "Yeah. It looks like."

From the corner of his eye, he saw the two deputies making their way around the room, nudging things aside with a shoe, but taking care not to touch anything.

But he'd seen some of the clothes on the floor before he'd forced Nia into the chair. The bed wasn't the only thing that got the knife job. She'd be lucky to find anything big enough to use as a rag.

Had he come here looking for Nia? Or was this just to scare her?

Law didn't know. Soothingly, he rubbed a hand up and down her back, watching as the color slowly crept back into her cheeks, watching as the shock in her eyes was slowly replaced by anger.

He saw her body tense only a second before she went to shove him aside. He let her, but when she tried to barge into the cabin, he stopped her. "Nia, it's a crime scene. They need to make sure there isn't any evidence. You go in there, it makes it harder for them."

"Damn it, Law," she snapped. She reached out to shove at him, but instead, she rested her hands on his chest. Then, abruptly, her hands fisted in his shirt. A harsh sigh, too close to a sob, escaped her.

"Hey . . ." Slipping an arm around her waist, he eased her up against him, pressed his lips to her brow. "It's going to be okay, baby. I swear."

"How? How in the hell can you swear that?" She buried her face against his chest, her voice muffled. "My cousin's gone. We don't know who is responsible. And he's fucking around with me."

"He's messing up, that's what he's doing," Law said. He hugged her close, wished there was some way he could protect her from this. Assuming she'd even let him. Hell, he'd tried to protect her earlier and she'd spent the day pissed off at him—he could still feel that wall between them.

Already she was trying to back away. And he couldn't force her to stay there, either. Reluctantly, he let her go. She wasn't pale now, and although her eyes were still a little off, she looked more pissed than anything. She stared through the door, but made no move to go inside.

Her head tilted to the side and he watched as her eyes narrowed, watched as a flush settled over her cheeks. "He cut up my clothes," she said quietly.

Law tucked his hands into his pockets, rocked back onto his heels.

She shifted her gaze his way and snarled, "He cut up my fucking clothes."

"Yeah."

Spinning away, she started to pace. "What the hell . . . I mean, shit. What the hell is he trying to do?"

"I'd say he's trying to run you off."

She stopped in midstep and looked at him. "What?"

He shrugged. "Makes sense. I mean, think about it. He can't risk coming after you, not if there's a chance you've shared your concerns with the sheriff, and everybody knows you've talked to him a few times. First thing anybody would think is that there's a connection. If you disappeared or got hurt . . ." *Or worse* . . . "It's going to just make things look that much more suspicious."

Fuck. His gut was in knots just thinking about the *or worse* possibilities. What he'd seen in that underground cellar—the tools. The bloodied cot.

The fucking saw—

Shoving it aside, he focused on Nia's face again. "Whoever this is, he's smart enough to realize that it's safer to just get you out of here. Trying to come after you is dangerous. So he wants to scare you. That's what this is about."

"Scare me. He kills Joely and thinks cutting my clothes up is going to chase me off?" Nia shook her head.

"Well, some people might be freaked out enough." He chanced lifting a hand, touching it to her cheek. "But I doubt he'd planned on stopping with this. This was just another step. He'll probably keep going."

"Except we found his place," she said softly. "He'll know about that now."

A cold chill ran down Law's spine.

"Yeah. He'll know." Grimly, he looked back at the cabin and then around the grounds. "Nia, staying alone, even with the deputies outside, it's just not safe."

She was gritting her teeth. He could tell. Curling a hand over the back of her neck, he massaged the tense muscles there, half-expecting her to jerk away. "It will get worse after this, you know. It only makes sense. Once he finds out his place was found, he'll get pissed or desperate or both."

"And coming after me does what? It's not like I *know* anything."

"But you'll be his focus. The problems started back up with you."

"Me . . ." She frowned and twisted her head around, looked at him. "This time. But is he going to focus on me, or Lena? Who really started the problem?"

Law wrapped an arm around her shoulders, pulled her back against him.

She didn't pull away. In fact, she snuggled closer, lifted her hands to curl around his forearm. Standing there together, they stared into the cabin, watching as the deputies continued to study the remains of her clothes.

"It really will get worse now," she said softly.

"Probably."

It was late. So fucking late. All she wanted to do was lie down and sleep.

Nia couldn't, though. Not yet.

It was like a burn on her brain, that driving need to know.

He thought she was asleep. She'd let him think that, waited until he slid out of bed, knowing he'd probably shower—he liked to shower before he slept, one fact she'd already picked up on.

Once he was in the shower, she slipped out of his bed and padded over to the door, listening through the narrow crack to the water splash. She eased the door open, peered inside. His phone was there. Just a few feet away. Easing the door open just a little more, she peeked around the edge, stared at him.

She could see him, his lean back to her, hands braced against the tile wall, head bent as the water pounded down on him. She slid her way inside and grabbed the phone, clutched it to her breasts as she backed away.

She didn't bother closing the door, just beat a fast retreat out of the room as she hit the button, wincing as the iPhone's bright screen flared to life.

*Photos . . .*

She hit the icon, hit another one, scrolled down.

*Shit.*

Nothing there.

He'd deleted it—

Then she remembered.

He'd sent it to Ezra. E-mail. It would be in his e-mail. She hit the icon for that. Shit. The shower cut off.

She hurriedly headed down the steps, swearing as the messages loaded. *Sent—*

There it was.

The message he'd sent to Ezra.

The picture was there, in the body of the message.

Her mind *recognized* it. But it didn't want to process it.

Part of it was too shiny, like Law's flashlight had reflected off it. Something dark and rusty stained the bottom of it.

A saw. It was a saw . . .

*No.*

On the bottom step, she stumbled and fell against the wall.

Dimly, she heard the strangest sound—an animal.

It sounded like a wild animal.

Whimpering.

Law swiped the towel over his head, weariness tugging at him. Although he didn't really want to sleep, he needed to. He just hoped when he slid into bed next to Nia, he could avoid the nightmares he feared waited for him.

Fuck, he wished he hadn't gone in there.

Ezra could have figured out some way to get people out there, right?

Granted, Law going in under the guise of curiosity and finding suspicious shit made it a lot easier, but still . . . he wished he could wipe the images out of his mind as easily as he'd been able to delete them from the damn phone.

He shot a look at the counter where he'd left his phone.

Then the bottom dropped out of his stomach when he realized it wasn't there.

"Aw, fuck," he muttered.

Just then, he heard something.

It was a sound that would haunt him, much like those images.

Snagging his jeans, he hitched them on in seconds and took off. She wasn't in the bedroom. Not in the hallway. He hit the lights and looked around.

That sound—there it was again.

And there she was.

Sitting down at the foot of the stairs, a look on her face that probably echoed what he'd felt inside when he'd figured out what he was looking at. His phone was a few inches away from her hand and she was staring at it like she expected it to attack her. Fuck—what the hell, he'd deleted it . . . oh, shit.

E-mail. He'd sent it to Ezra and it was in the *sent* box.

"Nia."

She didn't even seem to hear him.

Unsure what to say, how to say it, he came down the steps, knelt on the one just above her. He touched her cheek, but she didn't react, didn't move. Sighing, he lifted her feet and sat down on the step across from her. She shifted her gaze to him then and he saw the horror lurking in the golden depths.

*Why in the hell did you have to look, baby?*

That was what he wanted to ask her.

But he didn't.

It was bad enough that she'd seen. He didn't need to remind her that she'd had the option of *not* looking . . . that he'd tried to spare her this. Maybe she regretted it, maybe she didn't. Too late now, either way.

"It's a saw," she said, her voice soft, toneless. Her gaze clung to his face, like she couldn't bear to look away.

Law nodded.

"A saw. There's blood on it." She licked her lips, darted a look at the phone, like she feared the image would somehow morph into reality or something. "That . . . it was blood, wasn't it? Could it be something else?"

Blowing out a breath, he said softly, "It could be something else."

"Could be," she whispered. Then she giggled. It had a high, almost hysterical note to it and just hearing it hurt his heart.

"Nia . . ."

She shook her head. "Could be." The laughter died and she stared at him and now, the shock had faded, leaving nothing but the horror, so thick and dark, it threatened to drown them both. "It could be, but you don't think it is."

"No, I don't."

Closing her eyes, she rested her head against the wall. "You told me I'd have nightmares. That's why you didn't want me looking." She swallowed and then lifted her lids just enough to stare at him from under her lashes. "I wish I'd listened. I don't want that picture in my head. I'd do almost anything to get it out."

"I know the feeling. It's stuck in there, though. For both of us, I guess." He closed one hand around her ankle and started to rub the bottom of her foot. "Maybe . . . I dunno. Maybe I should have given you some idea of what I'd seen. That might have helped."

"No." She had her eyes closed again. "I still would have tried to look, would have been determined. I can't stand to have somebody trying to protect me, keep something from me. Even when maybe it's better."

With a watery laugh, she whispered, "I wish I'd let you keep this from me, Law."

"I'm sorry."

Silence fell between them, thick and tight, but no longer quite so strained. She sighed as he used his thumb on her instep, across the ball of her foot. When he put that foot down, she lifted her other foot for him. "I shouldn't have come down on you like I did," she said softly. "I get why you didn't want me seeing that."

Law stayed quiet.

"I'm just . . . hell. I just don't deal well with being coddled, with having somebody make a decision about what I can and can't handle."

"It's not about can or can't handle," he said, shooting her a quick look. "I'm starting to think there's not a damn thing you *can't* handle. It's a matter of why in the hell should you have that image in your head? I don't want it in mine. Ezra has to have it—it's his job, but you and me . . . ?"

He sighed and shook his head. "Wasn't trying to coddle you. You'd cut a guy off at the knees if he tried that with you. I was just trying to help."

"I know." She leaned forward and covered one of his hands with hers.

"And I'm sorry," she added as their gazes locked.

"It's okay."

She squeezed, gave him a smile. "No, it's not. But at least you tolerate me being a bitch . . . although I don't know why." She sighed and closed her eyes, only to open them immediately. "Damn it—I think I'm going to see it every time I close my eyes. I want to push it out of my head but my imagination is kicking in and I'm already thinking, *what did he do with that stuff* . . ."

"You need to stop wondering," Law said. "It's just going to drive you nuts."

"I'm already there."

"Why don't you come to bed?" He laid a hand on her knee, squeezed it. "Get some rest."

"I can't sleep with that picture in my mind and right now, it's all I can see."

She lifted her hands to her face, but stopped when she saw them shaking. A harsh laugh escaped her.

"Shit. Holy shit—I can't stop seeing it. Why did I look?" she whispered. Sliding her gaze past him, she stared at the phone, shuddered as the image loomed large in her mind once more. *Why . . .*

Abruptly, she tore her gaze from the phone and looked at Law. His hair, still damp from his shower, was darker than normal. He'd shaved recently. He smelled of soap, toothpaste . . . and himself.

Rolling to her knees, she half crawled until she was straddling his lap. "There's no way I can sleep with that in my head. I want it out. Will you make it go away, Law? Can you make me see something else?"

Her eyes had the look of something desperate . . . something just this shy of mad terror, Law thought.

If he was any kind of decent, what he should do was find some whiskey, hold her until she felt asleep, and just be there when the nightmares came. They'd probably come for both of them.

But he was a little too raw, a little too ragged to worry about being decent.

Her mouth was just a whisper away from his. Reaching up, he fisted his hand in her hair, holding her back when she would have kissed him. "What do you want to see?"

"How about you? Just you?"

"Don't close your eyes, then." Still staring at her, he brought her face close . . . closer . . . until their breath mingled, until his lips covered hers. He shifted around until she was sitting on the step above him. "Wrap your legs around me."

Nia did and he groaned when she pressed against him. Soft and warm, separated from him by nothing more than his jeans and her T-shirt. Her eyes, wide and wild, locked on his face as he reached out his hand and caught hold of the banister. With a slow smile, she said,

"What . . . you're not going to just ravish me here on the steps?"

"No." He nipped her lower lip. "By the time I'm done with you, I plan on the two of us being too damn weak and tired to move. So the bedroom's better."

Weak, tired, too damn exhausted for even nightmares to haunt them, if he had anything to do about it.

She smiled against his mouth as he stood. "You know . . . I'm no lightweight. I can walk up the stairs."

"And I can carry you." No . . . she wasn't a lightweight. She was a solid, sleek woman. Cupping her ass in one hand, he squeezed. "Haven't you ever had a guy carry you up the steps before?"

"Can't honestly say I've ever wanted one to," she murmured. She peered over his shoulder and then smiled at him. "It's a long way down . . . you better not drop me."

He swatted her butt. "I've got too many things I want to do to you. Dropping you isn't one of them, don't worry."

As he turned into his room, he hit the lights with his elbow.

They didn't need darkness right now . . . no darkness, no shadows.

There were too many shadows in her eyes already. He wanted to chase them all away. Carrying her to the bed, he set her on the edge and reached for the hem of the T-shirt. "You never did ask if you could use this, you know," he said. "I think I want it back."

"Not very good at sharing, Law?"

"I suck at it." He stripped it away and tossed it to the floor. Holding her gaze with his, he trailed his fingers up her side and cupped one breast. "When something's mine, I want to keep it . . . for me, only me."

Her lashes fluttered. "It's just a shirt, Law," she murmured.

"A shirt. A book . . ." Dipping his head, he raked his teeth down her neck. "Sometimes it's more. A lot more."

"And what are you talking about now?"

Sinking to his knees in front of her, he palmed her breasts, pushed them together. He captured one swollen nipple between his teeth and tugged. She hissed, her head falling back. "Hmmm. Maybe nothing. Maybe everything . . . I dunno. I could be speaking hypothetically, you see."

Her hands came up, one gripping his shoulder, the other dipping into his hair and fisting there. "That a fact?"

"Hmmm. You know something, Nia? I really love the way you taste," he whispered. He boosted her farther back on the bed and came up between her thighs, pushing them wide. "Fucking love it . . ."

"Is that . . ." Her breath caught as he used his fingers to spread the folds of her sex. When he licked her, she bucked upward, her hands shooting down to grip his wrists.

Grinning against her, he caught her clit between his teeth and tugged and then lifted his head. "Is that what?"

Blindly, she stared at him. "Huh?"

"You were saying something . . . is that? What were you asking?"

She groaned and caught his head, tugged him back against her. "Forget what I was saying and just go back to what you were doing."

Chuckling, he let her guide him back between her thighs. The tight black curls that covered her sex were already damp. Slipping his hands beneath her hips, he arched them upward and pressed his mouth to her.

She cried out when he pushed his tongue inside. When he began to suck on her clit, she shivered. The moment he started to use his fingers, she shuddered and started talking to him, low, pleading little demands, her voice husky and soft, her fingers twisting in his hair and clutching him close as though she feared he'd stop.

Like he would . . . like he *could*.

He didn't stop until he had her climaxing, and then he only stopped to let her calm, let her relax.

Then he started all over again.

No nightmares, he thought . . . not tonight.


"Law, please . . ."

Nia didn't think she even had the energy to say his name, but she had to say something—Hell, she didn't know she *could* come that many times, and he hadn't even taken his damn jeans off.

He gave her a slow, heated smile when he lifted his head from between her legs.

Her heart banged against her ribs, but she honestly didn't think she had the energy when he levered his weight up and came up to lie next to her, his knee pressed against the sensitized flesh between her thighs. Every last nerve in her body was singing, humming, so sensitive and aware, each touch was almost an excruciating pleasure.

He reached down and cupped her and she jerked. "Law, I don't think . . ."

"No nightmares, Nia," he whispered, pressing his mouth to hers.

She groaned, tasting herself in his kiss. "I'm tired."

"You won't be for long."

One finger pushed inside her and she cried out, the sensation almost painful. His mouth rubbed against hers, his lips soothing, almost gentle. Curling an arm around his neck, she shuddered under his touch. His hands—damn it, those hands of his. As he stroked a finger in, then out, her heart skittered a beat, proving already that she wasn't too tired.

His lips skimmed across her cheek and he teased, "Too tired, Nia?"

"Apparently you bring out the worst in me." She whimpered as he used his thumb to tease her clit.

"The worst . . . hell, if this is your worst, don't show your best. It will kill me." He pressed a hot, opened-mouth kiss to the side of her neck before lifting his head and staring down at her.

The look on his face made her heart ache. Something tender, hot, and wild . . . a little bit possessive and protective, too; all of it, it added up to something that made her ache in a way she'd never ached before.

"You're driving me crazy, Law." Lifting a hand to his cheek, she tugged him close, pressed her mouth to his.

"I plan on doing it for the rest of the night . . . be warned."

She sighed, even her body clenched, just thinking about an entire night of this sort of torment. "Not exactly the kind of crazy I was talking about, baby."

"No?" He peered into her eyes, brushed the back of his hand down her cheek. "What kind of crazy we talking about?"

She just shook her head. She wasn't ready to discuss the emotional upheaval she felt when she looked at him sometimes. Not yet. Pushing against his shoulders, she said, "Roll over. I think if we're playing a game of *chase the nightmares away*, I get to take a turn on top."

"Oh, please." He gave her a wicked smile. "Be on top. Be the top whenever you want."

He caught her around the waist and rolled, pulling her atop him, settling with her astride his lap, his denim-clad legs rubbing against her naked thighs. "Okay, Nia . . . you're on top . . . now what?" he asked, his hands stroking up and down her waist.

With a look of mock submission on his face, he laid there, staring up at her.

She stared down at him, her hands resting on his shoulders. Smiling, she caught his hands and lifted them, stretching them up overhead. "Somehow, I don't see you getting into the submissive mindset."

"Depends on who's in charge." He arched his hips against hers, his lids drooping down to half-mast. "If you promise to walk around in black leather, I just might be all over the idea of playing at the submissive. Can I buy you some black leather, Nia?"

She chuckled. "No. I'm not much for the *Mother May I* thing, sugar."

"Oh, trust me. I'm not thinking of my mother."

Laughing, she rubbed her mouth lightly over his. "Okay . . . not much for the *mistress* bit, either." Stretching out over him, she curled one arm around his neck and whispered, "Still, I don't mind taking charge. Open your mouth for me, Law . . . I want to kiss you. I want to make you as mindless as you make me."

*You already do,* he thought, his thoughts buzzing.

As her tongue rubbed against his, her hands stroked down his sides, light gentle touches—butterfly touches—that shouldn't have been able to drive him that insane. But each one, the brush of a fingertip across his nipple, the scrape of her nails over his belly, had his heart racing harder, his breath all but burning in his lungs.

When she reached the button of his jeans, his hips jerked and he squeezed his eyes closed, hoped he wouldn't make a fool of himself and lose it the second she touched him. He hadn't done anything like that in ages, not since high school, but Nia shattered his control like nothing else.

Nia shattered *him.*

She sat up, shifting her weight off to the side and although he hated not having her that close, when she moved away, it wasn't a bad thing—he thought. He could cool down, have a few seconds to compose himself . . . but then she shifted lower. Not just reaching for the button of his jeans, either.

Oh, she did that—freeing the button, lowering the zipper, and then, oh sweet hell—Law's eyes crossed as she bent over and took the head of his cock in her mouth, sucking him deep. She wasn't at all hesitant with it, either. She took him in one fast, hard motion until she'd taken as much of him as she could and then she pulled up, did it again, and again . . . Law swore and reached down, fisting a hand in her hair, tugging on her.

"Damn it," he swore. "Stop it."

She lifted her head just long enough to send him that smug smile. "No."

Then she went back to it, taking him hard and deep, her mouth a sweet, sweet torture. He twisted a hand in the sheets below him. "Fuck, Nia, I'm going to . . . would you stop?"

"No. And I want you to," she muttered. Then she wrapped one hand around the base of his cock and started to pump in time with her mouth.

Law's entire body stiffened. Reaching down, he buried his hands in her hair—torn between pulling her away and just enjoying . . . hell. He was only human. As she licked and sucked on his aching flesh, he started to rock against her, swearing and muttering under his breath, barely even aware of what he was saying.

She groaned around him and he felt the vibration of it clear down to his toes. When she scraped her nails over his balls, he lost it. Holding her head, he arched up, pumping into her mouth, once, twice. Then, abruptly, he froze, tried to pull her away. She leaned into him, her golden eyes flashing. Daring him. Slowly, she took him, sucking, licking . . . teasing.

"Nia . . ."

She did it again, and again.

Any bit of control he might have had died at the challenging look she shot him. Cupping her head in his hands, staring down at her face, he pumped up, meeting each downward stroke of her head with an upward stroke of his hips. She pumped him with her hand, squeezing him lightly, rotating her wrist just a bit before starting back up. His breath caught, hitched in his lungs.

Oh . . . holy . . . *fuck* . . .

With a harsh groan, he came, his hands clenching and unclenching in her hair.

Nia continued to move her head up, down, working him through it, teasing the slit in the head of his cock with her tongue. When she finally stopped and lifted her head to smile at him, he had about as much energy as a newborn kitten, his heart raced so hard he could barely breathe, and what he wanted, more than anything, was to pull her against him.

But he could barely move his damn arms.

Hoarsely, he muttered, "Come here."

She grinned and curled up next to him, stroking a hand over his belly. "Now is where I get to tell you that you can't be tired . . . I'm not done with you yet."

"Damn it." He sucked in a desperate breath of air, closed his eyes. "I sure as hell hope you're not done with me. I don't think I'll ever be done with you."

The hand on his belly stilled.

The second the words escaped his mouth, he wished he had been a little more aware, but it was too late now. Heaving out a breath, he stroked a hand down her back and cracked open one eye, hazarded a look at her face. "Don't go panicking, Nia," he muttered.

The look on her face, though, wasn't one of panic.

She was staring at him with a wondering, almost hopeful look on her face.

"Not done with me, huh?" she whispered, reaching up to touch his mouth. "What do you mean by that, Reilly?"

He caught her hand in his, lifted it to his mouth. "Just that you're in my head an awful lot, gorgeous. All the time. Not anything you need to go freaking out about, but . . ."

She sat up, curled down around him, pressing her lips to his. "I like hearing that I'm in your head a lot, baby. Because God knows I can't stop thinking about you, either. Even when I've got every reason to be thinking about other things . . ."

Her mouth tightened and her eyes went dark and sad.

Sitting up, he shifted in the bed, pulled her across his lap. "Not tonight, Nia. We're not thinking about anything tonight but us."

"Just us." She reached between them, curled her hand around his semi-erect cock, started to stroke. "Am I still on top? That where you want me?"

He saw her trying to find the lighthearted moment they'd briefly had, but just then, he needed her, just her. "You're where I need you to be already . . . right here with me." Her hand stroked up, down, and just like that, he was ready. He pulled her closer, then groaned, swearing. "Fuck, I need to get a rubber."

"No." She shifted closer, rubbed against him so that he felt the slick, wet folds of her naked pussy.

He tightened his fingers around her hips and swore. "Nia . . . ?"

"We don't need it, not unless you want it." Staring at him through her lashes, she said, "I haven't been with a guy without one in . . . hell, five years. The last time I was with a guy before this was almost a year ago. I'm on the pill, and I'm clean. I got tested a few months ago for a health insurance thing. So unless you want it . . ."

"Fuck." His eyes closed and he pulled her closer, taunted himself with the slick, wet feel of her. "Haven't been with anybody in a few years, and nobody without a rubber."

Trailing his fingers down her spine, along the curve of her rump, he stared into her eyes. "This is either a really fucking stupid thing or a really fucking big step . . . which is it, Nia?"

She pushed herself up onto her knees and reached between them.

"Up until you, I didn't even get close to touching the line of this, you know. It could be borderline stupid, Law." She squeezed him lightly and said, "Maybe it's stupid, maybe it's a big step . . . maybe it's both. You okay with that?"

"Fuck, yes." He gripped her hips and shifted his gaze downward, watching.

Holding his cock in one hand, she slowly sank down onto him.

Law, his entire body shuddering, watched as their bodies merged . . . became one.

*One* . . . complete. Whole.

"Damn . . ." Nia muttered, staring at him from under her lashes as she took him completely inside. She arched her back, the movement lifting her breasts.

Law swore, reaching up and curling a hand around her neck. "Come here." He pulled her close, pressing his brow against hers and rolling his hips upward. Slick and tight, so damn good. "Damn it, you feel good."

She hummed low in her throat, that smug, female smile on her lips. The one that drove him insane. "You feel pretty nice yourself."

He rocked against her again. She clenched around him and he shuddered, stroking a hand down her back to grip one hip. "Be still," he growled as she started to ride him.

"No."

"Damn it, Nia, be *still*," he growled. Already he could feel it building inside him, even though he'd just climaxed. Skin to skin—damn it, it felt like heaven, like nirvana.

Nia laughed and continued that slow, lazy stroking. "I don't wanna be still. Didn't I tell you I was going to drive you nuts?"

"You've already done it."

She did a little twist with her hips, used her internal muscles to milk him and Law damn near lost it then. With a snarled curse, he twisted and put her under him, catching her wrists in his hands, stretching them over her head.

"What happened to me being on top?" she asked, her eyes glinting.

"You had your turn. Now it's mine." He dipped his head, bit her lip, and then shifted. Letting go of her wrists, he settled on his knees, gripping her hips. He stared down at her, watching as she stroked a hand up her torso, teased one nipple. "Witch. You're a witch."

"Hmmm." She smiled at him, her lashes shielding her eyes.

He rocked against her, moving slow and easy, trying to ignore the vicious, driving hunger—the need that all but screamed in his head, in his blood. He used his thumb to stroke her clit, watching as her lashes flickered, as her breath caught.

She tightened around him and a flush settled on her cheeks. "Law."

She closed one hand around his wrist, twisted her hips, tried to move faster.

"My turn, remember?"

She shifted, moved around, a smile curling her lips. "How about our turn?"

As she sat up, sitting astride his hips, he gripped her ass. "Our turn. We drive each other crazy."

"Sounds like that's how it's been from day one, hasn't

it?" She draped her arms around his neck and started to ride him, as he arched into her.

Her cries grew ragged and his hands gripped her tighter, leaving faint red marks. The need inside him raged out of control, the need screaming louder. The need to take, to keep, to protect, to mark—

He'd had a need to be gentle, had wanted this to be slow and lazy, as though something sweet and easy could take away the misery of the day. It wasn't quite the sweet and tender seduction he'd hoped for, but as the climax rushed up on them, claiming them both hard and demanding, as she rested her forehead to his, their gazes locked, her mouth seeking out his . . . everything else fell away.

In those moments, nothing else existed but each other.

# CHAPTER
# SEVENTEEN

"Man, I really don't want to talk to Roz," Nia muttered as she climbed out of Law's car.

He came around and joined her by the hood, rubbing her back. "Why?"

Shooting him a sidelong scowl, she asked, "Have you forgotten the mess that was made of my cabin?"

He jerked a shoulder in a shrug. "Hell, that wasn't your fault."

"Doesn't matter if it's my fault or not." She sighed. "I still feel responsible."

He eased his hand up her neck, massaging the tense muscles there. "But you're not. Roz isn't going to blame you because some psychotic bastard went postal in your cabin, beautiful."

She frowned, shook her head. "If you say so. Seems to me that lady is sometimes a little high-strung."

Law grimaced. "Well, she can be that. But she's not stupid, either. She knows you can't control other people."

Nia knew that. But she still wasn't looking forward to this. She wasn't going to try to get her money back on the cabin—she'd signed an agreement, she'd honor it. Roz could keep the money, but there was no way Nia was going to stay at the cabin. Law was more than willing to let her stay with him and she felt safer there anyway. Plus, the sleeping arrangements were *far* more appealing.

Glancing back, she grinned as she saw the county car back there, one of the deputies climbing out. "So is he going to be telling everybody that I'm shacking up with you?"

"Nah. Ethan won't." Law shot him a look over his shoulder and then slid Nia a smirk. "But you should probably know that Roz more than likely will. It will be all over town by the end of the day. That what you want?"

Nia shrugged. "I couldn't care less." She caught his hand in hers. "What about you? Is it going to cause problems for you?"

He snorted. "Hell, no. Half the town thinks I'm either a drug dealer or that I run some sort of white slavery ring—or something along those lines. Other rumors include that I'm the bastard son of some rich mogul in New York and that's why I don't have to work and mingle with the common folk."

"You've managed to keep them from finding out what you do for this long? How?"

He shrugged. "I just don't tell them. My agent cashes my check and it gets deposited into a national bank, so it's not like I need to use their banking services. They can't figure it out that way. And small-town gossips have a lot more fun cooking up ridiculous stories like me dealing drugs than something as mundane as me being a writer."

"There's nothing mundane about being a writer." Nia shook her head as they mounted the steps.

Law laughed. "Oh, yeah? Ask a writer. It's a job, Nia. It's got high points, low points, like any other job. I still work my ass off—there's nothing glamorous or exciting about it. People think otherwise, but at the end of the day, it's still a job." He opened the door for her and stepped aside so she could enter.

She stroked a hand across his belly. "I think it's a sexy job—you gotta have brains to do it, right? Brains are sexy."

"I don't know. I've met a few idiots," he muttered. Then he caught her hand and squeezed. "Shush now."

She caught sight of the sitting room and some of the guests there. Smirking, she reached up with her free hand and zipped her lips. "I guess this serves as appropriate blackmail material, doesn't it?" she teased in a low voice.

"Shit, not you, too." He groaned under his breath, leading her down a long hallway.

Nia glanced around, curious, before shooting him a look. "Not me, too, what?"

"Hell, Lena's favorite threat is that she'll blab all over town."

"Why's that such a problem?"

"Because if I wanted everybody *knowing* what I do, I wouldn't use a pen name," he muttered. He tugged open a door marked *Private,* ducking inside without a qualm.

Nia arched a brow. "Well, I guess I don't need to ask if you're familiar with the place, do I?"

"Nope." It was another hallway, but he stopped at the first door—clearly an office.

And there was Roz, sitting down at a desk, talking on the phone. She smiled at them and gestured to the couch, holding up a finger—*one minute,* she seemed to be saying.

"Look, I don't care if you have to send it out on a sleigh pulled by eight tiny reindeer, you promised you'd have me my delivery by two, and I expect it to be here," Roz said, her voice cool and breezy.

She rolled her eyes, paused.

Nia leaned over and murmured, "Should we come back?"

"No." Law sat down, tugged Nia down to sit with him. "She's always either juggling calls, brides, or her husband . . . something. Roz doesn't do boredom well. If she only thinks she'll be a minute, that's all she'll need."

Then he pressed a kiss to her temple. "You'll feel better when this is over, anyway."

"Hmmm."

Something silvery flashed in the corner of her eye and she glanced back at Roz, watched as the woman slid something from one hand to another.

A bracelet.

A fist reached up.

Grabbed her around the throat.

Law felt Nia tense next to him, although he wasn't sure why. He reached up, rested a hand on her neck, rubbed the tense muscles there, not that it did any good.

She was still sitting there. Tense and stiff, getting more so by the second.

Staring at Roz as though she'd never seen her before.

Leaning over, he murmured, "Are you okay?"

She shot him a glassy-eyed look. "I . . . um . . ."

"Okay, then . . ."

Roz hung up the phone and Law looked at the other woman. "How are you two doing?" She flashed them a wide smile and winked. "Don't tell me you're here to set up a wedding."

"No. Nia needed . . ."

Nia shot up off the couch. "Is there a bathroom?"

Her voice, thin and strained, clued him in that something was wrong. Very wrong.

Her pupils were mere pinpricks, all but lost in the dark gold of her eyes.

Standing up, he caught her hand. "Nia, what's wrong, baby?"

"Just need the bathroom," she said, her voice a faint whisper. She stared at him, but Law could have sworn she was seeing *through* him.

"Use mine," Roz said, giving her a gentle smile. "It's just through that door."

Nia pulled away and headed toward the bathroom, her normally graceful moves awkward and jerky.

*What the . . .*

Roz arched a brow as the door swung shut behind her. "Everything okay?" she asked. She dumped something on her desk and pushed up, moving out from behind her desk to the small wet bar. Law liked to tease her about it, but he'd seen—from a distance—a few of the brides she'd worked with. More than a few of them probably were easier to handle if they had a glass of wine on occasion, not that many of them got into Roz's private office. She probably had the liquor back here just so *she* could handle some of her bride-zillas.

"I don't know. Hey, you got whiskey, right?"

Roz lifted a brow. "A little early for you to drink, isn't it?"

He scowled. "Me, but not you? And it's not for me. Give me a whiskey and Coke—I think she might need it." For whatever reason.

"Hmm. You might be right. She looks like something freaked her out real fast." She mixed up a whiskey and Coke and then grinned as she handed it over. "Maybe she doesn't realize I do weddings and she thought you were here for one."

Law snorted. "She doesn't spook that easy." Still, keeping it casual, he skimmed a look around the room. "Can't be anything in here. Even I'm not going to go ghost-white at the sight of a wedding dress, Roz."

He didn't see anything. At least, he didn't think he did.

Roz's office looked like it always did—a state of organized chaos. Glancing around the room, he frowned.

Something wasn't right.

The bracelet—

Bent over the sink, Nia sucked in a desperate breath of air.

Hell. It wasn't like the bracelet she'd seen in the pictures had been *unique*. Just the inscription engraved on the inside. And even that wasn't exactly a one-of-a-kind twist of phrase, right? She hadn't even seen it *close*.

But her hands were sweating.

Her gut was roiling.

Adrenaline crashed through her so hard and fast and she could hear the blood roaring in her ears.

The bracelet. Damn it. She had to see that damn bracelet. Had it belonged to Kathleen Hughes . . . the girl who died in Chicago? Was it the bracelet the killer had taken from her body? Why did Roz have it . . . ?

Nia's hands clenched on the counter.

Roz was married.

A man's face flashed through her mind.

The name eluded her.

But his face didn't.

Friendly eyes, Nia thought. He had friendly eyes.

Ezra watched as Lena hung up the phone.

The tension in her shoulders told him she wasn't pleased about this.

He didn't give a shit if she was pleased or not. He would be spending a good, long while dealing with his crime scene and he couldn't leave her alone either.

She had just about gone through the roof when he told her he didn't want her alone for the next week or so. He'd been being conservative, although he didn't plan on letting her know that.

Yeah, as nervous as he was about things, he knew she valued her independence.

So he'd played hard on the guilt factors and her desire for privacy—he could either spend so much time worrying over her, or he could put a deputy in the house, or she could spend today, at least, at the Inn with Roz, whether she was working or not. Reilly had been the initial suggestion but Law wasn't answering the phone—Lena had gone with Roz out of default.

Ezra wasn't too happy with that suggestion, but the Inn was one big place that was rarely empty, especially in June. So it wasn't bad middle ground—Lena wasn't with him, wasn't with Reilly, but she wasn't alone, either.

As she turned to face him, she had a brittle smile on her face. "Are you happy now, Daddy? I've got my babysitter lined up."

"Yeah, I'm happy." Then, trying to lighten her mood a little, he reached and slid an arm around her waist. "But if you're going to call me Daddy, can you put on a short skirt or something?"

She snorted. "No. Pervert." But some of the tension seeped out of her. "I hate this, you know."

"I know. But it won't last forever." *Just until I find a killer . . . and it may take awhile . . .*

His gut said otherwise, though. This guy wasn't going to wait much longer to make a move. Most likely toward Nia. Ezra wasn't taking chances, not with his wife.

Turning his head, he pressed his lips to her brow. "Come on. Let's get you over to the Inn."


Focused on Nia, worrying about Nia, Law barely heard it when the phone rang.

The drink in his hand was sweating and he set it aside, shoved a hand through his hair.

"What . . . ?"

"Huh?" He glanced up, saw Roz on the phone. She was frowning, staring off in the distance. She glanced at him and shook her head. Then, abruptly, she left the office. He could hear the sound of her heels clicking down the hardwood floor.

As the sound grew more and more distant, he stood up and moved to the bathroom door. He almost knocked. Decided not to. He turned the handle, a little surprised when it opened for him.

Nia stood at the sink, head bent, eyes closed. She shook. From head to toe, she shook.

"Nia?"

She slid him a quick look and then, just as quickly, her gaze bounced away. "I . . ." She stopped, licked her lips. "Where's Roz?"

"Slipped out. Somebody called." He laid a hand on her shoulder. "You okay?"

She shook her head. "We need to go," she whispered, her voice thready and weak.

"Okay. We can talk to her about the cabin later."

Nia laughed. The harsh, hysterical sound of it made him hurt—it was like a dagger scraping over the exposed flesh of his heart. He wanted to ask her what was wrong, ask her what had scared her so badly in the past few minutes.

But now wasn't the time.

Here wasn't the place.

Stepping aside, he said, "After you."

She gave him a wobbly smile, shuffled out past him. Lingering by the desk, she shot it a look. He watched as her gaze fastened on something. But he couldn't tell what.

Her shoulders stiffened, her breathing hitched.

"Nia . . ."

She swallowed. "Can you go ask Roz when would be a good time for me to call?" she blurted out.

He narrowed his eyes.

The smile on her face took a decided turn for the pathetic and although he knew, he *knew* she was up to something, he nodded. Hell, he couldn't figure out what she was up to if he didn't let her do it, right?

He headed out of the office, keeping his steps light . . . and his gaze focused on a narrow ornamental mirror that hung over a table just outside Roz's office. Nia barely waited until he'd turned the corner before she reached out and pocketed something off Roz's desk.

If he wasn't mistaken, it was the silvery bracelet Roz had been fiddling with.

It was almost two hours later than normal when Ezra got into the office, but he didn't give a damn. He'd been here until almost midnight last night and he knew he'd be spending far too much time in this place for the foreseeable future, as well.

So when he caught Ms. Tuttle's dark look, he scowled at her. "Damn it, don't lay into me. Did you hear the hell I had to deal with yesterday?"

To his surprise, she gave him a faint smile. "Actually, I did. And that look wasn't for you." She sighed and looked away, shaking her head. "It's for all the vultures who've been in here, demanding to know what's going on . . . you wouldn't believe the questions I've had to deal with."

"Don't bet on it," he muttered.

He headed toward his office but paused, looked back at her. "It's probably going to get worse, once word gets out, Miz T. You up for it?"

"Please." She adjusted her glasses and gave him an arch look. "Don't be insulting, Sheriff. It doesn't become you."

He smiled at her and headed into the office, leaving the door open. She'd be in shortly with the messages he'd missed for the morning, along with any news that had turned up. It was only 9:30, but in small-town America, that was pretty damn late, he knew.

He should have been here before the crack of dawn, but he wasn't forsaking his wife's safety for the job, and getting here at dawn wasn't going to get him answers any sooner, he knew.

Weary, he slid into his chair and rubbed his eyes. Coffee. Damn it. Should have gotten coffee before he sat down.

Too late now. He was going to make some headway on the messages he knew would be waiting for him before he got the damn coffee. The coffee would be the reward.

He opened his eyes and sure enough, there were messages.

Reports. One preliminary report—his eyes narrowed on that one and he grabbed it, but before he could start reading, a shadow fell across his desk.

He looked up, expecting Ms. Tuttle.

He found Carter Jennings. Roz's husband—Lena's sort-of boss. Sort-of because he did own half of the Inn, although Roz had more of a hand in running things.

"Hi, Carter," he said, leaning back.

"Hey, Sheriff." He gave him a tired smile, leaned against the doorjamb. "You look worn out."

Ezra shrugged. "Late night."

"So I've heard." Carter's grin flashed wider now. "You've figured out the small-town grapevine, right? You know how many tongues are wagging right now?"

"Probably all of them," he said mildly. "Now ask me if I give a damn?"

Carter chuckled. "Oh, I don't need to. You don't give a damn. But I'm hoping you can tell me something, *anything* to set Roz's nerves at ease. She's stressing something awful."

"About Lena?" He shrugged. "Look, it's more to put my mind at ease than anything."

Carter looked down, sighed. "No. Not about Lena. Just about . . . well. Whatever's going on." He looked up, his blue eyes intent on Ezra's face. "So much weird shit going on around here lately. And after last night . . . well, she's just worried sick. She was after me to go talk to Hank, but I don't want to do that, ya know?"

"It's not like he can tell you anything," Ezra said, shaking his head. "Right now, there's nothing to tell. Just let me do my job. So I have something I can tell you."

Carter continued to stare at him. Then he sighed, and nodded. "Okay."

As he turned away, Ezra leaned back, scowling.

Not a damn thing out of either of them.

Carter wanted to hit something, smash something. Break something.

He couldn't indulge, though. No, all he could do was head out to his workshop, get some work done on his projects—he had some pots that needed to be glazed today and Roz was on his ass to get some new designs in for the summer.

He couldn't change anything about his behavior. Even as that thought circled through his mind, he laughed shortly. Not a damn thing. Not when he was surrounded by nosy cunts, cops who were too busy listening to nosy cunts, and bastards like Law.

Sweat trickled out from under the hairpiece he wore, to run down his neck to his spine. A cool breeze drifted across the square, one that would have felt sweet if he could have fully let himself enjoy it.

But he couldn't do that—couldn't relax his guard. Climbing into his car, he shot another look at Ezra's window. He jolted when he saw the sheriff standing there.

Watching him.

He waved. And absently, he wondered why the sheriff had mentioned Lena at all.

Carter hardly ever even thought about Lena . . .

Law waited until they pulled out of the driveway before he asked.

"So what did you take?"

Nia stiffened. Her face turned a dusky shade of pink. Her eyes, still too wide and too unfocused, went glassy. "Huh?"

"What did you take from Roz's desk?"

"I didn't take anything," she snapped, her voice just a little too harsh, a little too defensive. She had her arms crossed over her chest, and if she hunched in any farther on herself, she might just disappear inside the seat.

Sighing, Law said, "Bullshit. I saw you in the mirror hanging outside Roz's office."

"What . . . you . . . I . . ." She ran out of steam and snapped her mouth closed. Thunking her head back against the seat, she sighed. In a quiet, almost desolate voice, she murmured, "It's a bracelet."

"Okay." His gut went icy and his hands went slick with sweat, but he kept his tone cool. So she'd taken a bracelet. He almost wished he could tell himself this was some latent klepto streak she'd developed under stress. But he knew better. "You want to tell me the significance of the bracelet, beautiful?"

She licked her lips and shifted, reached inside her pocket.

When she pulled it out, sunlight shining in through the windshield hit the diamonds and made it gleam. Somehow, Law suspected that wasn't some JCPenney purchase. "Nice sparkly there," he said, keeping his tone light.

She didn't respond, just flipped it over and studied the underside of it.

"Pull over."

He shot her a glance. One look at her face had him arrowing the car for the side of the road and slamming on the brakes so hard, the car behind him laid on the horn. She barely got out the door before she started to puke.

*For my angel.*

*For my angel.*

*For my angel . . .*

The words seemed to shriek inside her mind, danced around like a horrendous, speed-induced hallucination. They had teeth, nipping and tearing at her flesh.

*For my angel . . .* And that tiny little flash of blue.

She moaned and leaned forward, retching.

A gentle hand came around, supported her brow. "Easy, Nia," Law murmured. "Just breathe. Whatever it is . . . we'll get through it. Just breathe."

She focused on his voice—on him. So much easier than thinking about the words that mocked her and taunted her.

That bracelet. Oh, *fuck*. She'd been sleeping yards away from the man who'd kidnapped, raped, and tortured her cousin—renting a *bed* from him . . .

Another spasm of nausea hit her, doubled her over.

It seemed like ages before it passed, before it ended.

Her face stung and burned, and tears soaked her flesh.

But when she went to straighten, the nausea, while it lingered, didn't pounce on her anew. Something hard and round was pushed into her hand. Looking down, she saw a bottle of water. Puzzled, she glanced at Law. He shrugged. "Maybe I should have been a Boy Scout. I keep water in the back."

She nodded and twisted the top off. It helped, rinsing her mouth. She didn't trust her belly enough to drink anything. Spitting it on the ground, she closed the bottle and then eased herself down to sit on the car's seat, her feet still outside.

"We need to go into town," she said quietly. "Talk to Ezra."

Looking down, she stared at the bracelet she still held clutched in her hand.

"Okay." He knelt next to her, touched one fingertip to the glimmering piece of jewelry. "Mind telling me what this has to do with anything?"

Sympathy glinted in his eyes as he looked up at her. "Was it Joely's?"

Nia shook her head. "No. I think it belonged to the woman he killed in Chicago a few months ago. Her name was Kathleen Hughes."

He tugged on it gently, staring at it. Then he looked at her. "Baby, this looks like it could have been bought at just about any decent jeweler's. It looks expensive, but . . ."

With a shaking hand, she reached over and turned it, exposing the inscription. And the little sapphire. "Yeah. It could have been bought at just about any decent jeweler's. But the odds of Roz having the exact same inscription, and the exact same stone set on the inside?" Her voice shook, both with fury and fear. "No."

"Shit."

# CHAPTER
# EIGHTEEN

HE COULDN'T CONCENTRATE.

Something was niggling him in the back of his mind and Ezra couldn't focus on his work to save his life.

Swearing, he threw his pen down and leaned back in the chair, blanking his mind. Once he did that, a face settled there. A man.

Familiar. But . . . not. Something off.

He'd seen him before—

He squeezed his eyes shut, tried to remember.

Courthouse.

At the courthouse when Nia had been going through records. Something about him had struck him as familiar. But not.

The eyes . . .

The answer hovered just *there*, just right outside his reach. He could *almost* feel it forming, almost feel the pieces settling into place. Almost. Not quite.

Voices intruded on his thoughts, Ms. Tuttle's firm, insistent tones, then a low, softer voice—although no less firm, no less insistent. Accompanied by another voice, one that made Ezra scowl as he kicked his feet off the desk.

Concentration shattered, he stood up as Law Reilly appeared in the doorway.

"You know, the point of having a cell phone is so people can call you," he drawled.

Law frowned, patted his pocket. "Shit. I guess I left it home. Sorry." Then he nudged Nia inside, shutting the door in Ms. Tuttle's surprised—and furious—face.

Oh, he was going to get it later, Ezra thought. Really get it—and he'd be sure to take it out on Law. When he had a chance.

Sighing, he rubbed a hand over his face. "Law, I don't have time for this. I'm exhausted, I've got too much work to do, and I have to get back out to the site today."

"This is more important," Law said, his voice flat.

"More important." Smirking, Ezra hooked his thumbs in his pockets. Absently, he shifted his weight to his right leg, taking the strain off his bad one. "Just what is more important than finding whatever clues we can that will lead us to finding a killer?"

Law rested his hands on Nia's shoulders. Then he looked up, focused on Ezra. "How about this . . . I think Nia knows who it is."

In that moment, a gorilla could have danced by Ezra's window in a pink tutu and he wouldn't have noticed. Narrowing his eyes, he stared at Nia. She had her eyes closed, and she was pale—almost ashen, her breaths coming in rapid, shallow pants. Alarming, that.

"Nia?"

She swallowed and looked up. Then she reached into her pocket and pulled something out—a plastic bag. She barely touched it, holding it only with the tips of her fingers, like she couldn't bear to touch it.

"You're going to find fingerprints on it," Law said. "Hers, mine . . . probably from other people. We found it at the Inn."

Nia opened her mouth to say something else, but Law's hand shot out, caught hers, squeezed. He shook his head.

Ezra narrowed his eyes. "What's up, Reilly?"

"Nothing you need to know about."

"Why don't I believe that?" he muttered, shooting Law a dark look as he came out from behind the desk. He took the bag and lifted it. The second he saw what was in it, his heart sank to his knees, and then leaped up to his throat.

The bracelet. Kathleen Hughes—

Shit. He'd done some investigating on the girl's death after Nia had shown him her report. Yeah, this fit the description. But still . . . hell, Carter bought Roz jewelry all the time.

"It's inscribed," Nia said, her voice reed-thin. "I didn't tell you that. But her boyfriend had it inscribed to her."

Ezra turned it over.

*For my angel.*

There was also a small blue sapphire set there.

"It was Kathleen's birthstone," Nia whispered.

Ezra looked at her, his hand tightening on the bracelet. "You said you found this at the Inn."

Nia nodded jerkily. She opened her mouth, but then closed it without saying anything.

Ezra didn't need her to say anything, though. Because just like that . . . those missing pieces Ezra had been searching for fell into place.

The man he'd seen in the courthouse—he hadn't been able to place him because he hadn't *looked* right.

Carter.

Carter *fucking* Jennings. He'd looked different, because he hadn't had any hair—bald.

What in the holy fuck . . .

"Son of a bitch, Lena's over at the Inn," Ezra snarled.

\* \* \*

He was running out of ashes, Carter mused. He'd known he would. Couldn't get the ashes when he didn't have his special ingredients. He'd been hoarding what he had, but he was now just about out. Roz did love the pieces with that glaze, but what could he do?

Sighing, he added some more copper oxide. It was going to be lovely when he was done. A deep, burnished red glaze he'd use on a few of the pieces he'd fired—one of them was an anniversary present for Roz.

The glaze had to be perfect. He had used the last of his ashes for it, so it would be perfect. The ashes had a way of giving the pots a special gleam . . . like they glowed with some inner spark. A soul.

After leaving the sheriff's department, he'd come here. He'd been tempted to amble around town and see if he could learn anything. In the end, though, he had needed the peace of his workshop, needed to focus on something other than problems. That was why everything had become a problem, he knew. He let himself get so close he could no longer see the big picture.

He should have kept his distance.

They'd found his place. Carter had to deal with that. He'd been careful, even in his own territory, not to leave any sign of himself. Body hair was no issue. He wore condoms and he wore gloves. They would find blood from his victims—blood never really did come out easily, but even that would be hard to trace. Bleach broke down DNA and he used it religiously.

No, they wouldn't likely find signs of him and they weren't likely to even connect his place, for certain, to any specific crimes, because there were no bodies. Save for Jolene Hollister, and of course, Mara and Katia—his infamous Chicago fuck-up.

But only Jolene could be traced back to Ash. All they

had there was suspicion. No hard evidence. *Nothing*, he told himself. *They have nothing.*

And he'd be careful not to give them anything, either. From here on out, his games would stop. Perhaps later, he'd find a new game. But for now, it was done.

This was for the best. It had been too close, the game he'd been playing and he had been doing too many stupid, foolish things, and neglecting his work, even his wife.

Roz deserved better than that. He'd make it up to her. The present. Perhaps another special piece of jewelry. A trip, even. He smiled as he finished mixing the glaze, studying it with a critical eye. Yes. This would work.

His mind calm, he shifted his focus to the other task at hand—cutting himself off from the other loves of his life. His hunts, his games. For a second, the rage tried to emerge, rage at Nia . . . coming here, screwing it all up—

Then he stopped, made himself breathe, made himself think.

"What's done is done, right?"

The ringing of his phone interrupted the passive, placid pace of his thoughts. Frowning, he made his way to the dusty thing—he'd turned his cell phone off. He never used it in here and Roz knew better than to call him while he was working.

Only in emergencies. She knew that.

"Hello?"

"Oh . . . you are there." She sounded surprised. She paused and he could hear her agitated breathing.

"Yes, I'm here. I've got a lot of work to get done, too. What's wrong, angel?" *Angel* . . . she was his angel. He'd seen that on the bracelet he'd given her, liked to call her that while she wore it.

"Carter, baby, I know you hate it when I call you while you're working, but . . ." Her voice broke. "My bracelet. That beautiful one you gave me after you got back from Chicago? It's missing."

He stiffened. Through stiff lips, he echoed, "Missing?"

"Yes. I . . . well, I had a call from Lena. Nia and Law were over, and I thought maybe they were wanting to talk about a wedding package or something—you can see they are gone over on each other. The clasp was giving me trouble again and I just left it on my desk when Lena called. She was upset and . . ." She was talking so fast her words were running into each other.

Carter swore and reached up, skimming his hand along his smooth scalp. He never wore his hairpiece in here. It got too hot and when he sweated in it, it made it that much more often he had to clean it. It was a pain in the ass to clean, too, something he had to see to himself, because he didn't want others knowing.

Only Roz knew about his hair loss—something that had crept up on him after college. He'd hated it at first, but over time, he realized it was better. Without hair, he was less likely to leave evidence, a blessing in disguise.

But right now, the feel of his naked scalp was just another irritation, one that would boil out of control. Why in the *fuck* did things keep going *wrong*?

The calm he'd found in his short time here was threatening to disappear, but he clung to it. Forcing himself to speak quietly and coolly, he said, "Roz, you need to slow down. What *happened*?"

"I . . . well, I feel awful saying this, but I think Nia might have stolen it."

His calm exploded in a blast of fury. And more than a little fear.

Son of a bitch.

That cunt knew about Katia.

\* \* \*

Lena King might not be able to see, but she didn't need eyes to sense the storm of emotion cutting through the air.

With one leg drawn up to her chest, she tried to track Roz's movements, but the woman was moving too damn fast.

"You going to tell me what has you so mad?"

"What? Oh, nothing. You know, if you want, since you're here, if you want to go bake something fattening and chocolatey, I wouldn't mind," Roz said. Her voice had the high, harsh note of somebody who was clinging to her temper by a thread.

"Hmmm. I bet. I don't think you need the caffeine, darling."

"No. I just need the chocolate."

Lena could tell that much, she mused. "You know what? I think you're probably right. Chocolate is exactly what you need." She swung her legs off the couch and stood up. "Come on, Puck. Let's go whip up something fattening and chocolatey."

Roz laughed. "Lena, it's not necessary."

"Of course it isn't." She smiled as she felt around for Puck's leash. "But I want to. Forward, Puck."

She didn't mention to Roz what a relief it would be to get out of that small office. Whatever had her so on edge was about ready to send Lena through the roof. Roz had slipped outside a few minutes earlier and when she came back, her mood had been just as erratic, just as harsh.

In the name of sanity and friendship, Lena figured chocolate was the best thing she could offer since Roz didn't want to talk about it.

Her phone rang as she pushed into the smaller family kitchen Roz and Carter used. She wasn't going to use the Inn's kitchen—the day staff would already be working on lunch and dinner. Lena didn't want to get in the way. Pulling her phone out, she said, "Hey, gorgeous. Yes, I'm behaving for the sitter."

"Have you talked to Carter?" Ezra demanded, his voice flat and hard.

"What? No—"

"Good. Don't mention his name, don't be anywhere that he might be able to be alone with you. You have Puck, right?"

An icy shiver raced down her spine. "Ezra—"

"Don't ask any questions," he said, softening his voice. "I don't want anybody hearing you ask them—not Roz, not Carter, not *anybody*. Trust me, okay? I need you to trust me and just do what I ask . . . no questions. Please?"

As terror settled like a cold, slimy ball in the pit of her stomach, Lena whispered, "Okay."

"I'm on my way. I'll be there soon," he said. Then the call disconnected.

Swallowing, she lowered her hand. Puck leaned against her leg and whined. She reached down and rested a hand on his head.

*Carter . . .*


"I don't know if I want to get married here," Hope said, climbing out of the car and staring at the Inn. Then she sighed. She didn't want to mess with handling the details all by herself, either.

Yeah, she had a few months, she knew. They weren't in any big rush, but she needed to at least figure out what she *wanted,* right? Because Remy didn't care. He wanted whatever would make her happy. Hope just didn't *know* what would make her happy.

Hitching her bag up onto her shoulder, she headed into the Inn. It wouldn't be too, too busy, she didn't think. Not if she got here before lunchtime, and not in the middle of a workweek. Plus, this was a good way to keep her mind off everything else.

Which was actually why she was here. She needed to keep her mind off everything else.

Inside the Inn, just behind the hostess desk, she saw a woman who looked vaguely familiar. Hope hid her wince as the woman beamed at her. "Well, hello, Hope . . . I bet you're here to talk wedding plans . . ."

"Ah . . . if Roz has a few minutes . . ." She gave the woman's discreet gold name tag a quick glance. "Tammy."

"Normally we do prefer appointments, but you're a friend of Roz's." Then she winked. "And family to me. I'm Remy's third cousin—one of many."

"Many, many," Hope said before she could stop herself. This time, she didn't hide her wince. "I'm sorry. I'm still trying to adjust to tripping over soon-to-be relatives every time I turn around."

"It's okay. I still don't know who all I'm related to and I've lived here all my life." Tammy smiled. With a wave of her hand, she gestured down the hall. "Go down there and go through the door marked private. There's a hallway and you want the first doorway on the right. That's Roz's office. She should be in there or in the kitchen."

Hope smiled her thanks and headed down the hall. As she did, she pulled out her phone. She was supposed to be over at Law's, working there, but she suspected Nia would be there and she wasn't up to feeling the vibes between those two, plus she'd promised Remy she wouldn't be anywhere alone for the next few days.

This commitment and compromise stuff was a headache. Tapping out a message to him to let him know where she was, she sent it off before slipping through the marked doorway.

Roz's office was empty.

Hope started to head back—the kitchen was on the other side of the house, but she heard a familiar voice, one that sounded a lot like Lena's. Rather weird, because Lena shouldn't be working today. Curious, she headed down the hallway.

She passed by a set of glass doors that opened out onto a private patio, one she hadn't seen before. Glancing outside, she saw Roz. Carter was with her, his head bent close to hers, nodding.

Roz leaned against him, her shoulders trembling, shaking.

Embarrassed, Hope looked away and headed down the hallway, following what had sounded like Lena's voice.

She came to a kitchen—a smaller, trendier version of the kitchen where Lena did all of her cooking. But Lena wasn't hard at work on anything. She was standing with her hips against an island, her eyes shaded by the lenses of her glasses and head downcast.

"Hey."

Lena jumped, startled. "What the . . ." She listed to the side and slammed a hand against the island to get her balance.

Puck growled, responding to Lena, liquid eyes focused on Hope's face, lip curled to show those very impressive teeth.

"Hey, it's just me—Hope." Her heart banged against her ribs.

Puck barked at her.

Nervously, Hope backed away a step.

"Down, Puck," Lena snapped, righting herself. "Fuck. Damn it, Hope. I'm sorry. I'm just a little freaked out right now and anytime I'm afraid, he does this." She licked her lips and then said, "Ah . . . are you alone right now?"

Automatically, Hope glanced around. "Yeah. Why wouldn't I be?"

"Don't ask." She laughed sourly and then sighed, rubbing the back of her neck. "Did Roz send you back here?"

"No. I was looking for her—thinking about asking her to help coordinate the wedding even if we don't get married here. But I heard you." She shrugged nervously, smoothing a hand down her jeans as she wandered into the kitchen. "I thought maybe you were in here talking to her, but I saw her outside on my way back here."

"I was talking to Puck," Lena said. She bent over, scratching the dog's head. "Did you say you saw Roz?"

"Yeah. Outside talking to her husband."

Lena's hand faltered. Then her fingers curled convulsively in the dog's silky fur. "Carter. You saw her talking to Carter," she said quietly.

"Yeah." Okay, something about Lena's tone had a cold chill running down Hope's spine.

Behind her, she heard a door shut . . . and voices.

Slowly, Lena straightened. "Hope," she said, keeping her voice low, all but soundless. "Come on. *Now.*"

A very large part of her was dying to know what in the hell was going on.

But Hope understood fear. She understood the survival instinct. Without saying a word, she headed for Lena as the voices behind them drew closer. They slipped out of the kitchen, with Lena easing the door shut so it didn't swing and betray their presence.

Seconds later, they heard Roz calling out, "Lena, you in there?"

Lena turned her face to Hope, one finger lifted and pressed against her lips.

They moved down the hallway, Hope wincing as she moved along next to Lena, her steps sounding unbelievably loud, at least to her own ears. After a few seconds, Lena said in a quiet voice, "We're going to the other kitchen. The day staff is in there. Just don't say anything—don't ask. Ezra's on his way."

*Ezra*—

Hope slid a hand into her pocket and tugged out her phone.

Up ahead, a door opened.

Puck stopped in his tracks, growling low in his throat.

Even before he moved out from behind the door, Hope knew who it was.

Carter Jennings stood there. Behind the lenses of his glasses, she couldn't see his eyes. That bothered her, a lot.

She could see his smile, though.

And the smile really freaked her out.

"Hello, ladies."

"Carter." Lena sounded calm and cool.

Hope wondered if Carter could tell that Lena was shaking—oh so slightly. Edging in a little closer, Hope stared at the other man.

Where was Roz?

Where was Ezra?

And what in the hell was going on?

Puck growled again, low and rough, deep in his chest. Lena gripped his leash tighter. "Easy, boy," she murmured. "Easy.

"He's antsy today," Lena said. "I guess a lot of us are."

"Yeah." He continued to stand there, just watching them.

Hope swallowed. There was something about that stare that just unnerved the hell out of her.

Lena—how did she manage it—gave him an easy smile. "Speaking of antsy, I was dragging Hope along to the big kitchen. I promised your wife some chocolate chip cookies, but I want coffee and my blend is in there. I'll probably spike it with some Kahlua, too, and your wife doesn't touch the stuff."

A faint smile curled Carter's lips. "No. No, she doesn't." He stepped aside, using his body to block a side door leading down a hall. "I'll come by and grab some cookies later, ladies."

"You do that. If you wait too long, you know Roz will eat them all." Lena murmured to Puck, and Hope, still glued to her side, followed her along. As she did, she kept her head down. From the corner of her eye, she tried to glance past him.

Was that Roz . . . ?

She heard Carter sigh.

Lena stiffened, walking faster.

"You know, don't you, Lena?" he asked.

"Know what, Carter?" She didn't wait for an answer, shoving through the door, one hand coming out to grab on to Hope's, all but dragging her through. She didn't let go, either. They passed the kitchen and still Lena kept moving, long, confident strides of her legs. "Door, Puck," she said.

"Lena, what in the hell is going on?" Hope demanded, shooting a look back over her shoulder, half-expecting to see Carter appear in the doorway.

"I don't know." Her voice was no longer so cool, and not at all controlled. It shook, but it wasn't just fear in Lena's voice. There was fury there. Tightly reined in, but fury, nonetheless. "But something's up. I heard it in his voice. Puck's pissed. And Ezra . . ."

She snapped her mouth shut. "Come on. You drove, right? We'll get in your car and go wait at the end of the drive."

\* \* \*

Carter stood in the front door, watching the two women climb into Hope's car. They acted like the devil was behind them, he mused. Especially Lena. Although there was a marked amount of caution in Hope's eyes. A smart girl, his pretty little mouse. She saw him standing there, but pretended otherwise, her eyes bouncing away without making contact.

*Nothing to see here, nothing to see* . . . he thought.

As the car backed away, he retreated into the house, his mind whirling.

They knew.

Just *what* they knew, he wasn't sure. But they knew something.

He didn't need to waste any time wondering how, either.

The bracelet. Nia Hollister. Damn that bitch. How had she connected it? How had she connected Katia, some tramp in Chicago, to her cousin's death? Rage had him shaking and he made himself pause, take a breath. He needed to think.

He had plans in place for this. He'd always had plans. He just needed to think everything through . . . once he put things in motion, there would be no going back.

Clearing his mind, he pushed through the staff door, heading down the hall to the private door. They separated the private parts of the house from the public areas they shared with guests. Just inside, Roz lay on the floor. Her face was slack and he sighed as he crouched down next to her. He touched her cheek and listened as she moaned softly. She'd wake up soon.

" 'Til death do us part," he said gently. Slipping his arms under her, he rose.

There was a lot of work to be done now. Two thorns he needed to remove before he finished things. Then he'd take care of things with Roz.

He'd give her something, make sure she'd stay quiet

while he took care of business. He didn't want her to worry, didn't want her scared. Kissing her brow, he slipped out of the house as quietly as he'd come. He had everything he needed stashed in his shop. He would have had to go back for that stuff anyway. Certain things needed to be destroyed.

As did certain people . . .

# CHAPTER
# NINETEEN

SEEING THE LITTLE GREEN SEDAN SITTING AT THE END of the Inn's drive had Law's eyes narrowing. "What in the hell is Hope doing here?" he muttered.

Ahead of him, Ezra slammed on his brakes. Law did the same thing, putting his car into park. He didn't bother asking Nia to wait—it would have been a waste of breath.

She was out the door as fast as he was and moving on long legs to catch up with him as he came up to stand by Hope's car. Ezra was already bent over, peering inside, something oddly relaxed about his posture.

A familiar canine head popped up from the back seat, dark, liquid eyes peering at Law. "Hey, Puck." He bent over and saw Lena sitting in the front passenger seat. Well, that would explain why Ezra wasn't already back in the car, tearing his way to the Inn. "Lena. Fancy meeting you here."

"Hi, Law." She had her head back against the seat, her shoulders tense and rigid. "Any time somebody wants to fill me and Hope in, we'd be just fine with that."

Ezra scowled. "Yeah, that would be nice, darlin'. But I'm afraid I've got to figure out how to get a warrant. I want you to go back home with Law and Nia. And *stay* there."

Law narrowed his eyes as he straightened, glaring at Ezra.

Ezra stared back. "What do you want me to do? Take you two with me? Just how hard do you want to make it for me to arrest him, huh? *Think*, Reilly." Then he shifted his gaze to Nia. "You came to me for a reason, Nia. I'm hoping it's because you trust me to do my job. Now get the hell out of here and let me do it."

A heavy, tense silence fell.

Then, to Law's surprise, Nia reached up and rested a hand on his shoulder. "He's right. We've done what we can. Besides, he can't just send them off by themselves. He needs to be *here* . . . and he can't be worrying about Lena and Hope. He needs somebody watching them. And hell, you'd be worrying about them, too."

"Shit." He covered her hand with his. "Why do you got to go and be all reasonable?"

She gave him a wan smile. "I'm taking a leap of faith." Then she looked at Ezra. "I hope I don't regret it."

The sheriff scowled and then pointed toward Law's car. "Go. Now. I've got too many calls to make, lawyers to fight with."

"You didn't tell him I saw it on Roz's desk because I'd stolen it," Nia said as they drove along behind Hope's car.

"Yeah. Illegally obtained evidence wouldn't help him get a warrant and he'll need one. Hell, even without illegally obtained evidence, he's got a fight on his hands."

"It's him," Nia said quietly. "I know it. In my gut, I know it. Nothing fit—that's why I had to come back, because nothing about what they said with Joely *fit*. This *fits*."

"I know you think it does," Law said, keeping his

voice neutral and wondering if she had a gun stashed on her somewhere. Shit. It wouldn't surprise him. She'd gotten one illegal, unregistered weapon—she could get another. It wasn't that damn hard, if somebody knew how to look. Obviously, she knew how to look. "Nia, you need to let him do his job. Your cousin wouldn't want you blowing the rest of your life for her—let him handle this."

Nia smiled sadly. "You think I'm going to go after him with guns blazing?"

His hands tightened on the steering wheel. "Are you?"

"I want to." Her voice was husky and soft, shaking. "But I'm terrified right now. When I saw that bracelet, I was so damn sick, I could barely see. All I could think was I'd been sleeping *that* close to him, paying him money . . . and I was terrified. I keep seeing those pictures you took and I'm terrified. If I see him, could I even pull the damn trigger or would I turn into a wailing, screaming mess?"

He reached over and caught her hand, squeezed it. Bringing it to his lips, he kissed it and murmured, "Ezra's a smart guy, and he's a good cop. Let him do his job, okay?"

"I'm *trying* to do my job," Ezra growled.

"You're trying to prove you're nuts." Beulah Simmons gaped at him. "That's what you're doing. Why in the hell should I give you a warrant based on a bracelet that may or may not belong to a woman who was killed in Chicago months ago? What possible connection could Carter Jennings have to some cotton-candy-looking Barbie doll from Chicago?"

Ezra swore and wished there was some way he could have gone to Remy. But there wasn't. Remy couldn't be involved in this, no way, no how. But Beulah was a hard-ass of the highest order. Normally, that was a good thing. But she didn't allow any wiggle room and she wasn't too impressed with the one piece of evidence he had.

Hell, even *he* knew it wasn't much.

Slamming the report down on her desk, he said, "*Look* at it, damn it. The bracelet matches the description to a T. If it wasn't for the inscription, I wouldn't think much of it, but it matches. The sapphire matches. And Carter Jennings *was* out of town that weekend. There was a big arts-and-crafts show in Chicago—he was down as one of the vendors—I checked their website. He attends every year."

"So?" She shoved up from her desk, not even topping five foot five in whatever skyscraper heels she had on today, but what she lacked in height, she made up for in attitude. "A *lot* of people were in Chicago. It's *Chicago*."

"You're not going to give me the damn warrant, are you?"

"Based on a bracelet? One a disturbed, distraught woman gave to you?"

"Nia Hollister is *not* a disturbed woman. Distraught, I'll give you that, but she's not disturbed." Ezra grabbed the evidence bag and the report. Shit, shit, *shit*. "Fine. I'll find more evidence—I'm getting a damned warrant, Beulah. I've had a weird feeling all along about the way the Carson case went down—it was too fucking easy. If something that screwed up looks too simple, then maybe there's a reason for it."

He stormed toward the door.

"Ezra. You need to calm down. You've got a good career here—"

He paused and looked back at her, furious. "The career can get fucked, Beulah. What good is my fucking badge if I can't protect people against a killer who's been in plain sight for God knows how long?"

"You're wrong," she said, shaking her head. "Carter isn't a killer. You're wrong."

"What if I'm *not*?" He jerked open the door.

As he stormed out of her office, Beulah sank back into her chair, shaken.

The conviction in his eyes, in his voice, worried her.

Beulah knew cops. She might be a small-town county DA, but she knew cops. She'd be willing to bet the Jimmy Choos she'd just bought online last night that Ezra was a good cop—a smart one. He didn't strike her as the type who'd go off blindly.

Pressing a hand to her belly, she closed her eyes and tried to think.

If he was wrong, it was going to cost him his job. Ash, Kentucky, wouldn't forgive an outsider coming down on one of their own—especially not somebody like Carter Jennings.

But if he was right . . .

"Shit, boy."

The way Ezra saw it, he had two choices—well, three, but one of them wasn't really a choice. That third one— the *not*-choice—involved going to talk to Remy. Remy Jennings—Carter's cousin, and the other county DA. A *not*-choice of the highest order, as far as he was concerned, because if Beulah hadn't believed him, then why would Remy?

So scratch *that* possibility.

Second possibility—get a few of his men out, asking some questions. Even if he just took one or two of the men he thought he could trust the most—hell, even just one, like Keith. Maybe they could get somebody who had seen *something*. Could a man really hide that long without showing anybody his true nature? It didn't seem that way.

But it would take too long. Ezra didn't know how much time they might have. His gut was screaming a warning—*hurry, hurry, hurry*—time was something he didn't really have, he suspected.

Not to mention that every minute that went by was another minute Carter would have to bury his trail. He'd done a damn good job hiding already.

Other choice—go out to the Inn. Maybe he could find Carter, see if the bastard would fuck up. Or maybe Roz would be wearing another piece of jewelry—shit. The fucking jewelry . . .

As he climbed into his car, he pulled out his phone. He needed to know more about the jewelry. Had she uncovered other women? Were there other pieces missing? Just how much digging had Nia done? Would it be enough?

Remy stood on the steps of the courthouse, his briefcase in one hand, the other in his pocket. Puzzled, he stared at Ezra's car, then glanced back over his shoulder.

He caught a glimpse of Beulah Simmons before she slipped into her office. If she hadn't shut the door, he might not have thought anything of it. But that wasn't like her.

Shutting the door. Not to mention that she hadn't so much as waved to him.

Just like it wasn't like Ezra to not hear him calling.

Weird shit abounds . . . and Remy had been around too long to think the weird shit wasn't connected.

He debated for about two seconds—did he go talk to Beulah? Or see if he could get Ezra to talk? Ezra, honestly, was his best choice, he suspected. Beulah wasn't likely to open her mouth for anything short of a shoe-shopping spree and Remy had a wedding to pay for, a honeymoon . . . and a house he was thinking about showing to Hope.

Ezra, it was.

Of course, Ezra was pulling out of his spot by the time he reached the sidewalk.

Swearing, Remy headed for his car. He wasn't entirely sure what he was doing now. He didn't have anything else going on today—he'd expected to be in court this afternoon, but thanks to an unexpected offer from the court-appointed attorney, that wasn't going to happen. He could get some lunch, could call Hope. And he needed to do that, soon. She was supposed to be out at Law's and he wanted to make sure she was.

But he could make that call while he was trailing Ezra.

Trailing a cop—hell, could he do that without being seen?

Not likely. But he was doing it anyway.

He couldn't quite understand what instinct pushed him to do it, either.

Hope checked her phone. No calls. No messages from Remy. Sighing, she slipped it back into her pocket and got up from the kitchen table.

It was already almost two and Lena was working on a late lunch, not that any of them were really hungry. It was more to give the other woman something to do than anything, Hope suspected.

She could sympathize. She desperately wished she had some of her work from Law's. But she wasn't about to suggest one of them make a trip over there.

"You know, a lot of my books are audio," Lena said over her shoulder. "You're welcome to pick one out."

Hope winced. "Am I being that obvious?"

"No more than the rest of us," Lena said, shrugging. She slid a pan into the oven and closed it before stripping off the gloves she wore. "I can just hear you pacing and I know I'd be bored stiff if I was over at Law's place with nothing to do for hours on end."

Hope scowled. "I just hate not knowing what's going on."

"Me, too." Lena started her way, one hand outstretched.

Hope caught it and when the taller woman wrapped an arm around her, Hope sighed and leaned into her hug. "Life was supposed to get easier, right? Now that Joe's gone. Everything was supposed to be smooth sailing."

Lena chuckled. "I guess we forgot to inform *life* of that fact." She squeezed Hope gently and then eased back. "Life is just life, Hope. We get through this and things will be fine. You'll see."

"Don't see how things couldn't *not* get better, that's for sure," she muttered. Sighing, she pushed a hand through her hair and moved to stand by the door. The buzzing of the phone in her pocket had her jumping, muffling a shriek. "Damn it, I'm so on edge."

"We all are," Lena said, her voice wry. "I'll leave you to talk with your sweetheart. But . . . ah . . . maybe you shouldn't say anything about this. Not yet. He's pretty close to Carter."

Hope frowned and glanced at the readout. Yeah, sure enough it was Remy.

*Don't say anything . . . ? But what do we talk about? "Hi, honey, how was your day? I went by the Inn and had to leave, but I can't tell you why . . ."*

Normally, talking to Hope soothed him. Even as it turned him on.

But as he disconnected, Remy was anything but soothed.

She wasn't at Law's. She was at Lena's. With Law, Lena, and Nia. She'd been at the Inn earlier. That wouldn't bother him so much, except that was where Remy was sitting now. He'd seen Ezra turn in, but instead of taking the main entrance, Remy had driven on past and taken the second, more concealed employee entrance, parking in the back. He could see Ezra's car, see the sheriff climbing out, see the grim look on his friend's face.

*What in the hell . . .*

Remy would like to dismiss it. He wanted to. There was no evidence of anything weird, and if Ezra was here on serious official business, he'd have a couple of deputies with him. But he was here alone. That had to mean something.

But the sinking, crawling sensation wasn't *letting* him dismiss it.

That same sinking sensation had him climbing out of the car and moving toward the house.

He'd head off Ezra, find out what was wrong.

If that didn't work, he'd find Roz or Carter.

Because something was up.

He knew it.

Then Ezra shifted his head and looked at him, dead on.

The sinking sensation, that icy-cold feeling of dread hit, spreading through him like an insidious wave. Slowly, he started across the grounds, not bothering with the paths that Roz had carefully laid out—she worked damned hard on the grounds, but Remy didn't care. Tension had his muscles strung so tight, he felt he might shatter.

As he drew even with the sheriff, the look in Ezra's eyes had him wishing he'd just headed home. Or gone back to his office, dealt with paperwork. Done *anything* but followed Ezra.

"Any reason you decided to start tailing me, Jennings?" Ezra asked, his voice flat and hard.

"Yeah. I'm still trying to figure out what it is." He looked at the Inn. It was a beautiful place. Warm, inviting, cheerful.

But in that moment, it seemed . . . cold. Harsh.

"What are you doing here, Ezra?"

"Nothing you want to know about." He sighed and shook his head. "Go back into town, okay?"

"No." Remy folded his arms over his chest. "What's going on?"

Swearing under his breath, Ezra turned away. Then he looked back at Remy, his green eyes hard, sharp as broken glass. "You asking in an official capacity or what?"

"I'm asking because the look on your face means trouble. And you're standing in front of the house one of my cousins owns. What's up, did Roz forget to pay her damn parking tickets again?" he asked sarcastically.

"I don't think I'd get too bent out of shape over parking tickets." Ezra dipped a hand into his pocket and tugged something out.

Remy heard the soft crinkle of plastic and he looked down, but whatever Ezra held, he was keeping it hidden. "I'm asking again, Remy. Why are you here? This any sort of official thing?"

"Shit." Remy reached up and jerked at his tie, loosening it. It felt like it was choking him. "No, I'm not here *officially*. I've got family here—makes me anything but impartial. Aside from that, I don't even know why *you* are here, so how can I be here *officially*?"

Ezra stared down, like he was thinking something over. Then he nodded and turned back to his car, reaching inside. He pulled out a folder, flipped through it. When he straightened, he turned around and handed Remy a report.

Remy recognized the police report, found himself staring at a girl with a pretty face, hidden under too much makeup, a smile that hadn't quite hidden the misery in her eyes.

The next picture was so god-awful, he'd see it in his

nightmares. He set his jaw and skimmed the report, then gave Ezra a look. "Why am I looking at this?"

"You see the part about the bracelet the roommate claims was missing?"

Remy smirked. "I say there are good odds the room-mate took the bracelet. A diamond bracelet, Ezra?" He glanced up and that was when he saw what Ezra had been hiding.

A diamond bracelet. The evidence bag couldn't quite hide the way the diamonds sparkled under the sunshine. The sight of it sent a chill down Remy's spine. Still, they ran a damned Inn—people from all over came through the place. And just how unique was a diamond bracelet?

Shaking his head, he said, "Sorry. You'd have to do a better job than—"

Ezra dumped the evidence on top of the report. Remy had to juggle to keep it from sliding off. "Look at the underside of it. You can see it without taking it out of the bag."

"Shit." Flipping the bag, he peered at the underside—saw a flash of blue. And an inscription. "It's inscribed."

"Yeah. That makes it a hell of a lot more unique."

"Okay. Still, Roz runs a damned bed-and-breakfast. People come here from everywhere."

Ezra sighed. "I know. And I also know that your cousin was in Chicago the weekend that girl died. Now you go find someplace to stick your head in the sand. I told you that you didn't want to be here." He grabbed the bracelet and shoved it in his pocket, pulled the re-port from Remy's slack hands and tossed it into the car.

Remy barely noticed. Blood roared in his ears.

His cousin—

Carter.

Fuck—

It took him a full sixty seconds to get his legs moving and by the time he *could* move, he had to run to catch up with Ezra. He made it just before the sheriff opened the front door.

"I'm going with you—to prove you wrong," he snapped.

"If you do prove me wrong, I'll be damn fine with that." Ezra glanced around, looking for the hostess. But Tammy wasn't at her normal spot. "I don't want to be right about this. Trust me."

Remy muttered, "Trust you? Not damn likely." He started down the hallway.

"Where are you going?"

"To see if Carter is here or at his workshop—if I don't see him, I'll look for Roz. She'll know where he is." Remy headed down the hallway, tuning out the noise he heard coming from the kitchen. It was louder than normal, but he couldn't care less. He just wanted to find Carter or Roz.

But three minutes later, he was standing in the doorway of her empty office, Ezra at his back.

Remy scowled and headed toward the back of the house, taking the longer way around. He looked out the windows, but he didn't see her in the garden or on the private patio there, either. Just before the hallway split again, there was a door—it opened to yet another hallway, one that would lead to the private upstairs bedrooms, Carter's library. It also circled back to Roz's office.

As the door swung shut behind him, Remy called upstairs. "Roz, Carter?"

There was no answer. Swearing, he turned around. "Guess we need to check the kitchen."

But Ezra wasn't listening to him.

He was crouched on the floor just a few feet past the stairs, staring at something on the smooth, dark wood.

Something that gleamed even darker than the wood. Something that made Remy's gut clench.

"What is that?"

Ezra slanted an unreadable look in his direction. "It looks like blood."

The fist-sized circle was already drying, starting to go tacky.

"Doesn't mean anything," he said, shaking his head.

Ezra cocked a brow. "Blood? Doesn't mean anything?"

"Hell, this is a restaurant. One of the staff could have cut themselves." He swallowed and told himself that was a perfectly logical explanation. Perfectly. And it *was*.

*One of the kitchen staff cut a hand—came to look for Roz. She took them to the emergency room,* Remy told himself. He passed a hand over the back of his mouth. Tried to buy more completely into that idea. It wasn't completely whacked, right?

"Denial is a river in Egypt," he muttered as he stood at the door and waited for Ezra.

"Huh?"

He shook his head. "Nothing. Just talking to myself. Now what?"

"Can you call Roz?"

Remy nodded. He shot that hideous red another look as he reached for his phone. He squeezed it tight, the casing biting into his fingers. "I want to make sure she's not in the kitchen. Hell, one of the staff really could have cut themselves, you know. Maybe she's running them to the hospital and—what?"

Ezra just shook his head. "You go check the kitchen and then call Roz. If it will make you feel better to look at the hospital, go ahead."

Something that might have been pity flashed in the other man's eyes—it fucking pissed Remy off. Glaring at him, he turned around and shoved through the door.

Before he headed to the kitchen, he shot Ezra a dark look.

"Fuck, no, I'm not going to the hospital. I'm going with you, wherever you're going. You're so fucking certain Carter did something—fine. You think that. Seems to me I should stay with you to make sure you don't go planting evidence."

The second the words left his mouth, he regretted it. But damn it if he could take them back.

A muscle twitched in Ezra's jaw. "If that's how you want to play it, Jennings, so be it. Hurry it up, though."

His gut was already tied into knots, fear burning a metallic trail down his throat. Now he had guilt on top of that. Wasn't this just fucking perfect?

"Fuck." He headed for the kitchen. With every step, he said a silent prayer.

*Let Roz be in there. Let Carter be in there. They're both in there, and everything will be fine . . .*

# TWENTY

EZRA WAITED JUST OUTSIDE THE KITCHEN FOR REMY. Tammy, the hostess, almost crashed into him on her way out. Frazzled and flushed, she gave him a strained smile. "Sorry, Sheriff. We're a little crazy around here today."

"Everything okay?"

She shrugged. "Yes—well, no. I can't find Roz. She always takes shipments and we had a shipment, but she couldn't take delivery, so I had to do it, and then one of the kitchen guys got sick and had to leave . . . hell, it almost feels like Monday."

"Where did Roz take off to?"

"That's it, I don't know." Tammy lifted her hands helplessly and shrugged. "We don't *know*. She didn't tell anybody anything. She was just . . . *gone*. Nobody's seen her since this morning. She talked to Nia and Law, and that's it. Nobody has seen her since." She shifted from one foot to the other, chewing on her lower lip. "It's not like her . . . I'm getting worried, too. She's not even answering her phone—she *always* answers."

Remy came out at just that moment and he frowned as he heard Tammy. He gave Ezra a narrow look, but

Ezra wasn't about to waste another two minutes here. They'd wasted too much already.

As they pushed through the front door, Remy snarled, "You don't have any fucking right interrogating Roz's staff."

"I didn't interrogate her. She blurted it out," Ezra said shortly. "Now yank your head out of your ass. You're convinced Carter didn't do anything wrong—fine. Then prove it. I need to talk to him. Where is he likely to be?"

Remy swore. Shoving a hand through his hair, he said, "His workshop." He pointed off to the side. "It's about a twenty-minute drive if you want to take the car—we have to cut through on backroads. Or we can take the path he takes—it's about a ten-minute walk across their property."

"We walk." Grimly, Ezra headed down the sidewalk. His leg was already aching and he hadn't done a damn thing. It was going to be a bitch of a day—he already knew it.

As they started down the path, he pulled out his phone and pulled up Lena's number. She answered on the second ring. "Anything going on?" she demanded before he even managed to get a word out.

"No." He shot Remy a look, wondered how much he could say, how much he should say. "Everything okay over there?"

"Oh, we're just peachy keen."

The bite of sarcasm in her voice had him smiling. "When you talked to Roz this morning, did she say anything about going anywhere?"

"No. And she wouldn't be—too many shipments come in today," Lena said.

*Hell.* "Okay. Everybody still there?"

"Yes. Why were you asking about Roz?"

"I was just wonder—"

"Bullshit," she bit off. "What's wrong with Roz?"

"I can't say anything is wrong with her. I haven't seen her."

Lena fell silent. Even though he couldn't see her, he could all but feel her worry. "Do you think . . . ?"

"Don't start the *what-if* game, baby," Ezra said, sighing. "Just hang tight. If I hear anything, learn anything, I'll call. And if *you* hear from her, call me."

"Okay."

"And keep everybody there. Don't leave, okay?"

"Yeah, yeah." She paused briefly, then murmured, "I love you. You be careful."

"I love you, too, sweetheart." As he disconnected the phone, he was all too aware that Remy was watching him—too aware, but he was already walking on a hair trigger himself. Getting into a pissing match with a man he considered a friend wasn't going to help either of them right now. And Remy—hell, his life was about to get seriously unpleasant.

Carter was a killer. Ezra knew it in his bones.

"What's this workshop for? He paints, right?"

"No. Pottery." Remy's tone was level, measured, like he knew Ezra was carefully circling around the things Remy wanted to say. "Carter's a potter. Does the pottery you see in Roz's shop, in the bookstore on the square. Even gave you and Lena a platter at your wedding—the sign of a killer, for certain."

Ezra gave him a narrow look. "You're right. Killers always look like killers. Jeffrey Dahmer looked so evil, didn't he, Jennings?"

Remy tensed, his muscles bunching.

He could all but see the other man getting ready to lunge.

Ezra stilled. "Don't. We don't have time for this shit—and I think, if you'd just take a few seconds and listen to your gut, you know I'm not just making this up. I *want* to be wrong, Remy. Like you wouldn't believe. And if I

*am,* I'm willing to deal with the fallout. But are you prepared to deal with what happens if *you* are wrong?"

"Fuck you," Remy snarled. Then he started to walk,
moving down the gravel path at a fast pace, too fast.

Ezra didn't bother trying to keep up. Whether it was
his own nerves or what, the muscles in his leg were already knotting up and he could just see it buckling under
him, see himself flat on his ass. Not going to happen.

Remy got to the workshop ahead of Ezra, leaning
back against the door with a sour look on his face. "Surprise, surprise. The door is locked," Remy said, sneer-
ing. "And Carter isn't in there, because he'd be answering
if he was."

Blowing out a breath, Ezra pushed Remy out of the
way and peered through the narrow window in the door.
It didn't let him see much and most of what he could see,
he didn't recognize. Some benches, a huge metal thing
hulking over in one corner—a kiln, maybe? There were
smaller versions, too. Kilns, had to be. That's what pot-
ters used, right?

"Shit."

He backed away, reaching up to rub his neck. *Running around in circles.* Head bowed, he stared at the
ground, tried to think. He was so focused on trying to
figure out the next step, he had probably been staring at
it for a full twenty seconds before he *really* saw it.

It was small, much smaller than what they'd found at
the house.

Already dry, too. But the blood still looked pretty
fresh. At least that was what he'd say if he got asked. He
drew his weapon as he put a few feet between him and
the door. Remy had already started back down the
path—it wasn't until he heard Ezra kicking the door in
that he bothered to look back.

"Damn it, Ezra, what in the *fuck* are you doing?"

"There's blood on the ground and on the threshold.

Gives me reason to think there might be somebody inside here that's hurt," Ezra said, keeping his voice low. Remy came rushing up and Ezra caught his arm, jerked him to the side. "Didn't you hear me? If I think there could be somebody *hurt,* that means somebody who could be *doing* the hurting could also be in there. Makes sense that the person with the gun goes first."

Of course, Ezra knew Carter wasn't in there.

The bastard knew he'd been figured out. He was on the move. Ezra knew it as well as he knew the back of his hand. And as much as he was throwing procedure out the window right now, he didn't know why he was bothering. But he wasn't letting a civilian go in there, not until he'd checked it out.

It was easier to think that Ezra had lost his mind than to think about the alternative. Remy was very much clinging to his thoughts of the sheriff's sad future, how people would shake their heads and sigh about how he'd cracked under the strain.

It wasn't much comfort, though, because there was nothing about Ezra that he could totally write off as nuts. He'd even looked at the spot on the threshold, tried to convince himself it could be anything *but* blood. Hell, Carter glazed stuff here, right? Could be glaze.

But the longer Remy had stared at it, the more it looked like blood. His imagination—that was all. Getting away with him. Finally, Ezra appeared back in the doorway and nodded. "He's not in here. Nobody is."

"Then we leave, damn it," Remy snarled. "You'll be lucky if I can talk Carter *out* of pressing charges. He's insane about his privacy—" The second the words left his mouth, he snapped his jaw shut, wished he hadn't said anything.

Ezra's mouth twisted in a smile, but there was no humor in it. "Yeah, I bet he's insane about his privacy."

He ambled off, back into the workshop, not even re-motely resembling something that looked like he was leaving.

Remy closed his eyes and swore. He had to get the bastard out of here. Had to, before *he* ended up screwed as well.

"What are these things?" Ezra asked, stopping in front of a huge receptacle that took up most of the east-ern half of the workshop.

"His kilns." Remy started over to him, snagged his arm. "You can learn about pottery while you're in jail for breaking and entering. Come on."

"You might want to take your hands off me, Remy," Ezra said, keeping his voice light, easy.

Remy snarled at him, fisting his hand in Ezra's shirt. "Will you just get the fuck out of here before you screw *your* career *and* mine?"

Ezra glanced down at the hand that still held a fistful of his shirt. Then, eyes narrowed, he looked up. "You want to watch it there, Jennings. I mean it."

"We're leaving."

Ezra reached up with one arm, shifted the other, manag-ing to trap Remy's hand. As he did it, he whirled around, using his momentum to shift Remy's body around. Remy hit face-first into one of the smaller kilns—hard. For a second, he saw stars. Then he saw red. But he was hard-pressed to do much about it, which only pissed him off even more. He shoved back, but Ezra had somehow man-aged to get his arm locked and twisted high between his shoulder blades.

"Enough, Remy," Ezra snapped. "You got it?"

Remy shoved back, ignoring it as his shoulder screamed a warning at him. "Get the hell off of me." He managed to budge himself. About one inch. Shit. Taking a deep breath, he closed his eyes. Counted to ten. "You can't expect me to believe this shit. Carter's not just my cousin—he's one of my best friends. You can't just expect me to believe this."

He opened his eyes. Stared at the kiln just an inch from his face. "You can't."

Behind him, Ezra swore. Then said something.

But it was like bees buzzing in his ears. Slack, Remy sagged against the kiln, staring through the small, almost nonexistent peephole. It wasn't much of a space—just enough to get a glimpse inside.

But that glimpse was all he needed. That glimpse was too much.

"Holy shit. God, oh, God, oh, God . . . Ezra."

Ezra let go. "What—?"

The strength drained out of Remy's legs and he reached up, clamped a hand over the top edge of the kiln. This was a smaller one—maybe twice the size of an industrial fridge. Shaking, he lifted his hand, rubbed his eyes. Looked again.

What he saw didn't change.

"Aw, no. No, *fuck*, no."

# CHAPTER
# TWENTY-ONE

IT WAS A DECENT SIZED HOUSE, NIA KNEW, BUT SHE was absolutely certain she was going to come out of her skin if she had to stay there too much longer. Which meant she was going to come out of her skin, she supposed.

As much as she wanted to be out there doing something to find Carter Jennings, Nia wasn't about to do the dumb chick thing and put her ass out where it didn't belong. She was a photographer, not a cop. She'd done what she'd set out to do, even though it was mostly through sheer dumb luck and chance. But she'd done her part—she needed to let King do his job now.

But the tension in this place was driving her *crazy*. It was even worse now, ever since he'd called not too long ago to check on Lena.

The other woman hadn't said much, but Nia could tell she was worried. She'd like to do something, say something to help, but what could she say? *I know your new husband is out there chasing after a psycho, but I'm sure he'll be fine,* maybe? Didn't really sound like a Hallmark card.

By some unspoken agreement, they all stayed together. After lunch, they'd all migrated into the living room and none of them seemed interested in leaving. When one of them left, even if just to use the restroom, Law played their shadow. It was sort of embarrassing, yet still strangely comforting, at least for Nia. He wouldn't let anything happen, not if he could stop it. And while she'd never wanted or needed a white knight, she'd never realized how reassuring it could be to have one handy.

Right now, he was sitting on the floor at the coffee table, across from Hope, the two of them bent over a chessboard. For some reason, it didn't surprise her at all that he knew how to play chess. It was a game that confused the hell out of her. He'd offered to teach her, but she could barely hold a thought in her head today.

Lena sat in a fat, overstuffed chair, her legs tucked neatly under her, a weird-looking contraption in her hand. She'd offhandedly mentioned it was her PDA— and right now, she was running the tips of her fingers over it.

Reading, Nia supposed. The device was a lot bigger than any PDA Nia had ever used, but then again, she didn't have to rely on her hands to read.

Just then, Lena glanced up, a faint smile twisting her lips.

"Do I look that much like her?" she asked softly.

"Huh?"

"Your cousin. Do I really look that much like her?"

Staring at that face, feeling an ache in her heart, Nia said quietly, "Yeah. You look a lot like her."

"I'm sorry."

"Hell, it's not your fault." Because it hurt too much to think about Joely, she asked, "You can really feel me staring at you?"

"When somebody's staring at you, don't you feel it? Yeah, I can feel it." She shrugged and set the gadget on the table next to her chair. "You live without being able to see most of your life, you start to pay more attention to your other senses."

"So you used to be able to see?" Then she winced. "Oh, shit, I'm sorry. That was rude."

"It's okay." Lena shrugged. "I don't mind. Yeah, I used to be able to see. Out of one eye, at least. I was born with this thing called PHPV—persistent hyperplastic primary vitreous." She grinned. "Try saying that ten times fast. It only affected my left eye. Up until I was ten years old, I could see out of my right eye just fine."

She reached up and tugged off her glasses, revealing pale, almost crystal blue eyes. "People who have a vision problem on one side are like ten times more likely to have an accident that will screw up the vision on the other side. You know that? But I was one of those kids who didn't want to be seen as different. My mom was the overprotective sort who would have covered me in bubble wrap, put me on a shelf, and kept me there my entire life if I would have let her. Every chance I could, I did exactly what she *didn't* want me doing. Things like playing baseball without the safety glasses I should have been wearing. I got hit. That's all it took." She finished with a wry smile.

How in the hell could she tell that story with a smile? Nia gaped at her, stunned. "My God, I'm so sorry."

Lena laughed. "Why? *You* didn't make me not wear the glasses."

"You were *ten,*" Nia snapped.

"Yeah. I was ten. Kids never think anything bad can happen." She sighed and slid her glasses back on. "Actually, plenty of adults think nothing bad will ever happen. But it does. It's not like it was the end of my world, though. I can't even say it ruined my life. It *changed* my life, but considering how my life is going? I have to say it changed it for the better. How do I even know I'd be where I am, married to Ezra, with a career I love if my life had gone a different way?"

"You're one hell of an optimist," Nia muttered.

At that, Law laughed.

Nia shot him a look.

He glanced up from the chessboard, a smirk on his face. "She's about the most *un*optimistic person I've ever met. She's just realistic."

Lena made a face in his direction. Then she shrugged. "He's right. I'm hardly ever optimistic. But I love my life—I wouldn't do anything that might change how it's going now. Especially if it meant that I might not have Ezra in it."

"That's so sweet." Hope smiled.

"Yeah. I'm sugar, all right." Lena snorted and picked her PDA back up.

"It *is* sweet. Romantic." Hope shrugged and looked back at the chessboard. "I mean, there are probably a lot of people who couldn't say that—they'd *want* a chance to go back, undo what the ten-year-old kid did, you know? Your life could have been easier. But you don't care, because Ezra's worth it."

"It's not *just* about Ezra," Lena said self-consciously. Then she shrugged. "But yeah. He's worth it. And hell, would *you* change things if it meant you wouldn't have Remy? You had to deal with more hell than I ever did."

Hope glanced at Lena. Then away. "Remy's worth everything. Anything."

"When it's real, when it's right, that kind of love *is* everything." Lena focused on her PDA again. "And now I want to read—this much mushy talk is going to make me want to wear pink and dance on mountainsides or something stupid."

Envy, longing, stirred in Nia's heart. *Everything* . . .

Feeling the weight of his stare, she looked up and saw

Law looking at her. Her heart skipped a beat and then started to race.

*Everything* . . . Yeah. She could believe that. Maybe she wouldn't have a few years ago. Even just a few months ago. But Law was changing all sorts of things.

Remy tore at the door to the kiln, wrenching at the complicated mechanism even as Ezra tried to grab his arm. "Get the fuck away," he snarled. He got the door open just as Ezra managed to jerk him back.

Ezra froze as he saw what Remy had glimpsed through the kiln's tiny peephole.

It was Roz.

Bound hand and foot, her head lolling against the side wall of the kiln.

"Dear God," Ezra whispered.

Remy barely heard him.

He had to crawl inside to get to her. It wasn't one of the bigger kilns, but it was too big for him to pull her out without getting in. Part of him was terrified to touch her. He couldn't tell if she was breathing. Couldn't tell if she was alive. And he wouldn't know until he touched her. But he couldn't live in denial anymore.

There was only one way she could have gotten here.

Ezra had been right—Remy had been horribly, terribly wrong.

And he was going to kill Carter.

His hand was shaking as he reached out, touched Roz's neck, checking for a pulse. Her skin was warm and under his fingers, he felt a thready, erratic beat. Heaving a sigh of relief, he awkwardly eased her body out. "Thank God," he whispered.

"There's a pulse?"

"Yeah." Remy cradled her against his chest. "Roz? Roslyn, sweetheart."

She didn't move. Didn't seem to hear him.

He heard Ezra talking and glanced over, saw him on his radio. Calling it in, he realized.

Shit. This was really happening.

Carter—

Dazed, he looked at Ezra and shook his head. "I can't believe this is happening, man. I . . . what in the fuck is going on?"

Ezra paused, lowered the radio. "I don't know." He looked at Roz's still form, and then shifted his gaze back to Remy's. "I really didn't want to be right, you know."

Memories, fragments from their childhood flashed through his mind. Camping in the woods. Hunting. Fishing. Chasing after girls. Racing down the highway after Carter had gotten his first car . . . Remy had stood up with him at his wedding. Carter had been there when Remy's dad had died.

Brushing all of that aside, he swallowed and met Ezra's gaze. "I know."

"Sirens," Lena murmured, lowering her PDA.

Law climbed to his feet and moved to look out the window, even though he couldn't see more than a slice of the road. He caught a glimpse of red and blue lights, but that was it. "Heading east," he said softly.

"Wonder if it means anything," Hope said.

"It means they are heading east," Lena said flatly. "Toward the Inn, most likely."

Law turned and watched as she reached into her pocket, pulling out her phone. Gripping it like it was a lifeline.

"I wish Ezra would call already," she muttered.

"It's only been about twenty minutes or so since the last time he called," he said softly. He moved to sit on the ottoman in front of her. Taking her free hand, he squeezed it. "I know you're worried about him, but he can handle himself, sweetie."

She scowled. "This being married to a cop thing is going to have some rough spots."

"Just remember he's worth it," Nia said from across the room. "And that man of yours can handle himself."

Lena smiled faintly. "Yeah. I just don't like not knowing what's going on."

"None of us do. But we can't go bugging him, either, if we want him to concentrate. He's safer if he's got his mind on the job anyway, right?" Nia pointed out.

"Yeah." Lena sighed.

Law smiled at Nia. She jerked a shoulder in a shrug and crossed her arms.

Carter was a patient man under most circumstances, but today wasn't most circumstances. He kept his radio tuned into the frequency the local cops used as he turned the little BMW down Reilly's driveway. People recognized his van too easily. They didn't drive the BMW as much—hopefully, it was less likely to be recognized.

His head pounded as he slammed on the brakes in front of Reilly's place. Nia's bike was there, parked in front. Good. Take care of them both. The bitch, Reilly. Then he'd deal with Lena before heading back to his workshop, where he'd finish things.

He only had a couple of hours before the drugs wore off on Roz. Well, assuming she hadn't suffocated. He wanted to be back before she woke up. He'd give her more drugs before he took care of her, make sure she didn't know what was coming.

He loved his wife. Hurting her was something he'd never do.

Time was short. Because he didn't have time, he didn't bother knocking. He knew there was an alarm system and he'd planned on only being there a few minutes anyway. It didn't take long to aim and pull a trigger, after all.

But the three minutes he was in the house were wasted, because the house was empty.

Damn it.

Rage was singing in his blood by the time he was back in the car. He didn't have time for this shit. He'd be damned before he got his ass arrested. No fucking way.

Now he had a choice to make. He deliberated as he headed to Lena's. Did he waste any more time trying to find Nia? She was the reason for all of this.

"Well, actually, that's Lena," he muttered, his voice harsh, rough. All those months ago. When she'd heard the screams when his little bitch got away.

Just thinking about *that* had those memories flashing through his mind—her screams. Him tracking her. Catching her—

The way she'd sobbed as he hauled her back, her pitiful pleas . . .

Blood roared in his ears, so loud, so hard.

He didn't even hear the sirens wailing until the first deputy car came flying around him.

Spine stiffening, he looked in the rearview mirror and saw another.

Sirens wailing, the car flew around him, the same as the last one. Heading east down the highway . . . toward the Inn.

And his workshop.

Breathing raggedly, he gripped the steering wheel. Lena's house was coming up.

He made a split-second decision.

He had to know—because if they were at the workshop, he couldn't risk going back there.

Ezra still had a million and one things to do, and this was already a nightmare in the making as far as crime scenes went, but the lost look on Remy's face, when the man was normally so fucking cocky and collected, hell. It was killing him.

"I called for an ambulance, too," he said, moving to stand in front of the bench where Remy was sitting, cradling the unconscious woman.

"Ambulance," Remy echoed. "Yeah. Good idea. Why won't she wake up?"

Ezra had his suspicions. He lifted one of Roz's lids, peered at her eye. The pupil was a mere pinpoint. "I think he drugged her. I'll tell the EMTs—they'll probably look anyway, but they can let the doctors know, run some blood tests."

Remy nodded.

Still, that lost, dazed look remained on his face. Ezra didn't have time to shock him out of it, either. Hell, *Remy* didn't have time to sit there looking lost, or confused. There was too much at stake, too many people who could become potential targets and Remy, better than most, might be able to figure out who was most at risk.

"You going to sit there all damn night looking like he killed your dog or are you going to snap out of it and do something?" Ezra said, going for a cold, flat tone and hoping it would do some good.

Remy stiffened.

Then slowly, he looked up, his blue eyes shuttered. "You're going to have to give me some time to adjust to the fact that my cousin—my blood, my *friend*—is a killer."

"No. I don't have to give you some *time,* Counselor. Because *time* is something we don't have. Somehow I don't see him tucking his wife into an oven and just disappearing. He was going to come back and kill her, but he had a plan, damn it. He was going after somebody. He's pissed and I bet you can figure out best who is the most likely target. Nia? Since she came back and fucked it all up? Reilly? Lena?"

"What . . . why would he go after Lena?"

Ezra spun away, shoved a hand through his hair. "Hell. You really aren't thinking like a lawyer, are you? Are you thinking at *all*?" He looked back at him. "She heard one of his victims, Jennings. The screaming. Probably Nia Hollister's cousin."

Remy went white. Then he closed his eyes. Nodded. He took a deep breath and looked at Roz, then back at Ezra. "I can't process all of this—I just can't. Give me a few minutes—let me get her to the hospital."

As he said it, they both heard the sirens wailing. Remy rose, still cradling the burden of Roz's limp, practically lifeless body. He looked toward the window. "I need to call Hope, let her know what's going on."

Ezra softly said, "She already knows most of it. She was at the Inn this morning with Lena. Left when Lena did. She's at our place and she'll stay there."

A muscle twitched in his jaw. "She knows, then. About Carter."

Ezra inclined his head.

"Okay. I need to talk to her. I need a few minutes. Then I can think."

He headed for the door and then looked back. "It won't be Reilly, though. It would be too fair a fight. Even when we were kids, one thing Carter never could stand was a fair fight. He wouldn't call it that—had it in his head that it was strategizing or whatever. But he'll go after somebody he has a chance at taking down. He wouldn't have a chance with Reilly, and he knows it."

Then he paused. "Actually, he's most likely to go for the weakest one, the most vulnerable. While others are focusing on her, he'd have his fun with the rest. Mind games. He was all about mind games."

"Hope."

Remy's mouth twisted and he shook his head. "Hope's quiet, but she's not weak, man. And he doesn't have any reason to go after her. He'd only fixate on somebody who posed a problem to him. Hope's not the vulnerable one I'm talking about."

Ezra's gut turned to ice.

# TWENTY-TWO

THIS TIME, EZRA GOT THE WARRANT EASILY.

It was hell on earth, too, because this was now the last place he wanted to be. He wanted . . . *needed* to be with Lena. But instead, he had to be here. Doing the job he could have been doing earlier if Beulah had given him the benefit of a doubt.

Instead of being with his wife, he had to be a fucking cop. The only consolation was that he would be better able to protect her once he had what he needed to lock Carter up. And it would have to be a strong, solid case because the people of Ash, Kentucky, might just make that legendary Blue Wall of Silence among cops look mild. They weren't going to like seeing one of their beloved Jenningses go down—Remy was proof of that, and Ezra liked the guy.

He'd be damned if he left her unprotected, though.

He had Ethan and Keith out there. They might want to be *here,* but he trusted those two more than anybody else on his team and if he couldn't be with Lena, then it was going to be them.

He barely managed to keep himself from tearing into the place while he waited for the warrant. Once Beulah had it to him, though, Ezra and his deputies all but peeled the workshop apart, looking for a clue, a sign.

Granted, the deputies weren't too keen on it at first.

But Steve Mabry made a gruesome discovery that changed everything. It was dumb luck that he'd even found it, though. The kilns were heavy mothers that would need to be moved with forklifts—and those were the smaller ones. The bigger ones, Ezra didn't know how they'd even begin to move those bastards.

This kiln was a smaller one, the same size as the one Roz had been in. Identical, even. But Steve had noticed the internal dimensions were off. Because of that, he'd checked the make of the kilns. Identical.

Watching the big deputy crouch inside it made Ezra's gut clench—the thing was nothing more than a big oven, one that got really, really hot. He circled around it, checking the display. It was dark, but still, it freaked him out seeing one of his men in there. Almost as bad as it had been seeing Roz—

"Sheriff, there's something weird about the back wall of this thing."

"Something weird about this whole damn thing," he muttered, shaking his head. Then he sighed and headed back around to the front, peering inside.

Mabry tapped the strange white bricks that lined the back.

"They don't match."

Ezra frowned. "I couldn't care less if it matches or not, man. It's not like we're running a fashion show here."

Mabry shifted around more, giving Ezra a better view. "You're not using your imagination there, Sheriff. Look." He tapped the sidewall in front of him, then gestured to the other one. "See? These two, the material matches. The bottom, the top? All match. It's the back that doesn't. And look."

Ezra watched as Mabry used his flashlight and tapped it against the sidewall. Nothing happened. But when he tapped it against the back wall, the white brick crumbled.

"You know how hot these things get?"

"Really hot?" Ezra said helpfully.

Mabry snorted. "How does about two thousand degrees or so sound?" He pointed to the back of the kiln. "The brick is supposed to help insulate against fire and stuff. How safe you think that is?"

"Well, probably not very. But we're not here for fire safety—"

"This, here, Sheriff, is a patch job." Mabry pulled a pocketknife out, wedging it in between two of the bricks. "There's something behind this. I bet he doesn't even use this kiln. It's just here for show."

Narrowing his eyes, Ezra folded his arms over his chest and watched.

It took more than an hour.

But when they were finished, they found a small, secure little cache. Two locked metal boxes, long and skinny, the kind Ezra would expect to see in a bank's vault. The first one held hair. More than a dozen different swatches, different shades, different textures.

The other box, a larger one, was the most disturbing, though.

It held ashy fragments of bone.

Mabry looked up at him. "Is . . . ah, is that what I think it is?"

The rest of his men gathered around to peer inside.

Ezra blew out a careful, controlled breath as he studied the kilns. "How hot did you say these suckers could get again?"

"Two thousand degrees, easy."

Gently, Ezra placed the lid back on the metal box. "The human body can be burned to nothing but ash and fragments of bone when it's exposed to temperatures that high for a couple of hours."

"Oh, God."

He didn't know who said it, but he echoed the sentiment. Somehow, he didn't suspect they'd be finding many bodies. That was part of the reason Carter had gotten away with this for so long—there was never a trail. He picked women who weren't from here, women with no connection to him, and instead of burying the bodies, he'd burned them.

"Sheriff."

He glanced over. "Yeah, Kent?"

The deputy stood by one of the workbenches, staring down at something. Needing to get away from that macabre discovery, he joined Kent. "I saw this earlier. Didn't think much of it until you all pulled that out," he said, his voice thin and reedy.

Ezra frowned, looked at Kent, at his pale face, the sweat beading on his brow. Then he took the little index card.

The word *glaze* was written in neat block print at the top.

Most of the words on the card might as well have been a foreign language. *Silica, feldspar, quartz.* But there was one word that jumped out at him. One word that all but imprinted itself on his brain.

*Ash mix.*

His hand clenched spasmodically. *Don't jump to conclusions—don't.* "Ash mix, could be a lot of things."

Kent shook his head and pointed to a magazine that lay open on the workbench. "He's got an interview in there—it's a recent one, just came out last week. Somebody asks him about his glazing techniques. Apparently he has a gift for coming up with ones that others can't duplicate. He says he has a unique way of mixing his glazes. Cutting the wood ashes with a special mix of ashes that is unique, and only his."

Kent bent over and tugged open a drawer, revealing another large metal box, similar to the ones they'd found hidden in the kiln. There were only ashes in this one, but precious few, clinging to the cracks and crevices of the box.

"In the article, it also says that his special mix has been depleted, though, and he anticipates it may be a long while before he can get the right ingredients again. He even says he may never be able to get the *right* ingredients—says he may not be able to use that glaze ever again." Kent swallowed, his eyes glassy, but the rage was starting to burn through now. Rage. And horror. "People who have those special pieces should treasure them . . . each one is unique, each one glows with its own soul, its own voice . . . its own life."

Staring into that metal box, Ezra's blood roared in his ears.

Slowly, he shifted his eyes upward, staring at the neatly organized row of pots and vases lining the shelf just above the workbench. Some truly did seem to glow.

"My God," he whispered.


"You believe this crazy shit?" Ethan muttered, shaking his head and staring out the window at the big old white farmhouse. Lena had spent a lot of money having the place fixed up. Fresh white paint gleamed in the soft light of the late evening sun. The shutters were dark red, but nobody could glimpse anything inside the house.

The curtains were drawn, hiding everything inside.

"I mean, seriously, Keith. This is *nuts*," Ethan said, shaking his head. "Carter Jennings? A fucking killer? You don't believe that, do you?"

"I know I don't want to," Keith said quietly. Carter

was blood to him—very convoluted and distantly related, but still, family was family.

But the job was the job and when he'd taken the call from the sheriff, he'd heard the urgency, the sincerity in King's voice. The man wouldn't have them out here on some crazy ghost chase.

"Ha! See, I knew I wasn't the only one." Ethan smirked and leaned his head back against the headrest, sighing. "Damn it, this is going to screw Sheriff King up bad."

Keith slid him a narrow glance. "You didn't hear me very well. I *said* I didn't *want* to believe it. That doesn't mean I *don't* believe it. I'm going to withhold judgment there. But the sheriff wouldn't make this call without good reason."

The crackle of the radio kept him from hearing anything else that might have been said.

"This is Dispatch . . . got a report of suspicious activity . . . Deb Sparks . . ."

Ethan and Keith, as one, groaned.

Keith answered. "We're already busy at the moment, Dispatch. You'll have to send another unit."

"No one close—sounds urgent, heard her screaming."

"Fuck." Ethan rolled his eyes.

Keith groaned.

Ethan said in a low voice, "It's just Deb. I can leave you here, swing by, flash the lights. It will make her feel better while the other car gets closer. We're spread thin here as it is, with most of the team out at Carter's workshop."

"Against protocol."

"And what if there really *is* a problem?" Ethan gestured to the house. "There *isn't* one here."

The radio crackled again. "Closest car I have reports ETA in ten minutes."

"We're three minutes away." Ethan glared at Keith.

"You either get out and keep an eye on the place on foot, or you come along for the ride."

Keith glared at the younger deputy as he reached for the door. "You know I'm going to write your ass up for this."

Ethan flashed him a grin. "Go ahead. But I figure King's going to be in so much damn trouble for the shit storm he's bringing down with this bullshit on Carter, nobody's going to care."

That had to be the most faulty reasoning Keith had ever heard. But as he watched Ethan speed off down the driveway, he was torn—he liked Ezra. He liked Ethan. He'd known Carter most of his life. So did he hope Ezra was right—which meant Ethan wouldn't be getting off scot-free for insubordination—or did he hope Ethan was right and that while Ethan's little fuckup would get lost in the smoke of Ezra's screwup, Ezra's career would be shot?

"I didn't sign up for this political bullshit." He rubbed the back of his neck.

Hell. Too much political bullshit.

Deb's lifeless eyes watched him as he poured himself some whiskey from the stash she'd kept hidden in her sewing basket. He toasted her. "Cheers, Deb," he murmured, looking out the window.

He'd heard her calling the cops. He'd *wanted* her to call the cops.

After all, how could he make a move when they were all focused on the place where he needed to be?

The sheriff's department was spread thin as it was. So if he could cause enough chaos, hopefully he could slip in, quietly, do what he needed to do, and then be done with it.

When he heard the sirens, he smiled and left her sewing room, made his way to the living room. It was dim in the house now, almost dark with the oncoming night. He'd already taken care of the lights. Now he just had to wait, and watch.

Through the window, he could see the car well enough. Just one deputy. Sheffield, he thought. Wasn't positive, but he thought that was the name. Carter was happy it wasn't family.

Young. Stupid. Arrogant idiot.

He announced himself before he entered—Carter had left the door open. No reason to make him break it down, after all. He wasn't trying to hide.

Backing out of the living room, he waited in the formal dining room. It was a new game of cat and mouse, and it had his heart racing. His last game—that was what today was. His last game, and now that he'd settled down to play, it was turning out to be pretty damn fun.

Floorboards creaked as Sheffield came into the living room.

Carter watched the floor, judging by the shifting shadows as Sheffield drew closer to the open doorway between the two rooms.

"Miz Sparks? It's the County Sheriff's office. Can you tell me where you are?" Ethan called out. Not so much arrogance in his voice this time.

A wicked little smile curled Carter's lips. *Why, Ethan . . . she's dead. I'll tell her you dropped by . . .*

Ethan drew closer to the dining room and Carter backed away, edging out and circling around, carefully avoiding the boards that squeaked—he'd taken care to learn them, and he placed his weight with caution. When he peered around the doorway, Ethan had already made his way through the dining room.

Smiling, Carter moved faster. It was his own arrogance that tripped him up. He didn't double-check be-

fore he came around the corner and he found himself
staring down the business end of Ethan's service revolver.

"What the . . ." Ethan shook his head, gaping.

Carter might have been touched by the astonishment
in the boy's eyes—if he had cared.

He didn't, though.

Ethan shrugged it off, though, and he did it fast. In a
harsh, flat voice, he said, "Drop the weapon."

Carter smiled. "No."

He jerked it up, aimed.

He pulled the trigger just as Ethan got a round off.

The fiery pain that cut through his arm was a shock.
A brutal, burning one. In the end, it was also one that
didn't matter, because Ethan went down, his throat a
raw, bloody wound, blood gushing. Carter kicked his
weapon away and then bent over, grabbed the radio,
jerked it off. He'd be dead in no time.

As he was walking to the door, another fiery pain hit
him.

A bullet, ripping through the side of his calf.

He stumbled, slammed into the doorjamb. Looking
back, he watched as Ethan's backup weapon fell from
his hand. Watched as his eyes went empty. Lifeless.


Lena closed her eyes.

The sound of a gunshot echoing through the night
was like the start of the nightmare all over again. Except
she wasn't alone.

Her hand clenched in Puck's fur and every once in a
while, she rubbed her finger over her wedding ring. Ezra
was still out there. Searching, looking for evidence, or
something. Maybe even looking for Carter. Roz . . .
damn it, where the fuck was Roz?

There was a deputy pacing around her house.

Law, Hope, and Nia were here. And she knew she wasn't going crazy—knew people believed her. All good things.

So why was she still so terrified?

There was a thunderous bang at the front door and she jolted, barely managed to suppress a whimper. She hadn't even made it to her feet when Law said softly, "I'll get it, Lena."

She didn't bother arguing. Why should she? There was only a handful of people she'd let in right now anyway and two of them were already in here. The other three were her husband—and he lived there, so he didn't entirely count—Roz, and Remy.

And it turned out to be Remy, she learned in under twenty seconds. Hope's relieved sigh told her that without anybody even having to say his name. Lena smiled as she heard her friend rushing across the floor to him. "Oh, man, am I glad to see you."

"You, too," Remy murmured.

His voice . . . he sounded like he'd aged ten years. Poor bastard.

"Hey Remy." Resting her head on the back of the chair, Lena said softly, "I take it you've been told what's going on."

Silence fell, heavy and tense. Then he said, "Yes."

Lena nodded. "Don't suppose you know where Roz is, do you? I haven't been able to get ahold of her all day."

"She . . . is in the hospital. And don't ask anything else right now, because I don't know."

Roz—*hospital*—

Lena's heart leaped into her throat.

"Don't *ask* anything else?" she snarled, shoving upright. Next to her, Puck tensed. "Excuse me, but did you just tell me not to *ask*?"

"Yeah. I did. I can't tell you shit, so save us the head-ache and don't ask," he bit off.

"That's one of my best friends, damn it. You want me to just meekly sit here and not wonder why she's in the hospital?" Her hand curled into a fist and she all but shook with the need to do something violent.

"She's my cousin's wife and I'm *still* trying to figure out why she's in the damn hospital. I'm still trying to figure out a whole hell of a lot of things, Lena, and guess what, nobody's giving me any answers, either." He paused and then suggested, "Deal with it."

Her nails bit into the flesh of her palm. She wanted to hit him. She knew where he was standing and she sus-pected she could probably aim for that oversized, arro-gant head of his just fine.

But then a hand touched her arm. Law said quietly, "Lena . . . enough."

"Enough? *Enough?*" She jerked back. Fury burned in-side her, hot and brutal and ugly. She shook her head. Next to her, Puck tensed, snarled. She rested a hand on his head. "No. *Not* enough—"

"You didn't just find out your cousin was out killing people," Hope said. "And considering what all is going on, whatever *is* wrong with Roz, chances are it's from something Carter did—I think Remy's got enough to deal with. Give him a break."

Lena scowled. Then guilt started to settle in, slippery and nasty. "Well, hell." Dropping back into her chair, she pulled her knees to her chest and closed her eyes. Puck rested his head by her feet, whining gently. "It's okay, boy."

"This day isn't ever going to end, is it?"

Despite himself, despite the misery and grief and guilt that had choked him for the past few hours, Remy was able to look at Hope with something of a smile. She had a light glinting in her eyes as she stared at Lena, all but daring the other woman to say anything else.

Across the room, Nia said with a smirk, "Look at Tinkerbell going all mama-bear."

Hope snapped, "Oh, shove the Tinkerbell crap up your ass."

For about two seconds, Nia just stared at her. Then she started to laugh.

Ignoring her, Hope hooked her arm through Remy's and led him out into the hallway. "Where have you been all day?" she asked quietly. "I've been trying to call."

"I . . . I know. I should have called, but once we found Roz, I . . . shit. I needed a few minutes. I don't feel like I can breathe, Hope. This is choking me," he said, looking away. "I knew you were over here with Law, knew you were safe. I . . . uh. I've texted him a few times, asked him not to tell you. I just needed a few minutes." Then he sighed and rubbed his hands up and down his face. "Shit, I still can't believe this is happening. How can this be real?"

Instead of saying anything, she just leaned her head against his chest and wrapped her arms around his waist.

Remy tucked her head under his chin and held her tight. For a few seconds, he allowed himself that luxury. Then he eased back. "Ezra said he was sending a car out."

Hope nodded. "It got here a couple hours ago. One of them is here—Keith, I think? The other said there was a call he had to see to—left about ten minutes ago."

Remy frowned. "Ezra will have his ass."

"That's the impression I got when I heard Law talking to the deputy." Hope shrugged. "I don't think the other deputy believes what he's being told. It's the one who flirts all the time, Ethan, I think."

"Shit." Remy pressed his lips to her brow. "Go back

in there with them. I want to talk to Keith, see what's going on."

She glanced at the door. "I want to come outside, damn it. We've been cooped up in here all day."

"And that's how it's going to be for a little while longer. Sorry." He pushed a hand through her dark hair, then cupped the back of her neck, pulled her close for a kiss. "I'll be back in a minute."

She scowled and then headed back into the room, her hands shoved deep into her back pockets.

Remy watched her for a minute and then headed for the front door. As he was walking out, he heard footsteps behind him. Glancing back, he saw Law and he scowled, but ignored him.

He caught sight of Keith's shadow just as he was circling around from the back. "Where's your partner?" he called, striding down toward the edge of the porch.

Keith sighed. "Shit."

The front screen door banged open as Law came outside.

"Reilly, you're not supposed to be outside," Keith said. "Would you get back in there before the sheriff kicks my ass even harder than he's already going to do?"

Law shrugged. "Your ass ain't my concern."

Keith glared at him and leaped up on the porch. As Law headed their way, there was a cracking shot—as it echoed, Keith lunged for Reilly. Remy hit the ground.

Law's scream echoed through the night.

# TWENTY-THREE

NIA HEARD HIM SCREAM.

She didn't have to look to know who it was.

She bolted for the door, but Hope caught her arm. Wide-eyed, she said, "We have to stay inside."

"You do that—stay inside," Nia snapped.

"Damn it, if we go out there, that just makes it *easier* for him," Hope said, her small, slim fingers clutching Nia's arm with surprising strength.

"Fuck—"

There was another gunshot. Nia whirled around and hit the lights. "We need to stay down," she said, her voice brusque. "Let my arm go. We need to get the lights out. It's dark out now—with the lights on, we're too easy to see. And the guys outside, it's even worse."

Hope went white. Then slowly, her fingers uncurled from Nia's arm.

Nia didn't absolutely *plan* on going outside. Not if she didn't have to. But she had to know—

Crawling on her hands and knees made the few feet between the living room and the front door seem twice as long. She hit the lights with her fist and then gave her eyes a minute to adjust before she cracked open the door. She saw Remy out there, bent over Law.

Holy fuck—he was sitting up.

The color came back into her life, her heart started to beat and she let herself breathe. *Thank You, God,* she whispered. "Law," she whispered, keeping her voice low.

He shot her a pained look.

Remy was using his tie as a tourniquet, tying off Law's right leg. There was a wet, glistening pool of blood forming underneath.

Nia didn't see the deputy anywhere.

She cracked the door open wider. "Get in here," she said quietly. "Now—"

A bullet hit the door, shattering glass, splintering wood.

She barely managed to keep her scream behind her teeth.

Law shook his head. "I think that means I'm supposed to stay out here." He gave her a tight smile, then shifted his gaze down.

It didn't catch any light—that was the nice thing about the guns she'd picked up. That matte black made them damn hard to see in the dark. She recognized it from months ago. He'd kept it. For some reason, it made her smile. "I'm going to wait right here for a few minutes."

Remy slid her a look. "Get in there, the three of you stay together," he said softly. He glanced at Law's gun—a subtle glance, one that didn't move his head at all, then back at her. "You got another?"

With a mean curl of her lips, she whispered, "Bet your ass." It was in her bag in the living room.

"With you?"

"Yes."

"Get together. Find a place and hide." He had his body curled around in a way that hid his hands and that was when she saw his phone. "The cavalry will be here soon."

She swallowed. Okay. Could they stay alive, though? Then she wanted to kick herself. Hell, yes, they'd stay alive. She hadn't made it through all of this, found the bastard who'd killed her cousin, found *Law* . . . to die *now*. None of them had come through this hell to die *now*.

Backing away, she retraced her path into the living room. She kept low to the floor, scuttling along on her hands and knees. Seeing her bag there was a beautiful sight. Unzipping it, she reached inside, pulled out her gun.

The solid, heavy feel of it in her hand was reassuring and she let herself breathe just a little easier. She wasn't helpless—had never been helpless. He was a fool beyond measure if he thought she would go down easy. Taking one more, deep, steadying breath, she looked up and met Hope's gaze, then shifted her attention to Lena.

The two of them were crouched on the floor by the couch, Puck standing guard.

"Law's alive. The bullet hit him in the leg." She looked at Hope, saw her pale face. "I opened the door for them to come in, but as soon as I did, the bastard shot at the door—they try to come in, they'll get shot—at least that's the message I got."

Hope whimpered and then clamped a hand over her mouth.

Lena swallowed. "And the deputy?"

"I didn't see him." She glanced toward the window, hidden by the shades and the curtains. "Remy wants us to stay together and hide. He's already called for help. Now we just hide until help gets here. It's your house, Lena. Where do we hide?"

Law gritted his teeth against the pain, telling himself he wasn't going to break down and whimper like a girl. And hell, if any of the women in the house heard that? They'd smack him. Yeah—that's it, focus on anything

besides the fact that his leg was screaming like a bitch,
anything besides the blood that was still oozing out despite the makeshift tourniquet Remy had made of his tie.

Panting, he looked at Remy. "You need to get in there
with them."

Remy shot a glance at the door, then toward the trees.
"Any time I try, he sends a nice loud message."

Yeah. Law had heard those messages, all four of them.
Lena's house was getting fucked up, big time. With a
scowl, he said, "I don't *care*—Nia's in there. Hope.
Lena. You think he's cutting us off for jollies?"

"No." Remy looked down the porch. In a low voice,
he called out, "Keith?"

"I'm down here." The whisper was practically lost in
the night, it was so quiet.

"You hurt?"

"No."

Crouched in the dirt, his body hidden by the porch,
Keith Jennings held his service revolver and stared into
the night. He hadn't been entirely honest. The shooter—
and he had to assume it was Carter—had laid down a
line of fire and Keith had taken a graze to his left arm,
but it wasn't anything that would slow him down.

Remy's voice floated to him again. "We need somebody in the house and I can't—I move and he starts
shooting again."

Yeah. Keith had noticed that. The shooter wouldn't
do it forever, though. He couldn't, because *he* had plans
to get in the house. And unless Keith was seriously mistaken, he'd already started to move.

Still—going inside when he had a wounded man just a
few feet away . . .

His radio crackled. "Dispatch, come in. Son of a bitch,
we've got a mess—"

Swearing silently, he clamped a hand over it to muffle

the sound as he fought to turn it off. Another thunderous crack tore through the night. Something stung his face. Looking up, he squinted at the painted wood of the porch post.

The light was dim, but he was pretty certain there was some damage to it—a bullet.

The shooter had heard Keith's radio.

And judging by the angle, he was definitely moving through the woods. Circling around, heading to the back of the house. Damn it . . . "Are you two okay?"

Law's laugh was wracked with pain. "Oh, I'm just peachy, Deputy. Now would you get your ass in the house? He can't *see* you."

Keith doubted the shooter would have been able to see the other two after another minute, but he didn't point that out. He wanted those two out of the danger zone and if the shooter was heading around to the back, then the front was the safer place. "Remy?"

"I'm fine," he bit off. "Shit, I don't think he wants to shoot me. If he did, I'd already be dead."

Yeah. Keith had already figured that much out, too.

He didn't waste another second. They'd wasted too many already.


Just how stupid did they think he was?

Carter stood there, shaking his head as he waited for Keith to creep around the corner of the house.

He waited in the shadows until he had a good shot. It took some doing. Keith was careful, using the lack of light, the shadows of the house to his advantage. But as he came to the deck, Keith had to risk exposing himself and that was when Carter fired.

This weapon, unlike the shotgun he'd used earlier, was virtually silent. Save for the green laser, it made no sound. And he had to be quick, precise—if Keith saw the laser, it would be too late.

He waited until Keith went to slip into the house, his back turned for just a moment.

Then he fired.

Keith stumbled, fell.

As he jogged toward the deck, he checked the time. It had been three minutes since he'd shot Law. He had less than fifteen minutes before Ezra would arrive—no, he hadn't *seen* anybody call, but he knew they would have already done it. It didn't matter. He'd either finish the job and be gone by the time they got here, or he'd finish up when the sheriff got here.

He wasn't picky. He wasn't even worried, now that it was coming down to it.

He'd always known how he'd handle it if he was discovered.

Carter would be damned before he went into a cage—no fucking way. All he wanted to do was take some people with him. The people who had pushed this on him—namely Lena and Nia.

Although he hadn't heard any sirens, he imagined the radio he'd heard earlier was the sheriff's office discovering his surprise out at Deb's place. More of the sheriff's minuscule police department out there, dealing with the mess he'd left for them. That nosy bitch wouldn't be causing anybody any more problems now. Not ever.

He crouched by Keith, rolled him over. Keith's face was slack. Checking his cousin's pulse, he found it steady. Good . . . good. Didn't want the guy dead. He hadn't ever been a problem, after all. The tranquilizer would keep him under for hours, but Keith would be just fine.

Rising, he opened the screen door, checked the back door . . . locked. He used the butt of his gun to break the glass.

After all, no point in being quiet now, was there?

* * *

On winding country roads, ten miles could take forever. Ten minutes might as well be two hours. Ezra pushed his car as fast as he could, fear blistering through him, turning his gut to ice, his blood to acid, and his mind into a tangle of horror.

*What if . . .*

*What if . . .*

"Stay safe," he whispered, thinking of his wife.

He'd just found her. He couldn't lose her already.

Other deputies, whoever could be spared, were already heading to his house. But nobody would do a damn thing until he was there. Not when Lena was involved. Fuck . . . Lena.

"Please God . . ."

Lena buried her fingers in Puck's fur. The dog was trembling, but not with fear. Every now and then, a soft growl would escape. The dog might understand fear, but he reacted to her fear more than his own. And right now, he was pissed.

"Hush," she said, keeping her voice low. "Hush now."

She was hiding in a closet. A fucking *closet*, like a child. It infuriated her.

Tucked behind boxes and clothes and coats, Nia had said she wouldn't be seen from the door as long as she and Puck didn't move. But Lena didn't know how much longer she could stay there, frozen in terror, not knowing what was going, locked in and cut off.

This, here, was horror.

This, here, was helplessness.

Puck's body stiffened. Lena sank her teeth into her lip. The floorboards just outside the door creaked.

Nia, her hands resting under her face, dust tickling her nose, lay under Lena's bed, staring as the feet moved across the floor just outside the hallway.

Lena was in there. Helpless. Vulnerable. Yeah, she had the dog with her, but the dog couldn't stop a speeding bullet, couldn't tell her to run—

*Fuck*—

Carefully, she eased out from under the bed, still watching those feet. He was opening the closet door now. She'd be on the other side of the bed in a second, and unable to see him. Closing her eyes, she said a quick prayer. That she'd live through this, and if she didn't . . . well, maybe this would make up for some of the mistakes she'd made lately.

There were other things she wanted to include, but then a sound caught her ear.

An engine.

The crunch of gravel.

*No time*—

Shoving to her feet, she took off running.

Carter Jennings whirled around and caught her arm as she passed by him. She swung out, catching him in the nose with her right fist, and the sound of cartilage crunching was sweet. "Let *go* of me, you son of a *bitch*!" she snarled as he jerked her close.

Then she fell silent as he pressed the muzzle of a gun against the underside of her chin.

"Hello, Nia."

She spit at him.

With a cool, polite smile, he lifted a hand to backhand her. She blocked that one, but she couldn't move fast enough to block the next one and that hand? It held the gun. The metal of the gun grazed her face. Fiery pain exploded. She bit her lip to keep from crying out, tasting blood.

"Where are the others? Where is Lena?"

"She had a date with the Easter Bunny," Nia snarled. "Get off of me."

He hit her again, this time in the belly. Air exploded out of her and she doubled over, sagging to the ground.

"Where is she?"

"I'm right here, you son of a bitch."

Lena stopped in the doorway and let go of Puck. "Puck . . . attack."

She might not be able to see, but she could *feel* the intensity of a madman's gaze on her.

Puck snarled and the reassuring presence of his body was gone.

Ducking back behind the closet's wall, she closed her eyes, tried to breathe. Over the roar of blood in her ears, she could hear Puck snarling, a man screaming.

Then there was a whimper, a familiar whine.

*No—*

Hope wrapped her hands around the baseball bat she'd found in the makeshift home gym. It was ironic— supposedly she'd used a baseball bat to pound on Law, but she stood there needing to use one now and she didn't even know how to hold it. She flinched as she peered around the corner, saw Puck waver, then fall, his big golden body motionless.

"Stupid mutt," Carter growled.

When he kicked the dog, Hope bit her lip to keep from crying out, focusing on his shadow. When it shifted, she peeked out, saw him turning toward Nia. She was on her knees, trying to get up, clutching her belly.

As he reached for her, Hope moved.

She swung clumsily—she'd never make it on a baseball team, but it connected with his head and she watched as he hit the floor. Without waiting another second, she turned toward her friend.

"Lena, it's Hope. Come on, we need to get downstairs."

Lena appeared in the doorway of the closet, her face streaked with tears, her eyes glittering.

"Nia, can you walk?"

"Yeah." It came out on a pained gasp. "Can run if I had to."

Still clutching the bat, she held out a hand to Lena. "Take my hand."

"Puck—"

Seconds that lasted an eternity. The other deputies fanned out behind him as Ezra crept up the first few stairs, listening. He heard Hope's voice, then Lena's, and Nia's—thank God.

"I don't know, but we have to get out of here."

"But—"

"I'll get him," Nia said. "Just get the fuck down those steps, Lena."

Ezra didn't know if he wanted to kiss Lena, hug Nia, spank them both—

The stairs squeaked and two seconds later, he saw Hope and Lena. Hope gasped when she saw him, opened her mouth, but he lifted a finger, pressed it to his lips and gestured to the deputies waiting behind him.

Until he knew the situation, he wasn't advertising his presence, wasn't letting anybody know he had deputies crawling out of the woodwork now. Silently, he gestured for his men to part and he pointed toward the door.

Hope nodded her understanding.

He stared at Lena—saw her pause as she came down the last step. She lifted a hand, reached out. It came within an inch of touching him. Then she sighed and continued to walk, her shoulders trembling, tears continuing to fall.

Ezra didn't watch her as she left the house. Instead he

started the slow climb up the stairs, avoiding the areas that squeaked, placing each foot carefully. The skin on the back of his neck was crawling. He wanted to yell at Nia to get the hell out, wherever she was—

Then the stairs squeaked. He saw her foot through the wooden slats. Heaving out a sigh of relief, he opened his mouth.

"Had to get the dog, didn't you?"

Nia felt the muzzle of the gun against the back of her head. Her arms ached from the strain of holding Puck's weight, her head throbbed and she wasn't breathing all that well. Her ribs, they *hurt*.

Looking down at Puck's limp body, she sighed. "Yeah. What can I say . . . he hates you as much as I do. I couldn't just leave him here."

The gun pressed harder and she swayed, thrown off balance. She caught herself by shifting a foot to the next step, but she almost pitched forward down the next six steps. Which actually would have been fine with her, if it wasn't for the dog. She didn't want to hurt him any more than he already was.

"You should be more careful, considering I've got a gun in my hand, considering I'm pointing it at your head," he snarled. He enunciated each word with a harder push.

She stumbled down another couple of steps, swearing. "Be careful?" She laughed. "Why? You're going to kill me anyway."

He chuckled. "Well, there is that. I'd like to get both you and Lena. Wouldn't have minded killing Reilly. But you and her? I really wanted you two dead. I might have to settle for you."

As he drilled the gun's muzzle harder into her head, forcing her down two more steps, she said, "If you keep pushing me, you'll have to settle for me with a broken neck—it's hard to balance here with an eighty-pound dog."

"Then why don't you drop it?"

"No."

She heard an ominous click. Her knees turned to water and she tucked her chin, hunched her shoulders—like that would help.

"I said, drop it."

"Why?" she asked. She opened her eyes—from the corner of her eye she saw something—through the railing on the second level of the steps, leading down to the floor. Swallowing, she took a deep breath, tried to sound like she wasn't quite so terrified. "Why should I? We've already established I'm dead, right?"

"Well, this is true." He shoved her with more force this time and she fell, gritting her teeth against the scream and trying to curl her body around Puck's. The dog fell from her arms and she hit hard on her side, smacking her head against the small table tucked under the little window on the landing. She rolled away, tried to come to her feet, but she barely made it to her knees before he was there.

He fisted his hand in her hair, jerked it back. As he nestled the gun against her chin, he said, "Do you have any idea how badly you fucked things up for me? How much you ruined my life?"

"Not even half as bad as you fucked mine," she said, panting, trying to breathe around the obscene pain spreading through her. Her side—shit, it hurt. She saw movement—

Nia jerked and twisted, ignoring how much *worse* that made the pain.

"Stupid bitch—"

"Drop the gun, Carter."

The sound of the sheriff's voice was a welcome relief, but Nia didn't dare relax, barely dared to breathe. Fury blistered through Carter Jennings's eyes, and the hand he had fisted in her hair tightened until she thought for sure he'd rip it out by the roots.

"Hell, Sheriff, you made good time," Carter said, a vicious smile lighting his face. He moved the gun away from Nia's chin, but now it was pointed at Ezra. Not exactly an improvement.

"Let her go. Put the gun down," Ezra said. He held his own gun, steady and level, his eyes flat. "You can walk away from this. You hurt her, and you won't."

Carter chuckled. "But I don't *want* to walk away. And I want to *hurt* her. I can have everything I want."

Nia's gut clenched. A man who didn't care if he lived or died . . . or a man who *wanted* to die . . . was there anything more dangerous?

She swallowed, blinked back the tears. Damn it. She wasn't ready to die with this arrogant, cruel sack of shit—

"Nia . . ."

His voice was a ragged whisper, coming from too far off.

She could barely turn her head. Wheeling her eyes to the right, she saw him, standing in the doorway of the house. Law had his arm draped around Remy's shoulders and the other clutched at the door frame.

Maybe there was one thing more dangerous than a man who wanted to die, and that was a woman who was determined she *wasn't* ready to die. As the hard, hot knot of fury settled in her heart, it burned the fear away. Shaking under the onslaught, she shifted her gaze forward, blocked out everything. She didn't care about the deputies crowding in behind Ezra, didn't care about Carter.

She only cared about Law.

Carter shouted something at Ezra.

Ezra only shook his head in response.

Nia didn't know what they were arguing about, didn't care.

She had a shot, maybe only one, right then, while Carter was focusing on something *other* than her.

Fisting her hands, she swung up, catching him between the legs. At the same time, she surged to her feet as hard, as fast as she could, putting that extra momentum into it.

She wrenched away from him and stumbled toward the steps as Ezra lunged for Carter. Sobs threatened to choke her, tears—fear, relief, both—blinded her. But she didn't need to see just then.

What she wanted, needed, was standing in the doorway and his hand reached out and caught her the minute she was close enough.

"Law."

"Shh . . . it's okay."

She pulled back long enough to glare at him. "You fucking idiot—you were shot and you're telling me, it's okay?"

But then, she pressed her head against his chest, shuddering.

Maybe it was over . . .


"Put it *down*," Ezra snarled.

Nia had caught Carter off guard, but the man either had no balls or they were made of steel, because before Ezra could even reach him, he had recovered enough to point the gun at Ezra.

"I'm not going to jail," Carter said. His voice was polite. Almost pleasant. His blue eyes were vague and blank. And in the dim light of the house, his naked scalp gleamed as smooth as a babe's. "I always planned to end it if it ever got that far, and I'm not changing that plan now."

He still held the gun pointed at Ezra, his hand rock-steady, like he could hold that position all night.

Nobody could, though. Guns were heavy—nobody could stay that way indefinitely.

"Come on, Carter. You don't want to end it this way. Don't you want to see Roz? Your wife? You love her, right?"

"Of course I do. And that's a nice try, but no. I don't want to see her enough to let you arrest me, Ezra." He gestured toward the steps with the gun. "Why don't you just go on downstairs now?"

"You know I can't do that."

"Hmm." Carter frowned, his brow creased like he was thinking very, very hard. Then, slowly, he smiled.

A chill raced down Ezra's spine.

Carter's finger tightened on the trigger. "You know, you never were one I'd planned on killing, Sheriff. I had no problem with you. Never had a problem with Dwight, either. But he got in the way, there at the end. Just like that idiot Carson did. So I had to take care of him. Now you're in the way. So . . ."

"Don't, Carter," he warned. His life started to flash before him. Damn it—he'd made himself a promise, more than a year ago. He wouldn't take another life. *God*—

"I'm sorry. But you're in my way," Carter said, his voice so polite, so reasonable.

Ezra squeezed the trigger.

As Carter dropped to the ground, Ezra sagged against the railing.

Yeah. He'd made himself a promise, all right. Back when he'd been forced to kill his own partner. It was that action that had led him on the winding road to this small town, to this very house, in fact.

"Ezra!"

Hearing Lena's voice, he looked up. If he'd only stood

there, frozen by guilt, he would have been taking a life anyway. It just would have been his own instead of a killer's. Sighing, he looked at Carter Jennings. There was a neat hole between his lifeless eyes.

"I guess I'm not in the way now," he murmured.

Then he headed up the stairs. He had one gigantic mess to clean up, but first . . . he needed to hold his wife.

# TWENTY-FOUR

"REMY."

Dawn was still just a distant thought. In the cold, bright lights of the hospital, he couldn't hide from the truth anymore, although he was trying.

He also couldn't hide from Hope, it seemed.

She'd tracked him down to the small chapel and when he looked up and met her eyes, he knew she wasn't about to leave him alone, either.

As she rested a hand on his shoulder, he reached up and covered it with his. "Did you let the doctors look you over?"

She eased down on the small wooden bench next to him. "No need. He never even touched me." She brushed his hair back from his face, studying him with worried eyes. "Are you okay?"

Remy laughed bitterly. "Okay? I just found out my cousin was a killer. A brutal one." He paused and then said, "You know what one of the deputies told me? They found what they think are human ashes in the workshop, darlin'. *Ashes.*"

"Ashes . . . how?"

"The kilns." He looked over at her and said softly, "Last year at Christmas, he gave my mother this bowl.

It had the most amazing glaze—it shimmered, almost like it was alive. She asked him how he had come up with such a unique glaze. She'd done some pottery herself in college and she was in awe—apparently he did something really, really special."

He stopped, let his mind adjust to the horror. It was going to come out, all of it. "You know what he told her? He was using a special blend of ashes in some of his glazes. Ashes, Hope. He said it gave the glazes a special luster, a life of their own."

She went white. "Oh, God. Remy."

She went to slip her arms around him, but he came off the bench, shaking his head.

"No. For God's sake, how can you stand to touch me now, Hope?"

Silence. It was a heavy, awkward silence, broken only when he turned to look at her, making himself ask, "I guess maybe you don't want to, now that you've thought about it, huh?"

"Don't be an idiot," she snapped. She stood and jabbed him in the chest with a finger, hard. "Why shouldn't I want to touch you? *You* had nothing to do with what *he* did. Did *you* know what he was doing? Did you help him? Did you cover for him?"

"God, no!" He stared at her, horrified.

"Then why should my feelings for you change?"

He shook his head, still so full of the horror, the shock. He couldn't think. She shouldn't be near him now, shouldn't touch him.

Her hands, small, but so strong, closed around his shirt. "Damn it, you bastard." Hope shook him. "I *love* you. I've spent my entire life waiting for somebody like you and if you think I'm going to let somebody like Carter interfere with that, then you better get that out of your head *now*."

"Hope—"

"No." She cut him off, shaking her head. She let go of his shirt, reached up to cup his face. "I just need to know *one* thing, and only *one* thing. Do you love me?"

Staring into her soft green eyes, Remy sighed. Something was trying to work past the horror inside—something *true,* something *clean* and *real.* It was *her.* Hope. Pressing his brow to hers, he said softly, "More than my own life."

"Then nothing else matters. *Nothing.*"

Lena lay on the hospital bed, stroking a hand down Puck's side. She hadn't been hurt, but her boy had. Poor Puck. And Ezra wasn't about to let her go off to the vet to tend him, either. Thankfully, though, they could, and would, unofficially, check on broken ribs and stuff here.

"You did good, boy," she whispered, staring off into the darkness. Achingly alone. Puck was asleep, although unconscious would have been a better word. Apparently Carter had shown up loaded for bear, or close to it. He'd shot Puck with one of the tranquilizer darts and since he was still breathing . . .

Tears leaked out of her eyes. Squeezing them closed, she pressed her face against soft golden fur. "Hang in there, boy. You have to."

A hand caressed her hair.

"Ezra."

Shooting upright, she turned and clamped her arms around him. The sobs that had threatened her for the past few hours were perilously close, but she fought them back. Not here. Not while they were in this cold, sterile hospital.

"You okay?" he murmured, pressing his lips to her brow. "The nurses said you don't want anybody in here with you."

"The only people I'd want are all too busy," she said, trying not to let her voice break. "I guess you might have a few pieces of paper to fill out. And I guess one of the others is getting patched up—but hell, Law's leg can't be that bad, right?"

"Nah. Bet it's nothing worse than a paper cut," he murmured, humoring her.

"Yeah. So why is he being a baby and not in here with me? Or Hope and . . ." She almost said Remy, but then she stopped, ashamed. "Man, Remy must be reeling."

Sick at heart, she leaned against Ezra. "And Roz—damn it!" She stiffened and sat up. "Ezra . . . is Roz here?"

He stroked her hair. "Yeah, sweetheart. She's here. I'll take you to her in a minute. I just needed some time with you first." His arms came around her, tight and strong. "Damn it, Lena. I was so scared . . ."

"Yeah." Breathing him in, she relaxed against him. "Me, too."

"Roz?"

There was no sound. Turning her face to Ezra, she whispered, "Is she awake?"

"Yeah." Ezra blew out a breath and then glanced down at his wife for a moment before looking back at Roz. She lay on her side, knees drawn up to her chest, staring dully at the wall.

She'd been like that for hours. He'd hoped she'd respond to Lena, but . . . "I guess I'll walk you back to your room."

"No." Lena eased her hand from his and stepped forward, the collapsible cane in her hand going from side to side as she moved forward. When she reached the bed, she patted it with her hand, moving forward until she was at Roz's side. Then she sat down. "Hey, sweetie."

From his position in the doorway, Ezra could see Roz close her eyes.

Lena laid a hand on her arm and started to stroke. "I'm here. You know that." She patted along the bed until she found Roz's hand, then she squeezed it. "I'm right here."

And quietly, Roz started to sob. Lena curled her body around Roz, hugging her close. "There you go, sweetie. You go ahead and cry."

"Don't you look sexy."

Law, groggy from the pain meds, punchy from exhaustion, forced his lids to open, forced his eyes to focus. Nia stood in the doorway.

A wry smile twisted his lips. "I look like shit," he muttered. "You, on the other hand . . . you still look like an Amazon."

"An Amazon?" She snorted. "Whatever."

His lids drifted down, but he forced them open again. He didn't know how much longer he could stay awake, though. The drugs were too damn strong to fight. "Yeah. That was what I thought the first time I saw you. You were an Amazon. Strong. Sexy. Beautiful."

She came inside, limping a little. He saw the brace on her foot and fury, so useless, so fiery hot, burned inside. "Your leg?"

"It's my ankle," she said, shrugging. "Twisted it when I fell. All in all, I got off pretty light, seeing as how he came there solely to kill me."

"Fuck, don't say that right before I pass out," he muttered. "Don't need more nightmares."

"Sorry." She winced and put her hand in his.

He squeezed lightly. "You should be. Now you have to stay while I sleep. Keep the nightmares away. Will you?"

"Sure." A hand stroked his brow. "You sleep, Reilly. I'll keep the nightmares away."

\* \* \*

Nia stroked his hair back from his brow, watched him as he drifted off to sleep. Yeah. She could stay while he slept. She owed him a few hours at least. Actually, she probably owed all of them her life, and not just for saving it a few hours ago.

But now maybe she could move *on* with her life. Once she let herself grieve for Joely, maybe she could actually have a life. Something she hadn't let herself think about in far too long. Getting back to her life.

Yeah.

She thought about leaving Ash, Kentucky, leaving behind the ugliness of the past day, the awful memories and the knowledge of what had happened to Joely here. She could do it now.

And although it hurt to think about, she thought about leaving Law.

She'd left her life back in Virginia, after all, right?

Silent, she stayed with him, watching him through the night.

As dawn broke, she made a decision.

She'd done what she came for.

It was time to go.


Law woke to pain, brutal and ugly, and the cold hands of a nurse as she wrapped a blood pressure cuff around his arm. Groggy, he muttered, "What the—"

"Good morning, Mr. Reilly," she said, her voice cool and flat. "Just checking your blood pressure and your temperature and I'll be out of your hair."

"Wow, nice bedside manner you've got there," Nia said from across the bed.

Forgetting about the nurse, he turned his head, stared at Nia. "You stayed."

She gave him a vague smile. "You asked me to." Then she looked at the nurse. "You come in here at six in the morning without bothering to knock. I'm pretty sure that violates hospital protocol, by the way. You don't bother with an introduction, you jerk the blankets off an injured patient and start messing with him, without any regard to the fact that you'd just woken him up. You didn't give your name, you didn't knock, you didn't bother to draw the curtain for privacy *or* shut the door."

"Nia—"

The nurse sniffed. "I knocked. Neither of you were awake."

"Nice try." Nia bared her teeth. "I've been awake for the past three hours, ever since you came in to check his IV. You might have knocked then. You didn't knock this time." She peered at the nurse's name tag and then smirked. "Now why am I not surprised to see your last name is Jennings?"

The older woman clenched her jaw. She started to jerk the blood pressure cuff off Law's arm, but Nia's narrowed eyes must have spoken volumes. With exaggerated care, the nurse removed it. "Naturally, I always knock," she said stiffly. "Perhaps you were closer to sleep than you realize."

"Ahhh. Perhaps." Nia flicked Law a glance and then looked at the nurse. "And perhaps you should find another nurse to provide his care. Naturally, you're distraught about the death of your relative—that would explain why you're not acting with the concern for your patients that you *should* display."

Before the nurse could say another word, Nia uncurled herself from the chair and rocked back on her heels. "It really would be best if you did just that. How good would it look if you were reported to the licensing board for less than ethical behavior? Before you answer, be aware . . . I know how to make that report. And I will."

Without another word, the woman left.

Law lifted a brow. "Being a bitch isn't the same as being unethical," he said.

"It is if she's doing it just because she's pissed about her cousin." She jerked a shoulder in a shrug. "I wasn't asleep—and she's nowhere near as quiet as she needs to be when she's bitching. I could hear her out at the nurse's station. She was griping about cover-ups and conspiracy crap. If she can't separate her personal opinion from her professional job, then Nurse Ratchett out there needs to find a different nurse for you."

He gave her a weak version of a lewd grin. "You know, it makes me hot, seeing you get upset on my behalf."

"Yeah? What doesn't make you hot?" She smiled, but it was tight. Strained.

"Hmm. Nurse Ratchett. Doesn't do a damn thing for me." He grimaced and shifted on the bed. "Fucking leg. Hurts like hell."

"I bet." She came closer, brushed his hair back from his face. "You need anything for it?"

Probably, but he didn't want anything. It would just make him sleep and right then he wanted to sit there and enjoy being alive—enjoy seeing her. Enjoy knowing it was *over*. "Nah. I'm good."

"Yeah. I can tell—you look like you're ready for a walk on the beach." She bent down and pressed her lips to his temple.

Law took a deep breath, breathing her in. Her scent flooded his head, chased away some of the stink of antiseptic and blood. A little more of the horror faded. It really was over. Maybe now they could start to talk . . . to think . . .

"Well, Reilly . . . I've got to say. It's been an adventure."

Law blinked at her. "What?"

She shrugged. "Can't say it's been boring, right?" She

hesitated and then brushed a hand through his hair. "You take care of yourself."

For a second, he was caught off guard. Big time. As her lips pressed to his, his mind was spinning in circles, trying to figure out why it sounded like she was saying good-bye.

Then it dawned on him, as she turned away.

She *was* saying good-bye.

Reaching out, he caught her arm, just barely. "Wait— what—you're leaving? Just like that?"

Nia turned back to him. With a shrug, she said, "What else am I supposed to do? It's over now. Time for me to get back to my life. I need to start living again, right?"

"But . . ." He let go of her arm, uncertain of what he had to say. What *could* he say? Damn it. "You just leave."

"My life is in Virginia," she said gently. Then, without another word, she turned and walked away.

# TWENTY-FIVE

*My life is in Virginia.*

What life?

Nia stared at the four walls of her empty home and tried to figure out just what it was she'd been coming back to. Because there was nothing. That was exactly what she'd found. Absolutely nothing. The emptiness here threatened to drive her mad.

She'd been back for a week and it was already too long.

It wasn't the place, though, that was lacking.

It was her.

She was missing something. Something she was realizing just might have become vital—

Of course, it didn't help that every fricking day she had to hear his name. She hadn't even made it home before she heard his name. The calls from Ezra started almost immediately.

*Did you not realize there would be questions I needed to ask? Law said you took off, left town. What the hell, Nia?*

Then the next day. *Law's been discharged, although he's having a hell of a time getting around on that leg of his. Hope's going to help him out for a few days. I need to talk to you, ask some questions—you know, you could come back out here, stay for a week or two while he gets on his feet.*

Every fricking day. But it wouldn't have mattered. She'd still be thinking of him.

Yeah, maybe she'd gone to Ash for a reason, and maybe she'd accomplished everything she'd set out to accomplish. Maybe she didn't exactly have a *life* there and maybe there were ugly, awful memories there.

But Law was there, too. And she was starting to realize that if she really wanted to get back to her life, she needed to figure out just where Law fit into her life, just what place he filled. It certainly wasn't her past, though, because she couldn't stop thinking about him.

The phone started to ring. But when she saw the number for the sheriff's department in Ash, she ignored it. Flopping back onto her bed, she pulled a pillow over her head and tried to just *not* think.

Just let her thoughts drift . . . that's how she'd figure out how to solve this problem.

The problem being the massive hole inside her heart.

What would fill it? And the answer was easy.

*Law . . .*

Swearing, she kicked her legs over the side of the bed and stormed over to the closet. She grabbed her duffel bag and started to pack. She'd only gotten all of the clothes washed and put away yesterday and here she was again, packing them back up.

Damn it. She needed to talk to him. Face him. Figure out just what they had going and what they needed to do about it. He meant something—mattered, and she suspected if she let him, he'd come to mean everything.

The thought both terrified and elated her.

She should, if she was sane, take a little while to settle. Recover. Relax. But she couldn't because her mind wouldn't settle until she'd faced Law again. Until she'd figured things out.

So she packed. She did it with the ease born of habit, making a few calls on the side to let her contact know that she wasn't available like she'd thought—damn it, she was seriously screwing herself there, but oh well. She was getting so burned out on all the damn travel anyway, all the horror and grief and chaos they wanted her to face when they sent her out.

If she didn't have jobs lined up, then she didn't have jobs. She'd figure out something, right?

It took her less than twenty minutes to get ready. She was going back to Ash, damn it. With a much less dangerous agenda, but this one was every bit as complicated.

Her heart was racing as she strode to the door. A hard, determined smile curled her lips as she jerked open the door.

And then, she froze.

Law was standing there, sweating, gripping a cane, one hand raised to knock.

Gaping at him, she asked, "What are you doing here?"

"About to collapse," he said shortly. He nudged her out of the way, none too gently, and headed over to the couch. "Nice place. I'm coming in. Thanks."

"Ahhh . . ."

Then she winced as he sat down with a look of obvious pain on his face. "I thought you weren't supposed to be putting too much weight on your leg yet."

"I'm not." He glared at her.

"Then what are you doing walking around?" she demanded.

"You *left*," he pointed out. "Said you had to get on with your life. That your life was in Virginia. So fine. I'm in Virginia now."

Edging closer, she dumped her bag on the floor by the couch and shook her head. "Ah . . . I'm not following."

"Of course not." He scowled. "You only see what you want to see." He reached out, caught her arm and tugged.

She resisted, edging around his leg. "Damn it, you're going to make me trip over you—do you *want* to be in more pain?" She stepped over his legs and then let him tug her down so that she sat next to him.

He didn't say anything right away, just pulled her close, tucking her under his chin. Then he sighed. "I dunno if it's possible. Just being away from you hurts like a bitch."

"Yeah." She rested a hand on his uninjured leg. "I know the feeling."

He pulled back, a scowl darkening his face once more. "Then why did you *leave*?"

"Well . . ." She shrugged. "It seemed like the right thing to do. I'd done what I came for, just hadn't planned on you."

"I didn't plan on you, either. But there you are." He cupped her face. "So we didn't exactly meet under normal circumstances. So what? Does that mean we can't make it work?"

"No." She curled a hand around his wrist and leaned in, pressed her mouth to his. "It doesn't mean that."

"Then why did you leave?"

"I . . . shit, Law. I don't know. Maybe I had to leave, just so I could figure that out." She nipped his lower lip, then pulled back, staring at him. "And I was heading back. That's where I was going, actually."

Law stared at her. Then, slowly, he started to smile. "Yeah?"

"Yeah." Curling up on the couch, she tucked herself against him and rested her head on his shoulder. "I do need to get on with my life, I know that. But I think the best way to do that is going to involve you, Law. How do you feel about that?"

His arms came around her, strong and sure. For a second, he didn't respond. Then, his voice gruff, he said, "I feel pretty damn good about that, actually, seeing as how I came all the way out here to tell you that I love you."

She stiffened. "You . . . what?"

"You heard me. Now it's your turn. How do you feel about that?"

Something warm bloomed inside her heart.

Lifting her head, she laid a hand on his cheek. "I feel pretty damn good about it, too, if you want the truth. Because I think I love you, too."

He cocked a brow. "Think?"

"Hey . . . gimme some time, Reilly." She leaned forward, pressed her brow to his. "We got that, right?"

"Yeah." His hand curved over her nape. "We got all the time in the world, I guess."

As their mouths met, that heavy ache of pain in Nia's heart finally started to ease.

Yeah. All the time in the world . . . and maybe it wasn't going to be the long, dark walk she'd been expecting.

# Author's Note

Some creative license was taken with this trilogy. Carrington County is a fictional county set in Kentucky, roughly an hour away from Lexington.

While I spoke with several lawyers and law-enforcement professionals while writing the stories, I realize certain aspects are still not going to be completely true to life. I hope it doesn't take away from your enjoyment of them.

# Acknowledgments

There's just no way I can thank everybody I need to thank, I don't think. At least not without needing a lot more page space than my publisher can give me. But I do need to mention a few special people.

Thank God for letting me live my dream, allowing me to use it in a way that lets me provide for the family You've given me.

I know I've mentioned my editor Kate and my agent Irene and I could mention them a hundred times—it still wouldn't fully express how much I appreciate them.

Again, thanks to Terrie T, with the American Printing House for the Blind, and Kristeen H. Your help when I was trying to build Lena's character and lay the groundwork for this trilogy was invaluable.

The same to Detective Todd H—I'm sure he thought I was probably crazy when my husband and I showed up at his door one night and I started asking him a bunch of very *strange* questions.

Nicole and Lime for insight into things of a legal persuasion, and fellow writer and friend Rosemary Laurey, although I can't really explain why and how she helped me . . . not yet anyway.

There are other writer friends, like Sylvia Day and

Shayla Black, who routinely talk me down when I'm losing it or boost me up when I'm needing it. As well as the time Allison Brennan took to chat with me at RWA, and in various e-mails while I was having numerous freak-outs . . . whether or not you remember, you helped me out more than you can imagine.

Thanks to my readers as well. You are all so awesome . . . thanks for your support.

Read on for a preview
of the first two books in Shiloh Walker's
thrilling romantic suspense trilogy!

# IF YOU HEAR HER

and

# IF YOU SEE HER

# IF YOU HEAR HER

# CHAPTER
# ONE

Her name was Carly Watson.

The final hours of her life were brutal.

She didn't know where she was. She didn't know how long she'd been there. By that point, she was so wracked with pain, so desperate for escape, she barely remembered who she was.

She was twenty-three. She was going to medical school. She was bright, eager, and before she'd fallen into this hell, she had loved life. Now she just prayed for it to end.

She had been stuck in that hellish darkness for hours, days, possibly weeks.

And she knew she would die there.

She knew he was coming back—the door creaked. It was like a death knell, heralding his arrival. As the door swung open, the ancient hinges protested.

A sob bubbled up in her throat as he laid a hand on her calf and stroked up. She cringed away as much as she could, but the restraints at her wrists, waist, knees, and ankles didn't allow for much movement.

When he cupped his hand over her sex, her scream, long and desperate, split the air.

Her kidnapper, rapist, and soon-to-be killer watched,

amused . . . pleased with her terror. "Go ahead and scream, sweetheart. Nobody can hear you."

"Please . . ." her throat was so dry and raw from how she had cried. How she had begged. How she had pleaded. She almost hated herself, for begging. For giving him that pleasure. Some part of her just wasn't ready to accept the truth, wasn't ready to give up.

Even though, in her heart, she knew it was useless. "Just let me go. Please let me go . . . I won't tell anybody, I swear."

He sighed. It was a sigh of long-suffering patience, the one a parent might give a child. He even patted her shoulder as he murmured, "Yes, I'm sure you won't."

A loud sound rasped through the air and she whimpered as she recognized it. A zipper. He was getting undressed—no, no, no . . .

Hysterical panic tore through her and she started to scream.

He raped her again.

Her voice gave out long before she was able to escape inside herself.

This time, though, her escape was final. She had retreated somewhere deep inside herself—somewhere where pain didn't exist, where terror didn't exist.

When he ended her life, she never even knew—she was already gone.

Her name was Carly Watson.

It was a lovely day, the kind of day you just didn't get too often. The air was warm and mild, with clear sunshine beaming down. A soft breeze drifted by. Under the trees, it was just a bit cooler.

The perfect sort of day for a walk.

At least, Lena Riddle would've thought so. But halfway through, her dog started getting anxious. Puck didn't do anxious. Not in the four years she'd had him. But there he was, pulling against his leash, like he was determined not to let her take their normal route through the woods.

"Come on, Puck. You wanted to go for a walk, remember?"

She tried to take another step, but the big yellow retriever sat down. He wasn't going to move an inch.

Just then, faintly, oh so very faintly, she heard . . . something.

Puck growled. "Hush," she murmured, reaching down and resting a hand on his head. He had his hackles up, his entire body braced and tensed. "Easy, boy. Just take it easy."

Standing in the middle of the trail, with her head cocked, she listened. The faint breeze that had been blowing all day abruptly died and all those faint sounds of life she could always hear in the woods faded down to nothingness. A heartbeat passed, then another.

It was utterly silent.

Then it came again. Something . . . muffled. Faint. An animal? Trapped?

She scowled absently, concentrating. There it was again.

Her brow puckered as she focused, trying to lock in on the sound better.

Puck whined in his throat and tugged on his leash, demandingly. Lena turned her head, trying to follow that sound. It was gone, though. The breeze returned and all she could hear now were the leaves rustling in the breeze, the sound of a bird call, and somewhere off in the distance, a car's motor.

Still, the faint memory of that sound, whatever it was, sent a shiver down her spine.

"You know what, Puck?" she murmured. "I think you're right. Let's get the hell out of here."

She only had a few hours left before she had to go to work anyway.

*    *    *

"... there. . . ."

He stood over her, studied her hair.

The gleaming blond strands were shorn now to chin length, perfectly straight, even as could be.

Her eyes, sightless and fixed, stared overhead.

That blank look on her face irritated him, but he wasn't surprised. He had seen this coming, after all. Something about the way she had reacted, the way she'd screamed.

The life had gone out of his girl and once that fight was gone . . .

Well. That was just how it was.

Carefully gathering up the hair, he selected what he wanted and then bagged up the rest, adding it to the pack he'd carry out of here. Later. Few things still that he had to handle.

He studied her body, the long slim lines of it, her limbs pale and flaccid now, the softly rounded swell of her belly. Nice, full breasts . . . he did like a good pair of tits on a woman. The dull gleam of gold at her throat from the necklace she wore. Strong, sleek shoulders.

Stooping down beside her, he hefted her lifeless body in his arms.

What he needed to do now wasn't going to be pleasant, and he wouldn't do it here.


"So what do you think it was?"

"Hell, I don't know." A sigh slipped past Lena's lips as she turned to face her best friend. Just talking to Roslyn Jennings made her feel better. And slightly silly. It had probably been nothing. Nothing . . . although it had bothered her dog something awful. "It sure as hell had Puck freaked out, though."

"You sound a little freaked out, too."

"Yeah. You could say that."

Although, really, freaked out didn't quite touch it.

Grimacing, Lena forced herself to focus. Should pay

more attention to what she was doing or she was going to end up slicing up her fingers as well as the potatoes. It wouldn't do the Inn's reputation any good if word got out that the chef was adding body parts to the dishes, she thought morbidly.

For some reason, that thought sent a shiver down her spine.

"It sure doesn't sound like Puck. I mean, that's not like him. He loves his walks, right?"

"Yep. He does. And you're right . . . this isn't like him." She couldn't recall him ever acting quite like that before. He was a good dog, protective, loving . . . a friend.

"Let's talk about this noise you heard. If we can figure out what it was, maybe we can figure out what had Puck so freaked out. It probably had something to do with the noise, right? I mean, it makes sense."

"I can't place it. Weird grunting. Kind of muffled."

"Don't take this wrong, but do you think maybe you heard somebody going at it?" Roslyn's voice was a mixture of skepticism and interest.

"Going at it?" Lena asked, blankly. "Going at what?"

For about two seconds, Roz was silent. Then she burst into laughter. "Oh, sweetie, it's been way too long since you've gotten laid. Sex, girl. Do you remember what sex is?"

"Yes. Vaguely." Scowling, she went at the potatoes with a little more enthusiasm than necessary. Oh, yes, she remembered sex. It had been close to a year since she'd gotten any, and before that? It had been college.

But, yes, she remembered sex.

"So, you think maybe a couple of people were out there screwing? Although, hell, if some guy is going to talk me into stripping nekkid in the great outdoors, it had better be good sex. Bug bites. Ticks. Poison ivy."

"Sunburn," Lena offered helpfully. Perpetually pale,

she had to slather down with SPF 60 just for a jaunt to the mailbox. Well, maybe not that bad. But still.

"Sunburned hoo-haa. Heh. Doesn't sound like fun, does it? Although if the guy is good . . . but you were in the woods, right? So scratch the sunburned hoo-haa. So, what do you think . . . could you have just heard some private moments?"

"You're a pervert, you know that?" Lena grinned at her best friend. Then she shrugged. "And . . . I don't know. I really don't know. The only thing I know for sure is that Puck didn't want to be there—that's just not like him."

The dog at Lena's feet shifted. She rinsed her hands and then crouched down in front of him, stroking his head. "It's okay, pal. I understand."

He licked her chin and she stood up.

As she turned to wash her hands again, she heard the telltale whisper of the cookie jar. Smiling, she said, "If you eat all of those, you're out of luck until next week. I am not whipping up another batch tomorrow. You're stuck with whatever you bought from the store. With that wedding you've got planned, Jake and I are going to be busy enough as it is."

Jake was the other chef here at Running Brook. They split the week, Jake working Monday through Wednesday and Lena working Thursday through Saturday—they traded off on Sundays, but with the wedding they had going on tomorrow, they both needed to be here.

"That wedding," Roz muttered around a mouthful of cookie. "Hell, that wedding is why I need the cookie—and store-bought isn't going to hold me right now, sweetie. I need the real stuff. Good stuff. Shit. If I thought I could get away with it, I would have a White Russian or three to go along with the cookie."

"No drinking on the job. Not even for the owner." Lena smirked. "Hell, you're the one who had to go and decide to start doing these boutique weddings. You all but have a welcome mat out . . . 'Bridezillas accepted and welcomed.' " Shoving off the counter, she joined Roz at the island. "Gimme one of those before you eat them all."

Roz pushed a cookie into her hand and Lena bit down. Mouth full of macadamias, white chocolate, and cranberries, she made her way to the coffeepot. "Since you can't have a White Russian, you want some coffee?"

"No." Roslyn sighed. "The last thing I need right now is coffee. I'm supposed to be meeting the bride and her mom in a half hour to discuss the floral arrangements."

In the middle of getting a clean mug from the cabinet, Lena frowned. "Discuss the floral arrangements . . . the wedding is tomorrow."

"Exactly. Which is why I need cookies." She huffed out a breath. "Damn. I really do need that White Russian, you know. But I'll have to settle for the cookies."

Lena smiled as her friend went for another one. That emergency stash wasn't going to last the day, much less the weekend. She thought through her schedule and decided she might try to make up another batch. She could probably find the time. It sounded like Roz would probably need it. They were all going to need it, probably.

"Does she want to change the floral arrangements or what?"

Roz groaned. There was a weird thunk, followed by her friend's muffled voice. "I don't know. She just wanted to discuss the flowers. She had some concerns." There were two more thunks.

"Well, banging your head on the counter isn't going to do much good . . . unless you hit it hard enough to knock yourself out. Otherwise, all it's going to do is give you a headache."

"I've already got a headache," Roz muttered.

"Look, if she does have the idea of changing the arrangements around, explain to her that the florist here closes at noon on Fridays. Somebody will have already made sure the orders are covered, but changing the orders would just be too difficult, and it could be too chancy to try someplace outside of town. If you lay it on thick enough, she's not going to want to risk it."

"Hmmm. Good point." The stool scraped against the tile floor as Roz stood up. "I knew there was a reason I hired you."

"You hired me for my cookies," Lena said, her voice dry.

"Another reason, then." She took a deep breath. "Okay, no more cookies. I'm going to check on a few things before I go talk to my . . . client."

"Good luck. But do me a favor . . . if she decides she needs a last-minute menu change? Stonewall her. I don't care how, and I don't care what you say. Stonewall her."

"This woman can't be stonewalled." Roz sighed. "I think she might just *be* Stonewall. His reincarnation or something. You can't stonewall a Stonewall, right?"

"Figure a way out." There was no way she was doing a last-minute menu change.

# IF YOU SEE HER

# CHAPTER
# ONE

"SHE'S A DISTURBED WOMAN, I'M AFRAID TO SAY."

Remington Jennings pinched the bridge of his nose and tried not to think about the sad green eyes and silken brown hair of one Hope Carson. "Disturbed, how? Can you help me out any here, Detective Carson?"

On the other end of the line, the man sighed. "Well, I'm reluctant to do that. You see, I wouldn't have a DA on the phone, asking about my wife, if there wasn't trouble. And I don't want to cause her trouble."

"She's your *ex*-wife and she's already got trouble. Do you want her to get the help she needs or not?" Remy asked, his voice taking on a sharp edge. Hell, anybody with half a brain could see that woman wouldn't hurt a fly unless she was just pushed . . .

"You want to help her, is that it, Jennings?" The detective laughed, but it wasn't a happy sound. It was sad and bitter.

"If I didn't, I wouldn't have called. I'm not trying to lock her up and throw away the key here. Help me out, Detective." *Damn it, Carson, gimme a break.*

"Help you out. You mean help you help Hope." Once more, Joseph Carson sighed. He was Hope's ex and a cop from out west. He was also proving to be one hell of a pain in the ass.

Faintly, Remy heard a heavy creak. "Mr. Jennings, pardon my French, but you can't help Hope, because she doesn't fucking *want* help. She's a very troubled young woman. She . . . shit, this is hard, but we hadn't been married very long when she was diagnosed with borderline personality disorder. She's manipulative, a chameleon—she can make a person believe whatever they need to believe. You might *think* you're seeing a woman you can help—if she'll just *let* you. But that's not the case. You're seeing what she *wants* you to see."

Remy clenched his jaw, closed his hand around the pen so tightly it snapped.

Shit—that . . . no. Not right. Everything inside screeched just how *wrong* that was. It couldn't be right—it just couldn't.

But his voice was cool, collected, as he said, "Border-line personality disorder, you said? Does she have a history of violence?"

Long, tense moments of silence passed and finally, Carson said, "Yeah. There's a history of violence. Only against herself . . . and me. I kept it very well hidden. I didn't want people thinking bad things about her, and on my part . . . well, I was ashamed. For her, for myself, for both of us. It wasn't until things got really bad that I couldn't hide it anymore."

"You're telling me she was violent with you?" Remy knew he needed to be making notes, processing this.

But he couldn't—couldn't process, couldn't even wrap his mind around it. That woman lifting her hand against somebody?

No. The picture just wasn't coming together for him.

"Yes." Carson sighed once more.

"So you're telling me she *does* have a history of violence?"

"Shit, didn't I just go through that?" he snarled.

Remy clutched the phone so tight, it was amazing the plastic didn't crack. This was wrong—so fucking wrong, and he knew it, knew it in his bones.

*She's manipulative, a chameleon—she can make a person believe whatever they need to believe. You might think you're seeing a woman you can help—if she'll just let you. But that's not the case. You're seeing what she wants you to see.*

Damn it, was he just letting her lead him around, he wondered?

Right then, he wasn't sure.

He took a deep, slow breath, focused on the phone. "Can you give me some examples? Tell me what happened?"

"Examples. Shit." Carson swore and then demanded, "Why should I tell you this? Just answer me that."

"Because if she's got a mental disorder, then she *does* need help and if she needs help, I'd rather her get help then get locked up. You should know her better than anybody. So if you do care about her, help me help her. Come on, Detective. You're a cop. You're sworn to uphold the law, to protect people. If your wife could prove dangerous . . ."

"You fucking lawyers, you always know what to say," Carson muttered. But there was no anger, no malice in his voice. Just exhaustion. "Yeah, you could say she has violent tendencies. You could say she has a history of violence. She's very manipulative and all those violent tendencies get worse when she doesn't get her way. She becomes unstable, unpredictable. There is no telling what she might do to somebody she perceived as being in her way."

Abruptly, his voice lost that calm, detached tone and he snarled, "There. I gave you all the dirt you needed and don't tell me you can't use that. God help me, I hate myself even though I know she needs help. Now tell me what the fuck is going on!"

Remy blew out a slow breath and said, "She's in the hospital at the moment—attempted suicide. Plus, there was an attack on a friend of hers. It looks like she might be responsible."

"Fuck." The word was harsh, heavy with fury and grief. "She's tried to commit suicide before, so as much as I hate to hear it, that's not a big surprise. But the friend . . . you said there was an attack on a friend?"

"Yes." Remy scowled absently at nothing. "Maybe you've heard of him—it seems like the two of them go back quite a while. The name's Law Reilly?"

"Reilly." Carson grunted. "Yeah. I know Law. I wish I could say I was surprised to hear that she'd turned on him, but Hope's always had a way of turning on those who've tried to help her. Those who care about her."

Remy closed his eyes.

Damn it, was there anything this guy could say that would make it a little bit easier for him to figure out how to handle Hope?

Of course if he *wanted* her put away, this guy would be making his whole damn night.

But right now, he could almost hear the cell door swinging shut on her and it was just turning Remy's stomach. "So you think she could have hurt Mr. Reilly?"

"With Hope, I just don't know. The one thing I *do* know? She's capable of just about anything. I also know that I wish I could help her. Hell, I'd like to believe *you* can. But I know I can't, and I can't believe you can either. She doesn't want help, won't admit she needs it. Look, if there's anything I can do to make sure she gets that help, just ask. I don't want her in trouble, but I do want her to get help. Before it's too late."

Remy barely remembered the rest of the conversation.

He was too busy finally processing the fact that he'd more or less gotten the supporting evidence he needed.

Hope Carson's fingerprints had been found all over the weapon used to beat Law Reilly.

She had slit her wrists.

She had a history of violence.

A history of turning on people who cared about her.

According to her ex-husband—who seemed to care about her—she was manipulative, prone to doing whatever it took to get her way.

Fuck and double fuck.

Instead of feeling satisfied with what he needed to do, what he *could* do, he found himself thinking about those sad, sad green eyes . . .

*Fuck.*

By the time she landed at Blue Grass Airport, Nia Hollister was so damned tired, she could barely see straight, so sick at heart, she ached with it, and she longed to curl up in a dark, quiet room and just . . . sob.

Giving in to tears had never been her way, but this time, the temptation was strong, so overpowering, there were times when she felt the tears swelling in her throat like a knot. And a scream—just beyond the tears, there was a scream begging to break free.

She kept it held inside through sheer will alone.

Now wasn't the time to scream, or to cry.

Somewhere inside her heart, she still wanted to believe they were wrong.

All of them.

Joely wasn't dead. She couldn't be. They were like sisters—almost closer than sisters.

They rarely fought. They were best friends, in their hearts, their souls. Even when Nia was on the other side of the country for half the year—or *out* of the country . . .

They could be wrong. All of them—Bryson, Joely's fiancé, who wouldn't even go with her to identify the body, the cops who insisted it was Joely . . . everybody. They could all be wrong.

It might not be Joely.

But if it wasn't her cousin lying dead in a morgue in Ash, Kentucky, then where was she?

Her fiancé hadn't seen her in more than a month.

She wasn't answering her cell phone or e-mail.

It was like she'd dropped off the face of the earth.

*No . . . she hasn't dropped off the face of the earth. She's been lying dead in the deep freeze in the morgue, you selfish bitch, while you're off on assignment.*

Abandoned—because law enforcement always turned to family, although Bryson might have been able to do it if he'd pushed, especially since Nia hadn't been reachable. Out of contact—*fuck.*

She hadn't been around, while her cousin was kidnapped, hadn't been around while she was killed, hadn't been around at all and because of that, Joely was treated like some worthless piece of garbage.

Nia hadn't been around. Oh, *God* . . . Tears pricked her eyes. She'd been out of contact for almost three weeks. Joely could have reached her, but would she have shared that information with her fiancé? Probably not.

With weariness and grief dragging at her steps, she lugged her carry-on through the airport. Years of living out of a suitcase had taught her to pack light and the bag was all she carried. The rest of her stuff was being shipped back to her house in Williamsburg.

Soon, she'd have to find a Laundromat and wash her clothes, but that was a problem for another day.

Now, she needed to get a rental car. Rental car. Then she needed to . . .

She stopped in front of an ad—it was brightly colored, displaying a chestnut horse racing across a field of green grass. Numb, she just stared at it for a minute and then once more started to walk.

Rental car. Ash, Kentucky. She needed to get there. Needed to . . .

"Miss?"

Nia started, then found herself staring dumbly at one of the airport security guards. Blinking, she glanced around. She wasn't sure where she was, or how she'd gotten there.

He eyed her with a strange mix of concern and caution. "Are you okay?"

Nia swallowed. That knot in her throat swelled to epic proportions and she realized those tears were even closer than she'd thought. "I . . . rough few days."

"It looks like it." He gestured with his head off to the side. "You've been standing in the middle of the hall for the past five minutes. Can I help you find where you're going?"

Nia pressed the heel of her hand against her temple. Shit.

The ache in her chest spread.

Ash—she needed to get to Ash, wherever in the hell that was.

But if she was standing around like a zombie in the middle of an airport, the last thing she needed to do was get behind the wheel of a car. Reality breathed its icy cold breath down her spine and she sighed. "I guess I'm heading outside to catch a cab to a hotel," she finally said.

Getting to Ash would have to wait until morning.

She loathed the idea, but her pragmatic side was strong, even in grief. As exhausted as she was, it would be suicide to get behind the wheel of a car and she knew it. As desperate as she was to get to Ash, she had some damn strong inner demons.

Besides, maybe she'd luck out . . . she'd go to sleep and wake up, realize this was nothing but one awful, horrid nightmare.


The conversation with Detective Joseph Carson was still ringing through Remy's mind hours later as he tossed and turned on his bed, trying to sleep.

*Settling down* wasn't happening, though. It was past midnight when he finally slept.

There were nights when he hit the mattress and sleep fell on him like a stone. As one of the two district attorneys in the small county of Carrington, Kentucky, he had helped put away meth dealers, a couple of child molesters and rapists, more than a few drunk drivers, and several wife beaters, and he routinely dealt with petty theft.

Even in his small, mostly rural county, crime wasn't nonexistent.

He enjoyed what he did.

But tonight, sleep didn't come easy. Hell, screw *easy*—it didn't want to come at *all*.

Every time he closed his eyes, he thought of a green-eyed brunette and he thought about what he had to do in the morning.

It wasn't a job he wanted to do.

It was a job he'd give just about anything to *not* do.

But he hadn't taken this job just so he could walk away from the hard ones.

All the facts pointed to one thing: Hope Carson was a violent, disturbed woman.

His gut screamed *Screw the facts*. But he couldn't ignore what he saw, couldn't ignore the evidence, couldn't ignore what he'd been told and what he'd learned.

His job was clear.

And his job, sometimes, sucked.

It was well past midnight when he finally fell into a restless sleep, and into even more restless dreams.

Nightmares.

Dreams where he saw her as he'd seen her that night in the emergency room. Covered in blood.

Pale.

A disembodied voice whispering, *You did this . . .*

"*No, I didn't. No, I didn't,*" Hope said, her voice shaking, but sure.

Remy stood there, horrified. All he wanted to do was pull her into his arms, take her away from this, away from all of it. But then Nielson, the sheriff, was there, pushing a pair of handcuffs into his hand.

"*You want us to arrest her? Fine. You do it.*"

But that wasn't Remy's job—he wasn't a fucking cop. He didn't arrest people. He got warrants. He prosecuted.

"*Yeah, you make us get our hands dirty. But you want her arrested, you do it yourself.*"

And that was what he did. Remy put cuffs on wrists that seemed too slender, too fragile for such a burden.

Remy was the one who led her to a cell.

And when he opened the door, she walked silently inside. But he saw it in her eyes.

*I didn't do this.*

As he turned away, the screams started. Endless, agonized screams. But he didn't know if they were hers . . . or his own.

That was how he came awake.

With the sound of screams echoing in his ears.

"*Shit,*" he muttered, jerking upright in bed, fighting the sheets and blankets that had become ropes around his waist.

With his breath sawing raggedly in and out of his lungs, he sat on the edge of the bed and stared off into nothingness. His gut was a raw, ragged pit and his head throbbed like it hadn't since his college days. Back then, he had thought he could get by on naps and caffeine.

In a few hours, he was supposed to meet the sheriff at the hospital.

Hope Carson was being arrested today, and there wasn't a damn thing Remy could do about it. That woman had the ability to turn him into knots just by looking at him. No other woman had ever done that to him. Not a one. Shit. This was a mess.

Not that she knew.

Nobody knew, thank God.

At least he'd managed to keep that much hidden.

But shit, he had to get it together.

Had to get his head together, his act together, had to do . . . something.

Shoving to his feet, Remy shambled naked toward the bathroom. Maybe if he blasted himself with enough hot water, and then flooded his body with enough caffeine . . . maybe.

Maybe, maybe . . .

He turned on the lights, but they hit his tired eyes with the force of a sledgehammer and, groaning, he turned them off again.

No light. Not yet.

Shower. Caffeine.

Then light.

Maybe.

Not that he really needed light anyway. Not like he needed light to shower . . . or even to get dressed. If he didn't have any light on, he wouldn't have to worry about seeing his reflection, right?

And the last thing he wanted to do just then was look himself square in the eye.

No matter what the evidence said, no matter what the logic pointed to, it just didn't feel right.

It just didn't feel right . . . at all.

* * *

There were days when Hope Carson wished she'd just driven right through Ash. Instead of stopping in the small Kentucky town to see her friend, like she'd promised, she should have just kept on driving.

No matter how much she loved Law, no matter how much she'd missed him, missed having a friend, there were days when she wished she had broken that promise and never stopped.

Maybe she should have driven straight to the ocean.

Hope had never seen the ocean.

She'd wanted to go to the ocean for her honeymoon, but Joey . . . her not-so-beloved ex-husband hadn't liked the idea.

*Everybody goes to the beach. Let's do something different.*

They'd gone to the mountains.

Skiing in Aspen.

But Hope hadn't been very good at skiing. And she hated the cold . . . it was like it cut right through her bones. She'd fallen down so many times, and had so many bruises.

"Should have just kept on driving," she muttered as she listened to the voices just outside her door.

Would have been wiser, that much was sure.

Desolate, she stared out the window and wondered if she'd have a room wherever they were taking her next.

Would it be another hospital?

A jail?

She just didn't know.

*Another hospital, probably. One with* real *security.*

Dark, ugly dots swirled in on her vision.

Fear locked a fist around her throat. *Locked . . . trapped . . .*

She barely managed to keep the moan behind her teeth.

When the door opened, she managed to stifle her wince.

Barely.

It was just one of the nursing assistants—this time.

But soon . . . soon, it would be uniformed deputies. She knew it.

Hearing the quiet, muffled sound of shoes on the linoleum, she stared out the window and tried not to think about what was coming.

No matter what, she had to be grateful for one thing.

No matter what, she wasn't trapped back in that house in Oklahoma with her husband, and she wasn't trapped in that hospital where he had complete, total control over her.

She'd almost willingly be held for a crime she didn't commit rather than go back to that particular hell.

At least she wasn't anywhere close to Joey.

At least she wasn't under his control, in any way, shape, or form.

That counted, for a hell of a lot.

But it wasn't enough, and the longer she stared at the plain, white walls of the small hospital room, the more they resembled a cell. So instead, she stared out the window—a reinforced window, one she couldn't open. Not that she'd tried.

But the nurse had been a little too free with that information, right after she'd come in to check her blood pressure and *offer* her the medications—just an offer this time.

Nobody had tried to force it on her again.

Not since Remy . . .

She swallowed and tried not to think about that. It really, really wouldn't do her any good to think about that, about him. As humiliating as it had been, for anybody to see her like that, it had been nothing short of a miracle in the end. Whether he'd said something to one of the doctors after he'd left or just scared the hell out of the nurses . . . well, nobody had tried to force any more drugs on her.

No antipsychotics, no tranquilizers, nothing. That fancy law degree of his, Hope imagined. She didn't know, and honestly, didn't care.

As long as nobody was forcing drugs on her she didn't need.

Her head was completely clear. She should be grateful.

And she would try to be.

But her gut told her she hadn't seen the last of Remy Jennings, and the next time she saw him, it wasn't going to be over the drugs the hospital staff had been forcing on her.

No, the next time it would be over the night she'd been found unconscious, just a few days ago, her wrists slashed open, her prints on the bat that had been used to beat a man damn near to death.

Her best friend—the people here thought she was capable of that.

They wanted her in jail for it.

Closing her eyes, she rested her head against her pillow and sighed. It wouldn't be long now, either. She'd seen it in the doctor's eyes when he'd been in to see her yesterday.

Sympathy, knowledge . . . and a grim acceptance. She was no longer in need of the medical services a hospital could provide. And they weren't about to let her traipse away where they couldn't keep her *secured*.

In their eyes, she'd done something awful, and it was time she paid for it.

*But I didn't do anything.*

The sad, forlorn whine wanted to work its way free, but she swallowed it, shoved it down inside. She sure as hell wasn't going to go meekly along with whatever they had in mind, but she was done with wringing her hands and moaning, too.

She just needed to figure out what she *was* going to do . . .